THE GENESIS SIGNAL

Science Fiction Thriller

BRANDON Q. MORRIS
DOMINIK A. MEIER

This book is published by:

A7L Thrilling Books Limited

Visit the publisher's website A7LBooks.com for more thrilling science fiction titles. Happy reading!

All rights reserved.

Translation: Megan Bigelow

Editing: Marjorie Hicks

Cover: Andrei Gherman

Chapter One

A DEEP, piercing echo reverberated through the silence. The steel growl of mighty machines, awakening from their slumber and quickly sweeping away the monotonous emptiness of the station. It was a slowly swelling symphony; the interplay of countless devices and apparatuses. Their entire purpose of existence was fulfilled in those minutes.

Adrian Morris was only peripherally aware of all this, somewhere in the depths of his subconscious. It was a long, dreamless sleep from which he now awoke. The sensations that hit him were chaotic and confused, dragging him along with them mercilessly. Light and darkness, warmth and cold, pain and emptiness. All this narrowed into a single vortex, into a whipping storm that roared its way through his mind.

A hurricane-like roaring swelled in his ears, accompanied by an ever-increasing pressure that he could not escape. Caught halfway between sleep and wakefulness, he did not even comprehend what was happening. He only understood that something was happening; something abruptly different from what had been before: nothing. Dull, monotonous nothingness.

Suddenly a sharp pain. Where exactly, he could not make out. But it was there. Cold steel pierced his skin and bored deep into his body. Something was pressed into him. Something painful. His body felt like it was about to burst; he felt sick, his throat tightened - and then suddenly a gush of liquid burst from his mouth, forced out by air he had not breathed.

The pain disappeared, replaced only by a weary exhaustion that came over him almost as suddenly. For a tiny moment he remained motionless, unable to move or even think. But then an instinctive urge came over him that he only now realized he had almost forgotten. He needed to breathe; his lungs demanded oxygen.

Carefully, he sucked in air through lips that were almost completely numb and a throat that was far too dry, only to cough immediately. His lungs were on fire. As was the rest of his body. More and more punctures made him wince. They were no longer a distant pain, but immediate and direct. They hit him in arms and legs, in chest, neck, back. Everywhere. Needles. Dozens of needles. Some of them pumped fluids into his body, others sucked something out of him. They all hurt.

He was cold. Unimaginably cold. He felt that he was surrounded by a warm liquid; that the outermost layers of his skin were about to be scalded. Yet he was immeasurably cold. Every fiber of his body shivered and quivered in a desperate attempt to warm him somehow. It was almost unbearable and yet there was nothing he could do about it.

And then, all of a sudden, it stopped. The pain subsided, the cold disappeared and almost every other sensation left him, so that only exhaustion and paralyzing numbness remained with him. Now, finally, he managed to open his eyes. Slowly, carefully, blinking, he felt his way back to reality. Light greeted him, accompanied by colors whose names he simply could not think of now.

"Process complete," a cool computer voice resounded in his ear. "Crew member: Adrian Scott Morris. Vital signs normal. Duration of cryostasis: 2,000 years. Station systems operating within expected parameters. Minor damage to secondary and tertiary modules. Are you feeling all right, Mr. Morris?"

Adrian swallowed. Once, twice. He knew that meant him. Adrian Scott Morris. That was his name. But his mind felt strangely heavy, as if trapped in a thick fog. He wanted to answer, wanted to move his lips, but no matter how hard he tried, he could not.

"Mr. Morris, if you understand me, nod on my command," the computer voice continued, completely unimpressed. "Optical sensors activated. Facial patterns acquired. Please nod."

Adrian nodded.

"Head movement detected. Instruction followed. Probability of conscious movement: 99.9 percent. Acceptable. Mr. Morris, you are experiencing the after effects of cryostasis. Numbness, discomfort, and difficulty with coordination are normal. Symptomatic improvement can be expected within thirty minutes and full recovery within twenty-four hours. If you experience tachycardia, please notify the appropriate ward physician."

"Wahapend..." Adrian started, only to pause again immediately. Why was it so hard for him to speak? He had practiced it. He knew he had. Where and when it had been, he could no longer say, but he knew with every fiber of his body that he had experienced this before, that he had been trained for this. He had been taught how to hold back the effects and even resist them.

"Please repeat."

He took a deep breath and concentrated as best he could. "Wha... what... happened?"

"You were awakened."

"So is it time? Just us or...?"

"The whole station is being awakened."

"The entire station?"

"That's correct. Awakening process halfway complete. Survival rate so far at 70 percent."

"70?"

"Modules 1 through 4, 9 and 13 are down. Cause unknown."

Adrian blinked. He was still having a hard time seeing clearly. The shapes and lights around him blurred into a single distorted image. Cautiously, he raised his hands and rubbed at his eyes. Or at least he wanted to, though he could not. One hand landed on his chin, the other somewhere else entirely. Only on the third try did he manage to rub his eyes.

The words of the computer system echoed through his head like waves that would not subside. Only seven out of ten had survived the wake-up process so far; a full six modules were lost. Even in the worst-case scenario, the simulations had assumed a maximum loss of two modules. How could that be? The system had told him that the station was intact. Or had it?

"Damage report," he finally demanded, while he grabbed the two grip bars that just at that moment moved in front of his cryo-capsule and allowed him to leave it. His vision was still blurry, but he could at least see clearly enough to pull himself forward - even if he could almost feel his legs giving way on the spot.

A scream of shock burst from his throat as he fell forward by a hair - or at least he thought that was what happened. It took him a few seconds to understand that there was weight-lessness around him and that he could not fall to the ground. Nevertheless, he instinctively clung to the grip bars with far too much force. His heart raced and once again every fiber of his body trembled. Damn.

"It is recommended that you refrain from simultaneous activities within the first few hours," the computer system explained in a monotone voice. "In particular, it is recommended to avoid simultaneous movement and speech."

Adrian gave no reply, but continued to cling to the restraining bars. The initial shock had already passed, but he still felt unable to answer anything or even let go of the stir-rups. His rational mind knew that he was in no danger, that he was be exhausted and that nothing would happen to him in zero gravity. Still, he found himself unable to use logic and reason to stop his instincts that had him cowering here like a frightened child.

"Damage report!" he hissed. A desperate attempt to distract from his current plight. He knew that the system was utterly indifferent to the fact that he was crouching here stark naked, shivering, and covered from head to toe in preservative fluid, but that didn't change how uncomfortable this situation made him. He knew it all, had practiced it dozens of times! Why was he acting like a moron right now?

"Minor damage to secondary and tertiary modules."

"I already know that! Why did we lose six modules?"

"Unknown."

"You can't be serious! Retrieve log! Begin with first loss!"

"Cryostasis duration: 1191 years. Life support module 1 failure. System restart. Ineffective. System cascade. Life support module 2 failure. System restart. Ineffective. Emergency protocol alpha initiated. Ineffective. System cascade. Life support failure module 3. Emergency protocol beta initiated. Modules 1 through 4 jettisoned. System cascade stopped. Cryostasis duration: 1582 years. Life support module 9 failure. Jettisoned according to emergency protocol Beta. Cryostasis duration: 1875 years. Life support module 13 malfunction jettisoned per emergency protocol beta."

"Cause?"

"Unknown."

Adrian bit his lip. Even if it had not been explicitly listed in the error log itself, the cause of the modules' failure was obvious in his eyes: the system itself was defective. It was in control of the entire station and thus had the responsibility to protect the lives of every crew member. So if life support had failed for no apparent reason, and even a reboot had not helped, then only the system itself could be defective.

Once again, he felt his heart begin to beat faster. If he was unlucky, this failure also meant that not only he himself, but also everyone else on this station was now being woken up for no reason at all. 2,000 years of cryo-sleep was a far longer time than calculated in the simulations, but not beyond all possible scenarios either.

"What is the condition of the others?" he finally asked. Now, finally, he managed to get out of the cryo-capsule and dried himself with the waiting towel before retrieving his uniform from the small locker at the foot of the capsule and getting dressed. His body still felt weak, but it was gradually gaining strength. "Is everything going according to plan in this module?"

"According to standard procedure, as the lead engineer of this module, you were awakened an hour before the others, Mr. Morris."

"And the other modules?"

"Aside from casualties, the first twenty modules have already been awakened. Partial individual fatalities due to medical causes within functioning capsules. Modules 21 through 30 are currently being awakened."

"Is there any possibility of stopping the wake-up process for now until we find out more about the system cascade?"

"Negative."

"Of course."

Shaking his head, Adrian forced himself not to say anything more in response, reminding himself that he was merely talking to a machine right now. A highly intelligent machine and in its time the most modern thing mankind had ever developed, but despite all the progress it was still just a machine. An automaton that pretended to be a human being, but in the end was not capable of more than tackling precisely worked out scenarios under equally precisely written protocols.

It did not matter. No matter what had happened, and no matter what he thought about it: It was too late to prevent the entire station being woken up. He had to make the best of it. At least as long as he did not get more detailed information about what had happened in the first place. And that meant he had to take care of the other 29 people who were in that module with him.

He took a cursory glance at the small control monitor on his own cryostasis capsule and skimmed the vital signs recorded on it. Indeed, he seemed to have survived the 2,000-year cryo-sleep that had just ended relatively well. All organs were functioning normally and even his blood-brain barrier seemed to have survived the critical moment of thawing. If one could find a reason at all for the discomfort of the moment, then probably it would be there. A small consolation, after all.

Slowly, he made his way along the relatively narrow circuit in front of the other capsules, carefully checking the vital signs of the others. Except for some minor damage from the freezing, they all seemed to have suffered no drastic restrictions. A few frozen fingers and toes here, some minor tissue necrosis there. Nothing that could not be fixed. The central supply unit, which was enclosed by the capsules in the center of the module, also seemed to function without any major problems. The nitrogen supply was well above the calculated loss for that period, which meant that there had been no leaks or other damage to the capsules. A circumstance for which Adrian was more than grateful.

Overall, the entire module was in exemplary condition. Not only the cryostasis unit and thus the most important machine here, but also the other systems were working within almost perfect parameters. According to the logs, even the power supply seemed to have worked constantly during the past two millennia. Only once had the emergency generator kicked in - and that was 1,000 years ago - to automatically check its functionality.

Adrian suddenly paused. He had just reached capsule number 28 and thus almost at the end of his tour, when he suddenly noticed something: The vital signs of the young woman behind the glass also seemed to be in order at first glance, but unlike all the others, she was not naked, but wearing her uniform.

"Information on 28."

"Name: Cassandra Toussaint. Age: 25 years. Gender: female. Vital signs..."

"I don't care!" hissed Adrian, glancing up at the ceiling as he spoke, almost as if he expected to catch sight of the system there. Which, of course, was not the case. "She's wearing her uniform."

"Crew members are required, for hygiene reasons, to remove their clothing before..."

"Why is she dressed?" he interrupted the system. "Has her pod been opened?"

"Affirmative."

"When?"

"Two years, eight months, fourteen days, two hours and..."

"Why?"

"Unknown."

"Seriously, are you kidding me? Did she talk to you? Was she on any of the systems? How did she manage to put herself back into cryostasis? Retrieve log!"

"Error."

"What kind of error? Specify!"

"Unknown error."

Adrian closed his eyes and took a deep breath as he tried to keep his anger in check. There was no point. The system was obviously broken, and until access to the rest of the station was released, there was precious little he could do about it. However, under the current circumstances, waiting that long was not an option either. No one could foresee how severe the system's defects were and what that ultimately meant for everyone aboard the station.

"What's the last external event recorded in your logs?" he asked, pulling himself to a control terminal. Through it, he had limited access at best to the system files, but he could at least try to make a preliminary error analysis from what it said and what it told him - or find out if at least what it had told him so far was true.

"Cryostasis duration: 1999 years, 364 days, 22 hours, 55 minutes. Signal received."

"Specify."

"Priority: high. Type: call signal. Protocol: *Exodus*."

THE *EXODUS* SIGNAL. The drumbeat, the beacon. The moment that everyone on board this station had hoped would never come. And the moment that everyone had secretly been looking forward to, because it was the reason why they were all here. The reason why this station had been built in the first place. Back then, over 2,000 years ago. Because of this signal, each of them had separated with their old lives and accepted that they would never see their families again. Or never get to meet them at all.

Now the time had come - and yet Adrian could not believe it.

He stared at the monitor in disbelief. The *Exodus* signal. It had been sent. It had actually happened. The day his entire life had been leading up to; the day for which he had trained, trained every waking minute from childhood; the day that had been simulated over and over again. It had come. Nothing felt different than before - and yet it was completely different.

More than 2,000 years ago, the leaders of the old world had realized that humanity would not last forever. Scientists had calculated the end, strategists and generals had planned it. Everyone else had feared it. By God, there had been enough problems. War. Hunger. Climate change. Social tensions. Diseases and pandemics. Which of these had now come to pass, Adrian had no way to say. And until he set foot on Earth, he would not know for sure.

He felt his fingers begin to tremble at the keyboard and withdrew his hands. Behind him, he had long since heard the steel growl of the machines powering up once more, announcing the awakening of the others. Their bodies, just like his earlier, were brought out of cryostasis; air was pumped into their lungs and countless chemicals into their blood to awaken them from their icy cold sleep.

He swallowed hard. This was really happening. That thought echoed through his head. Again and again, with merciless violence and intensity. Perhaps because in those seconds he became truly aware for the first time of what this meant, that it was really happening. The *Genesis* was being awakened; the massive station in high orbit of Earth that was meant to be a safe haven for those who would come later. Then, when Earth was no more, and with it, the people who had previously inhabited it. The back-up. The fresh start.

Their only chance to do better.

Adrian shuddered, rubbed his face with both hands, and looked around at the others. From all around him came the voice of the computer system, quiet yet unmistakable. It spoke to the others, welcoming them to this new, old time. Men and women, like him - healthy, fit, young, and prepared from early childhood for this very day. Stark naked, they climbed out of their capsules, dried off and dressed. Some of them looked miserable, others had obvious problems coordinating their limbs, while still others made their first movements after waking up, seemingly untroubled. What they all had in common was the incredulous surprise written all over their faces.

Suddenly, a dull ruckus sounded to his left. A shrill creak followed by a series of muffled thuds and a muffled scream. Although he was not looking, he already knew it had to be capsule number 28. The capsule where Cassandra Toussaint lay. The woman who had been awakened almost three years ago. He had almost expected this malfunction. The capsules were not meant to be reused. At least not these ones.

While a few of the others had long since gathered around 28 and tried to help the young woman, Adrian pulled the box of special tools from under the module's central console, opened it and equipped himself. Inside the capsule, Toussaint was in no danger as long as the preservation fluid drained according to the rules. And since she was able to scream ever more shrilly for help, it looked that way. No reason to risk a mistake by rushing and acting hastily.

"Make way." With a few brisk moves, he pushed the others aside and made his way to the capsule. Most of them were already wearing their uniforms, but a few were still naked - and covered in liquid. "Dry yourselves off! Everything according to protocol! If the ventilation gets clogged, we'll have a problem!"

"Morris?" he was addressed by a sleepy-looking, chalk-pale fellow who was obviously having trouble not throwing up. Horvat was his name, if he was not mistaken. He knew him from before. From back then, that is. "What is going on here?"

"What does it look like?" replied Adrian, as he applied the ultrasonic saw to the caulking of the capsule and sent a few short, high-frequency sound waves through it. Toussaint inside immediately cried out, but it was nothing he could pay attention to. The reseal and the second freeze had probably caused some nitrogen to collect around the edges of the door. He had to make sure it disappeared.

"Jesus, Morris, just speak up!" whined Horvat. "I've got a headache so bad I could scream! You've been awake for an hour, right?"

Adrian gave him a quick look and was already starting to tell him to be patient, but then noticed that almost everyone had gathered around him, looking at him partly expectantly, and partly openly frightened. They, of course, knew as well as he what their awakening meant. Not only for themselves, but also for all people on earth. If there were any left.

"The *Exodus* signal has been sent," he finally said, as he continued to try to open the jammed door of the capsule. So far, without success. At least Toussaint seemed to have caught on that he was trying to help her and at least she was in no immediate danger. "It reached the station just under two hours ago," he said.

"So this is serious?" a young woman asked, audibly unset-tled. Diaz was her name. "It really happened? Earth is gone?"

"I don't know what exactly happened yet," Adrian replied, shaking his head, putting the ultrasonic saw aside and reaching for the hydraulic pliers. It didn't seem to be the nitrogen that was preventing the door from opening. It would have to be by force, then. "The modules are still separated from each other. Until they're all woken up, we can't get access to the rest of the station. And even then: it could take weeks before satellite photos and sensor data are analyzed. Maybe the station has received radio transmissions or other information, but I wouldn't count on it for now. In any case, we have to follow protocol and..."

He paused.

"And what?" asked Diaz immediately.

"The computer system blew off six modules," he growled over the low hum of the tightening hydraulic pincers. Now, finally, the door to the capsule opened. Slowly, but surely. "The error reports are incomplete. I'm afraid the system itself may be defective. There may never have been a signal."

"What? But..."

"Diaz, I know as much as you do right now!" he growled. "And I'm trying to concentrate here! Man, what are you all hovering around for? Get yourselves up and running! As soon as the station becomes accessible, everything has to run smoothly!"

A murmur went through the crowd, though the others followed his order without audible objections. They probably knew as well as he did that their time window was by no means that narrow, but that had no bearing for him right now. He wanted to work on the capsule in peace - and exchange a few words with Toussaint without anyone directly noticing what was going on. She had been awake once before, almost three years ago, so she was his best chance to find out more about what was going wrong here. And perhaps about the signal itself.

Although he kept prying the capsule open, it was almost another ten minutes before Toussaint was able to get out of it. A good portion of the machinery and injectors that had woken the others up fully automatically were hanging around in the capsule, more or less loose and obviously makeshift to provisionally rebuilt.

"Thank you." Toussaint smiled uncertainly at him, but not even that could hide how guilty she looked. "For a moment there, I was really afraid I wasn't going to get out of there."

Adrian returned her gaze, but said nothing.

"I know." She sighed and looked down at the floor. "I'm sorry."

"I don't need an apology, I need information." With a quick nod of his head, he motioned for her to follow him to a slightly quieter section of the module and pulled past the others at the restraints. "You were awake."

"That's right."

"How long?"

"Almost two weeks."

"Two weeks?" he repeated, frowning. "That's a long time."

"It was a long time, yes. The loneliness got to me. How long has it been?"

"Two years, eight months."

She winced.

"My thought exactly," Adrian grumbled. "Toussaint, if I remember correctly, you're an information technologist, right?"

"That's right. Specializing in recovering, reading, and repairing old systems. After the touchdown on Earth, my job is to establish stable communications and try to track down any survivors and old government servers. Aboard the station, I'm the deputy head of the communications team. Why do you ask?"

"Have you interacted with the onboard system?"

She narrowed her eyes. "Morris, what's with these questions? What's going on here?"

"We may be dealing with a zero situation here."

"What?" Though he hardly thought it possible, she blanched. "A zero situation? A malfunctioning onboard system?"

"Not only that. I don't think it's impossible that even the *Exodus* signal is just a glitch. Until the *Genesis* is released and I can get access to the mainframe, I can't find out anything more specific, but we should be prepared in case it's just our module that's been woken up."

"Or in case we're not allowed aboard the station at all," she added grimly. "God, this is bad. Are the failures really so widespread that you fear that?"

"I want to be prepared for anything," he replied.

"That does not sound very optimistic." She twisted the corners of her mouth into something that, with a lot of imagination, could pass for a bitter smile at best. "But to get back to your question: Yes, I did talk to the onboard system. At great length and in great detail. It was, after all, the only - excuse the expression - person awake besides me. It didn't give me the impression that it was defective. It..."

She bit her lip and averted her eyes.

"You were on the station, weren't you?" whispered Adrian.

"Yes," she replied tonelessly.

"How?"

"The lock was open."

"What?"

"The lock was open," she repeated, still softly, but at the same time with much more emphasis. "It wasn't my fault, if that's what you're thinking, and I didn't break anything either. I was woken up quite regularly. At first I thought it was a simple delay, especially since you were still asleep, but when I was still alone after two hours... I broke protocol, okay? I looked around and got to the airlock. It was open. I went into the station, but there was no one there."

"And no one else came either?"

"No. All the other modules were locked and the systems, scanners and everything else were offline, of course. The onboard system didn't respond to me at first, but luckily at some point it kicked in and realized that must have been a mistake. With its help, I tried to repair the cryo capsule. With success, it seems."

"And you didn't notice anything?" asked Adrian, raising an eyebrow. "Any irregularities? Anything?"

"No. Although..."

"What?" More impulsively than intentionally, Adrian grabbed her by the arm, but immediately let go and withdrew his hand. "I'm sorry."

"It's all right, Morris. I can understand why you're upset. I'm probably going out on a limb here, but in some circumstances an access attempt could explain these problems. I didn't develop the onboard system, but I know its functions inside and out. It's largely shielded against outside access attempts, but before the station was launched it couldn't be ruled out that it might be possible to bypass the locks after all."

"How is that possible?"

"It was necessary to allow for the possibility that the surviving humans would not be able to send the *Exodus* signal and activate us. Some sensitivity to more primitive or incomplete signals was tolerated because of this. Otherwise, we would inevitably have had to wait for the exit protocol, but that wouldn't have kicked in for 5000 years, which in turn would have magnified the chance of a critical system failure."

"So you think such a signal would be capable of messing up the system?"

"At least, I wouldn't rule it out right off the bat." She nodded. "Like you said, we can't get a decent diagnostic until we get access to the station. Until we do, that's definitely my best guess." She looked around and watched the others for a few seconds as they equipped themselves, prepared the module to leave, and made final arrangements at a few of the terminals and consoles to get the *Genesis* up and running.

Adrian followed her gaze. The initial fear and uncertainty seemed to have subsided somewhat by now, but there was a deep, underlying concern written all over their faces.

He could not blame them. All the simulations and theoretical situation briefings they had gone through over and over again more than 2,000 years ago might have provided a solid foundation for everything that was to follow, but being awakened meant something else entirely. If the system was 'only' defective and they had been woken up too early, that was an unpleasant to shitty situation. But if it was not a fault, it meant that the now almost 720 of formerly 900 people on the *Genesis* were the last representatives of their species. It meant that the Earth no longer existed and that all hopes for the continuation of mankind rested on their shoulders.

All at once, Adrian was overcome by a strange feeling; one like he had never felt before. A mixture of sadness and resignation overshadowed by unspeakable melancholy. A quick glance at Toussaint told him that she felt no different. Everyone on this station knew that their waking up meant that it was over. That everything that had existed on Earth had to be gone. That they were the last ones. And that this end had probably been accompanied by unspeakable suffering.

"Module 22," the flat monotone voice of the computer system sounded at some point. "Stand by for decompression. *Genesis* is opening, all station resources are being released. On behalf of those who sent us on this journey, I wish you success. The future of humanity is in your hands."

Chapter Two

SHAKING HIS HEAD, Adrian stared at the small portable monitor in his left hand and - more out of routine than necessity - checked the cables that connected him to the *Genesis* central computer with his right hand. He had been sitting there for five hours already - 'sitting' in this case being a well-meaning euphemism for hooking his knees to a grab rail - trying to figure out what in the world was wrong with the onboard system.

The only problem was that he could not find anything wrong. Hell, if the readouts on the monitor were correct, there weren't even any deviations from the routines, let alone bugs or anything else that could substantiate his suspicions. Despite the fact that he was more than a little critical of the whole thing and was waiting like a bloodhound to get off the leash and take the system apart.

The truth of the matter was that the computer was working fine. At least, as of that moment. And Adrian also wholeheartedly doubted that any of the system technicians would later discover anything he might have missed. He was just as good at diagnosing and reading out logs as they were. Probably even better. So, unless someone had just installed a predetermined breaking point with a lot of skill and patience... No, that was truly a long shot.

"Morris?" A voice beside him interrupted his musings at some point. He looked to the side. Toussaint was just pulling herself toward him. In her hand was a small tablet. "Am I interrupting?"

"No." He wedged the diagnostic monitor into its designated holder and tilted his head to either side. After cryostasis, he still felt somewhat immobile. "Do you have anything?"

"I think so."

"You do?" He raised his eyebrows and reached out, but she hesitated. "Toussaint?"

"Morris," she said in a low, almost conspiratorial voice, looking him straight in the eye. "I haven't discussed this with anyone, and I haven't cross-checked it yet."

"Just give it to me already!" He sighed quietly and, with a quick wave of his hand, motioned for her to finally hand him the tablet. "It's not like I'm going to sound the alarm. It wouldn't do any good anyway."

Toussaint nodded and handed him the small computer. Frowning, Adrian skimmed the data displayed while simultaneously trying to match it with the onboard system's log. Not impossible, but he still found it much more difficult than he wanted to admit.

"That's the com log," he finally stated without averting his eyes.

"Yes." She moved immediately next to him, pushed his hand aside, and made a few quick entries. "We have four major signal occurrences, though I use that word with caution. 1191, 1582, 1875, and now."

"The times when the modules failed."

"Exactly."

"But how is that possible?" Adrian took a deep breath and expelled it between his clenched teeth. "The system is shielded. Those signals should never have had that kind of impact!"

"I agree."

"And you're sure this isn't a mistake?"

Toussaint snorted. "Why would that be a mistake?"

"Maybe a reverse causal chain?" Adrian suggested, even though he knew the answer. "Automated distress signals from the jettisoned modules? That would explain the temporal coincidence."

"Don't be ridiculous, Morris."

"Okay." He put both hands to his mouth and breathed into his palms a few times. "So the station received three 'signals,' the first of which resulted in a system cascade that jettisoned four modules with a total of 120 people aboard. Then Emergency Protocol Beta was initiated, by which two more modules were jettisoned - also after receiving two signals - right after the first error message. And now the entire station has been woken up."

"You think there's a connection?"

"Don't you?"

Toussaint gave no reply. Perhaps it was for the best. In the end, they could only speculate. Actually, even less than that. Speculation would at least have meant that there was a basic possibility that it was true. That was not the case here. The system was demonstrably not defective, and thus there was not the slightest indication that a simple signal would have resulted in such a catastrophe.

But what did that entail? That this was nothing more than coincidence? That, for whatever reason, six modules with a total of 180 people on board had failed and been jettisoned, and that signals had come in at precisely those times that had absolutely nothing to do with it? Impossible. But how was he supposed to prove the connection? Or establish it in the first place?

"Where's the rest?" he finally asked.

"What do you mean?"

"Well, the rest." He held up the tablet. "This is the com log, but I only see the event log. Where's the content of the signals?"

"There weren't any."

"That's impossible. Every signal is a set of data. Every piece of data is received and stored."

"There's nothing there, Morris. As I said, I use the term 'signal' very carefully. Actually, I have no idea what kind of event it is. It's just recorded in the com log."

Adrian felt himself open his mouth involuntarily. Probably to start a retort, though he himself did not know exactly what to say. And although his thoughts were racing, he found himself unable to utter a single word. This could not - must not - be true! Was he stupid? They were on a space station that had been built to withstand whatever madness mankind could unleash - any storm, any war, any catastrophe. 2,000 years ago, the machines surrounding them had been the best and most modern that their species had been able to create; everything had been checked and put through its paces dozens of times. Absolutely every imaginable scenario had been calculated; solutions and emergency plans had been created.

And now this?

Again, Adrian had all the even remotely relevant data displayed. Again, he stared at columns upon columns of code, looking for errors or even deliberately programmed routines that could explain what had happened. But there was nothing, and he knew that even if he spent the rest of his life looking, he would find nothing.

Suddenly, there was a hand on his shoulder. Involuntarily, he flinched. Toussaint looked at him with a pitying, but at the same time somehow encouraging look; the way one would look at a child who had just fallen off a bicycle and needed to be encouraged to try again anyway.

"Morris," she said softly, bringing a hand to the monitor only to take it away and clamp it in its holder. "I know we don't know each other well. But I also know you're good at what you do."

"What are you getting at?"

"What do you think I'm getting at, you ox?" she snorted.

"I'm trying to cheer you up! Did you know I wasn't originally supposed to be on Module 22? I was assigned to 17; they didn't assign me to you until two days before the launch. I read your file, wanted to know who I'd be reporting to. And..."

"And what?"

"And I think if you can't find fault, there isn't any."

"So I'm supposed to accept that this was a coincidence?"

"Inevitably. Or at least that we can't explain it."

"Toussaint..."

"Call me Cassandra. Please. I hate my last name."

"Cassandra, I can't," Adrian growled, shaking his head. "So many people have died! There are only 30 modules on the *Genesis* - and we lost six of them! That's a failure of 20 percent! I..."

"What are you going to change?"

"What?"

"What are you going to change?" she repeated. "If you're that interested in finding out why, surely there's a way you're going to undo all this. I would be interested to know how, that's all."

"That's not my point, but..."

"But what?" she hissed in a suddenly more-than-just-angry voice, fixing him with a piercing stare. "The dead are dead, dammit! And have been for centuries! There's absolutely nothing we can do for them anymore! What we're doing here is a waste of time - and between you and me, the leaders of the other modules are already asking about you."

"Don't they care what's going on?"

"Yes, but they probably know we have more important things to do right now!"

Adrian bit his lip, stifling a retort. Instead he just nodded before gathering his equipment and stowing it in the pockets of his uniform. Toussaint watched him for a few seconds with a skeptical look and finally pulled herself toward the small airlock leading out of the module.

He knew she was right - and, worse, that he had been ignoring protocol for hours now. He could not help the dead anymore, and another module blast probably would not happen. Not to mention that enough engineers and programmers were awake by now to prevent such a thing.

Still, he could not get the matter out of his head. He couldn't just forget about it and carry on as if nothing had happened. While even the most optimistic scenarios calculated in advance had assumed at least a dozen deaths from individual capsule failure or medical circumstances, not even the worst predictions had assumed anything so catastrophic - not to mention the loss of the entire station.

And then, of course, there was the matter of Toussaint herself. She had woken up almost three years ago. Or been woken up. Two weeks alone on the station with, as she herself had admitted, full access to the parts of the *Genesis* that were actually locked. He did not want to imply that she had anything to do with the problems; after all, there were no clues in the data to suggest that. But had she, as an information technician, been able to change the log files? That was absolutely within the realm of possibility. But why?

"Morris, are you in there?" a voice he didn't recognize suddenly echoed through the small airlock to the central computer, which was barely three feet wide.

"Yes," he replied, pulling himself toward the exit. "Who's asking?"

"Joseph Mabena, module 11! Is everything all right with you?"

"I'll be done in a minute," Adrian murmured, pulling himself through the airlock only to nearly collide with a man waiting for him far too close behind. "I'm sorry. I..."

"I already heard," Mabena interrupted him. "The system cascade. Did you find out anything?"

"Unfortunately, no."

"I have three excellent IT experts in my module. Do you want me to put them on it? As long as we prepare the primary steps, we have spare capacity."

22

"If the guys have nothing better to do, they're welcome to try their luck."

"That pessimistic?"

"I just spent five hours completely tearing the system apart and found nothing. All you could do now would be to read through every line of code one by one. However, I doubt that would do any good. One of my information technicians was here just now. Apparently signal events were reaching us at the time of the outages, but I can't determine any causation. We don't even know if they were really signals or if the events weren't just stored in the com log."

"Morris, do you mind if I ask you a question?"

"Go ahead." Adrian felt a smile flit across his lips. Mabena hadn't said it, but a simple glance at his uniform already told him that he was far above him in rank: Executive Field Officer. Effectively number 3 on the food chain on the station; the one who carried out the orders of the two Directors and would make sure everything ran smoothly on Earth.

"I'm not asking as your superior," Mabena grumbled, seeming to have noticed his gaze. "But as someone who, like you, is interested in getting everyone aboard the *Genesis* back to Earth in one piece."

"Same answer," Adrian replied, tilting his head slightly. "Go ahead."

"Why do you feel responsible for this?"

Adrian blinked and stared at him uncomprehendingly for a moment before managing to regain his composure.

"What?" he finally asked.

"Why should you, of all people, feel responsible for this," Mabena repeated. "You're a decent engineer and head of 22, and - if I remember correctly - the head of the second emergency unit. None of that justifies or compels you to do this investigation."

"Mabena, with all due respect, don't you care what happened?"

"You're evading, Morris."

Adrian sighed and looked to the floor. "Sir, I have no

reason to. I was brought out of cryostasis and the system told me about the failures. I... It seemed like the obvious thing to do to take care of it in case there was a threat of more failures. Or that it was all a mistake."

"A mistake?"

"If there was a system failure, we should have checked to see if the *Exodus* signal had actually been sent. Whether we were right to be awake."

"We are, Morris." Mabena cleared his throat. "We sent the check signal to the automated listening post in Greenland two hours ago and have just received confirmation: The signal originated from Earth. We are the last humans."

"The initial satellite photos confirm our previous scans. It looks bad."

Dr. Svendottir, the head of the science department, folded her arms in front of her chest as a series of high-resolution satellite images were displayed on a large screen immediately behind her. Images that had been taken only minutes ago, showing what was left of the Earth. And that, by God, was not much. Deserts of sand and ice - dead, algae-eaten oceans - and the ruins of cities that looked like cancerous growths on the face of the planet in their shades of black and gray.

"Based on the information currently available to us, nuclear war seems to be the most likely scenario. All the metropolitan areas of the planet have been completely destroyed."

"What is the radiation level?" asked one of the other module leaders.

"The final measurements are still pending," Svendottir answered quietly. "For now, I think we can assume that the areas outside the cities are generally walkable. They are not free of radiation, but the level is below the critical range for the most part. Geiger counters will be issued for the teams that go down. The cities themselves..." She paused and shook her head. "It's likely that neutron bombs were used," she finally continued. Her voice trembled. "Or a comparable weapon that results in long-lasting radiation. We can't say for sure until the detailed scans are completed, but that will probably take several weeks. The secondary modules of the *Genesis* were hit by significantly more micrometeorites and space debris than we expected. Repairs could prove to be extensive and lengthy."

"What about survivors?" someone asked. "Are we picking up radio signals or other signal activity indicative of humans?"

"Negative."

"There's really nothing there?" asked another. "How long ago was this war? Surely there were bunkers! Someone must have survived!"

"The pictures are clear!" a young woman growled, giving him a meaningful look. "Just look at that! Deserts and ice! That means the Gulf Stream has dried up, and at the same time there are probably dozens more similarly widespread climate disasters. This is not something that happens overnight after a war."

"So the end of humanity has been a long time coming?"

"Inevitably."

"And why did they wait so long to wake us up?"

"Intentionally," Adrian grumbled, crossing his arms in front of his chest. "Fully intentional. Assuming we really are dealing with a nuclear war, Earth has been contaminated for a very long time, depending on the type of radiation. Neutron bombs are probably an apt estimate there, but it's also possible that something much worse was developed during our sleep. It would have made no sense to wake us up immediately after the war. There would have been nothing we could do, and we would have died from the radiation ourselves during the effort."

"Morris is right," Mabena agreed with him. "The scenario analyses have not yet been completed, but for such a case, delayed activation is absolutely within the realm of possibility.

If indeed no signal activity can be detected, we can assume that this war happened decades or even centuries ago. The listening post in Greenland should have recorded when and which signals were last sent."

"You want to go down there?" asked Svendottir, audibly disconcerted. "With all due respect, Mabena, I don't think that's a good idea."

"You said yourself just now that the repairs, and thus the detailed scans, could take weeks."

"Yes, but that's no reason to deviate from protocol! There's probably no one left alive down there for us to help anyway! So why risk our lives when we could do the same thing in a few weeks under reasonably safe conditions and controlled parameters?"

"Because every day of delay is another drain on our already stretched resources," replied a man in a dark red uniform that identified him as the chief of logistics. "A few days more or less won't matter, but weeks could mean we'll be short on important resources in the resettlement effort. I must vehemently disagree with you here, Dr. Svendottir. The risk to a small landing party more than outweighs the risk to the entire station and thus the operation itself."

For a moment, there was an almost eerie silence in the briefing room. The two dozen or so leaders of the remaining modules, as well as the designated command personnel and the specialists present, exchanged looks, some scowling, some openly uncertain, while new images of the destruction on Earth kept appearing on the screens around them.

Adrian did not really want to look at all, did not want to burden himself with the suffering and destruction. He was aware, of course, that it would not be pretty. He and the others had been prepared for this years before the start of their mission and had been taught ways to deal with the psychological pressure. Still, he would have been lying if he had claimed that it did not get to him.

Personally, he had always hoped for a less brutal ending. That humanity would not perish in the fires of war or in a planetary pandemic, but that it would slowly die out, as species have done since the dawn of all life. That it had simply gone downhill at some point and in the end there were simply not enough left to go on.

This was probably a hope that would have inevitably been dashed from the very beginning. A hope that could not have come true at all, because even if mankind had taken this path, it would have been its very nature to go for each other's throats in the struggle for resources and survival. It was not without reason that all analysts had assumed at an earlier stage that warlike activity was inevitable.

While the first discussions about how to proceed soon flared up around him, Adrian withdrew further and further into the depths of his own thoughts. What was being discussed now was nothing that directly affected him, and he cared little about the discussions as it was. All that mattered to him was what decisions were reached - and what he was supposed to do.

As Mabena had stated earlier, he was one of the leaders of the three emergency units of *Genesis*. This meant two things: on the one hand, that in the worst case, his module had all the necessary specialists to survive independently on Earth and thereby lay the foundations of a new civilization with a small probability. On the other hand, it also meant that he and his people were trained to operate under the most adverse conditions. For example, under those that currently prevailed on Earth.

With a brief nod, Mabena took him aside. "Morris, a word."

"What is it?"

"You spoke of signals reaching us before the failures - could you imagine those were earlier attempts to activate *Genesis*?" he asked in a low voice.

"You mean that the activation codes were basically correct, but the signals themselves were too damaged?" Adrian quirked the corners of his mouth. "That would be a question that would actually have to be resolved by a programmer. But I could certainly imagine it. It would at least explain the system cascade: It was an attempt to take the station online, however the signal was unable to do so and instead only retrieved individual modules."

"Which, in turn, the system interpreted as an error and reacted accordingly." Mabena nodded. "Exactly."

"An interesting theory. That would mean, then, that the war took place a good thousand years ago."

"Enough time to be reasonably safe outside the immediate detonation points."

"Let me guess," Adrian snorted, looking him straight in the eye. "You want my people and me down there?"

"Just a task force. Logistics is right - we can't afford weeks of delays. Don't even get me started on months. Our resources are designed to begin terraforming operations as quickly as possible and produce at least some of our own food in a timely manner. We would have to start rationing in as little as three weeks if we are to cope with even the most adverse scenarios on Earth itself."

"I understand."

"Are you sure?" Mabena grabbed him by the arm and squeezed much tighter than he should have. "Morris, I'm not going to lie to you: No one can tell you what to expect down there. Your people may not come back, or they may be so badly contaminated that we can't let them back on board."

"I'm aware of that." Adrian nodded. "That's why I'm going to go myself."

"Morris, this..."

"My people, my responsibility. Simple as that. How quickly can you give me a rough idea of the situation?"

"What do you need?"

"All the readings we have available, pictures of the landing zone, and protective gear. That should be enough for now. I don't plan to be there any longer than necessary. We'll try to install a digital uplink in Greenland, and if that doesn't work, download the data manually. If the terrestrial governments have held up their end of the bargain, we should be able to track what happened until the big crunch. So, how long?"

"One day."

"All right." Adrian pulled away from his grasp. "I'll put together a team. As soon as you're ready, let me know." With those words, he turned and retreated toward the sweeping airlock that separated the briefing room from the rest of the station. The fact that the meeting was still in progress and would probably continue for several hours was something he was fully aware of - and wholly unconcerned with. Even in the past, he had not been able to do much with the endless discussions and the theoretical running through of countless scenarios, and 2,000 years of cryo-sleep hadn't changed that. What counted were results.

Actually, he should have taken the direct route of gathering his people and putting together a task force. But first, he still had 24 hours left, and second, there was something that seemed more important to him right now - and for which the best opportunity presented itself in these minutes.

Concentrating, he made his way through the narrow tunnels that connected the larger rooms and halls of the station. It was not difficult for him to orient himself, as he had already spent weeks in an exact replica of the station during his training. But still, it felt strange to be here. Except for the minutes between his arrival, back 2,000 years ago, and the initiation of cryostasis, he had spent no time on the real *Genesis*. It was alien to him, and yet so familiar. Gliding through weightlessness here now meant the emergency his entire life had been geared toward has arrived. Maybe that was why it felt so alien?

Involuntarily, he shook his head. It was still difficult for him to understand the past time in the abstract and to accept that everything he knew was supposed to be gone. In his own perception, he had entered the cryo-capsule only a few hours ago, only to wake up more or less immediately. Not a particularly pleasant process; neither before nor after, but at its core no different than a deep sleep or anesthesia. And yet, 2,000 years had passed.

When Adrian finally reached the entrance to Module 22, he involuntarily squinted his eyes and stared for a moment at the small plaque next to the airlock. He had not even realized that he was already here; that his arms had made him instinctively take the right path without his intervention. The countless exercises earlier had apparently served their purpose.

As expected, there was no one in the module. His people were all at their stations or preparing for their assignments. That was a good thing, because it meant he could work undisturbed.

Without hesitation, he pulled himself along the grip bars to capsule number 28. While all the others had been sealed according to regulations and were waiting to be dismantled and recycled in the hospitals that would hopefully soon be built on Earth, Cassandra Toussaint's was still wide open. A thin film of preservation fluid clung to the inside, and the technical makeshift she had used to put herself back into cryostasis floated in zero gravity.

Adrian reached for it and looked at it from all sides. Actually, it was impossible to put oneself into cryo-sleep without trained personnel or at least outside help. Or to put it another way, doing it alone meant immense pain and a far from pleasant process of falling asleep. Most people would probably not have been able to bring themselves to do it at all, preferring the loneliness of the ward to falling back asleep.

Nevertheless, Toussaint had obviously succeeded. It showed finesse and ingenuity - and a willpower that should not be underestimated. Not exactly qualities he would have expected from an information technician. She had modified the access ports for preservation fluid and nitrogen with crude, manually operated nozzles. Presumably to buy time to prepare herself. She must have done the initial anesthetic injection manually as well - and had even managed to realign the oxygen injector for the recovery process.

"Activate onboard system," he finally said in a firm voice

as he looked closely at the repaired injectors. "Personal information on Cassandra Toussaint."

"Cassandra Toussaint," the onboard system replied monotonously. "Age: 25 years. Gender: female. Born in Toulouse, graduate of Sorbonne Université in advanced technical computing, information sciences, and cloud and network infrastructure engineering, summa cum laude in each."

"Sorbonne?" repeated Adrian. "She wasn't trained from an early age for the *Genesis* Project?"

"Negative."

"How did she get on board? Why is she participating in this mission?"

"Warning: information access restricted."

"Authorization code: Scott-Lambda-Epsilon-Four-One-One."

"Warning: information access restricted."

"I just told you my authorization! Give me the damn information!"

"Authorization level insufficient."

"Are you kidding me! Who is authorized to access?"

"Dr. Sara Abraham."

"Dr. Sara Abraham? She created the project."

"That is correct."

"She has been dead for 2,000 years. She cannot issue an access authorization! What is the protocol for this case?"

"Error."

"What kind of error?"

"There is no protocol."

"So I can't find out who Toussaint is?"

"Cassandra Toussaint. Age: 25. Gender: female. Born in Toulouse, graduate of the Sorbonne..."

"Deactivate onboard system!"

Adrian slapped his hands against the wall above his head and took a deep breath as he tried to keep the mixture of frustration and anger burning relentlessly inside him in check, but he knew by now it was only a matter of seconds before he failed. Cassandra was not part of the project. Even more: she had been brought in from the outside. Just in time to join his team. She was one of the few who knew about the signals that had reached the station - and had been woken up almost three years ago. Enough time to manipulate every system on board.

"God damn it."

Chapter Three

CAUGHT SOMEWHERE between actual thoughts and pointless musings, Adrian stared at the displays that flickered in tight columns across the small tablet in his hands. The mission parameters, all the information he had requested, and all manner of other data that might prove useful. Mabena seemed anxious to get his people back as quickly as possible and in one piece. Adrian could not agree more.

More than an hour ago, he had already reviewed the parameters and decided that the framework was acceptable, despite the dangers. What had actually happened on Earth and thus was the cause of the current 'problems', no one was able to say for sure yet, but as far as the effects were concerned, scientists and sensors were in relative agreement.

All the major ocean currents had stopped, and with them the Earth's thermohaline circulation. There was no temperature balance between the oceans, and apart from the tides due to the gravitational pull of the sun and moon, there seemed to be no movement in the world's oceans. The effects were as simple as they were frightening - unspeakable, hostile heat, especially along the equator, combined with desertification, while near the polar ice caps ever more enormous amounts of snow accumulated. As well as occasional areas where the remains of human civilization we visible.

Adrian could not imagine that a simple nuclear war could be the cause. That did not mean that he questioned the effects of such a furor, but in no simulation that had been calculated before the start of the mission had such a scenario resulted in this kind of impact. Something else had to have happened. An additional event. Maybe even the actual trigger?

He knew in the long run, it didn't matter. The task of the *Genesis* was not to rack their brains over the past, but to lay the foundation stones for a new and hopefully better future. What had happened was not the business of the present. At least, no more than was necessary to deal with the problems.

And yet Adrian could not help but think about it. He would have given a lot to be able to fast-forward time a few weeks and find out right away what the sensor experts and scientists would find out. But that was unfortunately impossible. And that, in turn, meant he would be going down there in less than two hours to see for himself on the ground.

"Morris?" a cautious voice suddenly echoed through the anchorage. Just moments later, Horvat pulled himself along the tethers into the spacious hall and looked around until his gaze finally lingered on Adrian. "There you are."

"What's up?" Adrian stowed the tablet in one of his pockets and returned his gaze. "You're early. It doesn't start for another two hours."

"That's why I'm here. I don't know if I'm much help down there."

Adrian raised an eyebrow. "Don't tell me you're scared."

"No." He shook his head vehemently. "Not afraid. Really, I'm not. I just don't understand why you requested me, of all people, for the expedition. I'm an agronomist and not suited for the first wave. I won't be much help to you down there."

"You will be," Adrian merely replied.

"And what makes you so sure of that?"

"Because the conditions aren't as lousy as you might think." Adrian tapped his finger on the pocket that held his tablet. "The mission parameters look good. And I need people I can count on."

Horvat narrowed his eyes. "Do you anticipate any problems?"

"It would be foolish not to expect any."

"That's not what I mean. Are you expecting problems that aren't from Earth? That someone will refuse orders?"

Adrian took a deep breath. He would have liked to tell him what was going on. That he did not trust Toussaint and by now even had a solid reason not to. That he actually did not want to take her on the expedition, but just as much did not want to leave her on the *Genesis*. That he hoped to be able to confront her on Earth, far away from the others, and if necessary to build up enough pressure to find out who she was. And why she was here.

Only he could not. Must not. As long as he did not know anything more precise, such an approach meant an immense risk. Not only if Toussaint had indeed been snuck in from the outside, but even more so if that was not the case. The *Genesis* mission was built on three pillars: Cohesion, Trust, and Protocols. Everyone on board - except Toussaint - had been selected at birth based on genetic traits and taken in for training when they were just three years old. Without exception, they had spent virtually every day of their previous lives side by side, grouped together in clusters of 30. Only before the onset of cryostasis had the groups in the modules been reshuffled to discourage overly close bonds and possible power struggles after awakening. Hence, 30 modules of 30 people each.

"Horvat, you know as well as I do how delicate any decision, no matter how small, can be," Adrian finally said. "We have dealt with each other a time or two before. I know I can rely on you."

"And I know you're lying to my face right now, yet telling the truth," Horvat growled. "All right, Morris. I'm with you on this. Maybe..." He paused and pressed his lips together as if to stop himself from speaking.

"What?" demanded Adrian, laughing softly. "Come on, tell me!"

"I know it's a little early, but do you think we could stop by Svalbard?"

"Svalbard? You mean the Global Seed Vault?"

"Exactly. Svalbard is less than seven hundred miles as the crow flies from the listening post. If fuel permits. Listen, Morris. I know we have our own special supplies on board. Seeds and all. And I also know that we are required by protocol to use only those so as not to jeopardize the breeding. But even you must realize what a loss that is! We have about 700 species aboard the *Genesis*. At one time, nearly 6000 were cultivated; don't even get me started on all the others that were essentially used!"

Adrian sighed.

"I know what I'm asking," Horvat continued before he could say anything back. "Believe me, I really do. I also wouldn't ask if I didn't think there was a chance of success."

"Success?" Adrian managed to stifle a derisive snort just in time. "You actually think this venture could succeed?"

"Yes." Suddenly Horvat sounded more than determined. "In 2051, the Vault was extensively renovated and expanded. The entire facility was embedded in a free-swinging frame capable of withstanding quakes of magnitude nine on the Richter scale, and in addition it has its own antimatter power plant, which in theory can keep the cooling system intact for almost 3,000 years. Unless the Vault took a direct nuclear hit or was contaminated, the seeds should have stood the test of time!"

"Are you going to salvage it?"

"No. I just want to get an overview. If the Vault is still intact, maybe I can convince the Directors to use it."

"All right."

"What?"

"All right," Adrian repeated. "We'll go there - provided you convince Mabena to allow it."

"Thank you!" Within a single moment, Horvat turned and pulled out of the anchor bay. "Thank you, Morris!"

Adrian looked after him for another short moment, then

snorted softly and took a deep breath. While he knew the importance of protocols and the importance of following them, he saw no salvation in following them unquestioningly. Obedience to corpses had never proven to be a useful means of dealing with problems. And honestly, if they could save a few more species through the Seed Vault, why not?

He felt a grin flit across his lips. Breaking out of his thought carousel for a few minutes had been a nice distraction, even if it did not resolve the real reason for his musings. But that was all right. It would have to be fine until he found a way to resolve this dilemma.

Finally, he unfastened his belt from the handhold and pulled himself a few feet to the side. From here, he had a better view of the massive anchor that would connect the *Genesis* to an equally huge orbital lift, which in turn kept the entire station in orbit around Earth. Although that was not quite right: if the anchor broke, they would be at a sufficient altitude to assume a stable and, of course, predetermined orbit around the planet. Nothing had been left to chance.

Nevertheless, Adrian could not help but feel a certain awe in the face of such advanced technology and such gigantic machines. At that time, this had been the pinnacle of human technology. Not so much the station itself, which was impressive as well, but rather the orbital lift and the technology behind it. For while the *Genesis* itself was within a Molniya orbit and accordingly flew a sweeping ellipse around the planet. To the south of Chile existed a titanic orbital lift into which the station could hook if needed - and in less than two hours it would do so.

"Amazing, this technique, huh?" a strangely mocking voice suddenly sounded somewhere behind him, making him wince involuntarily. Not even a second later, a young woman with pitch-black hair pulled herself to him and looked at him with an indefinable look. "Hey. I'm Iris Sato."

"Not amazing," Adrian replied, extending his hand to her. "Just well thought out. So you're my physicist?"

"Physicist, chemist and biologist," she grinned, chiming in. "Everything you can possibly imagine and more."

She nodded toward the anchor.

"Well thought out, then? No space magic?"

"I can assure you of that."

"Well, if you say so as an engineer... Probably going to be a good bang when this thing hooks up, right?"

"We'll see. It was pretty manageable in the simulation."

"You're just brimming with confidence."

"I have faith in technology." Adrian looked past her. "After all, the station doesn't thunder in full, to put it bluntly, but slows down before it does. We have more than just powerful thrusters. The worst that can happen is that the lift is broken, but at least so far everything looks good. A signal goes out every five minutes to confirm functionality, and so far we've always gotten a response."

"And if it does fail?"

"Then we can take a stable low orbit and go from there. Won't be quite as pleasant and we won't get back on board, but there are worse things."

"You're the sober type, aren't you?"

"Excuse me?"

"Restrained, rational, believer in technology."

"I'd be out of place if I weren't." Adrian gave her an appraising look. "Do you feel any different? I couldn't be here if I didn't trust technology."

"I'm not saying I don't trust it, but we're already stretching the laws of nature pretty thin. What we're doing here is the cosmic equivalent of an emergency landing on an aircraft carrier."

"It's not quite that bad." Adrian replied, doing his best to suppress a grin. "After all, we're not using a hook in the true sense, but high-power electromagnets. If it doesn't work, we just fly by it and try again in a few hours. Nothing can really go wrong."

"Really."

"If you have any doubts..."

"Never mind." She sighed theatrically. "I just wanted to tease you a little. See how my boss reacts."

"I'm not your..." he started, but she interrupted him almost immediately.

"Yes, you are. Adrian Scott Morris. Module 22, the module I've been assigned to - and I'm your intended, by the way, in case scenarios one and two fail."

"I'm sorry, what?"

"Oh." She grinned from ear to ear. "Right. That's one of the scenarios that's generally not yet known. As I'm sure you know, we've been thoroughly studied and our genes systematically screened. The brightest minds in humanity have calculated which of us must have children with whom in order to create the healthiest and most genetically diverse offspring possible. Aside from the fact that sooner or later it will degenerate into a protocol clusterfuck, you and I are supposed to father at least five children. But as I said, just in case we lose so many people that such measures become necessary."

"And you were chosen because you're the perfect pain in the ass?" returned Adrian, trying to make his voice sound as indifferent as possible. Still, he couldn't quite avoid a slight, almost nervous tremor. Sato wasn't unsightly, and he had been aware that he would have to reproduce, but the thought of having to father a set number of children was terrifying.

"So this is what it takes to get you upset?" She snorted. "Children? Humanity is screwed, we're floating around in space where even the slightest damage can kill us all, and you're afraid of kids? Geez, Morris."

"Let's just prepare ourselves," he replied tonelessly. "Let's see how fertile I am after the radiation down there."

"CONTACT with orbital anchor in ten minutes." The onboard system's voice echoed in a monotone yet strangely promising manner through the relative silence of the station. "Please evacuate areas 1 through 4 and seal airlocks A-1 through C-7. Emergency teams Alpha through Delta, stand by."

Adrian folded his arms in front of his chest - or at least attempted a gesture that came closest. The mix of space suit and hazmat suit he had donned did not leave much room for such movements. Not exactly what he had hoped for, but Mabena and the boarding officers in charge had probably agreed that a higher protection factor mattered more than unrestricted mobility for the time being.

He had been waiting for a few minutes with the rest of his team behind the window of thick bulletproof glass that separated the control room of the anchor bay from the rest of the facility. It had been decided that they would not take any chances and accordingly would lock down this part of the *Genesis* in case of material failure or other unforeseen problems. Not exactly a rosy outlook, but at least the control room offered some sort of modest security.

Hovering immediately beside him were Horvat and Sato, who, like him, held their arms in front of their chests in a half-crossed, half-stupid-looking position. The former had already put on his helmet, so that his face was no longer visible, but he was the only one of them who thought it was necessary. Besides the two of them, there was a relatively skeptical looking Toussaint and a slightly stocky-looking guy named Lars Aacken in the control room. A silent type, but according to his file, a specialist in salvage operations - and thus one of the few on board who had the skills to tackle problems relatively 'head on'.

"Contact in five minutes."

A dull rattle rippled through the station, followed closely by a piercing but relatively quiet whine as the massive generators kicked in to power the electromagnet in the anchor. And although there were only a handful of magnetic components in his suit, Adrian almost instantly felt the tremendous forces unleashed by the magnet. The steel components of the *Genesis* itself also creaked audibly. Fortunately, the anchor was lowered just a few seconds later.

"Is anyone else nervous?" asked Sato tauntingly, but could not hide a worried undertone. "No? No one?"

"Quiet on the radio, Sato."

"Oh, come on, Morris, don't be a killjoy!"

"This isn't a game."

"If I was always in as bad a mood as you, I'm sure I would have become the boss, too."

"You're supposed to shut the hell up!"

"What happens if I talk?"

"Besides you pissing me off, putting me in a bad mood, and making me more willing to leave you down there?"

"A whole planet to myself? Oh God, how terrible!"

"That's enough!" hissed Adrian. "I mean it! Enough!"

Sato gave him another half angry, half incredulous look, but then actually shut up. A circumstance for which Adrian was more than grateful. He knew that she only wanted to ease the tension and cheer up the moment a little, but that was not helping him in the least. He didn't readily admit it, but he himself was also considerably more nervous than he would have liked to admit.

"Contact in two minutes."

Adrian closed his eyes and reminded himself why nothing could go wrong, that both the *Genesis* anchor and the lift's anchor had to be equally magnetized to allow hooking up, that he himself had controlled how the station's thrusters powered up and slowed them down, that in the worst case they would simply shoot past the lift, correct their course, and try again in a few hours.

He knew all that. And yet there was a quiet voice full of doubt, somewhere in the depths of his mind, that kept whispering to him that sometimes only a single bolt or loose screw stood between such a maneuver and disaster, that even the smallest mistake could kill everyone on board and thus destroy the last of the humans.

He shook his head, reached for his helmet and pulled it on before sealing the suit. Instantly, dozens of different displays lit up; the most important of them projected directly into his pupils. Involuntarily, he squinted his eyes. How he hated this feeling. It was not painful, but the projection still felt like his eye was drying up.

"Contact in thirty seconds."

Adrian took as deep a breath as he could. He had long since grown accustomed to the stale and wan-tasting oxygen that had been preserved on the station for over 2,000 years, but breathing what one breathed in such a suit was a horror in itself every time. No chance of calming down like that.

"Contact in twenty seconds."

Actually, it was a strange thought to imagine that the crew of the *Genesis* represented the last hope of a doomed species, yet they had to rely on two millennia-old machines to work and do their job on the first try. In space, that was one thing, but the parts of the lift inside the atmosphere had been subject to war and corrosion. Even the best precautions and materials could not prevent it. What if the lift ruptured and pulled the entire station out of its orbit?

"Contact in ten seconds."

Suddenly Adrian felt all alone. If they died, it was all over. No one would come to their rescue. No one would even know.

"Contact in five seconds. Stand by. Three. Two. One. Contact."

The generators howled; a shrill, almost infernal whirring that echoed through the silence like a whiplash, followed closely by a dull thump and a shudder that made the entire station tremble. And then it was over.

"Contact made."

"Is that it?" rumbled Horvat's uncertain voice through the radio.

"Seems like it, doesn't it?" asked Toussaint. "Morris?"

"Hold on." Adrian grabbed the side of his helmet and pressed the radio control. "Morris here. Anchor control, do you copy?"

"I read you, Morris. Go ahead."

"Are we on? Did it work?"

"Affirmative. Contact has been made, both magnets are

operating at near full power. The cargo container is being prepared. You have lift clearance."

"Roger that. Any word from Earth, or are we really alone?"

"The automated systems have responded, but we're not picking up any signal activity indicative of humans. You shouldn't expect any contact, but if it does happen, avoid interactions for now."

"Understood."

"Avoid interactions?" asked Toussaint. "Why is that? If someone is still alive down there, we could help them!"

"That's not in the plan for Phase 1," Adrian replied. "Our own survival and the success of the mission take priority. You should know that."

"I... sorry."

Adrian bit his lip and stifled a comment. The very fact that she asked that question was further proof to him that he couldn't trust her. Anyone who had been trained for the *Genesis* Project had to know that assistance to survivors who did not have useful technical or strategic skills was not intended for the early years. That she asked anyway could have been dismissed as excitement or pity under better circumstances, but like this?

Shaking his head, he moved to the lock to the anchorage and opened it. He would have liked to follow up and call her out, but suspicion and distrust jeopardized the mission. Not to mention that in a few hours, with the threat of leaving her behind or dropping her off in a contaminated area, he had better means at his disposal than mere accusations.

Silently, he led his people past the massive generators into the center of the anchorage, where the pentagonal personnel pod, some ten yards wide, was already waiting for them. Ahead of them now lay a good four-hour journey via the orbital lift until they finally reached Earth. Actually it was ridiculously long, considering that the station was currently just shy of 400 miles above the Earth. But one should not expect too much from man and material.

Adrian was the first to enter the capsule and sat down on the side facing away from the access hatch. Despite its considerable size, the capsule was not particularly spacious. It had room for just eight people in full gear. Each of the inward-facing seats had an automated system that hooked into their suits, eliminating the need for seat belts, but other than that, there was nothing. No windows, no screens, and no way to influence transportation from the inside. For the next few hours, they were completely at the mercy of technology.

"Lock the door," he ordered after Toussaint was the last to board. "Anchor control, this is Morris. We're ready to go. Disengage as soon as you're ready."

"Roger that, Morris. There's a slight problem with the cargo unit."

"Specify."

"The power supply to the brakes is not working properly. We'll delay touchdown as long as possible and try to fix the problem remotely. You go ahead and go down and secure the landing zone. If we don't manage it, we'll go to lift protocol Zeta."

"Roger that. Send us down."

"Protocol Zeta?" asked Horvat.

"We'll get off and send the lift back up," Adrian replied as a dull jolt twitched through the capsule - the tell-tale sign that the ride was about to start. "Actually, both the capsule and the cargo module brake via a relatively complex system of electrical resistance braking and a series of increasingly powerful mechanical braking systems. The latter are primarily for safety purposes. I assume that the cargo container's resistance brake is not working properly. In that case, we can send the personnel capsule back up, magnetize it and thus break the fall. However..."

"It will break in the process?"

"It's not out of the question. We wouldn't be able to get back up, but at least we'd have our equipment on the ground. The rest of the *Genesis* would have to go out via the landing pods. Not the most elegant way, but it's doable."

"Wasn't that foreseeable beforehand?" Sato wanted to know. "Surely it could have been checked!"

"Ask me an easier one." He shrugged, but had no idea if the others could even see it. "I think it will work. As long as the cargo module doesn't enter the Earth's atmosphere, they've got all the time in the world. At least proverbially."

"Still, not particularly good omens," she grumbled. "Everything depends on that very thing. It would be a shame if it failed on that of all things."

"We have all the equipment on board in twenty copies," Adrian replied. "At least everything that really matters. Sure, vehicles would be helpful, but in the end, that's secondary. We could also start Phase 1 around the orbital lift in an emergency."

"Let's just hope it works," Horvat said. "I've been in discussions with Mabena for too long to just give up on the Global Seed Vault."

"Take it easy. No one is talking about giving up here."

"How long can the *Genesis* actually hold the geostationary position?" Aacken turned his head to the side, opened the visor of his visor and looked at Adrian with an indefinable expression. "We're four hours out here, and I guarantee you the brakes won't be fixed that quickly."

"Why do you ask?"

"I asked because there are humungous forces acting on the station right now," he answered immediately. "I'm no engineer, but even an idiot can figure that the *Genesis* can't take that forever. So how long before she has to decouple?"

"Actually, she should be able to hold position long enough to allow for the complete unloading of a module." Adrian returned his gaze. "Four hours for a trip down, two hours to get back up. So six hours for eight people, makes a day for one module. I haven't personally calculated through the resulting forces, but I can't imagine it would be impossible."

Aacken made an obviously disgruntled noise.

"What?" demanded Adrian immediately. "If you have doubts, out with it!"

"Of course I have doubts, otherwise I would have shut the fuck up! I..."

"Watch your tone!"

"I..." He paused for a moment and finally nodded. "You're right. I apologize, Morris. It may be that the station and the lift can withstand the forces in theory, but personally, I'm concerned about the anchoring on Earth. If the brakes on the cargo module are already having problems, who can guarantee us that the electromagnets on the anchor will work properly? If the mooring in Chile breaks and the magnets are not released immediately, the station is in danger of crashing. I think it's extremely risky to subject it to such stresses on the very first tour without first getting a picture on site."

"He's not wrong," Sato agreed with him in a low voice. "There are no control instances for the entirely mechanical anchorages on the ground."

"You understand, though, that we'll be sitting around down there for at least a day then, right?" retorted Adrian. "I can radio anchor control and relay your concerns, but under some circumstances it will be quite uncomfortable for us."

"I don't care. I'd rather have that than a total disaster."

Toussaint nodded. "I agree."

"Me too," Aacken agreed with her. "Horvat?"

"Likewise."

Adrian sighed and grabbed his helmet. "I'll talk to anchor control and see what I can do. Let's just hope they can get the brakes working in time. Personally, I don't feel like spending even a second longer down there than absolutely necessary."

Chapter Four

THERE WAS HARDLY MORE than a short, dull jolt to indicate that the capsule had reached the earth, followed by a few seconds of silence, which in turn was broken by a long, drawn-out rattle as the anchor's safety hooks moved into their intended positions. An unadorned, downright mundane event that did not even begin to do justice to the immense significance it held.

With a hand signal, Adrian told the others to prepare their equipment and wait for their protective suits to be released from the capsule. However, this could take some time, because at that moment the automatic scans of the measuring instruments installed on the capsule were still running. An additional backup to check the results that the sensors of the *Genesis* had provided. A bit funny, considering that they could not see any of the results here in the capsule and instead had to rely on the anchor control to do its job.

That was alright with Adrian, as the scans meant he had a few extra minutes to prepare for what lay ahead. While he did not feel particularly nervous, it would have been a lie to say that he was not excited. Whereas even that was hardly the appropriate word for his emotional state. Sure, on the one hand, he could not deny his excitement, his entire life had been headed solely for this moment, but at the same time he also felt a certain bitterness. A melancholy and resignation. After all, his presence, his entire existence was tied to the end of humanity.

"Morris, come in," the distorted voice of the anchor control operator suddenly rushed through the radio. Involuntarily, Adrian raised his eyebrows. Strange that there was interference now, of all times.

"Morris here."

"We were able to repair one cargo module and are slowing it down with the personnel pod. The rest of the cargo unit remains in orbit for now. ETA at one hour. Get an overview of the landing zone and report in if necessary so we can delay arrival. Otherwise, we'll bring up the personnel pod now."

"Roger that. What about my request?"

"The Directors share your people's objections. As soon as the cargo module is offloaded, we'll bring it back on board with the capsule and cut the station's connection. You will be on your own for 24 hours. You'll probably have to expect radio communications to be affected as well."

"Understood."

"You are cleared to seek shelter and hold tight there."

"Negative, anchor control. If the scans look good, I'd like to move forward."

"Scans are fine. Radiation level is within acceptable range. The responsibility is yours alone."

"Alright, anchor control. We're going to get started."

"Roger that, Morris. Good luck down there."

"You heard the man." No sooner had the anchoring of his suit come loose than Adrian stood up and stepped to the hatch. "Here we go. Nice and easy; we're in no hurry. Secure perimeter, clear landing zone. Watch your PPE and keep an eye on the Geiger counter. Maintain radio discretion."

With those words, he unlocked the hatch - and stepped outside. The first person from the *Genesis* Project to step onto the devastated Earth. The first of the hundreds who had been in cryogenic sleep on the station to give humanity a second chance. And probably the first human to set foot on this planet in several years. Possibly even decades or centuries.

He moved mechanically, almost as if remote-controlled, stepping out of the capsule like a puppet, leaving what was probably the only place on this planet that could offer him and the others protection and safety. How strange everything felt; every breath and every movement - and how normal and familiar. Even 2,000 years of cryo-sleep failed to fade his muscle memory of his former life.

Glaring sunlight shone down on him, but it did not blind him. The visor of his helmet transformed his entire surroundings into a monochrome, heavily darkened image; contours and outlines were artificially sharpened and emphasized by the system. A surreal world, tapped by ancient technology, but without it he could not possibly have found his way around.

A thick blanket of snow had buried everything around him. Even the anchorage of the orbital lift, a massive installation in itself, was only vaguely visible. The titanic steel claws, which had been driven dozens of yards deep into the rock, rose from the ground like frozen gods of a bygone era, clinging to the orbital lift. Almost as if they wanted to hold on to the hope that had always been associated with the project by any means necessary.

Adrian looked around. If it had not been for his visor, he would not have recognized anything at all in the white of ice and snow - although they were facing mostly ice here, as he noticed during his first cautious steps. Only the top few inches seemed to be covered by a thin layer of snow; underneath, dozens of inches of hard-frozen, impenetrable ice awaited him. It would be a real pleasure to clear the landing zone.

Sighing softly, he tapped the side of his helmet and activated the Geiger counter display. If there had been an immediate danger, the system would have automatically reported it long ago, but even so, he wanted to know how high the radiation levels were. Just under 100 microsieverts per hour. Not catastrophic, especially not because of the suits, but also not fun. The absolute bulk of the *Genesis*' equipment and machinery was designed for such levels and protected accordingly, but even the best shielding options could withstand too high radiation doses for only a limited time.

Of course, the fact that the level was so high out here at Monte Burney, and thus at the proverbial ass-end of the world, presented a different problem altogether, since it meant that the level had to be much higher elsewhere. Santiago de Chile alone was more than 1200 miles from here, and there were no other strategically important targets in the area. At least, Adrian could not imagine that anyone would have detonated a nuclear bomb in the vicinity.

In any case - and this was most important at the moment - the immediate vicinity of the orbital lift and the landing zone seemed to be relatively intact, apart from the ice. An eruption of the Monte Burney had probably not taken place. Which was something they would have at least been prepared for.

"Aacken," Adrian finally said, looking around at the others who were also leaving the capsule at those moments and cautiously entering the icy wasteland. "Your area of expertise. Protocol calls for the use of plasma torches."

"Inefficient," he replied. "We would have to cut out blocks and remove them manually. Without heavy equipment, we would be at it for hours. We don't have that much time."

"Alternatives?"

"None viable." He gestured toward some larger chunks of ice. "The lift modules automatically compensate for deviations in landing height. We operate with a tolerance of fifteen yards. We don't even have that here. I suggest we level the landing zone. The rest should fit."

"Agreed. You're in command."

"Horvat and Toussaint, you take that chunk up ahead," he ordered instantly, raising his hand and pointing to a chunk of ice about twenty yards from them. "I'll take care of the small stuff. Sato, you walk the perimeter and look for any other chunks that need to be removed. Anything less than three feet high is okay as long as it doesn't have a rock or piece of steel in it. We'll be leaving the LZ in forty minutes. Set your timers."

"Roger that."

"Morris," he continued, pointing in the direction of the control building that was set into the rugged ridge a good 200 yards away from them. "I see no reason why you should waste time. As far as I'm concerned, you can start looking around the terminal. We need a base of operations, and personally, with the radiation levels, I wouldn't mind if we could get by without a bivouac."

"All right." Adrian nodded. "Just let me know if you need more time."

While Aacken and the others instantly set about clearing the landing zone of the largest chunks of ice and other obstacles, Adrian picked his way across the ice and snow toward the control terminal. The protective suit, which weighed dozens of pounds, did not make it easy for him to keep his balance despite servo motors and stabilizers. But after a few yards he had finally gained a feel for the ground underneath him, so he was able to make reasonably safe progress.

He repeatedly looked around and stared at the ice desert that stretched in every direction. This part of the anchorage, supported by huge reinforced concrete girders, jutted out a good hundred yards above the actual ridge, giving a unique panoramic view of the surrounding terrain. Everything up to the horizon was white. Mountains, valleys and even the foothills of the Strait of Magellan. Desolate, barren, and dead.

Adrian shuddered. Meteorologically, it was supposed to be summer here. What could have happened to make the seemingly eternal winter bury everything so mercilessly? What kind of world conflagration had humans triggered to bring about such an all-encompassing climate collapse?

He had no idea, and he was not even sure he wanted to know. Some things were too bad to remember, and others should be forgotten forever for far too many reasons. However, none of this was within his scope of duties. He had to take care of the practical and technical aspects of the *Genesis* Project. Questions of what happened in the past, or whether it wasn't a better idea to start from scratch, were questions for the philosophers, historians, and other humanities scholars on the station to ponder.

Of course, it did no harm to recall the mistakes of the past to future generations, to teach them not to repeat them. However, humanity had already proven that this was not necessarily a very promising approach. Perhaps it was best to forget everything that had been and to hope that those who would follow them would not get those ideas in the first place.

Finally, he reached the control terminal - or what was left of it. Like the rest of the facility, it had been built to withstand the test of time and, if possible, all the insanity that mankind could devise and implement over the centuries. Nevertheless, weather and other environmental influences had left unmistakable traces.

The massive entrance to the facility lay exposed - aside from a few snowdrifts - and the structural integrity of the building seemed to have suffered little. For an area of seismic activity, a more than respectable result. The free-swinging anchors and columns seemed to have stood the test of time. Nevertheless, the walls were crumbling in many places and everything else looked more than a little run-down. A circumstance that was to be expected. The issue here was not aesthetics, cleanliness or accessibility, but very basic aspects such as accessibility, functionality and protection. And that was still the case.

At that time, no gate or other barrier had been installed at the entrance. Monte Burney was isolated and difficult to reach, and there was no fauna worth mentioning in the area. The more vital parts of the complex were protected further back, but here in front it was a matter of mere protection from the forces of nature - and of being able to accommodate a few vehicles.

Still, there seemed to have been more than a few visitors over the centuries. Used packages of snacks and provisions, cigarette butts, and even sleeping bags and things - whose purpose and use Adrian could not make out - covered large parts of the interior. Graffiti adorned the barren concrete walls and even traces of campfires could be seen. Obviously, some daredevils had taken the climb to enjoy the morbid character of the facility. Or had he and the other participants in the project at some point degenerated into a mere curiosity? A strange thing out there in space, a relic of the past that had been looked at in wonder and incomprehension, not knowing that it would serve its purpose after all?

Shaking his head, he paused and bent down to pick up a small, shimmering metallic device. It was barely larger than the back of his gloves and was shaped like a small horseshoe. It had no buttons, but a connector in the center of the object told him that it could be charged or at least connected to another device.

"Aacken, what's your status?" he asked, trying to make out the others through the gate, but the sharp contrast of light and darkness made it impossible.

"We're done and evacuating the LZ right now. Do you need anything?"

"Yeah, I found something here and I want Toussaint to take a look at it. Can you three unload the cargo module?"

"Can do."

"I'm on my way, Morris," Toussaint's voice rushed through the radio. "Be right with you."

Adrian said nothing in reply and instead grabbed one of the pockets on the chest piece of his suit. The device's connection was, of course, completely different from anything he knew from before, and thus different from anything used on the *Genesis*. Still, that did not mean he could not access the part. A lot could happen in 2,000 years, but at least at first glance, the port seemed to him like a serial transmission system. A classic USB.

Because of his gloves and therefore lack of fine motor skills, it took him a few moments to connect the cable ends of his suit's universal interface to the port, but when he succeeded, the device immediately began to hum softly.

"What's that?" sounded Toussaint's voice behind him, and not a second later she stepped up to him and reached out for the thing. "Did you find this?"

"Yes. I can't get data access, but it's still doing something. Take a look at this. Hang on a second, I'm creating a link to your suit and..."

He had just raised his other hand when suddenly a soft hissing sound came from the device and a small, dense cloud of steam rose. At first he thought that he had accidentally overloaded it and thus destroyed it, but then he noticed that the cloud of steam seemed to float in a kind of thin membrane. Fine lines of bluish light came from it, and within a few seconds it formed the blurred image of two faces. A hologram.

"And we're live!" a young man's croaky, distorted voice came from the device, and one of the light faces moved its mouth with a time delay. "We're on the Burney, speaking into the future!"

"Tom, this is silly," the second light face grumbled, audibly annoyed. A woman. "This thing is a tourist trap, nothing more, nothing less. You don't seriously think it's going to last hundreds of years!"

"Only one way to find out!" the man grinned. "Besides, I didn't climb this stupid mountain just to leave! So, people of the future: this is Tom Anderson from beautiful Newark, New Jersey. It's the year 2877 and you bozos have been sleeping up there for 300 years by now. We on Earth are doing just fine, thanks for asking. I don't know about you guys, but I'd feel pretty screwed. That's only fair, if you ask me, because I have to fork over five percent of my taxes every year for you fuckers and..."

"Tom, that's enough!"

"What, Anne? Those fools will never see it anyway! In a few thousand years, you take them down, put them in a home, and that's it. This crappy *Genesis* is costing us all a bunch of money and getting us nowhere! Time and time again we have to listen to the same shit! Ah, the world is coming to an end! Ah, we're so full of shit! Ah, guilt! I can't stand it anymore! I came all the way here to let these motherfuckers know what fucking idiots they are!"

The light face looked directly at Adrian. "You're fucking idiots! There, now I'm done! Let's go."

WITH PRACTICED MOVEMENTS, Adrian unlocked the doors that led deeper into the facility until he finally came upon the generator room and the antimatter power plant installed there. On the way here, he had found more than once that the actual layout of the rooms and machines differed from what had once been planned. Not bad, but still annoying, costing him valuable time that would have been better used elsewhere.

Even here, deep inside the sprawling facility, there were traces of people from earlier times. Not behind all the armored doors that could only be unlocked by a complex key system, but in front of them. Quite a few people had tried to gain access over the centuries. In some places, even drills and, judging by the soot residue on the walls, even explosives had been used.

Adrian tried not to think too much about it as he watched the antimatter power plant power up. All around him, even the emergency lights were already coming on, which personally would not have expected to be working under any circumstances after such a long time.

Nevertheless, he could not get the words from the recording out of his head. He had always been aware that the *Genesis* Project had swallowed up immense sums of money over many centuries, especially from the population of the wealthier countries, but he had never thought about the frustration of the general population. Dozens of generations had lived their lives without Earth going down, and yet had been obliged to continue maintaining the station. Enough reason for some to make the long and arduous journey here, to cross the cordon of the international protection forces and wreak havoc.

Or was it possible that there was no longer a protection force? Not just a few daredevils had been at work here, but obviously whole armies of tourists. Hell, he had even found children's toys further back! What if the project and everyone aboard the *Genesis* had been written off centuries ago and this facility left to its own devices?

"It's really getting to you, isn't it?", Toussaint's voice suddenly brought him out of his thoughts. "The readouts on your helmet are lighting up your face."

"Of course it's getting to me," he murmured, returning her gaze. "You heard the guy, didn't you? To him, we're just idiots floating around in orbit."

"That may be. But..."

"But what?"

"Well, he and his descendants are guaranteed dead. We're not."

"That's pretty cynical, Toussaint."

"I know, but it's the truth." She tried a half-smile. "What did you expect, Morris? That everyone would see us as heroes? The station was extremely expensive to maintain. It was agreed that as much as possible would be done from Earth to prevent wear and tear. Not only on the ground, but in orbit as much as possible. Somebody had to pay for it. And the majority of the population certainly did not grasp the full meaning and benefits of this mission. Nor could they. We are of no use to the living. Only the death of all gives us meaning."

"I know." Adrian sighed. "It's still unfortunate. I know I shouldn't care, but I do. In fact, if I'm honest, I feel screwed."

"Screwed?"

He nodded. "I never asked to be part of this mission. Someone else decided it for me. I had no childhood, no adolescence, no time as an adult. Always just training, training, training. As soon as I came of age, it was on to the final preparations and then cryostasis. And now here I am. This guy on the record at least had a life."

Toussaint was silent - and Adrian knew exactly why. This was something she could not relate with, since she had never been through the program. And even though he hardly felt like it right now for the life of him, this was possibly the moment he had been waiting for.

He took a quick glance at his Geiger counter and then nodded to her. "I think we can take the helmets off."

"Are you sure?"

He gave no answer, but instead undid the fasteners that connected his helmet to his suit and pulled it off his head.

After a moment's hesitation, she did the same.

"Toussaint," he said, looking her straight in the eye. "Who are you?"

"What?"

"I know you weren't in the *Genesis* program," he continued. "You were at Sorbonne University and joined this project after the fact. However, all information about it is classified and not even I can access it."

"I..."

"I'm not done yet," he interrupted her. "The others aren't listening in. I'm not going to risk any strife, and I'm not going to set you up. But if you lie to me, or if I even feel that you do, I will send you packing. Do you understand me?"

"Morris, I..."

"That's a yes or no question."

"Yes, Morris. I hear you."

"Good. So, who are you?"

"Cassandra Toussaint. The information about me in the onboard system is correct. What I'm surprised about is that it's retrievable. Actually, it was agreed that I would get a fake resume under my name."

"Agreed? With whom?"

"I can't say."

"Do you really want to stay behind in the desert?"

"You told me not to lie to you," she replied, "and I won't. It's the truth when I tell you that I can't tell you."

"Why not?"

She looked to the floor.

"Toussaint, does it really have to be this way?"

"If there's no other way, then yes," she whispered.

"Why?"

She fell silent.

"All right." Adrian cleared his throat. "I know you studied advanced technical computer science, information science, and cloud and network infrastructure engineering. With that, you're more than capable of easily overriding any onboard system, covering up intrusions, and doing whatever else you can with the systems. As far as I'm concerned, it's not even out of the question that you're responsible for the system cascade. If you don't want to talk, I'll radio Anchor Control now, inform them about you, and get permission from the Directors to leave you here to die."

"I belong to *Aegis Dawn*," she whispered suddenly.

"*Aegis Dawn*?" repeated Adrian. "What's that supposed to be?"

"A private initiative. The main funder of the whole *Genesis* Project."

"The main funder of the project was the United Nations."

"Officially, yes."

"So you're telling me that was just a lie?"

"Exactly. The United Nations was only able to raise a third of the money needed for the launch. The war between the U.S. and China put two of the main funders out of action. And with the European and African Unions busy with reconstruction aid after that, there was no one left to raise the money. The project failed by only a hair. So some of the biggest companies got together under the name *Aegis Dawn* to save the *Genesis*."

"If that's the case, there must be evidence," Adrian merely retorted.

"There is. A secret room exists beneath the reactor deck.

In it is a sealed, vacuumed glass vase containing a data storage medium and a handwritten and personally signed letter from Dr. Sara Abraham."

Adrian took a deep breath and tried to digest what he had just heard, but with only moderate success at best. Finally, he decided to just nod.

"All right," he grumbled. "Suppose you're telling the truth and this room really exists - what does that mean? Why are you here? What's your job?"

"I'm supposed to monitor the progress of the project and protect it."

"Protect?"

"Indeed. You know how fierce the opposition to the *Genesis* Project has been from some groups. Conspiracy theorists, environmentalists, religious zealots, the whole gamut. What we're doing here - *Genesis* - was the common denominator for them. The likelihood that there would be attacks or other sabotage was huge. On Earth, a wide network of security services and private military organizations provided security for the facility. At least during the first decades. The only sore spot was the station in orbit."

"The station whose crew, with the exception of you, had been trained and closely monitored since early childhood?" countered Adrian. "That doesn't necessarily sound like a security breach."

"Then how do you explain that four modules at once fell victim to a single system cascade?" She snorted bitterly. "Morris, that was sabotage!"

"Can you prove it?"

She bit her lip. "No. But I think it was someone in our module."

"Why?"

"What I told you after you pulled me out of the capsule was the truth. I woke up almost three years ago. However, it wasn't what you think. My capsule was rebuilt before launch. After any system failure or unexpected event, I was supposed to automatically wake up and take a look. That didn't happen in cryo year 1191, or 1582, or 1875, although there were large-scale failures that ultimately killed 180 people. I haven't had time to look at it yet, but I'm sure someone knew about me and kept me in cryostasis on purpose."

"Why didn't they just kill you?"

She tilted her head and raised her eyebrows. "Come on, Morris, you can't be that stupid. What do you think would have happened if you'd been woken up and found me with a broken neck or stab wound in my chest? It takes some knowledge to kill someone in cryostasis and make it look like an accident or a medical problem. By keeping me asleep, our perpetrator could continue to pursue his goal without immediately arousing suspicion."

"And you think it was someone from our module because ..."

"Because the airlock was open," she interrupted him. "Exactly. I know it closed before the mission started. When the module was abandoned, there must have been an error that prevented it from closing again. Until I did, three years ago."

"Whoever did that would have had a chance to do the entire station, right? Why these modules of all things?"

"Not necessarily. The onboard system was active, after all, and we can't underestimate how well it worked despite that. I don't think it was tampered with; otherwise, you would have found traces. Presumably, the person knew exactly how to bypass it and not be discovered. But he couldn't complete his plan. It intervened and adapted."

Adrian held both hands in front of his mouth and breathed into his palms a few times. "This is getting worse. I'm going to have to report this to the Directors."

"That will be the best way. However, doing so risks escalation."

"What do you mean?"

Toussaint was silent for a moment. "*Genesis* has started; humanity is at its end. Even the most deluded idiot must now realize that our existence has a purpose. If we take offensive action against him now, he may feel cornered and trigger a catastrophe. Morris, I... I know this is a lot to ask, but with your permission and your access code, I could try to track down a pattern in the six lost modules. We don't have to succeed, but we might find a connection through which we can in turn draw conclusions about the perpetrator and his motivation. These signal events in the com log may actually just be background noise or anomalies, but I may find out more about them."

"That is indeed a lot to ask."

"Was that a 'no'?"

Adrian shook his head. "I didn't say that. While I didn't think this conversation would turn out this way, for now I believe you, Toussaint. And as you said, *Genesis* has started. The priority is the listening post in Greenland. We'll finish our mission, and as soon as the others have left the station, we'll deal with this saboteur."

Chapter Five

A SINGLE CARGO module approached the Earth's surface, roaring and howling; a massive juggernaut of technology, dozens of tons of steel. Anchor control, as expected, had failed to get the brakes back on in time, so it slid slowly and almost reverently over the orbital lift cable, carried by the personnel capsule. Although it was only a single module, detached from the rest of the cargo unit, it was an awe-inspiring sight.

Normally, the unit was reminiscent of a spider carrying a cocoon full of eggs. More than a dozen cargo modules, each one a cube thirty yards across, were clamped into a massive central unit, held together by myriad connectors, supports, and brackets that in turn connected the individual modules to the carrier body and its spider-legged braking devices.

Normally. Now they had to do without them. However, at least anchor control had managed to slow down at least one module via the personnel pod and send it down to them - which meant they didn't have to wait out a whole day of waiting here first.

"Cargo module looks good," Adrian said into the radio as he watched the last few yards of the landing procedure along with the others from a safe distance. "Anchor control, ground contact has been made. Thank you for your efforts. Can you tell me how things are going on your side yet?"

"Affirmative, Morris. You've been assigned cargo module 7. For the time being, we feel it is appropriate to execute landing protocol Alpha-3."

"Alpha-3?" repeated Adrian, while trying not to let his surprise show through. "No offense, but why all of a sudden? I thought we were supposed to approach the listening post in Greenland?"

"That's correct. In cargo module 7 you will find a long-range, environmental protection class 1 aircraft, designed for three people. Use it to advance to the listening post, secure the data at all costs, and return to the starting point on Monte Burney. Meanwhile, two of your people will hold position and prepare the landing zone for the arrival of additional personnel. Have the control facility fully operational within twenty-four hours so we can begin running the *Genesis* protocol at our next lift contact."

Adrian remained silent.

"Morris, please confirm."

"Understood," he finally growled. "But next time, please figure it out sooner. Do we still have clearance for the Global Seed Vault?"

"Affirmative."

"Roger that, anchor control. We'll check back in twenty-four hours."

With those words, Adrian disconnected, clasped his hands over his helmet, and sighed with all his heart. If there was one thing he did not need, it was this. Now that Mabena had ordered him to Earth and given him more or less free rein, the corset of a protocol was more than a hindrance, meaning that he was now only allowed to react to deviations from the calculated scenarios in a very limited way. At least not without having to justify himself at length afterwards.

"How do we divide up?" asked Aacken tonelessly. "Three people for the listening post isn't a lot."

"No, it's not." Adrian agreed with him. "I have to go because I have the command codes for clearance. Toussaint is an information technician. I'll need her if the system gives me trouble. By yourself, you'd still be useful in case we need to clear something or find an alternate route, but on the other hand, we'll need Horvat if we want to go to the Global Seed Vault afterwards."

"No chance of squeezing four people on the plane?"

"And then I'm supposed to stay behind here alone?" hissed Sato immediately. "How am I supposed to manage all this, huh? What if something goes wrong and I'm stuck lying around somewhere until you guys get back?"

"We'll let the Seed Vault be," Horvat interjected, even before Adrian or any of the others could retort. "And put it off until later. If their power supply is intact now, it will be in a few weeks. I have Mabena's permission, after all. Time doesn't matter."

"Are you sure?"

He nodded. "Yes. Really, it's okay. The listening post is more important. Sato and I will take care of the base and get everything ready here."

Adrian raised his hand and gestured for him and the others to follow him to the cargo module. "Then we'll do it that way."

He took a quick look at the readings on his Geiger counter and then pulled his helmet off his head again. Protocol actually called for wearing protective gear continuously and, more importantly, completely on one's body until a certain terraforming level was reached, provided one was outside a shelter, but at least in those minutes the radiation levels weren't even close to high enough to justify it. Not to mention that he could no longer stand the smell of the air filter.

"Sato?" he finally asked as he continued walking toward the cargo module, looking around repeatedly. "You're a biologist and chemist. What's your assessment of oxygen on Earth?"

"What exactly do you mean?"

"Well." He raised his arms and made a sweeping motion. "Let's assume that the climate didn't just collapse the day before yesterday. Still, the air seems relatively normal to me, except for the altitude of the base. Can that be? Does that mean there are still plants somewhere?"

"That's a tough question, Morris."

"Is it?"

She laughed softly. "Yes. We don't know of any point of comparison to such a scenario, and at least prior to the launch of our mission, there were many different theories as to how such a causal chain might play out. The simplest explanation would be that there have been too few major events since the climate collapsed that would have depleted oxygen or contaminated the air with other gases."

"Is that what you think?"

"I think it explains it at least in part. The satellite scans have shown that there are hardly any oxygen-producing plants left on land - but at the same time we know that the oceans are practically overflowing with algae. These produce considerable amounts of oxygen. We may be dealing with a relatively stable global biosphere here, which would be beneficial to our terraforming efforts."

"Let's hope for the best, then," Adrian said, just as they reached the cargo module. "I..." he automatically paused and shook his head. He was not quite sure what he wanted to say himself, but whatever it was, it did not seem important enough to think about further. Instead, he approached the massive cargo module and opened the cover over the console next to the main gate. In an emergency, he could have opened the module purely mechanically, but since it was functional and had sufficient power, at least for the moment, he could fortunately save himself the effort.

It took only a few seconds for him to type in his command code and give the order to unlock the gate. Almost instantly, a low whirring sound was heard, confirming the start-up of the generator and machinery, and just a few seconds later, the steel began to move.

Inside the module, the lights now sprang on, illuminating not only the two dozen crates of equipment and supplies hanging from robotic arms on the ceiling, but also the handful of vehicles and aircraft that were waiting below that, secured by robotic arms as well. One, of course, was the small tractor Horvat and Sato would use to pull the cargo module out of the way; another was an all-terrain vehicle that looked quite futuristic with its curved shapes. There was also a hybrid bull-dozer-dredge equipped with a wide variety of tools, as well as a cargo helicopter and the long-range aircraft heralded by anchor control.

"I hated the simulations," Sato suddenly murmured, step-ping past him and putting his hands on his hips. "Unloading the stuff in the right order, securing everything, towing the thing... God, I hated it with all my heart."

"Why is that?"

"I don't know. There was always a kind of reluctance. An instinctive aversion. I can hardly explain myself."

"Then go back to the complex and get started there already." Horvat nodded at her. "We'll get the plane out, and once Morris and the others are launched, I'll manage the rest on my own."

"Are you sure?"

"Yeah, I think so. It's against protocol, but with the hybrid engine, you can unload the module quite nicely on your own."

"Morris, would that be okay with you, too?"

"Sure," he replied. "But first make sure the shelters are accessible. Protocol Alpha-3 is very clear on that. And maybe see if you can find a broom somewhere. Mabena will wring all our necks if the base is overflowing with centuries-old trash."

She chuckled. "I can see it now. You got it. Thanks, Horvat."

As she made her way to the base with quick steps, Toussaint, Horvat and Aacken moved into position. From the console, Adrian was already controlling the plane's tether, slowly extending the powerful robotic arm from which it was suspended. A creak ran through the entire cargo module, so loud that at first he thought the arm would break, but then it started moving, jerking and rattling, until the plane finally touched down on the ground and slowly rolled out into the open.

"Rust," Aacken growled.

"Are you sure?"

"Look." He raised his arm and pointed to a small brown spot on one of the robot arm's hydraulic joints. "That's rust."

"How can that be?" breathed Adrian, staring at the component. "Not a single component on the station should be rusting! Heck, I was there personally during the final stress tests! The corrosion rate is 0.0001 millimeters per year! Even at 2,000 years, we shouldn't have more than 0.2 millimeters of corrosion! That's nothing!"

"Then someone must have been sloppy," Aacken returned dryly. "That was to be expected. You don't have to get upset about it. As long as it works, it's all good. It could have been worse."

"Like what?"

"Well." Behind the visor of his helmet, a rare grin twitched across his lips. "The magnetic trap on the antimatter reactor could have failed. That would have made quite a bang."

"You Germans really are an optimistic people," he said.

"I consider that a cultural asset that I want to pass on to future generations. Just like our sense of humor."

"I'm laughing my ass off, Aacken. You flying?"

"Don't you want to? It's your mission, after all."

"Not exactly my comfort zone," Adrian returned. "I'll be glad to have a few hours to look at sensor data. With a little luck, we'll even get an uplink to some old satellites and find out what happened."

BRANDON Q. MORRIS & DOMINIK A. MEIER

"Well then." Aacken entered the cargo module, carried out a ladder and leaned it against the hull of the plane. "I need five minutes to get everything ready."

"Roger that." Adrian turned to Horvat, who stood beside him with a thoughtful expression, staring off into the distance somewhere. "Everything all right with you, Horvat?"

"I don't know."

"Why? Do you feel sick?"

"No, not that, but ... I don't know. I think I'm just getting my head around what happened for the first time. Or understand what it means in the fullest sense. Don't worry, I'll be fine. It's just weird."

Adrian was about to respond, but then thought better of it. He could well relate to how he felt and knew that words were nothing that could change that. This feeling - whatever you wanted to call it - would eventually affect every single participant of the *Genesis* Project. There was no other way. No matter how well they had been trained, no matter how many simulations and exercises they had gone through, in the end they were all just human beings. The last of their kind.

Finally, Adrian straightened his shoulders, banished these thoughts from his mind, and looked at the plane they were about to take to Greenland. A distance of just over 8,000 miles, which would take them just under three hours. A flight just below the stratosphere, in an aircraft that had been built to remain operational in the most adverse conditions. It could probably best be described as a cross between a vertical take-off, a space shuttle and a hypersonic rocket. More of a steerable projectile than a true aircraft.

When Aacken finally signaled that he and the craft were ready for takeoff, Adrian climbed aboard without fuss and squeezed into the small alcove behind the pilot's seat, from which there was access to the onboard systems, sensors, and possibly any old satellites remaining in orbit. Meanwhile, Toussaint took a seat a bit farther back, boxed in by emergency equipment and spare parts.

"Ready?" asked Aacken.

"Ready. Get us in the air. It's time we found out what's happened here."

"WE'RE AT MAXIMUM ALTITUDE." Aacken leaned to the side and flipped a series of switches. "All systems are operating in normal range. Shipshape."

"Did you expect anything else?"

"After that business with the grate? I wouldn't have been surprised."

"Don't make it worse, Aacken!" Toussaint growled from the back. "I'm already having trouble keeping my nerve!"

"Fear of flying?"

"No, but I don't particularly enjoy it. Especially since there's nothing back here for me to distract myself with."

"Aren't there any scanners or gauges lying around that you could adjust?"

"No."

"Then you must be very bored."

"You're a real study in human nature, Aacken."

Adrian raised both eyebrows and felt an amused smile flit across his lips, even as he followed the exchange of blows between the two rather casually. His main focus right now was trying to connect with an old satellite in orbit. He had long known that there was at least one out there; after all, the onboard systems were picking up some distorted signals. It did not take much for them to be too weak to be traced, but at least for now, that wasn't the case. He had to hurry.

He concentrated on attempting to triangulate the satellite's position, while at the same time manually adjusting the plane's highly sensitive antennas, hoping to get a better signal. So far, all attempts had been futile, but since they would still be en route for just under two hours, he had more than enough time to...

Suddenly: a signal! He had a connection!

"There we go!" he exclaimed triumphantly.

"What?" asked Toussaint immediately.

"Yes! Just a second, I'll try to transmit the signal to your suit, then you can see the interface through your helmet... Oh man, that's interesting!"

"Is that a cellular satellite?"

"I don't think so. It looks more like a GPS satellite to me. That thing is almost 2,000 years old and it still works! The solar cells have taken a beating, but they still power it! That's the jackpot, Toussaint!"

"And yet the information technician sits uselessly in the hold of the machine, having to rely on the engineer to know what he's doing," she returned tonelessly.

"I'll figure it out - and if I don't, you can tell me what to do."

Cautiously, Adrian headed for some of the satellite's subsystems, trying to get an overview. At first he had feared he was dealing with one of the older models, which would have made access much more difficult, but if he was not mistaken, it appeared to be one of the models that had been released around 2050. So unlike most of the rest of the electrical junk flying through space, this wasn't a high-tech toaster, but actually something he could work with.

"The log memory ends over 1,000 years ago," he finally grumbled, intently eyeing the displays.

"The time of the end of the world?" asked Aacken.

"Negative," Adrian muttered, continuing to work his way through the log. "We have normal signal activity until about the year 2500, then a rapid increase and a sudden drop almost to zero. That must have been the war. After that, there was off and on communication with the satellite for almost 400 years. Individual points on Earth that contacted it. Berlin, Paris, Pretoria, Delhi - a whole series of cities around the world. With the exception of the U.S., Russia and China."

"I guess those were the main warring parties then," Toussaint said, audibly resigned. "A predictable development. The contact attempts appear to have been deep bunkers. Government installations?"

"I suspect so. But there are repeated individual signals from other locations. Probably groups of survivors, though none of these signals were active for more than twenty years at most. They must have died off."

"Or they realized that the technology was no longer of use to them. In 2942, the protocol ends. A memory problem?"

"No. There was no communication from then on."

"Nothing at all?" asked Aacken quietly.

"No. Nothing. A few automatic pings of other satellites still, but nothing more. If Toussaint is right, technology was abandoned and people moved on after that. With the radiation levels, that makes sense. No device can withstand that in the long run."

"And neither can any human," Toussaint replied. "If the radiation doses are still that high now... I'm not an expert on this, but that long ago, people outdoors must have gotten lethal doses within a few years. That's surely when life expectancy dropped massively. I hate to say it, but they probably just died out."

"I think so," Adrian sighed. "Climate change will have done its bit. God, what a mess... I... Damn."

An oppressive silence settled over the plane's cockpit, broken only by the low, monotonous whine of the engines and the murmur of the tiny remnant of atmosphere that still existed at this altitude.

Adrian continued to work his way through the satellite's subsystems, but it was little more than routine. A task owed to his will to perform his duty. He had no remaining hope of finding something else; something that might have allowed a different interpretation. There was only cold, bleak resignation. The knowledge that there really was no one left out there. That they were the last.

He felt empty. Completely empty. Even the resignation was merely a brief flare in the midst of all-encompassing, abysmal monotony. Four hundred years. People had survived this madness, this atomic world conflagration, for more than 400 years, had held out and hoped for improvement. They had fathered children and released them into this devastated world, knowing that they would die young, a cruel death from radiation sickness. That is, if they survived infancy at all.

The very idea of how these people must have felt; the thought of the ever-elusive hope that must have been dashed each time; the knowledge that one was at the mercy of man-made hell on this planet - and could not escape it. It was horrible.

Finally, he disconnected the satellite. It would have been severed in a few minutes anyway, and there was nothing more he could do. He had retrieved all the subsystems, had read all the logs, and had even tried to ping other satellites or points on Earth - to no avail. There was nothing left out there.

"We're going on approach," Aacken said tonelessly. "ETA twenty minutes."

"Roger that. Get us as close as you can."

"Roger that."

"Are we receiving a signal from the listening post?" asked Toussaint.

"Affirmative. Normal signal ping. Station appears to be intact."

"At least that's good news."

"Uh-huh."

"What is it?"

"Nothing important."

"Spit it out. We don't have too much to do right now."

Aacken made a half groan, half sigh sound. "It's really nothing. Just one of many thoughts."

"Do I really have to pull it out of your nose?" hissed Toussaint. "Please say something, Aacken. I can't stand my own thoughts right now."

"Then what I'm going to say is hardly going to help you," he snorted. "I was just thinking that in a few days the terraforming crews will begin their work. That ultimately, each of us will be cooperating in this task in one way or another. And that we'll probably be doing this for the rest of our lives."

"The rest of our lives?" asked Adrian. "Do you really think it will take that long?"

"You should know that, Morris. Shouldn't you?"

"Terraforming has never been my strong suit. But it never really interested me either. Too abstract and intangible. Sure, I know the basics. But I didn't think it would take this long."

"Well, there's no big red button we can push where everything will be fine," Aacken explained. "If everything goes without a hitch, we'll proceed in three phases: First, we undertake a hypervitalization of the planet, meaning we extract nitrogen from the air on a large scale, primarily via the Haber-Bosch process, and put it into the soil. At the same time, we are pushing back deserts in temperate climates, planting primarily legumes, and enriching soils with nodule and blue-green bacteria to make better use of nitrogen. If all goes well in the process, we'll be ready for Phase 2 in fifteen years."

"Large-scale reforestation and pushing back ice and sand deserts, right?"

"Exactly. With a little luck, we'll be able to start genetically diverse cloning and releasing the first animal species. Mainly microbes, insects and worms to further stabilize the soil. Then, with Phase 3, we move on to restoring the earth's climate, breeding larger animal species, and creating genetic diversity. This is where the engineers come into play: the *Genesis* is disassembled and a grid is formed from its modules to keep solar radiation within the ideal range, while at the same time we try to artificially restore ocean currents and filter harmful gases from the air. Assuming everything continues to go according to plan until then, we'll be in a position to establish the first independent settlements in sixty to eighty years."

"And that's only if every woman on board is actually able to play birthing machine for a good twenty years," Toussaint added bitterly. "And thus produce enough children to keep the effort going."

"That's in the nature of things, I'm afraid," Aacken

replied, shrugging his shoulders. "It just takes a lot of women and tends to take few men to populate. That's true of almost all animals, too."

"I know. And I'm also aware of the studies that say women give birth to more girls in times of crisis, which is why I'll have to start swallowing artificial stress hormones in a few months."

"We knew the mission wasn't going to be pleasant," Adrian said dryly. "Especially not for women."

"Still, fifty percent of the crew are men. Had we taken more women, such extreme measures might not have been necessary."

"That's true, but for this it is provided that - if possible - men take over the dangerous tasks with a high risk of death."

Toussaint remained silent and Adrian did not reply either. He was fully aware that this arrangement and what the mission required of women was anything but fair; that they were reduced, at least in part, to procreation and raising those who would take their place in a few decades. That this behavior, this necessity, if you will, was pretty much contrary to everything the old world had considered achievement and equality. And was also contrary to all the principles that probably everyone aboard the *Genesis* shared.

What Toussaint, and presumably most of the rest of the crew, did not know was that there was another way. One way, in case this plan failed and they did not succeed in producing enough offspring. Deep inside the *Genesis*, hidden behind nearly a dozen airlocks that only the heads of the 30 modules could open and not listed in the inventory or onboard system, was the *Human In Vitro Embryo Database*. Or, for short, the *HIVE-D*.

Adrian shuddered just thinking about it. Knowing about this place and the machines there was probably one of the biggest burdens he had to shoulder as the head of a module. A piece of information that he himself had received only hours before the start of cryostasis and that he had not managed to process until today. So far, at least, he had successfully managed to keep the thought of it away from him, but now that the conversation had come up, the memory returned with a vengeance.

About 1,000 embryos with completely identical genetic characteristics were lying there in a kind of cryostasis, although he was not sure if their state could even be called such. These embryos had not been conceived naturally, but were the result of decades of research. The seeds of human beings, bred solely to grow up within a few years and in turn create offspring that would represent an ever broader genetic spectrum for generations to come. No hereditary diseases, no defects, but diversity born from sameness, unfolded by the process of birth. A genetic manipulation, as it had probably not existed in the history of mankind also after its start. Only in ten generations would the effects of this manipulation disappear, but until then these people would live only to reproduce and die young. An emergency measure that he hoped with every fiber of his body would never be necessary.

"Is everything okay, Morris?" Toussaint's voice suddenly snapped him out of his musings.

"Yeah, why?"

"Because I just spoke to you twice and you didn't respond."

"I'm sorry. I was in my own thoughts. What's wrong?"

"I was asking you if there was anything I needed to be aware of that I might not know," she growled in a tone that told him unequivocally that she was demanding information she couldn't possibly know, having been smuggled into the *Genesis* Project from the outside. A request and reminder not to let her get ahead of Aacken. "I'm sure you, as module leader, know more about that," she said.

"A normal database," he replied, turning to look at her. "A self-sufficient system in a deep bunker, protected against all environmental influences and equipped with an autonomous power supply. No cable-based connections. Retrieval of databases is possible only on site. Three mechanical and four digital security measures. I'll explain them to you on site."

"On-site only?" she asked, audibly surprised. "No system is immune to outside access."

"This one is, and you know it," Adrian returned emphatically. "A *CONE* System. A funnel that lets information through in only one direction. Only the *Genesis* can get a response through its pings. Concentrate, Toussaint, or people might think you slept through your training."

Chapter Six

WHILE THE PLANE's engines were still shutting down, Adrian unfastened his seat belts, opened the cockpit and jumped outside. But as soon as his boots touched the thin, shimmering sheet of ice, he collapsed and sank knee-deep into the snow. Just in time, he managed to cling to the fuselage of the machine.

Cursing, he looked around. The swirling snow made it impossible to figure out exactly where the entrance to the listening post was, and frankly, he would not have even been surprised if it had been buried somewhere under ice and snow, invisible to the naked eye.

With a quick flick of his wrist, he switched his helmet's gauges to the Geiger counter. Ever since he had opened the pulpit, the device had been rattling rapidly and consistently. Not so fast as to cause him acute concern, but not as slow and erratic as it had been a few hours ago in South America. The area had received significantly more radiation. Possibly the result of a nuclear explosion? But who would have bombed Greenland? Either way, the radiation level was more than 200 microsieverts per hour. That was not good.

"Aacken, I need a fix on location," he said.

"Forty yards ahead in the extension of the plane."

"Roger that. Toussaint, come with me. Aacken, you stay

here for now and make sure the plane stays operational. With the radiation levels, I'd rather leave sooner than later."

"You got it, Morris. Be careful."

Adrian took a deep breath and headed out. Without the servo motors and stabilizers of his protective suit, he would have been hard pressed to wrestle down the masses of snow and push forward yard by yard. And although his every move was supported by machines, he felt a biting exhaustion wash over him after just a few seconds. 2,000 years in weightlessness did not seem to be beneficial to a body's muscle mass, even in cryostasis.

Toussaint did not seem to fare any better. No consolation in the real sense, but at least they shared the misery of their way. As before, Adrian could see absolutely nothing that would have even hinted at the listening post or its entrance. In his mind he already saw himself trudging back to the plane to fetch spades and pickaxes. If there was anything like that on board at all. Goddamn it, what if they had to go back to South America for equipment? Why had he not thought that far ahead? Of course there was snow in Greenland!

"Aacken, do you have us on the systems?"

"Affirmative. Thirty more yards."

"Thirty?! Are you kidding me! I've been on the move for at least five minutes!"

"I didn't say you were going particularly fast, either. Do you want me to get out and push?"

"You really are a humorist, aren't you?"

"I've been told."

"As soon as we reach the entrance, you let me know."

"You got it, Morris. I..."

He paused.

"What is it?" demanded Adrian immediately.

"I'm not sure. I'm getting a signal in right now."

"From the listening post?"

"Seems so, but... No, it's not coming from the listening post. At least not directly. It's a feedback loop. I... Morris, you were on the sensors when we were on approach. Didn't you notice that?"

"There was nothing there, Aacken."

"That can't be!"

"There really was nothing," Toussaint agreed with him. "He put the readouts on my suit; I saw what he saw, and I guarantee you there was nothing there. At least nothing that could have picked up the plane's onboard systems. It's possible the signal just started up? Can you trace it?"

"Hang on a second, I'll climb in the back and take a look."

"Do that and get back to me when you have something."

Adrian bit his lip and glanced back toward the plane. Through all the swirling snow, he could only make out the plane as a shadowy veil behind a wall of white. And he would have loved to return to that very spot. He did not like what was happening here.

A signal that appeared suddenly and completely out of the blue, now that they had landed here? That could not be a coincidence.

But what was it?

His thoughts raced as he continued to fight his way through the snow. Actually, there should have been nothing here at all. Neither a signal nor a feedback loop or anything else. Especially not now, hundreds of years after the end of mankind and at the time when they landed here. Had they possibly triggered something without noticing it? Damn it! What if this was a trap? What if the governments of the old world, for whatever reason, had wanted to prevent them from entering the listening post?

No, it couldn't be. It just could not be. Right now, it was just stress and uncertainty talking, and he knew it. There would be a reasonable, understandable explanation for this signal. Maybe it was just an attempt to communicate with them? Perhaps the facility was no longer accessible and they were trying to provide them with the necessary information by other means?

"Five more yards, Morris."

Adrian stopped, squinted, and activated his helmet light. There was nothing there. Absolutely nothing. No building, no elevation, no entrance. But there had to be something. They had picked up the listening post's signal pings on the *Genesis*. It had to be here. They just had to find it - somehow.

"Toussaint, right now I'd really appreciate any suggestions."

"Well, if we don't see the post ahead, it must be below us."

"That's what I thought. So how do we get down there?"

"A shovel would be a great idea."

"We don't have one," Aacken interjected. "Just looked."

"Do we have anything?"

"I'd have an idea, but it's against protocol."

"Speak up."

"I can bring the plane over and melt the snow with the thrusters. Vertical takeoff is a hell of an invention."

"All right. Do it."

"Are you sure?" asked Toussaint immediately. "That seems a little extreme. What if the entrance gets damaged in the process?"

"I'll be careful."

It took only a few moments for the plane's engines to roar to life and for Aacken to slowly maneuver the plane in their direction.

Immediately, Adrian and Toussaint struggled through the snow a few paces away from the listening post until they were at a reasonably safe distance. Despite the distance and his protective suit, he could clearly feel the heat from the thrusters. An unconventional route, he was aware, but unfortunately the only one they could think of in those minutes.

While Aacken slowly flew a circle about twenty yards in diameter, melting deeper and deeper layers of the snow cover, Adrian was already trying to make out something behind the rising cloud of steam, but it was an impossibility. He probably had to wait until the German had finished his work.

Actually, he could have used this waiting time as an opportunity to take a deep breath and calm his nerves, but unfortunately, despite all his attempts, he did not succeed. Nervousness and insecurity had clung to him and sunk their claws deep into his body; merciless predators that would not let go of him until they had hunted him down.

Finally, Aacken turned and brought the plane back to the position where he had landed it earlier, and just a few seconds later the steam cleared, revealing the entrance to the listening post.

The dome-like building made of solid reinforced concrete was buried a good five yards under the surrounding snow cover. Even with shovels, they would have worked themselves to death on it.

"Are we still receiving the signal?" asked Adrian, climbing carefully into the meltwater-filled crater in the snow.

"Affirmative. I'll try to find out something about it and get back to you when I'm ready. And Morris, I'm just letting you know ahead of time. When you guys get down there, you might lose radio contact."

"Roger that. We'll be quick."

Adrian trudged through the meltwater toward the dark gray dome until he finally reached a hatch, a good ten feet in diameter, set into the reinforced concrete. Centuries under ice and snow had left hardly any traces on it, apart from some rust. At least that was good news. If it could still be opened now without any problems, that almost compensated for the effort they had had to make to find it.

Unlike the Monte Burney facility, the existence of this listening post was generally unknown. At least it had been when he and the others had set out on their mission 2,000 years ago. So unless things had changed, no one had been here in the last millennia. As far as he knew, even all records of the construction had been destroyed, and the *CONE* System made it virtually impossible to track them from the outside.

With a deft flick of his wrist, Adrian opened the two flaps behind which the door's unlocking mechanisms were located and heaved out the two powerful levers. At least, it tried. One of them moved easily, but the other didn't budge an inch. Probably rust. Damn.

"Toussaint, give me a hand."

"What do you want me to do?"

"Use the other lever. Maybe the movement will help get this one free."

"Got it."

Adrian grasped the jammed handle with both hands, braced his feet against the reinforced concrete, and prepared to pull with all his might. Toussaint now stepped up beside him, placed her hands on the other lever and nodded at him. Immediately he pulled with all his might - and indeed: with an infernal screech the lever came free. They had done it.

"Thank you."

Breathing heavily, Adrian pulled the second lever until, a few seconds later, the door's mechanism finally began to rattle, clearing the way into the listening post millimeter by millimeter. It took almost two minutes before the entrance was open wide enough for them to enter.

Adrian saw immediately that, despite all the technical gadgetry, the entrance could had not been completely sealed. Thin sheets of ice stretched along the walls and floor. Frozen meltwater. The devil alone knew how long it had been here, because at least Adrian could not imagine that the temperatures in this place had reached the melting point again since the climate collapse.

Slowly and carefully, he picked his way down the steeply sloping stairs, taking concentrated care not to accidentally slip. If he hurt himself here, he was almost certainly lost. Not only because protocol dictated not wasting resources on serious injuries for the first few months, but also because there was no way Toussaint and Aacken could have gotten him out of here, even with their suits' servo motors.

"Strange," Toussaint grumbled suddenly. "Morris, what does your Geiger counter read?"

Adrian looked at the small display on his visor. "About 240 microsieverts per hour. Why? We..."

He paused. In the seconds alone that he had answered her, the reading had climbed to a good 400 microsieverts. And it was still rising.

"So you're reading it, too." Toussaint sighed. "Up at the entrance, the level was still just under 220."

"That means we're heading for a radiation source," Adrian concluded tonelessly. "But how can that be? There shouldn't be any nuclear material in the listening post. Aacken? Aacken, can you hear me?"

"Distorted, but you're still there. I have already initiated a scan. If the readouts are correct, the facility is in the middle of an irradiated area about 400 yards in diameter. The center is more or less directly in front of you. However, the readings out here are all around 200 to 500 microsieverts. Not pretty, but not the end of the world either."

Adrian cursed silently and kept walking. With each step, the radiation level continued to rise, and after only a few yards it was close to 4,000 microsieverts per hour. A level that was far beyond the permissible limit exposure that his equipment could handle. Under these conditions - and if the value did not rise even further - he could stay here for a few hours at most without having to fear devastating consequences. But things were looking rough already.

"Morris, I hate to say it, but given this level of radiation, we have to assume that the plant's engineering has been damaged," Toussaint said. "After the Chernobyl reactor accident back then, the Soviets sent a Lunochod rover and a German police robot to the roof of the power plant. Both failed virtually immediately after launch."

"What are you getting at, Toussaint?" asked Adrian dryly.

10,000 microsieverts.

"I'm just saying that we should prepare for the possibility that the technology may..."

"Damn it, say what you're trying to say or don't say anything at all!"

"Morris, I think the feedback loop is a consequence of the

radiation-based system failure. And possibly the *Exodus* signal as well."

BREATHING HEAVILY, Adrian bent over the central controls of the listening post and made the entries necessary for Toussaint to begin her work as quickly as possible. The air filter and cooling unit of his suit had long been howling so shrilly that they drowned out almost every other sound, and by now he could also feel an intense pain pulsing through his head. The radiation level had settled at a good 60,000 microsieverts per hour. Too much for his equipment; the systems were visibly failing. And too much for his body, too. He had long since tasted iron on his tongue. Blood. Not yet irreversible, but borderline.

Toussaint was working right next to him at one of the consoles she could already access. Through the visor of her helmet, he saw how sweat stood on her forehead, too, how she kept gasping for air and squinting her eyes. Radiation sydrome. Still, she tirelessly typed her inputs into the console, displaying logs upon logs, retrieving data, and transferring everything possible to her suit's internal memories.

Adrian swallowed hard. He felt sick, barely managing to hold back the hot bile that kept creeping up his throat. Although he tried to concentrate solely on his work and on finally giving Toussaint full access to the listening post's systems, his thoughts kept wandering. His subconscious and survival instincts had allied against his rational mind, trying to calculate how much radiation his equipment and especially the air filter were probably keeping out and how much was actually getting into his body. But no matter how hard he thought about it, he could not reach a conclusion.

"Okay," he finally gasped, easing away from the console. "Full access granted. Download everything, Toussaint. We're checking the data at the base. How long do you need?"

"One second," she muttered. "I'm initiating the data transfer... God, it's a lot..."

"How long?"

"Morris, I've got 1.24 petabytes of data to transfer right now. Even with my equipment and best possible compression, I'll be busy for at least an hour. Plus, the radiation is interfering with the data transfer. It's quite possible that it will take significantly longer."

"We don't have an hour!"

"We have to." She panted in exhaustion. "Protocol Alpha-3, we are first command. The execution of the entire *Genesis* mission depends on this data. If we fail, humanity fails. An hour isn't pretty, but the radiation won't kill us immediately. We have enough time to make it back to the plane. That's all that matters."

Adrian bit his lip, only to immediately let it go as he felt blood running down his chin almost instantly. They didn't have an hour left and he didn't care what the protocol was. He had no intention of dying here. At least not if there was anything he could do about it.

Without so much as a moment's hesitation, he stepped back from the console and turned around. The light from his suit was already flickering. Only very slightly, but still clearly visible. The technology was beginning to fail. They did not have much time left. When the light finally went out, they would be stuck in the dark. And no one could say if they would find a way out then.

"Where are you going?"

"I'm going to find the source of the radiation."

"And then?"

"Then, hopefully, I'll find a way to eliminate it."

"This... Morris, you can't leave me here alone! Please!"

"We'll stay in radio contact, Toussaint. Do your job. We're not dying here."

With those words, he ran off, leaving the facility's central access point. He understood Toussaint well; he, too, was reluctant with every fiber of his being to split up. Radiation was a treacherous, cowardly enemy. An enemy that attacked you relentlessly yet lacked the courage to confront you directly. The fear of it was only natural. Nevertheless, it had to be.

The listening post was a massive facility, jutting dozens of feet underground, but the absolute majority of the rooms were not designed to be entered at all. Servers, back-up systems, power and emergency power - all these things had been built more than 2,000 years ago for a proverbial eternity. He only had access to a few rooms that were essential to his mission. Or for repairing the failed, or possibly destroyed, equipment in case of emergency.

With each step he felt it getting harder and harder to move at all. His legs felt weak - he was exhausted, and the nausea, coupled with the almost unbearable headache, was doing the rest. He was no physicist or biologist, and could hardly gauge how serious his radiation sickness actually was, but it felt bad. Really bad.

After only a few yards he figured out in which direction he had to go to locate the source of the radiation: to where the radiation level kept rising. A value around 60,000 microsieverts per hour actually seemed to be more or less the maximum. The changes amounted to a few hundred microsieverts. At least there was that.

Quick as possible, Adrian picked his way through the barren corridors, bordered only by unplastered, reinforced concrete, and across the bundles of cables that repeatedly crossed his path. He was fully aware that, over time, everything around him had become completely contaminated and that even eliminating the actual source of the radiation would not change that. But anything helped, even if it was only a little. Theoretically. Perhaps it would help Toussaint manage to transmit the data a little faster.

He had just stepped around a junction when he paused in place and squinted his eyes in disbelief. The corridor ahead was almost completely buried under snow, frozen into ice. Even through that, he recognized a dark gray object hidden just behind the top layer, sticking out in some places. An unexploded missile.

"Goddamn it!" he gasped.

"You got something?!" wanted Toussaint to know immediately.

"A missile."

Cautiously, he stepped closer and tried to determine as much as he could about the projectile, though he could not see any inscriptions or markings. Over the centuries, it must have faded with age. If they had existed at all. In any case, he now knew the immense danger he and the others were in. He had no idea how the ignition mechanism worked. It was possible that even the slightest vibration was enough to detonate it.

"It's relatively small," he finally continued. "I suspect a tactical warhead to specifically take out this facility. It did not detonate, for whatever reason."

"Shouldn't we have seen that from the outside?"

"There's a lot of snow here. There's probably a drift several yards high directly above it. We're lucky Aacken didn't fly this way, or he definitely would have blown it up."

"Can you do anything?"

Adrian looked around. A few feet away, he spotted a fire gate. That this was his best option, he knew immediately. Assuming the thing could even be closed. He didn't want to imagine what all the radiation and centuries of ice had done to the mechanism.

Nevertheless, he immediately let go of the rocket and made his way to it. Tenderly, step by step. Under no circumstances could he risk triggering a detonation with a careless movement. An undertaking that was made more difficult by the fact that he ultimately had no idea whether it even worked that way. This weapon might have been here for centuries, but to him it was still future technology. No one could foresee what strokes of genius had been devised by those who were to blame for the end of the world.

Finally he reached the fire door, and with it, the lever-driven mechanism that was supposed to close it. Actually, it should have locked automatically after the missile had penetrated the bunker ceiling, but presumably the electronics had been damaged in the process. Lucky, otherwise the explosive charge might have detonated after all and everyone aboard the *Genesis* would not have been awakened by the exit protocol for a few thousand years.

Carefully, he set about lowering the door, doing his best to mitigate the rattling vibrations as best he could and allow the door to move reasonably smoothly. It was probably only thanks to the radiation that it could be lowered so smoothly at all, since it slowed down the corrosion of most alloys.

Even when the door was halfway down, the radiation level dropped noticeably. While it had been over 60,000 microsieverts per hour just a few seconds ago, it now dropped to just under 50,000 - and the further the door closed, the more it dropped until it finally settled at just 40,000. Still a far from nice figure, but a noticeable improvement nonetheless.

"I've closed a fire door," he now said into the radio and headed back. "The radiation here has dropped noticeably. How about you?"

"I'm at 20,000 microsieverts, and I don't want to jinx anything, but the system is running much more smoothly. Thanks, Morris."

"You're welcome. Let's hope we get off lightly again."

"I think we will. Radiation as a result of nuclear war was finally considered one of the most likely scenarios. We have means of doing something about it."

"I'd love some of your optimism."

"Now I'm not going to die of radiation while I work here," she replied. "I have every reason to be optimistic. Don't you?"

"No."

"Why not?"

"Why?" He laughed bitterly. "Seriously? Toussaint, someone tried to destroy the listening post during the war! This isn't just a random hit! Hell, do you know what could have happened in the process? If that bomb had detonated, we might have been woken up right away - or not at all! God, I don't even want to imagine what could have happened!"

"Nothing happened," she returned dryly. "Besides, I don't think it was intentional in the sense you imagine."

"What's that supposed to mean?"

"That practically no one knew about this place and therefore its significance. Presumably a reconnaissance pilot spotted the dome during a flyover and the listening post was subsequently classified as an enemy facility."

"I guess you could be right about that."

"I know. It doesn't change anything factually, of course, but I take comfort in the fact that at least they didn't willfully try to sabotage our mission."

"How much longer do you need?" asked Adrian.

"I'm making pretty good progress right now. I've copied most of the data. I'm still copying over the government internals and..."

"And what?"

"I don't know. Somehow it's strange that humanity continued to exist for centuries and all the major systems around the world transmitted back-ups of their data to this place without anyone knowing about it. Every word and every decision was fodder for the day after it all ended. Foundation of our work. This *CONE* System... I still don't understand how it works."

"Well," Adrian replied tonelessly. Just at that moment, he entered the facility's central access point, where Toussaint was still working on the systems. "Initially, yes, they knew. It was the grand bargain. Probably the last time humanity agreed on anything. Each nation sent developers who checked each other's work and made sure no one put in a backdoor. The perfect system, the ultimate software for surveillance and data analysis - trusting that only we would use it. And that maybe we'd find a way to do it better."

"I hope we succeed."

"So do I."

"Morris..." she continued hesitantly, but then said no more.

"Yes?"

"I'm sorry I didn't tell you the truth about me right away."

"Why is that? That was exactly your mission, after all."

"Yes, but it might have been better if more people had known about it. Then maybe the sabotage would never have happened."

"What's done is done. If you told me the truth..."

"I did!"

"Then there you go - you couldn't have stopped it, and I doubt anyone else could have. I'm not angry with you for that, and I'm not disappointed. I'm just giving you the benefit of the doubt and assuming you're on the right side. Personally, I think we're through the worst of it in that regard anyway."

"What do you mean?"

"Quite simply, if someone had tampered with the modules on the *Genesis*, and that someone also knew about you, then he would have had more than enough opportunities to strike again. But he didn't. The log memory of the GPS satellite ends more than 1,000 years ago. About 200 years later, the first system cascade occurred on the station. At the very least, I don't think it's out of the question that he could have accessed the *Genesis* sensors and realized that humanity really had perished."

"You think he suddenly became empathic?"

"I think it's possible, yes."

"What about the other two lost modules?"

"Emergency protocol beta. The onboard system jettisoned them to prevent further cascades, even at the smallest errors. It couldn't have known about the sabotage. An indirect consequence, but probably not direct sabotage."

Toussaint took a deep breath. "I hope with all my heart that you are right. It would make a lot of our worries null and void."

"I hope so, too. Believe me."

Chapter Seven

BREATHING HEAVILY and trembling with exhaustion, Adrian brought the plane's diagnostic scanner to his neck, pushed his head forward slightly, and did his best to ignore the rapidly increasing heat and rhythmic vibrations emanating from the machine and jolting through his entire body. The protocol called for measuring the level of radiation in his body and that would guide the type and duration of treatment. However, he wasn't even sure he wanted to know how badly he had been hit.

As the diagnostic machine continued its work, sending an increasingly intense heat through his throat, he closed his eyes and tried to keep his nerve and calm down a bit.

Immediately after he and Toussaint reached the plane, their suits had been decontaminated. The stench of the mixture of various alkalis and far too many chemicals still hung intensely in the air. It probably would have been best if they had simply left their equipment behind, but unfortunately that was not possible. It was simply too valuable for that.

He could only hope that the decontamination had at least washed away most of the external radiation, so that he 'only' had to deal with the residual radiation in his body and not be further contaminated while he sat here waiting for Aacken to finally take off and bring them back to South America. God, what was taking so long?

"Lucky," Toussaint's voice suddenly snapped him out of his thoughts. "I'm at 2.3 sieverts."

"Severe radiation sickness," Aacken snorted. "Congratulations. Morris, what's your status?"

"Diagnostics are still running."

"That doesn't sound good."

"Man, give him a break, Aacken! Morris single-handedly made sure this mission succeeded!"

A piercing beep sounded. Adrian opened his eyes and looked at the small display on the back of the diagnostic device.

"Three sieverts."

"Well, that's something to be proud of."

"I agree," Toussaint agreed with him. "Not as bad as I feared. You got off lightly there, Morris."

Adrian didn't reply anything, but just continued to stare at the small display, which by now showed him that the medication dispensing had been adjusted and initiated. Only a few seconds later, a small compartment to his left opened as well, where he could just see the last milliliters of a rather large syringe being filled.

He shuddered and pulled it out of the compartment, but hesitated to push it into the injection port of his suit. Every fiber of his body rebelled against the idea of ramming this thing into his skin and jetting this cocktail of chemicals into his blood. Of course, he knew it had to be done. He knew the protocols - and more importantly, he knew the consequences of an untreated radiation dose of three sieverts.

Finally, he reached out with his left arm, opened the small access at elbow level, and fixed his suit's servo motors. True to protocol. Dozens of times he had practiced this scenario, yet he winced as the cold steel of the needle pierced his skin and injected the burning chemical cocktail into his blood.

"I hate this," he growled, pulling out the needle and releasing the brace on the servos. "God, how I hate it."

"It allows you to live," Toussaint retorted. "That's not such a bad idea, is it?"

"When did you become a cynic?"

"Sometime between my being stuck in the cryo-capsule and working in a fully irradiated listening post where an undetonated nuclear missile has been rusting away for centuries."

"That's an argument."

"You guys may as well settle in for now," Aacken grumbled, getting the plane in the air. "A few hours of rest for our heroes."

"Mmm. You do know that we won't be allowed back aboard the *Genesis* with those levels of radiation in our bodies, right? And neither will you, because we'll be contaminating you for the next three hours as well."

"I didn't go into cryostasis to escape back to a space station at the first opportunity," he replied. "On Earth, despite radiation, it's a thousand times better than up there."

"You think so?"

"I wouldn't have said it otherwise."

"What actually happened with the signal?", Adrian changed the subject and closed his eyes again. He could feel the chemicals crawling through his body already. A sickening, unpleasant feeling. Like he was being bloated from the inside out and collapsing in on himself at the same time. "That feedback loop?"

"I couldn't do anything useful with it," the German replied. "There's a copy of it on the onboard system so we can take a look at it later, but from what I found out... I think it's just a bug. Maybe the radiation actually damaged the listening post. Or maybe the systems were overwhelmed with the *Genesis* releasing the moorings."

"That's possible," Toussaint agreed with him. "It's possible that anchor control simply forgot to inform the listening post, and the system is now trying to make contact while the station is out of range."

"And another mystery solved."

While Toussaint and Aacken engaged in some harmless verbal banter, Adrian tried to get some sleep to skip at least the first few hours of the effects of the chemicals in his blood, but he could not. The burning sensation in his body was too unpleasant, and he felt the effects of the radiation too clearly. Sleep was out of the question under these circumstances.

Finally, with a silent sigh, he activated one of the consoles and had the sensor logs of the plane displayed. He would have liked to start analyzing the data of the listening post directly, but they were in the internal memories of Toussaint's suit. There was no way to access such amounts of data with the computing capabilities of the machine. Only with the equipment of the cargo modules would that be possible.

Fortunately, that did not mean he was doomed to do nothing for the rest of the flight. The plane's sensors had collected more than enough data. Mainly on the environment, radiation levels and atmospheric readings, but also some interference; old scraps of signals, too weak to be picked up by the *Genesis*. Probably remnants of ancient technology, which against all odds were still active somewhere on the planet. And so was the signal. The feedback loop.

At first glance, the signal actually looked more than ordinary. A simple signal ping to the *Genesis*; an automatic communication between the listening post and the station. A few ordinary data interrogations to confirm mutual functionality. However, it was not apparent why it had looped.

Involuntarily, Adrian squinted his eyes. Actually, he could not have cared less; it was little more than a mistake, a minor glitch without any effect on him, the mission, or anything else. However, he certainly was not going to let slip what was probably his only chance to keep himself busy on this flight. And so he began to pick apart and analyze the signal piece by piece.

"Strange," he said absentmindedly.

"What's strange?" asked Toussaint immediately, obviously glad to be able to say something. She probably felt no differently than he did. "What are you working on?"

"The feedback loop. Actually, it looks like a normal signal ping, but there's also a data query."

"Every signal ping is a data query, Morris."

"That's not what I mean," he grumbled. "Hang on a second, I'm transmitting the reading to your helmet. See that third entry? That's an explicit confirmation that the *Exodus* signal has occurred and we've been awakened, but..."

"But it's hidden," Toussaint took the words out of his mouth. "Or rather, it has been hidden."

"You think so?"

"I'm sure of it. But it's still not what it seems."

"You'll have to explain that to me."

"The confirmation query is hidden," she confirmed. "Not because it was meant to be hidden, but because the signal isn't even good for making that kind of query. Someone went to a lot of trouble to modify the signal so it could get that information."

"I'm not an information engineer," Aacken interjected. "But then doesn't that mean someone is alive out there?"

"Inevitably," Toussaint breathed in a quivering voice. "I... God, do you understand what that means? There's somebody there! Someone has survived! Someone who knows exactly that we're in orbit! That we were coming!"

"We might need to consider this as a distress signal." Adrian activated a couple of the other consoles and initiated a detailed analysis of the signal. "It's just odd that we didn't pick up on it on the *Genesis*."

"It takes more expertise to send a signal into space, pinging a station that's moving quickly, than it does to reach a stationary location on Earth," Toussaint replied. "Besides, the listening post is the only way to communicate with the *Genesis*."

Adrian opened his mouth a few more times to say something, but he was no longer able to make a single sound. This signal had actually managed to leave him speechless. No, not only that. It made his heart race, as well as his thoughts, because it meant that there really was someone out there.

That someone had survived; that all his fears and the results of the *Genesis*' sensor sweep were wrong!

"Aacken, can we manage to contact the *Genesis*?"

"I think so. Once we reach the stratosphere, I should be able to make contact. I don't know yet, though, if it will be enough for more than transmitting a message."

"When in doubt, that's enough. We need to let them know about the signal. Have them mobilize all resources to locate the transmitter and..."

"Morris, you're aware that protocol doesn't allow for that, right?" he interrupted him. "Phase 1 doesn't provide for that."

"I'm aware of that!" hissed Adrian. "But we're not dealing with some club-wielding Neo-Stone Age people here, we're dealing with someone capable of understanding complex technical issues! Someone who knows about the *Genesis* and obviously has advanced technology! That could be a huge advantage for our mission!"

"Morris is right," Toussaint interjected, even before Aacken could retort. "There may be a self-sufficient, self-sustaining enclave or even a larger state entity somewhere. If we manage to mobilize additional manpower, we could tackle and complete the individual terraforming phases much faster! We can't let this opportunity pass us by!"

"Don't discuss this with me, discuss it with Mabena and the Directors," Aacken simply replied. "I just wanted to point out to you that this may not be as easy as you think."

Adrian was silent. Aacken was right. No matter how vehemently common sense might dictate tracking the signal and the contacting of any survivors, even he was powerless against the strict regulations of protocol. Hell, he could even understand the reasoning behind it himself. One had to weigh whether such cooperation, the conflicts that might come with it, and the sharing of their own supplies, would ultimately bring better results than the actual protocol. Humanity was something that humankind could not afford, especially under these circumstances.

Nevertheless, he had to try. It was his duty to inform

Mabena and the Directors, and to initiate the necessary steps to make exactly this weighing, this calculating of the possible merits. Even if at the end of these discussions, there would likely be a decision to proceed for the time being according to protocol.

It did not take long for Aacken to bring the plane to the edge of the stratosphere and to calibrate the com systems on board accordingly. Nonetheless, Adrian hesitated for a moment, considering how best to proceed.

"This is Adrian Scott Morris," he finally said in a firm voice. "Calling *Genesis* anchor control. Please respond."

There was a rustling sound.

"This is Adrian Morris," he repeated a few seconds later. "*Genesis*, do you copy?"

"Anchor control here," the operator's distorted but still intelligible voice finally sounded. "I read you, Morris. What's your status? Any problems?"

"Negative, anchor control. We have reached the listening post, secured the data, and are now on our way back to the Burney base. A suspected live nuclear missile has penetrated the bunker ceiling and contaminated the listening post. Toussaint and I were exposed to doses of two and three sieverts, respectively. Initial treatment has been given."

"Roger that, Morris. Follow the protocol for dealing with acute radiation. We'll send down a decontamination chamber with advanced treatment options with the next cargo module."

"Thank you, Anchor Control. There's one more thing. We received a feedback loop at the listening post that has a specific query embedded in it about the Exodus signal and the wake-up procedure."

"Specify."

"We suspect the cause to be the existence of a survivor enclave that has advanced technology and knowledge of the *Genesis* Project. We cannot rule out the possibility of them initiating the signal. In accordance with my position as module leader, I request immediate notification of Mabena and the Directors. My personal recommendation is to trace the signal immediately and make contact. Please confirm."

"Acknowledged. Return to Mount Burney, proceed according to protocol, and await further instructions."

THE SUN WAS SETTING. Very slowly, almost majestically, it disappeared behind the horizon and cast a few last red-golden rays over the world. Adrian watched it, lost in thought. He sat on the edge of the landing platform of the orbital lift, his arms resting on the helmet on his lap. Cold wind blew towards him, carrying a few scattered snowflakes to his face every now and then.

They had already landed a few hours ago and were now waiting for the *Genesis* to reach the orbital anchor again, but that would still take a little while. Time enough to get some rest and even some sleep, but he did not succeed. An after-effect of cryostasis. In his training, he had been prepared for it. Sometimes it took three or even four days for a body to break down the last remnants of the various anesthetics and return to a normal biorhythm.

But that was okay. At least for him, right now. Watching the sun disappear and knowing it would soon rise again was comforting, putting his outlook on events in perspective. The cosmos was not interested in the lives and deaths of people. The sun rose and set again, no matter what happened, completely independent of the success or failure of their mission. It would still do that in 100,000 years. Until it went out sometime and pulled this system with itself into eternal silence. And at some point, the universe would end, too. Actually it did not matter how long mankind delayed its own end. It could not escape fate.

Soon the sun had finally disappeared behind the horizon. Only a fainter and fainter distant shimmering still indicated that it was there and continued its way inexorably. Adrian now activated the light of his helmet and the position lights of his suit. Protocol prescribed it that way, even if he would have preferred complete darkness right now.

"Hey, glow stick." Suddenly a soft, mocking voice behind him. Sato. A few seconds later, she sat down and looked at him. "Are you alright?"

"Mind the minimum distance," was all he replied.

"You're not Chernobyl, Morris."

"I feel like it, though."

"I'll take your word for it. Are you all right to some extent?"

"Other than the fact that I feel like all my organs are trying to crawl out of my mouth at the same time?" He snorted bitterly. "Yeah, otherwise I feel pretty decent. You guys did a good job with the landing zone."

"Horvat did most of it. I got the base up to snuff. At least the main departments. It's unbelievable how much garbage is lying around. This must have been one of the most popular tourist attractions in the old world."

"I had that feeling, too."

"Toussaint told me about the device you found." She reached into a side pocket of her suit and pulled out five of the horseshoe-shaped objects at once. "I found a couple more. Apparently some resourceful businessman made these things explicitly so anyone could leave us a message for a little money."

"So?"

"Well." She tossed all five of them in a high arc over the edge of the plant straight down the steep cliff of the mountain. "Practically all insults."

"Does that surprise you?"

"Honestly, no. Cultural assets, information, and knowledge were explicitly preserved for us. What was there for the common man to contribute, other than his frustration? Although a simple 'good luck' wouldn't have hurt my feelings any."

Adrian was silent.

"Can't sleep or don't want to?" asked Sato quietly.

"Both. You?"

"Don't want to."

"Why?"

"Don't know. I just don't. I've been asleep for 2,000 years. At some point, enough is enough."

Adrian laughed involuntarily. "It doesn't work that way."

"I know. I still just don't want to. I... Morris, can I ask you something?"

"Go ahead."

But Sato said nothing.

"Sato?"

"Forget it."

"Tell me."

"That's just it." She shook her head. "I don't know what I wanted to ask myself. Actually, I wanted to talk just to talk. I can't stand the silence anymore. A planet shouldn't be so... empty."

"You're not going to lose your nerve on me now, are you?"

"No." All at once her voice sounded completely monotone. She stood up. "Of course not, module leader."

With those words, she marched away.

"Sato!" Adrian stood up, ran after her, and grabbed her by the shoulder. "Sato, wait. Did I say something wrong?"

"No, of course not. It's just..."

"You may speak freely."

She raised her eyebrows. "Am I really allowed to?"

"Sato, please."

"All right," she muttered, taking a deep breath. "The thing you asked: if I'm losing my nerve. We're not human, Morris. We may have been born as humans, we may think and feel like humans, and it's our job to save humanity. But we - you, me, and everyone else aboard the *Genesis* - we're not human. We are not supposed to be. We are machines made of flesh. We must function. Weakness is not allowed, failure is not an option. Your question brought that back to me."

"I'm sorry about that, Sato. I didn't mean it that way."

"I have no doubt about that. It's still like that. I mean, look what happened to you! God, you got heavily irradiated!"

"It had to be."

"Exactly! And if it has to be that one of us jumps into an active volcano, then that's what we're going to do. We are dehumanized."

"Weren't you aware of that?" asked Adrian after a moment's hesitation.

"Yes I was, but that doesn't mean I like it."

Again he was silent.

"Don't you have anything to say about that?" demanded Sato in an emphatic tone.

He laughed softly. "Yes, I do, but it's probably better if I remain silent."

"Oh, come on, Morris."

"I don't think there's any point in thinking about it," he said slowly, weighing each word carefully. "Others have decided our fate. Our whole purpose for existence is what we're doing right now. And yes, in the end, this path will require much and sometimes everything of each of us. But there is nothing we can do about it. Sure, we could scream 'Fuck it!' and use all resources just for us, but to what end? It is what it is, and that is the purpose of our lives."

"You're speaking as a module leader right now, aren't you?"

"No, as a human being, I see it the same way."

"Why?"

"As I said, there's nothing I can do about it, and being in a bad mood about it doesn't help me. But if there's something I can help you with, please tell me."

"No, Morris." She pulled away from his grip. "You can't."

It took only a few moments for her to leave the landing platform and disappear into the now brightly lit base. Adrian still watched her go until he could no longer make out her silhouette, but decided against following her. He would have liked to claim that he could understand her feelings, but that would have been a lie. What he had said to her was indeed his deepest conviction: It was what it was. It had been decided for him, whether he liked it or not. And to rack your brain over things that you cannot change anyway was not expedient.

Adrian himself could not say exactly how he spent the rest of the night. Time flew by without him knowing how it happened, but either way it felt... wrong. As if his instinctive sense of time was fighting tooth and nail against taking the alternation of day and night as it was. It was possible that this was also an after-effect of cryostasis - or a consequence of his radiation sickness.

When the sun rose again sometime in the east and cast the first warm rays over the snow-covered wasteland of South America, he finally stood up and put on his helmet. It could not be long now before the *Genesis* reached the anchor. Until once again the powerful electromagnet was activated. And until more equipment and additional personnel were sent to them - hopefully.

Adrian smiled. He had never thought about it beforehand, but now that he had experienced what it was like to be one of the only handful of people within a radius of tens of thousands of miles, the thought of additional personnel on the *Genesis* was something that pleased him wholeheartedly.

He had just begun walking the landing zone, making sure one last time that everything was in order, when the massive orbital lift suddenly tensed. A deep rumble rippled through the air, accompanied by the creaking of steel. The space station must have reached the orbital anchor just in those seconds.

"Morris here," he said immediately into his radio, looking up, almost as if he hoped to actually catch sight of the station, but of course that was not the case. "Welcome back. Did everything work out?"

"Affirmative, Morris," the audibly relieved voice of the anchor operator answered him. "Everything's fine on our end. What's your status?"

"I'm walking on sunshine here."

"I can imagine that. We'll get everything ready and send

down the cargo unit in ten minutes. The first personnel transport will follow five minutes later. Is the landing zone clear?"

"Affirmative. Landing zone is clear. Who are you sending down first?"

"A ground crew from Module 27 and a medic from Module 11. Wait until the personnel pod has landed before unloading the cargo unit. We'll transmit instructions on unloading sequence in a moment."

"Understood. Have Mabena and the Directors decided how we're going to proceed regarding the signal?"

"Negative. We'll let you know."

"Understood. We are awaiting the cargo unit and will remain on standby. Morris out."

Sighing in frustration, Adrian left the landing zone around the orbital lift and leaned against the already unloaded cargo module that Horvat had parked a good distance away. He had been convinced that at least Mabena would give top priority to the feedback loop and locating their origin, but he had obviously been wrong about that. If he and the Directors decided to proceed further according to protocol, they could kiss a search for the origin of the signal, and thus for surviving humans, goodbye. And there was precious little he could do about it.

Soon, the others stepped out of the facility where the *Genesis* Project's base of operations would be built within the next few hours and days. The last bastion, the citadel of humanity. It might not look like much yet, but this place would become the cradle of their future with a little luck. The only bitter part was the idea that such a cradle might not be needed at all if more attention was paid to the signal.

The time until the arrival of the cargo unit was spent by Adrian and the others mostly doing nothing and waiting senselessly. They had long since completed the steps the protocol had given them and the mission they had been sent here to fulfill, and since anchor control had not given them any new instructions, that probably meant that their manpower was not needed, at least for the moment. Presumably a sub-protocol existed that not even he himself was aware of, forbidding him from further activity until he had been checked over by a doctor.

When the massive cargo module finally appeared in the sky and bridged the remaining distance to Earth, Adrian caught himself breathing a sigh of relief. Although there was hardly a thing that could go seriously wrong, part of him had feared until the very end that some kind of catastrophe might occur. The fact that this had not happened was a positive development of events.

Even as the cargo unit extended its spider-like robotic arms and positioned the individual modules so that they could be unloaded and transported away as quickly and smoothly as possible, the personnel capsule appeared at the elevator and touched down on the ground a short time later. Almost instantly, its hatch also swung open and eight men and women, fully loaded with protective suits and additional equipment, stepped out.

"Welcome to Earth." Adrian raised a hand and waved at them. "Had a good trip?"

"A little bumpy," one of them murmured, stepping toward him as the rest wordlessly set about unloading two of the cargo modules. "I'm Michael Hansen, chief medical officer of Module 11, and I've been told there's severe radiation exposure here?"

"That would be the two of us." Adrian nodded toward Toussaint. "She's at just over two sieverts, I'm at three."

"You did the initial treatment as per auto-diagnosis?"

"Yes."

"When?"

"About two hours later."

Hansen sighed in annoyance.

"What's wrong?" asked Toussaint immediately. "Is that bad? Were we too slow?"

"No," the doctor growled. "I'm just wondering what I'm doing here then. Your initial treatment was within the relevant time frame. For these doses of radiation, that's perfectly adequate. It's hard to explain to a layman, but think of it this way: The medicine you received extracts the radiation from your bodies, binds it, and ensures its elimination within five to six days, while any damage to your tissues that has occurred is already being treated. This is 'state of the art,' so to speak. If it makes you feel better, I can offer to look down your throat again. God, that's one time you rely on communication to be decent..."

"Sorry, Doc."

"That's not your fault, Morris. Personally, I'm glad you're both okay. I got a report of severe radiation poisoning. I thought that would put you somewhere between seven and eight sieverts. But two to three is well within our means. The only pity is that I would have been more useful on the *Genesis*."

"More useful? Is there a medical need already?"

"Nothing bad. The general post-cryostasis aches and pains. But while I'm here, I might as well start setting up the medical section. I'm afraid we're going to need it sooner rather than later."

Chapter Eight

THE *GENESIS* PROJECT WAS UNDERWAY. The fight for a second chance. Not only for mankind and Earth, but possibly for all intelligent life in the universe. With all its power, humanity reached out from the grave to grasp the throat of fate, to show it that it had not yet been finally defeated. That it had an ace up its sleeve and was willing to play it against all odds.

New personnel were steadily arriving on Earth via the orbital lift. The Directors had decided to relax security protocols to reflect conditions on the ground and allow transport by any means possible. As a result, not only was the personnel capsule in use, but so was a hastily converted cargo module, among other things. Nearly half of the remaining crew was already on Earth, working to initiate Phase 1 of terraforming.

Although only four days had passed since Adrian had reached the listening post in Greenland with Toussaint and Aacken, the base on Monte Burney had already developed into a more than imposing outpost of humanity. All sectors of the facility had been cleared and put into use; laboratories, factories, greenhouses and more had been set up. Planes and helicopters took off and landed every minute, while mighty bulldozers opened up a land route down from the mountain. Even on the shores of the Strait of Magellan, outposts had already been established, through which the Atlantic and the Pacific could be reached in equal measure.

Adrian could not help but admire what had been created here in such a short time. Of course he knew the protocols, knew about the division of labor and the procedures in the individual departments. Nevertheless, it was impressive. Knowing in the abstract what was going to happen was one thing, but seeing it with his own eyes was something else entirely.

Looking around slowly and attentively, he strolled through the extensive facility in the rock of the mountain. He had barely half an hour left before his next shift began. This was not free time in the true sense of the word, since he was required to try to the best of his ability to optimize what he saw, to eliminate errors, and to ensure greater efficiency overall.

Despite this - or perhaps because of this - he was impressed by what he saw and by those who worked for it. Sure, one or two personal conversations could have been stopped, or at least made sure that they were conducted during the work and not in between, but he didn't want to do that. What Sato had said stuck in his mind. They were machine people, living solely for their task. There was nothing he could do about that. But he was at least able to make sure that humanity didn't completely fall by the wayside.

"Morris," a voice suddenly rushed out of the small headset Adrian had put around his neck instead of wearing it on his head. "Mabena here. Do you copy?"

"Copy." He pulled the headset on. "I hear you. What's up?"

"Are you busy right now?"

"My next shift starts in just under half an hour."

"Then please come to my office immediately. We need to discuss something."

"Understood."

Adrian turned around on the spot and marched with quick steps back in the direction from which he had just come. Mabena and the two Directors were the only members of the crew who were privileged to have their own offices - or rooms for that matter. Everyone else, including the module directors, lived in shared quarters that corresponded to the modules on the *Genesis*. The only privacy was provided by the six-by-three-foot bunks. If you ignored the fact that you were allowed to spend a maximum of eight hours in it and shared it with two others.

As he hurried through the facility, he repeatedly encountered men and women in heavy, dark green protective suits. Members of the first expeditions to the devastated and most likely massively contaminated metropolises of the old world. The task was to get an overview of any production facilities that might still be intact, or at least to evaluate whether the debris could be reused.

An ice-cold shiver ran down Adrian's spine. The memory of his own radiation exposure and the brief interlude with the nuclear missile in Greenland still sat deep in his mind, and he would have been lying if he had claimed to feel completely fit again. However, even that was nothing compared to the nuclear madness that lurked in the cities.

When he finally reached Mabena's office, located in the farthest part of the facility, he paused for a moment outside the door and took a deep breath. Exactly what the Executive Field Officer wanted from him, he could not say, but he hoped with all his heart that he had news about the signal - and perhaps even permission to search for its origins.

"You wanted to see me?" said Adrian after entering the windowless office. But no sooner had he closed the door behind him than he noticed Toussaint leaning against the wall with her arms folded in front of her chest and her eyes fixed on the floor. "Toussaint, what..."

"Sit down." Mabena reached out and gestured to one of two chairs that stood in front of his meager desk. "Morris, I'm disappointed in you. Toussaint has just informed me of your suspicions regarding sabotage and explained the circumstantial evidence that points to it. Why did you not contact me immediately?"

"Sir, I am sure that Toussaint has also explained the reasons for my - our - silence."

"She did, but she is not a module leader and thus is not under immediate obligation. You, on the other hand, report to me and are in a much more exposed and responsible position. Your loyalty is indispensable."

Adrian took a deep breath. "So I'm out of a job?"

"I didn't say that."

"Then what did you say?"

"Morris, save the snarky tone. You and your people have done a good job. Not only here, but especially in Greenland. Considering the unexpected dangers you faced, you did a very level-headed and goal-oriented job. I know that I can rely on you. And Toussaint confirms this impression. Nevertheless, we must face the fact that your hesitation may have led to the saboteur's inability to be tracked down."

"How should that be understood?"

"Once the landing operation is complete and all personnel have arrived on Earth, the *Genesis* logs will be erased," Toussaint took over. "A sub-log I didn't know about - and that Mabena just told me about."

"What?"

"That's right." Mabena nodded. "The protocol calls for us to take over the station's computing capabilities, saving resources here on Earth for the time being, and respectively, or using them elsewhere. The archived databases will remain, but all system logs will be deleted to free up computing capacity."

"Then stop it!"

"I can't."

"Then the Directors will have to stop it!"

"Morris." Mabena looked him straight in the eye. "No one can. We are not supposed to interfere with established protocols and deviate from them only if necessary. That's exactly why these protocols exist. They were devised to keep our mission's chances of success as high as possible against all odds. Any change or deviation could result in a potentially dangerous loss of effectiveness."

"So, sticking to it must lead to potential disaster?"

"Sabotage from within was not considered as a possibility."

"Wonderful." Adrian threw his hands up. "Just wonderful! Mabena, with all due respect, why am I here?"

The Executive Field Officer looked to Toussaint and with a nod of his head motioned her to sit down as well, which she did with visible reluctance.

"The fact that *Aegis Dawn* was able to infiltrate a sleeper agent - on our side, to be sure, but an agent nonetheless - via Dr. Abraham shows that there are massive vulnerabilities," Mabena explained slowly. "That our system is not as airtight as we believed. And especially not as unassailable."

"That doesn't answer my question."

Mabena was already preparing for a presumably angry reply, but then paused and sighed before nodding slowly. "You're right. Morris, you looked at the system after the station became accessible. I know we've talked about it before, but I want an authoritative assessment from you as to whether or not we can find clues in it. If so, we could at least try to delay deleting the logs, even if it costs us a lot of resources."

Adrian bit his lip and remained silent. It was a good question, and he was tempted to answer it directly in the affirmative. However, not because he saw any basis for that answer, but rather because he hoped that someone with presumably better qualifications than he would be more likely to be able to read something from the logs. However, that would...

Suddenly it dawned on him: he had found nothing, because there was nothing. No one could destroy all traces; especially not when an advanced artificial intelligence like the onboard system was active. The logical conclusion was to try not to leave any traces at all, which had to be hidden afterwards. So, what if the saboteur had tampered with the modules directly - and not at the system level, but purely mechanically?

"You look like you just thought of something," Toussaint said cautiously. "What is it, Morris?"

"There are no traces," he started slowly, only to immediately pause again for a moment to put his thoughts into words. "There can't be any. The tampering has been done on a mechanical level! The system log recorded the failure of life support as the cause of the system cascade! Modules 9 and 13 merely had life support failures and were jettisoned per Emergency Protocol Beta to prevent further cascades. This was the logical consequence of the original cascade and the 'fault' of the onboard system. Modules 1 through 4 were deliberately mechanically manipulated. That would also explain the signal events – the *Genesis'* own sensor sweep to verify the damage!"

"And could that be proven?"

"I think..."

"Stop!" interrupted Toussaint. "It must be possible to find out who woke up, right? Even for mechanical manipulation, someone must have woken up from cryostasis! And I can tell you from personal experience that it's not that easy to get in afterwards. Has anyone looked at all the cryo capsules?"

"We have," Mabena replied. "It's standard procedure."

"And?"

"There was nothing there."

"The wake-up log is stored in the modules," Adrian whispered more to himself than to either of them. "Not in the onboard system."

"Those were checked, too."

"Then it was someone from the first four modules," Toussaint breathed.

"What?"

"It was someone from the first four modules," she repeated in a quivering voice. "Kind of like a suicide bombing. That's the only explanation. Right?"

Almost looking for help, she looked to Adrian.

"It would be a possibility," he agreed, returning her gaze

before looking to Mabena, who was staring at the *Aegis Dawn* agent with a pale face and unconcealed horror. "The modules are self-sufficient in their own right in terms of life support, however, under normal conditions, a common circuit is established around the station's central processing unit to conserve resources. If someone in Module 1 triggers a sufficiently large event, this circuit could possibly collapse and lead to a system cascade. The onboard system inevitably needs some time to cut the circuit, boot up the individual life support systems, and fix the problem. Jettisoning four modules seems realistic."

"No one expected an attack from within," Mabena breathed tonelessly. "We were prepared for anything, for any eventuality, no matter how ridiculous. And now this is supposed to have happened?"

"You don't believe us?"

"Yes, I do." He folded his arms in front of his chest. Probably an attempt to hide the trembling of his hands. He didn't succeed. "I do. And that's what makes it so terrible. I'm going to discuss this finding with the Directors and have it reviewed by two independent teams. Morris, Toussaint - dismissed."

Adrian hesitated for a moment, but then did as instructed and left the barren office with Toussaint. He was not sure himself how he managed to move his legs. Everything felt mechanical; his perception itself seemed numb and dull. That the system cascade had been triggered, as Toussaint and he had concluded, he had no doubt. Whether that could ever be proven was another question, but with luck at least they need not fear further sabotage now.

He looked at Toussaint, who returned his gaze and also opened her mouth, but said nothing. She was thinking the same thing he was, he knew it. But what would be better if they discussed it again? If they had the same discussion only for the certainty of redundancy? Nothing. What had happened might be horrible and tragic, cynical and also difficult for a rational thinking person to comprehend, but with any luck it would remain an episode that would not be repeated. Maybe now they could look ahead.

WITH A SOFT CURSE on his lips, Adrian wiped the sweat from his forehead before reaching for his water bottle and taking a few generous sips. He had been sitting here for hours, huddled and sweating, trying to figure out why one of the generators wasn't producing as much power as it should. He already knew that it was not a major problem, but that was all. And since neither he nor the other four engineers and technicians sitting with him in this ember hell could find anything, it could really only be a matter of what he always liked to call asshole protocol: at some point, after loosening every screw, removing every part, and checking absolutely everything, they would come across a tiny contaminant that was responsible. Not worth mentioning, but still reason enough for this effort.

He would have liked it much better if they could have at least taken this generator offline for the duration of the repairs, however, that was not possible. The base needed all the power available and the loss of power meant that some of the less important departments and stations had to be taken off line. Unacceptable, especially this early in the mission. Even if it meant he was sitting here in full gear, working like a maniac.

The Directors had launched an official investigation to verify Toussaint's and his suspicions, and two teams had independently concluded that this explanation was the only possible one. That was a good thing, because it meant that the deletion of the station log could proceed as planned, and it meant that they probably had no further sabotage to worry about. At the same time, everyone knew what had happened. That there had been an attack from among them and someone had become a traitor with whom 29 others had grown up and shared their lives. And that Toussaint was an agent of *Aegis Dawn*. Not particularly good conditions for building lasting trust, but perhaps time would at least heal those wounds.

Involuntarily, Adrian shook his head and once again wiped the sweat from his forehead, even if it hardly did any good. It felt strange to be crouching here now, going about his work. Not only because of everything that had happened, but also because it felt mundane and normal to do so. The activation of the *Exodus* signal and the launch of the *Genesis* mission had always been almost mythical events for him, the goal and purpose of his life. Something big, something powerful. His personal eschatology, if you will. Sitting here now with a screwdriver in his hand did not do it justice.

Many on the base seemed to feel the same way. He had heard from other module leaders that they sometimes had to do quite a bit of work to motivate their people and keep morale high. The initial euphoria had faded and now everyone had to find a way to cope with the fact that the first tangible results would come in a few years at the earliest, more likely in a few decades. If all went well by then, that is.

"Jackson, I'm getting nowhere here," Adrian growled at one point, looking off to the side. A few feet away from him, one of the other engineers was working upside down in a tiny ventilation shaft. "You got anything?"

"Some dead bugs in a voltage transformer," he replied, breathing heavily. "But I hardly think they're responsible. Probably got trapped in there during construction. We should come to terms with the fact that this thing is just broken. It's not going to help anyone if we slave away for days and find nothing."

"We need the power."

"Then we'll put up a wind turbine!" Jackson pulled his head out of the shaft. "Or we'll use one of the photovoltaic arrays! God, we've got double and triple everything! I just don't see the point in fixing this garbage!"

"Antimatter provides us with a virtually inexhaustible source of energy," Adrian retorted.

"So does the sun."

"True again."

"So? Abort?"

"You're running the repair," Adrian snorted. "Your responsibility."

"Afraid of Mabena?"

"I could do without listening to another telling off."

"Telling off? Why? Because of the sabotage thing?"

"Yup."

"Hmm."

Adrian raised his eyebrows. "What?"

"You'd think he'd be grateful to you. After all, if it hadn't been for you, no one would have thought of..."

"Exactly," Adrian interrupted him. "That's just it, isn't it? No one would have known. Now everybody knows, and we can't do anything about what happened, and we don't expect any more sabotage. So, in purely factual terms, all I've done is create discord and cause distrust."

"That's bullshit!"

"It's not," he grumbled. "But that's okay."

"And Toussaint?"

"What about her?"

"Do you trust her?"

"I have no reason not to."

"God damn it, Morris!"

"What?!"

"Talking to you is like pulling information from the onboard system." Shaking his head, Jackson struggled to his feet. "Cold, emotionless, purely pertinent statements. It's impossible to make small talk with you. I... Oh, forget it. We're breaking off here. There's no point. Let..."

Suddenly, there was a rattling, whirring sound that grew frantically louder. Jackson squinted in surprise and turned around, but before he could even react, a bright light suddenly flashed right next to him. An arc of light erupted from an open electrical box and bored into his body. Instantly, a thunderous bang sounded, sparks flew off in all directions, and Jackson fell to the ground in a heap.

"Emergency shutdown!" yelled Adrian on the spot. "Emergency shutdown now! I need a medic!"

A deep, yowling sound rang out not a second later. The generator was shutting down. Adrian ran to Jackson and was about to reach for him, but then stopped. His hazmat suit looked like it had been charred, his skin was pitch black, and the pervasive stench of burned flesh rose from him in smoke. He was dead.

"Morris! Morris, where are you!!! The paramedic is on his way! What happened!!!"

"Arc," Adrian replied tonelessly and without taking his eyes off his dead colleague. "Jackson's dead."

"What?!"

"He's dead, damn it! How could this happen!!! That section should have been kept under micro-voltage! I... Shit! Damn it! The entire generator room is being evacuated, shut everything down! I want a full report in an hour on how a goddamn surge ionization could have happened! Get a chemist down here; we need an air analysis!"

"Morris, we can't just take the generators offline! We..."

"I don't give a shit! That's an order!"

"With all due respect, I'm refusing the order. If we take them offline now, we'll set the entire mission back days!"

Adrian shook his head, turned and walked out of that part of the generator facility. There was no point to this. If these morons didn't follow his order, then he'd just have to take the plant offline himself. Until it was established beyond a doubt how such an arc could occur in a section of the generator that was at best under extra-low voltage, he would not allow anyone to enter that room. Every single death was one too many; every hazard unacceptable. Not only because of the loss of life, but also because the mission could not afford to expose any more specialists to such a risk.

It took him a few minutes to finally reach the hatch of the maintenance shaft and pull himself out, but no sooner did his feet touch the ground than he felt someone grab him by the arm and push him roughly against the outer shell of the generator. Two men in servo-supported work uniforms stood in front of him. No chance to fight them off.

"What are you doing?!" hissed Adrian immediately. "Get the hell off me!"

"Orders from above," one of them replied. "The generators stay online."

"This is madness!" he shouted. "Jackson is fucking dead! Until we figure out what..."

"The generators stay online," the man repeated, barely perceptibly shaking his head. "Morris, I'm sorry, but orders are orders. Either you leave the generator room of your own accord or we'll escort you out."

Adrian was already opening his mouth to yell at him and throw every one of the countless insults that were running through his head at that moment, but finally he just let it go and slowly raised his hands. The two of them hesitantly let go of him now, whereupon he instantly marched to the door and left the generator room.

He did his best not to let on, but he was seething with anger. Some risk was one thing, just like accidents or bad luck. None of that could be prevented. But knowing, seeing idiocy? Ignoring danger and accepting further loss? No, that was insanity. Insanity. Were protocol and strict adherence to it really so important that they couldn't even spend a few days to solve such a problem? Hell, what if one of the generators didn't just arc, but blew up and blew the entire base to hell? What if...

"Morris." Suddenly, Mabena stepped toward him. "Come with me. Now."

"With respect, sir, but I'll be damned if you think you're leaving the generator online after Jackson dies..."

"What the hell are you talking about, Morris?!" Mabena's eyes widened. "Jackson is dead? What about the generator?!"

"The..." Adrian cleared his throat. "The order didn't come from you?"

"Morris, I have no idea what you're talking about!" the Executive Field Officer growled in a cutting tone. "What happened?"

"We were repairing one of the generators because of a

loss of power. Jackson was in charge. It... He was killed by an arc, even though our section was only at extra-low voltage. I was going to have all the generators taken offline to look for the cause, but... Please forgive me, Mabena. They said there was an order from the top to keep them online."

"That could only have been the Directors," he muttered. "I'll look into it, Morris. That's an irresponsible decision. But that's not why I came looking for you. It's about the signal they received. About that feedback loop. The analysts are done."

"So?" demanded Adrian immediately.

"It was not possible to determine the original transmitter. We did include the *Genesis* sensors and scanners in the analyses, however, even they were unable to. However, based on some of the signal's peculiarities, we're relatively certain it wasn't sent directly to the listening post."

Adrian frowned. "What's that supposed to mean?"

"We were able to make out remnants of a very specific identifier; an automatic attachment, if you will. The signal was inter-processed by the *Sarasvati* radio telescope. That's a facility near Kanpur in India. It was built about 300 years after the launch of our mission, and until the end was considered the most powerful facility on Earth - at least according to the listening post's records. It was capable not only of complex radio astronomical measurements, but also of sending large amounts of data in a targeted manner."

"Why would they have done that?" asked Adrian. "Such an intermediate step is completely unnecessary and risks failure. The listening post can be directly accessed from any point on Earth. The *CONE* System..."

"It is possible that the sender did not know how to reach the listening post and chose this detour instead," Mabena interrupted him. "Or perhaps there are entirely different reasons that are currently beyond us. The fact is, we don't know, and it doesn't matter for now. Judging from scans of the *Genesis*, *Sarasvati* survived not only the war, but also the ensuing period relatively well. So if we want to find out where the signal is coming from, we'll have to look locally."

"So we have clearance?"

"Affirmative. I will personally lead the mission. If you have no objections, I'd like you to be there."

"Absolutely." Adrian nodded. "Thank you, sir."

"No need to thank me," he snorted. "This isn't going to be a walk in the park, Morris. Scans from the *Genesis* show high levels of radiation and probably larger amounts of chemicals from a nearby chemical industrial complex. Not to mention damage from the war and subsequent decay."

"Sounds like a bigger deal."

"I wish it were. We'll get a long-range transporter and appropriate equipment, though I've only been given permission for a six-person team because of the risk involved. Make sure Toussaint comes along, and fill another seat with one of your most resilient people. I'll take care of the rest. We leave in an hour."

Chapter Nine

THERE WERE STILL JUST under thirty minutes until the arrival at the *Sarasvati* radio telescope. Half an hour that Adrian already knew would seem like an eternity. He had been feeling nervous ever since they took off. Restless, exhilarated and almost rushed. He was fully aware that he hardly had a logical reason for this, but it changed nothing.

With a few quick moves, he undid the fastenings of his gloves, took them off, and stroked his face with both hands. His eyelids were heavy and from his temples a dull throbbing pulsed through his head. Fatigue and exhaustion, coupled with the last after-effects of his radiation sickness. Not exactly ideal conditions, exposing himself to a completely contaminated area again, but it had to be done.

Of course, he could have considered this a normal mission. At least as ordinary as it could be, given the circumstances. However, that would have been a lie. This was no ordinary mission. Not only because of the feedback loop and the fact that it was reasonably likely to involve survivors, but also because Mabena was personally accompanying them. He, as Executive Field Officer, oversaw the practical implementation of the sections of the *Genesis* Project as determined by the Directors, but had no business in the field. That he was here anyway underscored the importance of the signal - and how important the Directors thought it was.

Was that why he felt so fired up? He was not used to working under the direct orders of his superiors, nor had he been trained to do so. Actually, as module leader, he held the greatest possible autonomy and could carry out missions as he saw fit, given the circumstances. Still... he could not imagine that being the reason.

Adrian turned his head to the side and looked at Toussaint and Aacken, who were both sitting next to him and staring ahead with an indefinable look. Unlike himself, they did not seem nervous, but rather annoyed. A circumstance he could well understand, since Mabena had spent the first hours of the flight lecturing everyone on board about how important it was that they obeyed his orders to the letter.

The two specialists he had brought on board seemed to be no different. They, too, stared stubbornly and silently ahead. One of them, a burly fellow named Rosenblatt, was an information technician just like Toussaint, but with an explicit specialization in astrotech, those machines and devices that had been used explicitly for space exploration in the past. The other, Jinjin Xun, was a language specialist. The official language of the *Genesis* mission was English, which meant that India might need someone who spoke Hindi.

"Something's wrong," Mabena grumbled at one point as the landing approach neared.

The sound of his voice alone was enough to make Adrian wince.

"What's wrong?" he asked immediately.

"I'm not sure. The systems are showing me warning messages that I can't do much with. Come up front, Morris. Take a look."

Adrian unfastened his straps and squeezed past the others toward the cockpit. It was an undertaking that was anything but easy due to the powerful protective suits, especially since they were all still wearing a cover of thick rubber over the actual suits to protect them from the chemical exposure on the ground. Finally, he reached the cockpit and, breathing heavily, lowered himself into a seat next to Mabena.

"Here." The Executive Field Officer reached out and pointed to a series of readouts on one of the displays. "Can you do anything with these?"

Adrian squinted his eyes and stared intently at the alerts. Mabena was right: this was indeed strange. The radiation level was at extremely high levels, as expected, and countless different toxins had long been detectable in the air as well, but there was also another warning message. One that he had never seen like this before, and one that he couldn't place at first glance either.

"This is really strange," he muttered, flipping through the readouts, but even the details didn't provide him with an answer. Far too many different parameters were related to each other without making any apparent sense to him. Finally, he turned to the others. "Warning message *NIOC*, threat level 1, category *IIGE*. Does that mean anything to you?"

There was silence for a moment, but then Aacken gave a clearly audible sigh. "*NIOC* means '*Nuclear Induced Orbital Catastrophe*,' and *IIGE* means '*Irreversible Incident of Global Effect*.'"

"And what does that mean?"

"That we're screwed, Morris. That the mission has failed."

Adrian felt his heart skip a beat, only to immediately contract painfully and pump such adrenaline into his bloodstream that he had to gasp for air, while at the same time an unspeakable feeling of emptiness spread through his stomach. It was as if he were suddenly falling, as if he were suddenly caught in the middle of a nightmare that he knew was a dream but could not wake up.

"What?" he merely stammered.

"Extensive measurements would have to be taken for more accurate information," Aacken replied slowly. "But the most likely *NIOC* scenario is a complete and most likely irreversible rupture of the ozone layer, probably by a combined nuclear and aerosol bomb of great explosive power. One of the *NIOC* scenarios involves a very complex process in which ozone and oxygen mix and burn, tearing a huge hole in the ozone layer. You can guess what *IIGE* means: global and, more importantly, irreversible impacts."

"That can't be," Mabena said, shaking his head vehemently. "There is no circumstantial evidence for such an event! The sensors of the *Genesis* have detected nothing, and the data of the listening post do not offer any conclusion either!"

"As I said," Aacken cleared his throat, "one would have to take further measurements, but the warning messages are clear. It may be a relatively localized event. Even the *Genesis* sensors didn't scan the entire planet - or they misinterpreted the chemical contamination. I... Mabena, permission to speak freely?"

"Granted."

"An *IIGE* means de facto mission failure," he said slowly. "It means that we are unable to reverse or even combat the effects. There's still a chance that the scans are wrong or that there's some other explanation, but the chance is not very high."

"And your point is?"

"According to protocol, we should withdraw to the *Genesis* and try to get the cryostasis pods operational again. I..."

He paused.

"What?!" wanted Mabena to know immediately.

"Sir, I am by God no expert on the evolution of Earth's atmosphere, but such an event could reset the planet's clock. I think a complete collapse of the atmosphere is conceivable - and possibly a development of a new atmosphere at some point based on that. In the past, the planet has gone through several atmospheres, and the current one was formed just over two and a half billion years ago - as a result of the so-called Great Oxidation Event."

"Aacken, I still don't see your point!"

"This is probably the best thing that could have happened to the planet."

"What?!"

"Such a collapse could lead to extensive processes being set in motion that would not only reverse the radiation, but also the chemical stress on the Earth. That at some point a restart would become possible and evolution would start all over again."

"God damn it, man. You do know the goal and purpose of the *Genesis*, don't you?"

"I do."

"Then shut the fuck up! We're not going to allow ourselves to go extinct, nor are we going to retire to the *Genesis* for billions of years and wait for us to decay alive! We'll find a way to stop this madness! That's an order!"

"Sir, you do understand what 'irreversible' means, don't you?"

"As soon as we land, you will take all the relevant measurements necessary to confirm or disprove the warning message," was all Mabena replied. "Rosenblatt, can you use *Sarasvati* Station's technology to boost our sensors?"

"Under certain circumstances," Rosenblatt replied. "I'll have to look at it first, but depending on how many functions the radio telescope has, we could definitely access some old measuring equipment. I'll figure something out."

"Then do that. Toussaint, Xun, Morris - you come with me. We need to trace this feedback loop. There may be survivors who can tell us more about this ozone hole."

No one on the plane replied anything, although Adrian would have given a lot not to have to endure the cruel silence that now settled over them. While he admired Mabena's stubborn refusal to face reality and his conviction that a solution would be found, he doubted it wholeheartedly. Aacken was not one to make a statement lightly. That combined with the sensor data.

He sighed softly. God, this just could not be true! Unless a miracle happened and it all turned out to be faulty readings or defective sensor technology, it was all over. Everything. The *Genesis* mission would fail before it could even get underway, and each of them would spend the rest of their lives knowing they were the last of a long-dead species. A terrifying thought.

However - the war was centuries in the past. That meant that the nuclear and aerosol bombs must also have gone off centuries ago. The atmosphere had held until now and this crack in the ozone layer had not destroyed the entire earth either. That had to mean then that the danger was at least not completely immediate, right? Even if the atmosphere lasted only a few hundred years, that might be enough time to find a way to save it. Possibly even with technology that wasn't even conceivable today.

Adrian took a deep breath and exhaled slowly. A nice thought. He would have liked to cling to it to displace the cold fear that had so mercilessly taken possession of him. And he was even tempted to do so, had it not been for the rational part of his mind, which knew perfectly well that such hope was no basis for planning a future.

Meanwhile, Mabena had begun his approach to land and was steering the plane toward a small open area. Adrian could not see a radio telescope anywhere, though that did not necessarily mean anything. For one thing, he had paid no attention to whether they had already flown over it, and for another, he had no idea whether his idea of it was even correct. No one could foresee how the technology had evolved during their cryogenic sleep.

Still, he caught himself staring out the window, trying to make out something amidst the reddish-brown desert around them. It was impossible. Huge clouds of dust and a strangely pale, almost sickly light made it impossible to see further than a maximum of fifty or sixty yards.

He shook his head absentmindedly. While he would never have thought it possible, Earth looked sick. Unhealthy. Dead. Like a fallen god. Gaia, the earth mother, had died. This place was the tumor that had ruined her; the poison of humanity reached deep into her body and polluted her remains for centuries.

Perhaps they deserved to die just as she had.

"The observatory is about 500 yards east of us," Mabena said after the vertical launcher touched down and the thrusters slowly shut down. "Check your suits. Radiation levels are over 100,000 microsieverts per hour. Even a small tear in your equipment is tantamount to a death sentence."

"How long can we safely stay here?" wanted Xun to know.

"With the preventive medication and iodine block, we should have five hours," the Executive Field Officer replied tonelessly. "At least that's what the doctors calculated. Up to seven hours, the effects are reversible. After eight, we're dead. I'd be very happy if we could make it in five hours or less."

"Might be difficult."

"I agree," Aacken agreed with her. "With the weather conditions, it will probably take us an hour or two to even find the facility! What if it's partially or even completely buried?"

"Let's just do our best, then."

With those words, Mabena stood up, stepped past the others, and pulled on his helmet. Adrian did the same and just a few moments later the loading ramp at the rear of the machine opened. On the spot, such intense heat hit him that he had to gasp for air. And when he stepped outside, he felt like he was in another world. A strange, hostile world.

All around their landing site there was nothing but reddish-brown dust and a few debris of old buildings sticking out of the ground like skeletal ribs. The Geiger counter in Adrian's suit howled so quickly and shrilly that he turned it off, and all the other systems in his equipment jumped into the red zone in no time.

What that meant had long been clear to him. Here, at this place, unimaginable things must have happened. For such a radiation level on the surface alone, enormous weapons must have been used - and that only if the weapons had been explicitly built to do that. Could neutron bombs even do that? Or had mankind constructed something even more terrible?

And why here of all places? Kanpur was a city with millions of inhabitants in the immediate vicinity, but at least in the past it had neither been particularly important nor strategically relevant in any way. So why had such an inferno been unleashed here of all places? No. This was not just an inferno. This was where atomic hell itself had descended upon the earth and engulfed it.

"The radio telescope," Adrian finally said into the radio. "That was the target of the attack."

WHAT HAD HAPPENED HERE WOULD PROBABLY REMAIN a secret for all time. One that the old world had taken with it into the grave it had dug for itself. The fact that the *Sarasvati* radio telescope must have been the target of the attack was beyond question for Adrian. There was nothing else in the area that could have justified such a complete destruction. Whereby 'justify' was a very strong word. Nothing excused such a skyscraping madness.

Nevertheless, the same question remained: Why on earth had the telescope been attacked in this way? It could have been destroyed by conventional means. Even with nuclear means, a small tactical missile would have sufficed. There must have been a reason why they had decided to contaminate this spot of earth until the end of time. A reason for the fact that above their heads the ozone layer had been shredded, and with that the planet had been doomed.

But try as he might, Adrian could not imagine that this question could be answered with rational common sense. Had this place possibly possessed military significance? Had things been done here for which the radio telescope had not been built? Or had it possibly been built for such a purpose and had only met its inevitable end? Had its builders possibly even tried to make it indestructible, so that such radiation had been the only way to shut it down?

Adrian tried his best to put these thoughts out of his mind and focus instead on what lay ahead. Several hours of work in the worst possible conditions and in the place that was the closest thing to hell on this planet. He could not afford to be distracted if he wanted to have even a chance of getting out of this alive.

And so he followed Mabena and the others at a run across the reddish-brown sand that completely covered this place. With every single step he sank deep into the ground and it was only thanks to the servos of his suit that he could not only keep upright, but move at all with the equipment. The heavy protective overcoat alone weighed over forty pounds, and underneath he was also wearing a regular suit of the highest protection class. In theory, he could have used it to take a quick dip in a volcano. Presumably, that would have been less dangerous than this.

How Mabena managed not to lose his orientation was a mystery to him. The wind ensured that visibility was at most around fifty yards. Most of the time it was much less. And the radiation had caused the compass to malfunction, at least on Adrian's equipment.

"According to the data from Greenland, *Sarasvati* was a relatively conventional facility for the time," Mabena's distorted voice came through the radio at one point. "Twenty-four arrays, each with twelve individual antennas. Apparently, a combined system of smooth-surface parabolic mirrors and grid structure; plus advanced reflectors, about which we have very little information. Each array has its own control and computation room, but the entire system can be coupled as an interferometer and is then controlled by a central complex. For now, that's our target. If we don't find anything there, we'll work our way systematically through the individual control rooms."

"Understood," Adrian replied. "Did the analysts find out anything else that might help us? About the identifier, for example?"

"The identifier just tells us that the signal was processed here. That means by implication that there must be active processing capability. But at least with the aircraft's onboard systems, I can't see anything. The interference from the radiation is too strong."

Adrian nodded, though he knew Mabena could not see him. Active computing capabilities. Actually, it made sense when he thought about it, and it was another indication of what he had long feared: *Sarasvati* was not a civilian facility. It was remarkable in itself that it had survived the war and the centuries that followed, at least with its technology, but that after all this time, and especially in the face of such radiation, it still had power and computing capacity... That could only point to military use and corresponding bunkers.

All at once Adrian felt sick. Just thinking about how the world had ended made hot bile crawl through his throat. Back then, when he had made his way into cryo-sleep, there had been peace. Not complete lack of conflict, but peace by and large. The most powerful nations on Earth had realized, after the brief war between the U.S. and China, that advancing technology in the weapons sector would ultimately only lead to the complete annihilation of humanity. That war, no matter how precisely thought out, would invariably lead to two losers.

So what had happened that nations had suddenly forgotten agreements they had thought secure and had turned on each other? That such a war not only devastated entire regions and swallowed up the people, but also developed into a global cataclysm? Had no one tried to avert this madness? Or at least to stop it, if its outbreak had been inevitable?

What on earth could justify such a thing? Resources? Power? Hatred? Intrigue? Fanaticism? Or had it ultimately been, as so often before, just blindness?

"Mabena?" he finally asked, just as they reached a massive circular wall. Behind it had to be *Sarasvati*.

"Yes?"

"The data from the listening post. Do we know why the war broke out?"

"We have a guess."

"And?"

He sighed. "Morris, I don't think this is the time."

"You really don't?" asked Toussaint. "We're probably dying a horrible death from radiation, and you won't even tell us why?"

"She has a point, sir," Xun agreed with her.

"All right." Mabena took a deep breath. "From the data of the last twenty years before the war, we were able to draw some conclusions. Climate change, large-scale migration, and a resulting economic crisis seem to have caused instability around the world, resulting in populists coming to power. We suspect that they spun together simplistic, mass-market solutions for peoples out of fears and resentments, and thus entered a kind of downward spiral."

"You mean they couldn't back away from their own statements in a face-saving way?"

"Something like that. Old conflicts became heated, and they turned on each other. Local riots became regional uprisings, which in turn ended in civil wars and real wars. War has always been an effective way for our species to get rid of surplus labor and young men eager for conflict, no matter how cruel it sounds. We suspect for this reason it was also allowed to happen. And at some point, control was lost. The world practically slid to its doom. But it's ultimately impossible to know who fired the first missile."

"It doesn't matter, either."

"Probably not."

"And is there any evidence of this bomb that Aacken mentioned?" asked Toussaint. "This combined nuclear and aerosol bomb?"

"No."

"He didn't mean a combined bomb," Adrian said quietly. "But a two-stage bomb. Or rather, a two-stage attack."

"Does that make a difference?"

"A big one, yes. A combination would mean amplifying the explosive force, which makes no sense in a nuclear response. A two-stage attack, on the other hand, could produce an effect like we see here. A nuclear bomb by itself has a tremendous vacuum effect. Depending on what was detonated here, the mushroom cloud could penetrate the ozone layer with relative ease and even reach the mesosphere. If one subsequently blows up an aerosol bomb in the ozone layer, the ozone could serve as a burning accelerator for the oxygen - with consequences such as we see here. However, that would still require a preceding global enrichment with 'fuel' to explain the chain reaction. Perhaps chemical waste products that have become trapped in the atmosphere."

"But there must be some benefit to that, right?"

"Inevitably." Adrian nodded. "The purpose of the atomic bomb is clear. It was to destroy structures on the ground. However, as for the aerosol bomb... As you say - it must have had a use. So why purposefully destroy the ozone? It mainly keeps out UV radiation. Was that the way to disrupt the place? It can't really have that kind of effect."

"Unless something was done here that we don't know about," Xun replied. "Here - or in the air."

"You think the bomb was targeting a target in the upper atmosphere?"

"It's possible. A few years before our mission was launched, the first experiments with free-flying miniature factories were started in the stratosphere. The idea was to synthesize various substances as part of a series of experiments on artificial photosynthesis. It may be that this, or something similar, had developed into a promising future technology?"

"It's possible." Mabena's tone alone was enough to let everyone know that the conversation was now over. "At the end of the day, this is all speculation. We don't know the purpose, and as of now, I want everyone to focus on our actual mission."

He raised his hand and pointed to a pile of rubble on the wall, which Adrian only realized at second glance was the rubble of a building. A building that, upon closer inspection, turned out to be relatively intact, except for sand deposits and a few collapsed walls. The sheer thickness of the walls and the mighty steel elements that repeatedly protruded from the concrete were a clear indication that this facility had been built to withstand the worst of the shelling.

Or possibly even the direct hit of a nuclear missile?

Adrian bit his lip. If this was indeed ground zero, the building had survived the hit extremely well. A fact that even the attackers might have been aware of, since it had led them to ignore the material aspects of the facility and instead focus on killing the people inside through radiation exposure. Cold military logic. Nothing more, nothing less.

Silently, he followed Mabena toward a pile of sand behind which a path seemed to lead into the building. For the fact that there were relatively strong winds in this place, this was probably an optimal scenario. He had long since noticed that the wind was constantly changing direction. Possibly a consequence of climate collapse? If that was the case, then it was to their advantage. Otherwise, they would have had to spend hours clearing a path. And that was only if they had found the building at all.

"Okay." Mabena stopped and gestured for them to do the same. "I'm strongly assuming we're in the right place. I hope the radiation level drops further down. In the interest of time, we'll split up. Toussaint, you come with me. We'll work our way systematically from the top down. Morris and Xun, you try to get as far down as you can and start from there. With any luck, we won't have to look very far. Once we've got something, we have to make every move count. Any questions? No? Then let's go!"

Chapter Ten

How come you, of all people, are involved in this?" Xun's voice rushed through the radio, slightly distorted. A channel on which only the two of them talked, except for the occasional interference from old equipment that sounded like echoes from the past. "After what happened at the listening post, you were supposed to be off-limits for missions like that, right?"

"Supposed to be." Adrian felt a bitter smile flit across his lips. "Yes, actually, I should be. According to protocol."

"And how come you're here anyway?"

"Didn't Mabena tell you?"

"If he had, I wouldn't be asking."

"I guess that's true. We were at the listening post where we received the feedback loop. It was our guess that it might have come from survivors, and..."

"None of that justifies breaking protocol," she interrupted him in an almost cutting voice, though Adrian wasn't sure if that was really her intention or rather a result of the interference on the radio.

"I wouldn't have taken you for someone who clings to protocol," he replied.

"I'm not, but it doesn't help anyone if you get killed or become useless."

"Useless?"

"For reproduction. I've spent a lot of my training with Sato, and I know she's your assigned mate. It would be a shame if the two of you were to fail because you fried your genetic material."

"I'm sure suitable and willing replacements can be found."

"You know what I mean."

Adrian slumped his shoulders and nodded. "Yeah."

"What?"

"If there's any point in fathering children at all," he grumbled. "It all depends on what Aacken and Rosenblatt find out. I... Never mind. Xun, about that signal, I think Mabena trusts me. That's why I'm here. We could have kept it quiet or dismissed it as an anomaly, but my people and I decided to push for an analysis. I think Mabena appreciates that."

Xun said no more. A circumstance for which Adrian was more than grateful. Not because he didn't want to talk to her, but rather because he needed all his attention to orient himself in this radiation-infested hellhole.

By now they were seven stories deep underground, and nothing indicated that they would reach the end of the facility in the foreseeable future. On the contrary, the further they got, the more extensive the yellowed but still legible metal plates on the walls became, indicating the path network of the respective level. There were barracks, officers' messes, equipment stores, supply rooms, generators, and everything else one would expect to find in such a place. Whatever had been done in this facility, it had been built to withstand even the most adverse conditions.

Adrian snorted softly. Most adverse circumstances. An apt description. The atomic bomb had indeed unleashed the most adverse of circumstances. Even here, dozens of feet underground and with several thick blankets of reinforced concrete between them and the surface, the radiation level continued to be well over 60,000 microsieverts per hour. He could only speculate what physical and chemical tricks were required to achieve this, but either way, no one had been able to survive here. And increasingly, he doubted the protective effectiveness of his own equipment.

Nevertheless, he went on. It had to be done, was part of his mission. And depending on how the measurements of Aacken and Rosenblatt would turn out, not only the survival of the *Genesis* Project, but also of the entire human race depended on the success of this mission. If the feedback loop could indeed be traced back to other humans, then they had learned to live on this dead Earth and defy its adversities. And with any luck, they might have even known a way to avert the impending apocalypse.

Adrian knew how unlikely this hope was. But that was exactly what hope was. It was not a probability and definitely not a certainty, but an attempt to wrest something good from the worst. Even if it was only a tiny chance.

They had just reached the ninth basement floor when the staircase they had followed so far ended all at once. Unlike the floors of the facility behind them, there was no maze of corridors and halls waiting for them here, but a single wide gate of rusted steel. It stood open just wide enough for them to squeeze through despite their protective suits.

"Here we are," Xun said tonelessly, cautiously taking a step toward the gate. "Forty thousand microsieverts per hour. I... Morris, you noticed we didn't see any bodies upstairs, right?"

"What are you getting at?"

"The plant personnel will probably have retreated as far down as they could after the bombing," she explained slowly, her voice trembling. "That's the only way they could at least hope to find shelter from the radiation and ride out the fallout. This could be a graveyard."

Adrian nodded at her. A movement she couldn't possibly see because of his protective suit. But no matter. He stepped past her now, pushing past the rusted steel of the gate. His helmet lights had long since begun to flicker. An effect of the radiation. Even the best technology could not withstand such a level of radiation indefinitely.

As his lights illuminated the space beyond the gate, he paused momentarily. Xun was right. Before him lay the partially skeletonized and partially mummified remains of dozens, if not hundreds, of people. Remnants of uniforms and protective suits covered their bones. Glasses and remnants of hair covered their skulls. They all stared at him, out of their dark, dead eyes. Just about every one of them had looked toward the gate at the moment of their death.

Perhaps they had hoped for redemption. For the radiation to subside. That someone would come to save them. Or at least that their corpses would not remain locked up down here for all time.

Adrian knew that they had little time for this. There were no systems here, nor were there any paths to other parts of the complex. This place had to have been the last citadel; the last remaining point of retreat. No command center, no control room. It possessed no utility except to provide protection. Or at least a promise of it.

Still, he could not bring himself to just turn back around and go back upstairs. It did not feel right. No... more than that, it felt plain wrong. No matter what had happened, no matter if these people were partly responsible for the planet's nuclear apocalypse, they too were only human, born into the circumstances of their time; their lives at the mercy of the tides of fate. It was not right to simply leave them here.

"Every epoch is immediate to God," Xun's soft voice suddenly came to him. "Its value consists not in what emerges from, it but in its own existence."

"Who is that from?"

"Leopold von Ranke. A German historian."

"I was just thinking something similar."

"I know. I don't believe you can think anything else in a place like this."

"You think?"

"Death makes everything void. Everything the same. None of us is entitled to judgment because we don't know how we would have acted in their place. And even now we don't know what will be one day. What if, what we do today, eventually leads to something bad, even if we think we're doing the right thing? I... Imagine what it must have been like: The world is ending, you're sitting here, and you know that everyone you care about is probably long dead. You're scared, and then it hits you. You retreat to here, and wait to die."

"It's almost like what we're doing now."

"Maybe. Come on. We should go."

"You're right."

Adrian took a deep breath, heard his breath rattle through the filters of his protective suit, and turned. They had lost enough time already. Nonetheless, it felt good to have paused for a moment and paid respect to the dead. They were probably the first people to enter this place since the apocalypse.

It wasn't long before they reached the eighth basement level again and immediately began making their way through the pitch-black but otherwise surprisingly well-preserved corridors. In a few places, the concrete walls had cracked open and deep fissures stretched across the ceiling here and there. But other than that, there was virtually no damage. Even the desks and control terminals all looked as if they could be worked on at any time.

In itself, this was a circumstance that benefited them, since otherwise they would have had to find their way through rubble and debris. But at the same time, it also meant that their progress was very slow. Any terminal, console, control unit or computer could be responsible for the feedback loop. If most of them had been destroyed, that would have at least reduced the choice.

"I wish we had more time," Xun sighed at one point as she checked another console.

"Why?" asked Adrian.

"Imagine how much data must be on those computers! Of course, we have good equipment, but we must never forget that between our time and the end of the world there were centuries of technological progress. Discoveries and possibilities that we may not even be able to imagine. It would be a shame to let it all fade into oblivion."

"I doubt most systems would have survived the radiation," Adrian replied.

"A few definitely did. Otherwise, we wouldn't have been able to trace the signal back here."

"It's still just a feedback loop." He bent over another console and wiped the dust off the screen. "The identifier merely tells us that it was processed in this facility, but not when that happened. We may be chasing a ghost."

She turned to him. "So this is for nothing?"

He shook his head. "I didn't say that. I'm just saying it might be harder than we think. The signal certainly hasn't been buzzing through the ether for an eternity. It would have been best if we had sent out a ping through the aircraft's onboard sensors and tried to generate a response that way, but..."

He paused.

"But what?" asked Xun immediately.

"A ping," he repeated softly. "That's it!"

Without wasting another second, he grabbed the chest section of his suit and felt around for the controls located there for his individual equipment modules. The thick rubber covering made it difficult for him to find the controls, but after a few tries, he finally managed to access the radio controls.

The entire *Genesis* mission relied on analog and digital radio for reliability, but the systems on the suits and vehicles were much more powerful and capable of some technical gadgetry. That is, if you knew what to do. It was good to be an engineer.

"I'm about to go offline," he said as he began reprogramming his equipment. "On the radio. We won't be able to talk anymore."

"What are you going to do?"

"In a nutshell, I'm going to send out some kind of locator signal through my equipment. A sustained ping. Over that, we'll try to get a response from one of the systems - or rather, from its electromagnetic field. I can't guarantee it will work the way I think it will, but if it does, you'll get a faint signal over your radio. All we have to do is follow it to where it gets stronger."

"That's possible? Don't we need a receiver for that?"

"In this case, no. It's more like an echo sounder. I'm going offline now. Talk to you in a bit."

With these words, he deactivated the radio, made the last few entries and followed up on the displays in his helmet to see if everything was working as he thought it would. He could not say with certainty if it would work, but back in training he had at least run through a similar scenario. An active system always generated an electromagnetic field. A weak one, but with a little intuition it was still possible to detect it. Of course, there were much simpler ways to do this, such as a simple measuring device. Unfortunately, he had none with him. The radiation would have destroyed any measuring device anyway.

He paused for a tiny moment and sent a prayer to the heavens that his plan would actually work and that they would not have to spend any more time in this contaminated hell-hole. Then he sent out the ping and immediately looked at Xun, who was standing motionless next to him. For a few seconds she remained where she was, but then she suddenly raised her hand, signifying to him that she was receiving something, and took a few steps into the room.

In itself, Adrian was tempted to follow her, but he knew she had to test out where the signal was getting stronger and where it was getting weaker. For a few minutes he watched her walk between the control consoles and chairs, until she finally raised her hand again and pointed up to the ceiling. So they had to go up. He had almost suspected it.

As fast as their suits would allow, they rushed back to the stairwell and up until, after some back and forth, they finally entered the fifth basement floor, where Toussaint and Mabena met them only moments later. Xun seemed to say something to them - at least that's how he interpreted her gestures -

before she stepped past them and disappeared into a room further back. The two of them followed her on the spot, as did Adrian, until he finally found himself in a relatively small, inconspicuous side room that lay behind a heavy metal door.

He deactivated his makeshift sonar and looked around. The room looked inconspicuous only at first glance, because on second glance he realized that the walls had been built of thick composite material and obviously also kept out a considerable amount of radiation. Otherwise, he could not explain that currently only about 15,000 microsieverts per hour were hitting him.

"Of course," Toussaint's voice now came through the radio, already bent over a large console-like machine in the center of the room. "We should have guessed."

"What is it?" asked Adrian, looking at the device.

"An *EMU*."

"A what?"

"An *emergency message unit*." Toussaint's fingers raced straight across the machine's keyboard. "An emergency system designed to ensure that a facility can still be reached from the outside, even after a critical failure. Either communicate with possibly buried or trapped personnel, or to allow continued system access after such a failure."

"Which, in this case, you could not."

"No. There was no one left, after all, and... Oh."

"What?"

"Nothing," she muttered, "I think I made a mistake. This can't be right. This... Oh shit."

"What, damnit?!"

Toussaint didn't answer, but stared at the screen as if paralyzed. Adrian leaned toward her now, looking past her at the flickering displays. He couldn't do much with the absolute bulk of the data, but he did not have to, because he immediately saw what was bothering Toussaint: according to the displays, the feedback loop was not coming from a point on Earth, but from another source. And that source was Ross 128 b. A planet eleven light years away from Earth.

"I TRIPLE-CHECKED." Toussaint slapped her hands on the wall above her head and leaned against it. Even through the visor of her helmet, Adrian could see the desperation in her eyes. Her voice quivered. "I've triple-checked it. All sensors are operating within normal parameters. I can rule out damage to the radio telescope. And I am willing to bet that the system is working properly. The calculations are correct, the result is unmistakable."

"So that means the signal really came from Ross 128 b?" asked Mabena quietly. "And not from Earth?"

"Everything points to it, yes."

Adrian opened his mouth to say something he had not the faintest clue what it was supposed to be. Again and again he moved his lips, but he did not produce a single sound. What Toussaint had said; what the systems indicated; yes, damn it, what he had seen with his own eyes - he could not fathom it, could not believe it. And he knew with every fiber of his being that he did not even begin to comprehend the significance of those moments.

Ross 128 b. He knew this planet, had read more than enough about it, back before the mission had begun. Besides the planned but never really fleshed out colonization of the solar system, the planet had always been considered one of the most promising, if not *the* most promising, candidate for a permanent human colony. It lay within the habitable zone of a red dwarf, most likely had an atmosphere, and liquid water - and thus everything needed for a human colony.

The facts were obvious, the explanation was clear: Sometime between the beginning of the *Genesis* mission and the nuclear end of humanity on Earth, a ship must have been launched to colonize the planet. A ship that, even with the most advanced technology, must have been centuries in the making. A formidable challenge, but cryostasis had been a mature technology before. At least that didn't make such a journey impossible.

"Mabena," Adrian finally said into the droning silence, looking to the Executive Field Officer standing near the door with his arms folded in front of his chest. "The data from the listening post..."

"Nothing," he interrupted him tonelessly. "There was nothing there, Morris."

"Are you sure?"

"Our analysts went through the data in its entirety while we performed computerized analysis of cross-references and possible encryptions. The protocol calls for us to explicitly look for human settlements on the Moon or Mars, and also to consider possible missions outside the solar system. None of this has yielded any results. So if anyone has colonized Ross 128 b, they've done it without the *CONE* System noticing."

"Wouldn't that mean the ship must have launched before *CONE* was activated?" asked Xun.

"Possibly," sighed Mabena. "That or a very great effort was made to keep this trip secret. I don't know. Morris, you're the engineer. What do you think?"

"It's hard to say," Adrian admitted hesitantly. "When *Genesis* was launched, initial tests began on an antimatter drive that could accelerate a larger spacecraft to two percent the speed of light. That would have made the trip to Ross 128 b take a good 550 years. If we assume that the technology has developed further, and if we include certain limits, I would consider around five percent speed of light to be halfway realistic. A trip would still have taken 220 years with that."

"And this signal?"

"Well, electromagnetic waves travel at the speed of light. So it was sent eleven years ago. That much is certain."

Mabena sighed again. "That's true. I... God, I don't know what to say."

"Then perhaps it would be wise to give the order to withdraw, sir," Xun interjected. "We've been here for a good three hours already. Let's pull back and send a specialized team to evaluate the system."

"There's nothing left for us to evaluate," Toussaint replied, pointing to the screen. "*Sarasvati* received the signal and relayed it to the listening post. And as far as I can tell, a response was also sent back. That's all. There was no one left who could contact the *EMU*. This planet is really dead; there are no survivors. And whoever sent the signal will know we're awake in eleven years. With that, we won't have to come back for another 22 years to see if they respond. That's if the facility can even withstand the radiation that long."

"Why wouldn't it?" asked Xun.

"We opened the door," Adrian replied. "Until now, this room lay isolated and sealed. Now the radiation is getting in and damaging the system."

Xun answered nothing and no one else said a word. Adrian was sure they knew what that meant as well as he did: this was a one-time thing. Even if there were actually people there on Ross 128 b, they would most likely have no way to communicate with them. The resources to keep *Sarasvati* maintained and functioning despite the radiation were not available to the *Genesis* mission, and certainly no capacity existed to build such a powerful radio telescope elsewhere.

However, this was a circumstance of only secondary concern to Adrian. First and foremost, his attention was focused on a completely different matter: The *Exodus* signal seemed, at least according to the current state of knowledge, to have actually been sent from Earth, respectively from the listening post. So the space station had been awakened in a regular and designated way, most likely after a predefined waiting period. However, since the feedback loop and with it the signal from Ross 128 b had reached Earth practically simultaneously, this meant that its sender had known about it. That they had known exactly when the *Exodus* signal would be sent and the station would be awakened. And that was only possible if one knew about the end of the world.

"They started after the war," he finally whispered. "They knew when we were going to wake up. When the *Exodus* signal would be sent."

"I was just thinking the same thing," Toussaint agreed

with him. "Or at least just before this madness was foreseeable. What if the ship to Ross 128 b was some kind of evacuation mission? Maybe even a second attempt to save humanity if we failed?"

"You think the *Genesis* was in danger of being destroyed?" asked Xun uncertainly.

"Inevitably."

"Or the orbital lift could have been damaged," Adrian said. "It may be in an isolated location, but that doesn't necessarily mean anything. There may even have been fears of an active attack on it or the station. Toussaint could be right: They could have had some kind of... colony ship as a backup for if we fail."

"Not 'if,'" Mabena muttered. "It was 'because'."

Adrian instantly felt his throat tighten. He wanted to counter with something and tell Mabena he was wrong, but he knew full well he was right. The Executive Field Officer was right: you did not need an alternative if you believed that the original plan worked. The fact that this spaceship had taken off and was on its way to another planet could only mean one thing: Earth was irretrievably lost. And with it also every single one of them.

All at once he felt numb. Like a puppet on the strings of fate. He distantly heard Mabena finally gave the order to extract the data from the system and to evacuate the facility, and felt his legs carried him up the staircase, which suddenly seemed so unbelievably long, but he did not remember making even one movement consciously.

The ensuing march through the red-brown wasteland that remained of Kanpur also seemed to him like a distant, horrible dream. Like something he had to do because he could not do otherwise. An automation, carried out in a world without a future, in a life without a way out.

At one point he heard Mabena's voice over the radio.

"Aacken, Rosenblatt, come in," "What's your status?"

No answer.

"Rosenblatt!" barked Mabena. "Aacken! Come in!"

"Aacken here," a soft, monotone voice finally replied.

"What's going on? Where are you? Why isn't Rosenblatt reporting?!"

"Rosenblatt is... he's gone, sir."

"He ... What?!"

"He's dead, sir," Aacken repeated. "He took off his equipment and committed suicide. He died an hour ago. I tried to reach you, but..."

"What the... Why? What happened?!"

Aacken gave no answer, but he did not have to. Adrian already understood what had happened. What Rosenblatt's suicide meant. The measurements did not look good. The earth was lost.

"Aacken!"

"We'll have to get the *Genesis* to confirm the results first and do further calculations, but... It doesn't look good, sir. The ozone layer is visibly decaying, and at a considerable rate, too. I can't pinpoint the exact cause, nor the processes taking place, but we... I expect the Earth's atmosphere to collapse within fifteen years."

"Fifteen years?" breathed Mabena.

Any words spoken from that point on did not reach Adrian.

He could feel his legs weakening all at once; how he tried to drag himself up to the plane and hold on to its hull, but he didn't even come close before they finally gave way and he sank to the ground, into the hot sands of the desert.

Fifteen years. That number hammered through his head with unrelenting force, echoing off the walls of his mind and rising to an unbearable cacophony. Fifteen years. The last breaths of a planet that had made life possible for billions of years. That had seen entire species come into being and die out. That had survived asteroid impacts, volcanic eruptions, floods, earthquakes.

A planet that mankind had already worn out within a few millennia and now finally killed.

Panic and despair swept over Adrian. Like ravenous

beasts, they raked their claws over his body, tearing and ripping him apart, only to swallow him whole. Fifteen years. What was the point of even one more movement, one more thought, one more breath? Rosenblatt had done the only sensible thing and ended the misery without exposing himself to it for years to come and falling apart.

There was no consolation, no hope, nothing. Of course, they could have returned to the *Genesis*, repaired the cryo-capsules, and slept again for millennia, but not even that would have changed anything. Neither the capsules nor the station itself were designed to last eons, and it was probably lucky that they had lasted that long at all. Even if one day a new atmosphere would form and new life would emerge, it was far too late.

Adrian knew that failure had always been a possibility. That success had not been guaranteed even under the best of circumstances. He had prepared for it and, at least in theory, had also learned to accept it or at least come to terms with it. But here, now, in reality? No, he couldn't. He was too weak to fight back the despair.

"Morris?! Morris, can you hear me, damn it?"

Adrian winced and looked up. Mabena was standing right in front of him.

"Yes, sir."

"We're pulling out. Get on the radio and contact anchor control."

"And say what?"

"*Genesis* has failed. Phase one is being halted. We are evacuating Earth."

Chapter Eleven

RED-GOLD SUNLIGHT BROKE over the horizon and made the snow-covered expanse of South America shine like a sea of gold. Countless billions of snowflakes, each of them unique. An object that existed only once in the entire universe, born from the specific peculiarities of this planet. So delicate and fragile, yet a force of nature. They would perish with the earth.

Adrian lowered his eyes and looked at the back of his helmet, which he had placed on his lap. He knew he would be one of the last people to see this sight. One of the last people who would leave this planet and give up all the wonders it had produced over the eons. This world and all the beauty in it; all the wonders of nature, all the treasures of culture and art that humankind had produced, would be consigned to oblivion.

Genesis had failed. The great back-up, mankind's Plan B of. They had failed without failing, had failed without being struck down. When the great war had broken out, their fate had been sealed. No. Not only their fate, but the fate of humanity, nature and the planet. All the machines and resources on board the space station, the genetic databases of all known species, the *HIVE-D* - all that did not help them anymore, because even the greatest technical achievements of their species were not able to stop the global cataclysm.

This was no longer a mere assumption; no longer a cruel fear, but a terrible certainty. The scanners and sensors of the *Genesis* had checked and repeatedly confirmed what Aacken and Rosenblatt had already suspected: The ozone layer was dissolving. Not only over Kanpur, but globally. The biggest crack was certainly in the sky over *Sarasvati*, but the collapse could already be detected all over the Earth. It was only a matter of a few years until it finally disappeared and finally cleared the way for the atmospheric catastrophe.

What exactly had happened could not be determined with certainty, but all investigations indicated that their assumption was correct in this respect as well. The remaining atmosphere had become enriched with gases and chemical residues in its higher layers and especially just below the ozone layer. Presumably consequences of an industry that had been developed during their cryostasis. The nuclear war and its climatic effects had set in motion a kind of chain reaction that caused the atmosphere to increasingly and irreversibly collapse. Only the immense amounts of algae in the oceans seemed to have slowed this development.

Of course, there would have been ways to delay the atmospheric collapse for a few years and buy the mission more time to find a solution, but that was the problem: there was no solution. With their technical capabilities and scientific understanding, it was impossible to save the ozone layer on a global scale. It was beyond their capacity. In every way possible.

Nevertheless, the more optimistic of the crew vehemently demanded that they at least try. That all resources should be concentrated on buying as much time as possible and saving what could be saved. At the same time, dozens of field teams were to scour every corner of the planet, hoping to find some technology somewhere that could save them.

Wishful thinking. That was all it was. Even if Adrian would have given a lot to be able to join these hopes with conviction. But for one thing, he wholeheartedly doubted that such technology existed, and for another, he didn't believe that such a titanic power as the atmosphere of an entire planet could be saved so easily. Not to mention that such an approach more than stretched the resources of the mission.

No. Earth was doomed. Perhaps not all of humanity, assuming that Ross 128 b had actually succeeded in establishing a self-sufficient and prosperous colony, but what difference did it make? Even the most optimistic calculations gave human colonies on other planets a survival probability of barely one percent. That was not a card to bet on.

Suddenly, Toussaint appeared beside him and also lowered himself to the edge of the anchor platform. "Well."

"Toussaint," he said merely.

"What are you doing here?"

"Nothing."

"You never do nothing."

Adrian turned his head to the side and looked at her. Just like himself, she wasn't wearing a helmet, so he could see her bloodshot eyes.

"What do you want, Toussaint?"

"I'm trying to talk to you, but you're not making it very easy."

"What's the point anymore?" he retorted. "Every word and every breath - it's all for nothing."

"I never would have taken you for one to bury his head in the sand so lightly," she returned at once in a cutting tone.

"It has nothing to do with frivolity, believe me," he snorted bitterly. "I'd give a lot to have an alternative."

"So you don't think that..." she continued, but he interrupted her immediately.

"No. No, I don't. I've done the math. Over and over again. It's not going to work. The *Genesis* sensors predict the final collapse of the ozone layer in about ten years. The collapse of the Earth's atmosphere will probably begin in as little as seven years. Even if we try to artificially strengthen the ozone layer while doing everything we can to stabilize the atmosphere, we gain maybe three or four years by doing that - if that."

"And you don't think there's a technology that..."

"Don't you think the *CONE* System would know about it?" he interrupted her again. "Or that if they did, they would have sent a starship to Ross 128 b? That's wishful thinking, Toussaint. It's more likely we'll find the Holy Grail."

She remained silent.

"I... I'm sorry," Adrian murmured after a moment's hesitation. "I didn't mean to..."

"There is an alternative," she said suddenly.

"What?" he asked instinctively, although he had understood exactly what she had said.

"There is an alternative," she repeated, returning his gaze. "I'm the only one who knows about it. Besides the Directors."

Adrian eyed her. He looked into her eyes, looked at the barely noticeable twitching of her facial muscles, at the tears gathering in the corners of her eyes as the wind blew icy cold air into them. There was no trace of a lie on her face. And yet he could not believe her, though he would have liked nothing better.

Finally, he decided to say no more, and looked again at the sun, which had long since risen completely above the horizon.

"You don't believe me, do you?" echoed Toussaint.

"No." He shook his head. "No, I don't."

"There aren't 30 modules on the *Genesis*, there are 31," she whispered. "All but one are registered and covered by the system. The extra one is on the side of the station facing away from Earth. It is coupled to the station by a purely mechanical anchorage and is accessible only from the outside. And - more importantly - it is completely self-sufficient and has its own propulsion."

Adrian laughed softly. "Oh?"

"You still don't believe me, do you?"

"No. I know the *Genesis* inside and out. There is no such module."

"It's called the *Hercules*."

"That's no reason to believe that story, either," was all he replied.

"That may be, but I'm asking you to." she growled. "The *Hercules* has an antimatter reactor that can keep the module active for 1500 years while accelerating the drive to two percent the speed of light. On board are 19 cryostasis pods, each with a separate life support circuit, and all the equipment that the *Genesis* has - including its own compact terraforming unit."

Adrian sighed. "Why are you telling me this?"

"Because activating the *Hercules* requires the approval of three people. The two Directors and myself. Each of us is allowed to fill two slots freely, while the remaining twelve are each taken by a specialist at random. The Directors are not allowed to come along, but must accompany the *Genesis* to the end, while I am forced to participate in the mission in case of activation. I would like to fill one of my two seats with you."

"You're really telling me the truth right now, aren't you?"

"Yes."

"Damn it, Toussaint..."

"Morris," she interrupted him. "I know this is a lot to digest. And I can understand you being skeptical, too. God, I'm sorry I didn't say something sooner, but I had hoped it would never come to this. Even I wasn't told about it until just before cryostasis started. And now that it's come to this... I'm scared."

"I can understand that." Adrian took a deep breath and exhaled slowly before brushing both hands over his face. "I think I feel the same way. So - this *Hercules* module. If I understand it correctly, it's a small version of the *Genesis*?"

"Exactly."

"And what is its purpose?"

"It has several functions. For one, it could have acted as an emergency back-up in case there was a critical system failure on the *Genesis*. But at the same time, it could have been used to reach potential human colonies on the Moon or Mars. And..."

"And theoretically, you could also use it to reach Ross 128 b," Adrian completed her sentence.

Toussaint nodded.

"At two percent the speed of light, that would take 550 years," he continued. "That's a long time."

"That's right," she said. "We set a course and go into cryostasis. The system flies completely autonomously. In the event of a malfunction, we'll all be awakened, but we can put ourselves back into cryostasis. Morris, I personally consider the signal we received from Ross 128 b a call for help. They have hidden a status request in another signal rather than contacting us directly. It's possible that, for whatever reason, that's all they could do."

"You think they were hoping we would draw the right conclusions and trace the signal?"

"That's exactly what we did."

"Then they must assume we can reach them," Adrian muttered more to himself than to her. "Which must mean they know about the *Hercules*. So they must also be aware that it's going to take us more than half a millennium to reach them. Not exactly a good option when you're in trouble."

"Not for them. But for us."

"What do you mean?"

"Well." She stood up and made a sweeping hand gesture. "The earth is doomed. We're sure they know that. So, what if they want to give us a second chance to use our equipment to build a functioning colony that they may have failed at? It's no great feat that they know about the *Hercules*. After all, a simple scan from Earth will reveal the module."

"We're hardly going to establish a colony with 19 people."

"No. But with the *HIVE-D*."

"You know about the *HIVE-D*?!"

She nodded, but said nothing. Adrian was silent now, too, although he wanted to say something back with all his heart. A mixture of wonder, surprise, and perhaps even anger rose in him. Anger that Toussaint was obviously informed about all the possibilities of the *Genesis* and even had knowledge that not even he himself possessed. It wasn't even due to the fact that she hadn't said something sooner - for he could even understand that - but rather that he was now unwilling to trust that anything at all was as he believed.

"If you're requesting my participation in the mission, I'll do it." he finally said.

Toussaint looked at him. Suddenly, her eyes seemed to just sparkle. The hint of a smile flitted across her lips, but she said nothing, simply nodded to him one more time, stood up, and walked with quick steps toward the base, where the entire ground crew was by now working to undo everything they had managed to do in the last few days.

Adrian watched her for only a few seconds before he turned his gaze back towards the sun slowly moving across the sky, sending warmer and warmer rays down to Earth. It was more than obvious that she was happy about his agreement, but he himself was anything but sure whether he was even permitted to allow himself such a feeling.

All at once he felt completely empty. As if hollowed out. If he left, he would save his own life and possibly even face a future on a distant planet, but at the same time that meant leaving everyone else here behind. Hundreds of people he should have spent the rest of his life with. The men and women from his module for whom he was supposed to be a role model and a leader. For whom he had a responsibility.

Didn't responsibility sometimes mean dying, even if you had the option of staying alive? Didn't that possibly outweigh the pitifully small chance of actually leading Toussaint's venture to success? Was it not better to go to his death here with eyes open, but sincerely and dutifully, than to save his own skin? Or was he not entitled to such a consideration, since the survival of mankind itself was at stake here?

He truly did not know. And no matter how intently he thought about it and from which angles he looked at these questions, he came to no answer. There was no answer to be had - at least none that would have been able to ease his conscience. Finally, he stood up as well and made his way to the base, even though he had no idea where he was going.

"Morris," A voice suddenly sounded from his helmet just as he reached the entrance. He didn't recognize that voice. "Do you copy?"

He stopped and pulled on his helmet. "Morris here. What's up?"

"This is Dr. Martens. Can we talk without being interrupted?"

"One second."

Adrian swallowed hard. Dr. Martens was one of the two Directors. He immediately whirled around and marched back outside until he reached a spot on the anchor platform where no one else was.

"I'm ready. What do you want to talk about, ma'am?"

"Toussaint has informed us that you have already been briefed on the the *Hercules* protocol."

"That's correct."

"I'm sure you're aware that you're bound by confidentiality for the time being?"

"Of course."

"Good, that's where it will stay. We have decided not to announce the launch of the module."

"What? Why not?"

"We want to avoid unrest. Officially, you will be considered lost."

"The crew deserves to know the truth!" retorted Adrian in a quivering voice. "If they have to stay here and die, at least they should know that there is hope!"

"Your sentiment is honorable, Morris, but our mind is made up. We will see this mission through to the end and do all we can to wrest a future from destiny after all, but you have a different path waiting for you. Toussaint's second place choice was Lars Aacken and we have decided to use our choices on your assigned mates and partners to increase your chances of reproducing on Ross 128 b."

"I see. When do you leave?"

"In twenty hours. Proceed to the *Genesis* to undergo a final health check. Toussaint will then conduct the final situation briefing. We will transmit a list of the members of your module who will also be attending in a moment. Order them to the station as well. Good luck, Morris."

ADRIAN WAS NERVOUS. Perhaps even more excited than he had ever been in his life. Everything was prepared; nothing stood between him and cryostasis. He had completed the medical check and the final briefing with Toussaint was long behind him. Hell, he was already aboard the *Hercules*, staring blankly for half an hour at the cryostasis capsule in which he would spend the next centuries.

He felt his heart practically pounding in his throat. This was the final break; the final conclusion of everything that had been. Though he had given up everything back then when he had boarded the *Genesis*, at least he had Earth left. Earth and his comrades. The people he had grown up with. They fell away now. When he woke up again - if he woke up again - they would be gone. Earth would be desolate and empty, the others dead for centuries.

Perhaps it was this very thought that frightened him so. He was relinquishing control and would possibly never wake up again. A fate that could have also befallen him aboard the *Genesis*, albeit with much less probability. Knowing that he would fly billions of miles through the complete emptiness of space was an idea he could hardly bear.

But it had to be.

Somehow, everything was happening awfully fast. Much too fast for him to have been able to keep up with what was happening. Only the day before yesterday, he had flown to India to track down *Sarasvati* and find out the origins of the signal. A trip that, in retrospect, he probably never should have made, since it was responsible for everything that was happening now.

Perhaps it would have been better never to learn of the impending collapse of the Earth's atmosphere, but to blindly follow protocol and hope for the best, only to face an end as sudden as it was unexpected. It would at least have spared him and the others all the agonizing thoughts they were now suffering through. It made no difference whether it was his feelings of guilt at his journey, or the knowledge of facing certain death as everyone else did.

Finally, a short, piercing signal sounded. The order to move to the cryo-capsules. Adrian looked around at the others, wanting to know if they were doing it, but just like him, they hesitated. They too looked around, seeking eye contact with each other. It was a silent plea for confidence and encouragement. For comfort and hope. For the certainty of not falling asleep and never waking up, of actually meeting a distant future someday. In other words, something that no one was capable of providing.

A second signal sounded. The request to follow the previous one. Now, finally, the first ones climbed into their capsules and lay down on the holders provided for them. Adrian, too, did as he was told. He put one foot in the capsule, turned around and pressed himself into the bed. His throat felt as if a rope had been looped around his neck and was strangling him.

He felt not only his breathing but also his heartbeat quicken, every fiber of his body tense, expressing his instinctive, primitive aversion to subjecting himself to the rigors of cryostasis again. It was no help that he knew it had to be and was his duty. None of that mattered here and now, for right now he was little more than a frightened animal.

The capsule closed. It moved quickly, and yet so incredibly slow. A coffin, constructed to keep him alive. With a soft, whirring rattle, the machinery came to life; sensors and gauges kicked in, and a low hiss revealed that the preservation fluid was also ready to envelop him. Or drown it. Depending on how you looked at it.

The glass in front of his eyes fogged up because of his

frantic breathing. It took all his strength not to succumb to the naked panic that was so mercilessly trying to take possession of him. He did not know if he would win this fight, but he reminded himself that he didn't have to. He only had to hold out long enough until...

Suddenly, a sting in his arm - a short, burning pain, and then - nothing. He felt an indescribable fatigue come over him almost instantly, sweeping him away on the spot. He surrendered to it far too willingly, until his vision finally blurred and his eyes slid shut.

And then, at some point, there was an echo in the silence. A sound that Adrian already knew; like he had heard in his perception only recently. Machines that, just like him, were waking up from their sleep. Their sounds combined into a soon-to-be deafening symphony as Adrian himself emerged further and further from the deep unconsciousness into which he had slipped.

But this time something was different from the last time. There was no droning swoon that overwhelmed him, nor a storm of impressions and sensations that whipped at him, nor confusion, nor anything else. No. Rather, he was fully aware of what was happening; he remembered that he had just entered cryostasis, remembered the sting in his arm and the deep anesthesia into which he had been forced.

Even though he could not yet move his limbs and could barely feel them, his mind was long awake and clear. Alert, sharp - and above all, fully aware of what that meant. He had woken up. They must have reached Ross 128 b. Centuries of cryo-sleep had passed them by, in the blink of an eye. At least he hoped so, because anything else meant trouble.

It took only a few seconds before he finally felt the sting in his chest that pumped air into his lungs and forced the preservation fluid out of his body. He had expected the pain, just like the cascade of gag reflexes, spasms and so much else that came over him. And yet it still felt so sudden and unexpected.

Then he took a breath. A single, liberating breath. He had made it. His body was back; a flood of sensations rushing at him. He had survived cryostasis, awakened from it once more and hopefully for the last time. And since he did not hear any sounds - especially no alarm sound - except for the hissing and whirring of the machines, it meant they must have reached their destination.

Soon the cryo-capsule unlocked with a soft hiss. Immediately, he pressed his hands against the glass and pushed it open further, while at the same time the memory that he was currently in zero gravity welled up inside him. While he could still barely make out anything to confirm that impression, at least it felt that way. The...

"Welcome back," an exhausted, though unmistakably relieved, voice greeted him. It was Toussaint. "How are you?"

"Toussaint?" he asked, looking in the direction from which he thought he had heard her, and thought he could make out blurred outlines there. "You're awake already?"

"Surprised?"

He blinked a few times until his vision finally cleared. "I'm just used to being the first one awake."

"I'm just a few minutes ahead of you." She grinned. Only now did he notice that she, like himself, was of course stark naked. A fact that didn't seem to bother her at all. Nonetheless, she now pressed a towel into his hands. "Dry off and get ready for action."

Adrian laughed involuntarily. "Aye aye, ma'am."

"Don't call me that."

"Sorry."

"It's all good." All at once the grin disappeared from her face. "I'm really glad to see you, Morris. It was a terrible feeling to be the first to wake up and be completely alone."

"Is everyone else okay?"

"Yes. Everyone came through it just fine. I..."

She paused and looked down at the floor. She remained like that for a tiny moment before simply nodding to him and starting to get dressed.

Adrian did the same to her. He knew exactly what was going on, because he was no different: the initial joy of having survived not only the journey through space, but also centuries of cryostasis, faded and was replaced by the bitter realization of what it meant.

Everyone they had left behind on Earth had been dead for centuries, just like the planet itself. Mabena, Horvat, the Directors, and everyone else, too. They had probably died only a few years after they left; a few of them might still be in cryostasis on the *Genesis*, hoping that by the time the station's resources were depleted, Earth would have recovered from the apocalypse. A hope they must have known was futile.

Adrian rubbed both hands over his face and sighed softly. The knowledge of what must have happened on Earth paralyzed him; he barely managed to move, much less to form another thought. In his perception, there were only seconds between his last breaths on Earth and the here and now. Seconds that had stretched outside his head to centuries and had swept away everything he had ever known.

The feeling he had felt back on Earth now came over him with merciless force; the knowledge that he was finally stranded far away from everything he had ever known. The certainty that he and the others on board the *Hercules* module were possibly the last people who existed. And that he would probably never know what fate had befallen his comrades and his home planet.

Finally, he looked around. The others had also woken up in the meantime and were either still getting dressed or were starting cautious, quiet conversations about what was also bothering him. There were not particularly many familiar faces among them. Toussaint, Aacken, and Sato, of course, besides Elias Nikolaou, a physicist and Toussaint's assigned reproductive partner, and Irina Kowaliw, a geneticist and Aacken's assigned partner. Both members of his module.

Involuntarily, Adrian shook his head. Including himself, there were thus six members of Module 22 aboard the *Hercules*. Almost a third of the crew. Whereby the mere thought of asking about module affiliation after everything that had happened seemed ridiculous to him. Everything they had trained for, everything they had been trained to do - none of that mattered out here anymore. From now on, it was just a matter of bare survival. No matter how devastatingly bad their chances might be.

"Listen up!" Toussaint's voice suddenly echoed through the *Hercules*. It sounded serious, penetrating - and unlike on Earth, it also had an unmistakable tone of command. It was probably her training as an agent that finally came to the fore, since this situation was probably the most important reason why she had been on board the *Genesis*.

Toussaint now paused briefly while the rest of the crew gathered around her.

"According to the *Hercules'* sensors, we have arrived at our destination," she continued now in a much softer voice. "Ross 128 b. Our journey has taken 574 years almost to the day. Crew, equipment, and the module itself survived the trip well, as did the *HIVE-D*. Scans of the planet are ongoing, but at least we haven't picked up a signal yet and don't appear to have been contacted. However..." She paused and cleared her throat a few times, but couldn't hide how much her voice suddenly trembled. "However, there is a message from the *Genesis* recorded in the logs." Her voice broke. She cleared her throat again. "It reached us eleven years after our launch. I have not yet listened to it, and I would like to do so now with you. It affects all of us. The *Genesis* is – was - our family." She pulled up to a terminal and made a few quick entries.

"This is Joseph Mabena, Executive Field Officer for the *Genesis* mission," came a murmur from a speaker. "I'm contacting you to... God, who am I kidding? There are two pages of text in front of me that I was going to read to you, but right now it seems awfully ridiculous. What difference does a few fancy words make? I - we - did the best we could. The crew of the *Genesis* have fought in an exemplary manner and made unimaginable sacrifices to save the Earth. For a while it even looked as if we would succeed, but in the end we had to admit defeat. We retreated to the space station two weeks ago. The Earth's atmosphere collapsed. There are barely 200 of us left. The rest..." Mabena broke off for a moment. "Well, each of us did our best, and I am proud to have served with these men and women. Attached to this transmission is a detailed log and all the discoveries and calculations we have made. Perhaps they will be of some help to you. We have decided against a return to cryostasis and instead are attempting from the station to initiate processes that will allow Earth to eventually recover. With any luck, it will one day bring forth new life. As for us, all our hopes rest on you. All our prayers go out to each and every one of you. Good luck and farewell. Joseph Mabena - over and out."

Chapter Twelve

THERE WAS SOMETHING OUT THERE. Adrian could not say exactly what it was yet, but it was there - and it was big. At least as big as the *Genesis*, but was likely a considerable amount larger. An object made of metal and technology. At least, that's how he interpreted the sensor data; the crude radar scan and the results from the various other scanners. The *Hercules'* instruments were not particularly precise, and they did not offer nearly as many capabilities as the *Genesis*, but they were enough. Even if that meant he had to resort to makeshift improvisations here and there.

With a few quick hand movements, he adjusted one of the sensors, which the system immediately thanked him for with shrill warning messages. Actually, he was controlling a laser that was meant to send signals to theoretical objects in space, but it could just as well be used to scan asteroids, meteorites and other things, if you knew what you were doing. Such as the one a few thousand miles away from them in orbit around Ross 128 b.

He had just adjusted the laser when suddenly Toussaint leaned over, gave him a more-than-annoyed look and muted the warning signals. But that was almost an exaggeration. The *Hercules* was almost one-to-one like an ordinary module of the *Genesis*. The few differences worth mentioning were mainly related to a number of cargo modules connected to her, a few modifications in the internal structure - and the two tiny sensor rooms installed as superstructures on her hull.

A bitter snort made its way out of his throat as he set about continuing with the sensor scans. Although this room - or rather, this alcove - measured barely more than four square yards and every free inch was covered with consoles and machinery, three other crew members had squeezed in beside him and Toussaint. A necessary circumstance, since they had to gather as much information as possible at all costs in order not to unnecessarily strain their already minimal resources.

Unfortunately, that was exactly the problem. There was nothing out there. Or at least, nothing they had hoped for. Adrian had been firmly convinced that they would receive another signal during their journey here. That the people on Ross 128 b would make sure that they had not only received the feedback loop, but also drawn the right conclusions from it. And at the latest when they reached the system, he would have expected another contact.

But there was nothing. No signal, no contact, and nothing else that would have indicated anything of the sort. From the surface of the planet, they were receiving a considerable amount of signals, however they were so distorted and indistinct that they could make little sense of them. For the moment, they were only good as confirmation that there must be some kind of activity on the surface. But at worst, even that was just an anomaly.

The only exception was the object that appeared on Adrian's sensors. It was the only really solid evidence of human activity. By now, fortunately, a couple of the scanners had completed their scans and calculations, so Adrian could at least read off some useful information.

"The object is a space station," he finally summarized his most important finding and looked to the others. "They..."

"Are you sure?" Toussaint interrupted him, audibly doubtful.

"Pretty sure," he replied, pointing to the displays in front of him. "The construction is not unlike that of the *Genesis*. A composite hull, advanced alloys, and a stable, undisturbed orbit around the planet. I would not put money on it, but I think some of the superstructure could be sensors. The only thing that puzzles me is the complete lack of activity. I'm not picking up any evidence of signal activity or any power supply whatsoever."

"You mean this is an empty shell?"

"Seems like it."

Toussaint made an unintelligible noise and then cursed softly. "God, what if we're too late?"

"That was always a possibility, wasn't it?" one of the others asked.

"Yes, but I was at least hoping we wouldn't be."

"Let's not get ahead of ourselves," Adrian grumbled as he continued to keep an eye on the sensor readouts. "This station is almost certainly no longer in use, but that doesn't mean there aren't people living on the planet. After all, we're picking up significant signal activity, it's just that there are too many interfering factors for us to be any more specific."

"I agree," the physicist, Elias Nikolaou, agreed with him. "The activity is there, and that's the important thing. Toussaint, based on our current data, I think a disturbance in the planet's magnetosphere is the most likely explanation. Since we can't find any evidence of an external cause out here, the reason must be on the planet itself. Perhaps that is also the explanation for the station's condition."

"You mean it was abandoned because there are magnetic storms?"

He nodded. "Exactly. It's hard to say how long-lasting they are, but in some circumstances, they pose a considerable potential hazard to an orbital station."

"Wouldn't that apply to us as well?"

"Not necessarily. We are still some distance away. I think currently we are safe. The greatest danger we face is during landing."

"All right." Toussaint took a deep breath. "Let's stay positive, then. Morris, what's your assessment?"

Adrian raised his eyebrows and returned her gaze. "Regarding?"

"Are we boarding?"

"Toussaint, that would be suicide."

"Why?"

"If there really are magnetic storms, we can't foresee the effects on the station or personnel aboard," he growled. "Not to mention that we hardly have any capable equipment for it and would put the *Hercules* itself in danger."

Toussaint remained silent.

"What's the problem?" asked Nikolaou.

"Nothing," Toussaint replied grudgingly. "I'm just trying to make sense of this situation. Forget it. We did what we could. Contacting the people here wasn't and isn't possible, and we haven't received any signal from them that was explicitly directed at us. So if there really are people living on the surface, they may not know about us. After all, their ancestors contacted us almost 600 years ago. Initiate the landing. Nikolaou, you are in command."

"Roger that."

As Toussaint now pulled herself out of the small sensor bay and into the rear of the *Hercules*, Nikolaou made a few more quick inputs, but then nodded to Adrian and with a quick wave of his hand told him to follow Toussaint's direction and initiate the landing procedure.

Adrian now left the room as well and moved through the module towards the cockpit, whereby the rather makeshift control system embedded in a small alcove could only be called that with much effort. Still, it would have to do. Even if he struggled to believe that it would work.

Of course, the module - just like the ones on the *Genesis* - was capable of surviving atmospheric entry and landing safely, at least in theory. But as an engineer, Adrian was fully aware that there was sometimes a world of difference between theory and practice. Whereby, there were not many alternatives open to them either. They could not simply remain in space.

With a deep sigh, he activated the control console and began to power up the systems necessary for the landing, although there weren't exactly many of them. And not very sophisticated ones either. Basically, he used the *Hercules'* engines to enter the planet's atmosphere and hoped that gravity would pull it down afterwards. Some heavy-duty parachutes then took care of the rest. Only just before landing would a short engine pulse slow them down again.

The only problem was that all of these were only theoretical and pre-determined procedures that matched their actual situation only in some basic elements. Not only did they possess very sporadic information at best about the atmospheric peculiarities of Ross 128 b, but they also knew very little about its gravity, winds, and ground conditions. Not to mention that they still had the *HIVE-D* with them, which meant several tons of additional weight, which in turn had to be balanced by parachutes and thrusters.

Adrian sighed again. And those were only the factors they could influence directly or indirectly. No one could foresee how the people on the planet would behave. If they had even basic sensor technology - and there was no doubt about that - they were bound to at least register their entry into the atmosphere. Even if their ancestors had once known about the *Genesis*, a lot of time had passed since then. A lot of time.

"Well," Sato's voice suddenly sounded beside him. "Are you going to join us?"

"On what?"

"We're playing cosmic bingo and guessing how we'll get killed," she grinned. "So far in the lottery pot are: Nuclear missiles, ballistic missiles, fighter planes – jet, propeller, and antimatter machines - anti-aircraft guns, drowning, burning, and my favorite: getting beaten to death by cannibals."

"Then I'll throw incineration at atmospheric entry into the pot."

"Urgh," she mused, "I hadn't even thought of that. And

this from the man who's supposed to take us down there. Is your pessimism justified?"

"There's at least reasonable cause."

"Too bad." She theatrically held both hands to her cheeks and made a pout. "And I was so looking forward to making love to you!"

"Don't be silly, Sato," he merely returned.

"What? Don't you like me?"

"I'm not going to say anything about that."

"Why not?"

"For one thing, because I know full well that you're just teasing me, and for another, because my concentration right now is on trying to keep us all alive. But if you want me to rip your clothes off right here, you have to realize that the price could be the death of us all."

"You're a mood killer, Morris."

"And I think you're using that extroverted nature to compensate for your own anxiety."

"Where's the alarm button? You're a psychologist masquerading as an engineer."

Adrian was silent.

Sato twisted the corners of her mouth into a forced smile, but she could not even begin to hide the melancholy that was suddenly written all over her face. For a few seconds she just stared stubbornly before finally nodding.

"You're right," she whispered, "I'm scared. And honestly, I wish I didn't have to be here."

"You would have rather died on Earth?"

"Where every person related to me has died, too," she countered. "Where my parents are buried. My sisters and my brother. I barely remember them, but I know they existed. I don't know if what we're doing is right."

"I don't understand."

"I don't think humans are made for this." She made a sweeping gesture with her hand. "For space. For life on other planets. I never had a choice about my participation in the *Genesis* Project, but I always took comfort in the fact that it was about Earth. That I would stay where I came from. But now... It feels wrong."

"I'm... sorry about that, Sato. I didn't know you'd be forced to come."

"I wasn't. I'm just doing my duty. For one thing, my skills are certainly useful, and for another..." She paused and looked at the ground.

"What is it?" asked Adrian immediately.

"It's been hammered into us over and over again how important it's going to be one day that we have children," she murmured. "So not just us in general, but especially the female participants in the mission. I don't know why, but I feel shabby even thinking about letting this opportunity pass."

"If there are people here, you don't have to do anything like that."

"Do I really not have to?" She made a snide sound. "Or have I been so indoctrinated that I can't help it?"

"I'm certainly not going to coerce you into anything," Adrian grumbled, not taking his eyes off the displays. "If that even needs to be said."

"I wouldn't have thought so."

"Why not?" He glanced sideways for a moment before turning back to the landing control. "I know the protocol, and I'd like to have kids someday, but I'm certainly not an idiot to put my own offspring through that kind of life. If we run into problems down there that are beyond our capabilities, it's better to let it go. We've done everything we can, but I'm certainly not going to bring children into the world just so they have to grow up in hell."

Sato said nothing more, but simply watched him in silence as he continued to make calculations and prepare the *Hercules* for entry into the atmosphere and the subsequent landing. Adrian would have liked to talk to her further, but he also kept silent and concentrated on his work instead.

The subject of reproduction had always been a delicate one. Not only in the *Genesis* mission in general, but especially in personal interactions. That this was the central aspect of the project, with all its largely negative consequences, was part of the basic knowledge of every participant. That it was inevitably drilled into them to reproduce as humans, and women were even reduced to a kind of childbearing machine. It was a necessity that no one could deny, unpleasant as it was. But it just had to be that way.

However, what their potential offspring would face was a different story. Having children in a stable ecosystem and raising them in harsh, but at least not hostile, conditions was one thing. It was a way of living up to one's responsibility as a parent and as a human being if you at least gave them the chance to lead a fulfilling life and to build a future. But if you saw them only as a resource in the battle of attrition against a planet, then you had to ask yourself whether the end really justified the means.

THE WAS five minutes left until atmospheric entry. The *Hercules'* systems were running stable, although the first disturbances from the magnetic storms raging on the planet were already making themselves known. It was mostly problems with the sensors and electronics. Lights that flickered. Negligible at this point. The engines were active, and the heavy-lift parachutes would be deployed via a mechanical system. They would make it.

Adrian looked around. Just like himself, everyone on board had long since been wearing their spacesuits and, except for him, everyone had also already hooked themselves into the specially designed moorings. A few were additionally clinging to the tethers on the ceiling, but these would hardly help them in the event of a crash. He himself had secured himself rather makeshift via two straps directly to the control console. Enough to cushion the turbulence of atmospheric entry. Apparently, it had not been considered in the construction of the module that someone would also have to control it.

Nevertheless, the landing was under ideal parameters. He

had managed to adjust the drive and the parachutes to their current weight and to find a halfway acceptable landing vector. If all went well, they would land on a relatively flat open area with no settlements or topographical anomalies in the immediate vicinity.

If it all went well.

More involuntarily than intentionally, Adrian tilted his head to either side and let a few vertebrae crack. His back felt as if someone had forced him into a vice. Tension and nervousness were taking their toll - even if there were no problems on the Hercules and their landing continued to go well, there were still dozens more factors that could put them at risk.

Sato may have meant it as a joke earlier, but it was definitely within the realm of possibility that a defensive reaction of some sort by the humans on Ross 128 b would occur. After all, they had been on this planet for centuries, and any knowledge, no matter how well guarded, faded with time. And since there had been no communication so far, it could well happen that their presence was regarded as a hostile act. Possibly even as an arrival of aliens.

Adrian was aware of how ridiculous this thought was, but that did not change the fact that he had to think it. If he put himself in the situation of people on Ross 128 b, and assumed on top of that that they might have gone through a technological and civilization regression, such a reaction was more than likely.

If there were any humans down there at all.

What Toussaint had said just before they left suddenly reverberated through his consciousness with tremendous force. What if humanity had perished here, too? What if the colonists had known that not only they themselves would fail, but that the *Genesis* was doomed as well, and had therefore led them here? If the 19 people aboard the *Hercules* were all that were left?

Suddenly, there was a violent jolt, closely followed by the infernal creaking and howling of steel. They had entered the atmosphere. Almost instantly, Adrian felt himself plummeting downward, his feet lifting from the ground. Just in time, he managed to hold on to his straps.

A few warning messages flashed on the control console, accompanied by the piercing beeping of alarms from some secondary systems, but nothing that was an immediate danger to them. Adrian gave a sigh of relief. The first hurdle to a successful landing had been overcome. Now he just had to make sure that the rest went smoothly.

A few moments later, a piercing bang thundered through the *Hercules*. The first parachutes had just opened and now not even the harnesses managed to keep him upright. He was jerked to the ground and hit with a thud, but immediately struggled back to his feet, ignoring the throbbing pain in his head. The suit had absorbed most of the force. He had to keep going.

Currently, they were still a good 30 miles above the surface, falling at a speed of about 300 miles per hour. A much better value than he had calculated for the first para-chutes. Up to 430 miles per hour would have been within acceptable limits. In a few moments, the main chute would deploy and, if all continued to go well, slow them down to fractions of that.

Still, Adrian was unable to chalk that up as a success. There was still far too much that could go wrong. The *HIVE-D* in particular gave him cause for concern. On the *Genesis*, it had been relatively easy to separate it from the station and attach it underneath the *Hercules*, but that was exactly the problem now: It would be the first to touch down on the ground and thus ran the risk of being damaged.

They continued to approach the ground until at some point the main screen was activated and slowed their fall further. Only now Adrian allowed himself a short breath. They were only a few miles above the planet's surface and their fall had slowed to just under 25 miles per hour. Now it would literally have to be the devil's work for anything else to go wrong.

"*Genesis* crew!" a voice suddenly rushed through the radio. "Calling *Genesis* crew! Come in!"

For a moment, the world seemed to stand still. Adrian stared at the displays inside his helmet, unsure if this had just really happened or if he had just imagined it. But the displays left no doubt: they had been contacted.

"This is Cassandra Toussaint of the *Genesis*." Toussaint was the first to manage to say anything, though her voice trembled unmistakably. "We read you. Who... who are you?"

"My name is Gunthar Feystaal," the voice replied. "I am the High Commissioner of the Rossur Council for the Repatriation of the *Genesis*. Welcome home. Do you have control of your ship, or are you in a designated approach?"

"We..." Toussaint turned her head to Adrian, seeking help. "We..."

"Our landing vector is fixed," Adrian took over. "Ground contact in seven minutes. Any problems?"

"No problems," the man named Feystaal replied. "We will adjust our contact. I will be expecting you personally. Please forgive my emotional outburst, but you cannot imagine how glad I am that you are finally here. While we were sure our signal had reached Earth, we didn't know if you had received or understood it."

"Because of the magnetic storms?"

"They are indeed the main reason. The time windows to send signals from the surface into space are very short, but they can be met. As for reception, we understandably face much bigger problems. But that's something we can discuss more later. Did you experience any problems on your flight? Do you need medical assistance?"

"Negative," Toussaint said. By now, she had managed to firm up her voice. "We are doing well under the circumstances. Mr. Feystaal, we would be very grateful for any further information. After the activation of the *Exodus* signal, we were only able to work on Earth for a few days before your signal reached us and alerted us to the collapse of the ozone layer. This all came very hastily for us."

"I can well understand that, Miss Toussaint, believe me. Nevertheless, will you allow me to postpone answering this question until later? I would like to be face to face with you and not have this conversation over the radio. That doesn't seem appropriate to me."

"I understand." She looked to Adrian and raised a hand. He responded to her by raising three fingers. "Ground contact in three minutes."

Although Feystaal replied something else, Adrian stopped listening to him and stared intently at the displays of the Hercules module. By now the thrusters had kicked in and were continuing to slow their fall, and fortunately they seemed to be functioning flawlessly. They were steadily approaching the ground. It would be a soft landing. Hell, even if something went wrong now, they were unlikely to be harmed.

Much more interesting, however, was the fact that the few sensors that were still online were now picking up countless signals. There was more than just lively radio traffic out there, and there were also forms of communication that at least the ship's systems could not easily decode. It almost reminded him of a beehive. The laser scan even indicated several dozen vehicles that had taken up positions around their landing zone.

Suddenly, a feeling came over him like he had never felt before; a strange mixture of relief and apprehension. Relief because there was actually life on this planet, because humanity had managed to establish a colony that had now existed for centuries and obviously had not inconsiderable resources. And concern for exactly the same reasons, only considered from the point of view of why they had taken the trouble and brought them here.

But he had no chance to think about it any further, because with one more jolt, the *Hercules* touched down on the ground. For a moment, there was absolute silence inside the ship. A brief interlude, a last breath - and perhaps the last step that finally separated the future from the past. No one moved, no one said a word.

And then the hatch was opened.

Not from the inside, but from the outside. Tall figures in pitch-black full-body suits without recognizable visors or other external modules entered the *Hercules*. The sight of them was enough to make Adrian shudder, but unlike what he had feared, they did not advance deeper into the ship, but paused at the entrance until a similarly tall man in a dark red robe decorated with countless golden ornaments entered. This had to be Feystaal.

For a few seconds he stopped at the entrance and looked around, before he approached Adrian with a broad smile, held out both hands to him and touched his forearms just behind his wrists.

"You must be the captain of this ship!"

"No." Adrian shook his head. "I'm just the engineer, Adrian Morris. Cassandra Toussaint is in command."

He released one hand from his grip and pointed in her direction.

"It's such a pleasure!" Feystaal turned instantly, stepping toward her and grasping her forearms as well. "After so long, may I finally welcome you to Rossur!"

"Rossur?" asked Toussaint, trying to free her arms from his grasp, but barely succeeding.

"Forgive me!" Feystaal's grin grew even wider. "Rossur is our term for Ross 128 b. In the long run, it does get tiresome to pronounce it every time. Rossur has proven to be a viable alternative. So, you are Cassandra Toussaint? May I ask what function you held on the *Genesis*?"

"I am the assigned *Aegis Dawn* agent."

"Then it only makes sense that you are in charge." Feystaal nodded. "I'm sure you'll be pleased to know that Rossur was also colonized under the auspices of *Aegis Dawn*, although we decided to gradually break down the old structures."

"So this was Plan B?" asked Toussaint without responding to him, finally escaping his grasp before loosening the anchors of her suit. "You left Earth to colonize this planet?"

"That is correct. A journey of nearly 240 years, spent in cryostasis by our ancestors. A colony ship of similar capacity to your *Genesis*, but equipped with much more advanced technology and extensive equipment."

"Because Earth was unsalvageable? Because our mission was bound to fail?"

Feystaal was silent for a moment, but then nodded and took a step back.

"Unfortunately, that's correct," he said in a low voice. "The outbreak of war was not unexpected, but its ferocity did take us by surprise. Within a very short time it degenerated into a world war. As you must have noticed, the ozone layer was targeted in the process and ultimately irreparably damaged. We were forced to leave the planet."

"Why didn't you wake us up?"

"Miss Toussaint..."

"Please," she whispered, pulling her helmet off her head. "Please, Feystaal, answer this question for me. Everyone who was with us on the *Genesis* has been dead for centuries. They gave everything they had to save Earth, and we abandoned them to follow your signal. Please tell us why."

"It didn't work."

"What?"

"It simply wasn't possible." Feystaal shook his head. "I know the records of that time inside out. When the colony ship launched, they tried to take the crew of the *Genesis* with them. Since you were already in cryostasis anyway, this idea was obvious. Connectors were even built according to old blueprints to couple the modules. Unfortunately, it was not possible to achieve a detachment from the station, and if it had been tried by force, it would probably have come to a catastrophe. The onboard system seems to have been to blame. It was programmed to release the modules solely on the command of the *Exodus* signal. Fearing an attack from Earth, our ancestors decided to leave without you. Since then, we have been searching for clues to your awakening."

"So you brought us here to do what, exactly?"

"To save you. Or at least part of you. We didn't realize that you would only arrive on this ship. We were hoping for more. Not the entire *Genesis*, but not just... Are you carrying any special equipment?"

"None that is not probably long obsolete for you," Toussaint replied dryly. "Why do you ask?"

"Just curious." Feystaal gestured toward the exit. "You've had a rough time and should get some rest. We can discuss any further questions in detail later."

Chapter Thirteen

ADRIAN CLOSED his eyes and leaned against the bare steel wall. Water splashed on his head. It was ice cold and relieving. It washed the sweat from his body, just like the exhaustion that held every inch of his body so relentlessly in its grip. For far too long he had been standing here, allowing the cold to penetrate deep into his body. It felt so incredibly good.

He didn't know where he was or how long he would be here, but none of that mattered right now. In those minutes, he allowed himself to give in. To be weak. To let himself fall. For the first time since he began his training all those years ago, there was nothing he had to do. No training sessions, no program, no simulation, no lessons, no mission, and nothing else. Right now, right here, there was just him. Him and the ice cold water.

Hours ago, he and the others had been brought here. They had been led out of the *Hercules* and put into alien, yet unmistakably advanced flying machines and flown over the planet for hours until they finally arrived here. Food and water were available to them in abundance. Admittedly, it had taken some time before he had dared to taste it. Or to take off his spacesuit and wash himself. Not because he feared anything bad, but because he had to remind himself what it was like to be relieved of duty.

Finally, he turned off the water and stepped out of the shower stall, only to be immediately greeted by a fierce blast of lukewarm air that dried him completely within seconds. He grinned. Luxury. Not high-tech, after all, such systems had existed back on Earth, but luxury nonetheless.

His eyes wandered to his spacesuit, which lay disassembled in a corner of the windowless room. The heavy boots, the modules of composite materials and technology, the massive, almost armored chest plate, the helmet, and the life support unit. They seemed clunky and alien in the face of the perfectly formed elegance of this room.

On instinct, he would have put his spacesuit back on, or at least the uniform he had been wearing underneath, but then his eyes fell on a pile of clothes neatly folded on a curved chair in the corner. Knee-high, shiny boots with golden ornaments, relatively wide trousers and a top that reached down to his knees at the sides with sleeves that were excessively wide at the wrists. Not exactly his style, but a thousand times better than his uniform. The fabric felt unlike anything he had ever felt before.

When he had dressed, he lowered himself onto a semi-circular bed that stood against one wall of the room and looked around. Although these quarters measured just twenty square yards, they seemed anything but small to him. Part of that was surely because he wasn't used to so much space for himself, but a good part could also be explained by the fact that an entire wall kept disappearing to make way for beautiful landscape shots. Whether this was a projection, a massive screen, or even a hologram, he was unable to tell.

Nevertheless, the images were so detailed and razor-sharp that he almost forgot that they were not real. In front of him, images of vast desert landscapes interspersed with coral-like reddish-yellow structures, dense forests with the most colorful plants, incredible mountain landscapes, and so much more opened up. He couldn't get enough of it.

Suddenly, a soft ringing sound to his left. A blue light shone next to the door. A bell?

Adrian stood up. "Come in?"

The door opened and Toussaint entered, clad from head to toe in a dark red robe covered with black trim. The top resembled his except for a discreet neckline, and she too wore boots, but instead of pants, a sharply tailored skirt that started at her right hip and ended at her left ankle.

"I can't believe how different you look without a uniform," he greeted her, gesturing for her to enter. "Is everything okay?"

"Everything's fine with me." She hesitantly entered and closed the door behind her. "I was just making the rounds, making sure everyone was okay. You're the last one on my tour."

"So, is everyone okay?"

"Most are asleep." She smiled uncertainly. "I don't blame them."

"Me neither."

"What about you? Not tired?"

"I wouldn't have taken you for someone who makes small talk, Toussaint."

"Gotcha." She blushed. "I'm sorry, Morris. I didn't mean to disturb you."

"You aren't, but you don't have to beat around the bush, either."

"Sorry. I just wanted to talk to you. Of everyone on board - and everyone left now - you're the only one who's kind of a friend to me. God, I never thought I'd say this, but I trust you. I doubt we would have gotten this far without you."

Adrian was silent.

"I'm afraid coming here wasn't such a good idea," she whispered, leaning against the wall over which the most incredible images continued to drift.

"What do you mean?"

"Well." She crossed her arms in front of her chest. "To these people, we are apparently little more than a curiosity. I can't estimate how their level of technology relates to that of old Earth, but at least to us they are vastly superior. There is nothing we can contribute to their civilization. I feel like an animal in a zoo right now, and these rooms are our enclosure." She looked around. "I wouldn't even be surprised if they were watching us," she added, growling.

"Don't you think that's a little excessive?" asked Adrian. "Where did the sudden distrust come from?"

"Not distrust." She shook her head vehemently. "I don't want to go so far as to accuse them of evil intentions. But you heard what Feystaal said: they saved us. An act of charity, if you will."

"I don't know anyone who would be upset about that."

"You don't want to understand me, do you?" she hissed.

Adrian narrowed his eyes and look at her. The way she leaned against the wall and crossed her arms in front of her chest, the way she looked and contorted her face - that alone told more than a thousand words. She hated being here. She hated the clothes she wore and the comfort they all experienced. She hated her uselessness.

Why?

"You feel guilty?"

"We should have died, Adrian."

"Adrian?"

"Do you prefer Morris? We agreed on first names in the very beginning. Remember?"

"Your choice."

"It doesn't matter." She fixed him. "We should have died, Adrian. And now we're here and... then this! So yes, I feel guilty. Our lives had a set, clearly defined purpose: Rebuilding Earth. Saving humanity. We failed to do either. We failed, we were defeated. More than that, instead of facing the consequences, we came here and..."

"You could almost forget that you're an agent of *Aegis Dawn* who didn't go through all the years of training and hardships that everyone else had to endure," he interrupted her in a cutting tone.

Toussaint's eyes snapped open. For a tiny moment, incredulous surprise was written all over her face, but then it was followed first by indignation and finally sheer anger.

"And that makes me what?!" she hissed, clenching her hands into fists. "A traitor? Worth less?"

"I'm not saying that," Adrian calmly replied, standing up. "I just didn't think you'd feel that way. That's all."

"I was sixteen when I signed up for *Aegis Dawn*." Breathing heavily, she stepped toward him until she was standing directly in front of him. "One of nine fit candidates world-wide. My intelligence and physical fitness met the *Genesis'* requirements, as does my age. When a recruiter contacted me and told me about the dangers you face, I knew I couldn't refuse. I wanted to do my part to save humanity. My parents were told I died in an accident. I went to my own funeral. That is where I saw them for the last time. A few years later, I went into cryostasis with you. Do you really think I would have taken that on myself if I didn't care about your mission?"

"That..." Adrian took a deep breath and averted his eyes. "I didn't know that. I'm sorry, Toussaint."

"Cassandra." She cleared her throat and looked up at the ceiling. "Please call me Cassandra. Toussaint was the agent. Here, I'm not anymore."

"All right."

"Is... is it okay if I stay here for a bit?" she whispered. "I don't want to be alone right now."

Adrian nodded but said no more, and Toussaint was silent as well. She paused in front of him for a moment before slowly stepping away from him and a few steps into the room. She seemed indecisive, as if she had no idea what to do with herself. An impression that was probably very close to reality.

While she remained in the middle of his quarters for a few seconds before taking a seat against the wall opposite the pictures, Adrian examined her again attentively. She looked different, but it was not because of her clothes. No. Rather, it was small nuances in her face. The tension and stress she had felt on Earth had fallen from her like the dirt she had washed from herself. In their place had come a deep resignation and a no less pronounced melancholy.

All at once he felt incredibly sorry for her. Since he had first awakened from cryostasis, he had spent almost every minute at her side or in close association with her. And now, seeing her so depressed before him, he understood that she was more than just a comrade in the mission. She was a friend. Perhaps the only one he had left.

"We can do this." He sat down with her and put a hand on her shoulder. "Toussaint... Cassandra... I think we can make it. We've gotten through worse. So much worse. I have no idea what else is in store for us, but somehow we'll get through it."

"Thank you." She lifted a hand and clasped his with it. "How do you actually handle it? Have you been trained to do that, too?"

"What do you mean?"

"This. The... loss. That everyone you knew is dead. That you're skipping whole centuries."

"We've been taught ways to deal with it," he replied hesitantly. "Methods to calm ourselves down and focus on what is essential. We learned to accept it. But I could never do much with it. I found my own way for myself."

"Would you like to tell me about it?"

"Everything that exists is energy." He felt a smile flit across his lips. "The particles that make us up have existed since the Big Bang, and are not lost when we die. Energy never disappears. That means we never really disappear either. I take comfort in that. Everything has always been there, and everything will always be there."

"I never would have believed you would have such thoughts, Adrian," she whispered.

Adrian was about to answer her, but then said nothing more. He could well understand why she thought that way. Sometimes it surprised even him what trains of thought he found comfort and confidence in. It was one thing to stand with both feet in reality and try to find practical solutions and sensible approaches, but he doubted that anyone could do completely without ideas that gave comfort and confidence.

For quite some time they sat in silence, side by side, here on this strange planet, in the middle of a windowless room, surrounded by nothing familiar, gazing at the images that trailed across the wall before them. Adrian had long since ceased to feel wonder and curiosity as he watched them, but only a deep melancholy and pain that he thought would never go away.

This was indeed something for which he had not been prepared, for which he could not have prepared. It had never been planned that he or any of the others would leave Earth for good. Every conceivable scenario of the *Genesis* mission had been designed to save and repopulate Earth; to rebuild the planet and restore everything that had been there before.

And now here he sat, feeling at the other end of the universe. Whether it was eleven light years which separated him from his homeland, or eleven billion, did not play thereby any role. He had arrived in this foreign place and with everything foreign there was always a loneliness that differed from everything that was known.

Perhaps that meant that he had to reorient himself. That he had to say goodbye to everything he thought he knew and to all the certainties he believed to be immovable. That he no longer looked for his personal anchor on a planet or in a mission, but in the people who were left to him. In Toussaint and the others who had come here with him.

And maybe - just maybe - together they would succeed in mastering their lives in this new world.

IN THE MEANTIME, more than a week had passed since they had reached Ross 128 b - Rossur - in the *Hercules*. A lot of time, especially compared to the few days they had spent on Earth after their cryostasis. And maybe it was an aftereffect of just that, but Adrian felt like he was stuck in time. The minutes and hours just would not pass.

But maybe that was also due to the yawning boredom that dominated almost every waking moment. The idleness… no, idleness itself would have even been bearable. Rather, it was the feeling of being useless; the complete powerlessness in the face of the apparently immense technical possibilities of the people on this planet. They were not here to help, not to seize opportunities and rebuild, but for an end in themselves. Their lives as the result of a philanthropic pursuit.

A curiosity, as Toussaint had so aptly put it.

As before, Adrian spent most of his time alone and secluded in his quarters; only occasionally did he converse with any of the others. Mainly with Toussaint, Aacken, and Sato. But that was okay.

He knew that it was mostly up to himself. That he should have just let go. That he needed to finally accept being here and stop clinging to Earth and his own past. If he would only allow it, a future awaited him on this planet. But the question was not whether he wanted that, but whether he could at all.

The others seemed to be in a similar, if not the same, situation. They spent most of their time in their quarters, came together only occasionally and did not leave this part of the facility, even if they were officially allowed to do so.

Facility. Yes, that was an apt description. Rossur's capital did not resemble a city as it was known from Earth; neither in its structure and appearance nor in its purpose and use. It could best be described as a gigantic half-dome, built on the back of a no less immense mountain and blocking out all sunlight, so that inside it was mostly complete darkness.

But there weren't many open spaces to hang out in anyway. Almost every yard of the dome was covered from deep below the surface to high up in the ceiling. Mostly with fabrication plants, automatic farms, water purifiers and other autonomously working structures. People were seen only sporadically, if at all. There also seemed to be only a small number of residential buildings. At least, that was the little information Adrian had gathered from hearsay. He himself had not yet left the complex and saw no reason to do so.

Since Feystaal remained silent about how many people lived on Rossur, the first rumors already arose. About the fact that the last survivors of the *Genesis* were needed. For reproduction or as workers. That the planet was possibly dying.

As for Adrian, he thought that was nonsense. Apart from Feystaal and the hooded figures, he hadn't seen any other locals, but in his eyes that was mainly because they were housed in a separate part of this domed city, and it probably made little sense for others to come here - if they were allowed at all. In the end, they knew next to nothing about the social, societal and political structures of this world. What they considered standard may not have applied here at all.

With a quiet groan, Adrian got up from his bed, stretched and took a few deep breaths before heading out. Which was just a euphemism for leaving his quarters. If he was honest, he had no idea how to even leave this facility.

He had just stepped out of the door when he was suddenly met by one of those tall figures in a pitch-black, full body suit. The same kind who had also entered the *Hercules* after their arrival. He stopped on the spot and pressed himself as close to the wall as he could, but the figure didn't seem to pay any attention to him. It just marched past him and disappeared around a bend further down the corridor.

It wasn't until he was sure that they were indeed not coming back that Adrian detached himself from the wall and went on his way. He could not tell what it was, but he could not stand those things with all his heart. They scared the hell out of him - though he was not even sure what exactly they were in the first place. Humans? Robots? Something in between?

He was halfway to the comfortably furnished common room they had been given when a door suddenly opened a few feet in front of him. Aacken and Sato stepped out - with disheveled hair and clothes that were anything but kempt. Together with their more than satisfied look, a rather clear indication of how they had spent the last few minutes. They seemed to be aware of the fact that it was unmistakable as well, as the two instantly flinched when they noticed him, and turned bright red.

"I'm the last person you have to justify yourselves to," Adrian cut them off, raising his hands placatingly and stepping past them. "Do what makes you happy."

"It's not what it looks like!" exclaimed Aacken immediately.

"What does it look like?" Adrian returned his gaze with a grin. "I thought you guys were having an intense scientific discussion?"

The German stared at him, completely perplexed, but Sato immediately joined him, running.

"Morris..." she continued, but he immediately raised a hand.

"I really don't care, Sato," he said. "Believe me. You guys are adults. Do what you want. We're not married."

"But you and I..."

"You mean I should be consumed with anger and envy because the woman I'm supposed to procreate with is sleeping with someone else?" He snorted in amusement. "Please, Sato. We are not together. And if that ever worries you again, just remember that our genetic compatibility was probably calculated by ancient scientists who haven't had sex in years."

"Urgh."

"Thought so. A real mood killer."

"So what are you doing, then?"

He grinned. "When you ask like that..."

"What?! With who?!"

"I'm just teasing you, Sato."

"I don't think so."

"I have a sense of humor, too."

"Nope." She shook her head. "I don't believe that."

"I'm on my way to the common room," he said, hearing

the quick footsteps behind him as Aacken caught up to them. "I can't stand it in my quarters anymore."

"Mind if we tag along?"

"Don't you want get to round two?"

"Who says we don't need a break before round 4?"

"Uh-huh."

"Oh come on, Morris!"

"What?"

"Can I ask you something, Morris?", Aacken changed the subject before Sato could say anything back. "Did Toussaint say anything else?"

"What exactly do you mean?"

"Well - about everything. How things are going to go. What we can do. Or what we should do. She keeps talking to this Feystaal guy, doesn't she? We've been here over a week now, and I still know almost nothing about this planet. Or about the people here."

"No." He shook his head. "I last saw her the day before yesterday."

"I don't like any of this."

"Neither do I."

"Then you noticed it, too?"

Adrian stopped, narrowed his eyes, and looked at him questioningly. "What are you talking about?"

"Those black things that walk the corridors. They follow fixed routes and always patrol at the same time. And when you get too close to them, you hear a very soft beeping."

"A beeping sound?"

"I think it's some kind of sensor. These things are monitoring us."

"Don't you think that's a bit far-fetched?"

Aacken didn't reply, but merely nodded at him with a meaningful look. Adrian immediately turned around, only to catch sight of another - or the same? - figure marching down the corridor in their direction. Now, for the first time, he noticed how silently they moved. Their footsteps could be heard, but at the same time they were so quiet that one had to pay explicit attention to them in order to notice them.

Visibly unimpressed by their behavior, the thing walked past them and shortly thereafter disappeared into one of the adjacent corridors. Adrian was not one hundred percent sure, but he actually thought he had heard a soft noise. Whether he would have heard it if Aacken hadn't said anything, however, was another question.

"Well?"

"Yes, I think there was something."

"That's it?!"

Adrian sighed. "Aacken, what can I say? I don't know if they're monitoring us. Maybe they're just robots using these signals to check the technology of this facility or receive orders. We're not prisoners and we're free to leave whenever we want. God, I don't like being here either, but that doesn't mean these people mean us any harm!"

"That's exactly what I'm telling him!" growled Sato. "The boredom is getting to him!"

"You two are actually bored?"

"Damn it, Morris!"

"Sorry."

Just at that moment, for the first time, he became truly aware of the situation he was in. A human colony on an alien planet was one thing, just like the technical gadgets that his quarters were equipped with, but none of it was science fiction, if you will, but it was all things that had already existed on Earth at that time, even if not as sophisticated.

However, as far as these black figures were concerned, it was quite different. They were perhaps the clearest proof that he and the others had arrived in the future; that things had been developed which they could not imagine and certainly not comprehend. Not only the meaning and purpose, but also the function and structure eluded Adrian's understanding. Probably that was one of the reasons they unnerved him so much. That and their humanoid form.

When they finally reached the common room, they found

it empty. Only a few empty water bottles and used glasses testified to the fact that someone must have been here not too long ago.

"Finally!" Suddenly Sato marched past him, grabbed a pair of small black glasses from one of the tables, and threw herself belly-down on a sober-gray, though more than comfortable, sofa. "I'm off."

Adrian laughed softly but said nothing. There were four of those glasses here, and so far, at least, they had been in use every time he had come here. He hadn't tried any of them himself yet, but they were probably some sort of VR interface that was good for killing time. Not necessarily his world, but he could at least understand it if the others sought distraction with it.

He sat down at one of the tables, picked up a bottle of water and poured himself a drink, but then hesitated to take a sip. It was an understatement to say that he didn't like the water on Rossur. He hated it. When he had first drunk it after his arrival, he had suffered through hours of stomach cramps, and even now it felt anything but good. A result of the processing and the minerals that had been stored over time. At least it wasn't toxic.

"Mr. Morris?" Suddenly a voice by the door. Adrian looked around. Feystaal entered the common room. Unlike the last time they had met, this time he wore a sober garment that resembled his own, at least in principle. "Do you have a moment?"

"I wonder how he knew we were here," Aacken murmured, barely audible.

"I have time," Adrian replied without responding to Aacken, then stood up and faced Feystaal. "What is it about?"

"Miss Toussaint informed me that you were the only module leader aboard the *Hercules*? *Genesis* leadership person-nel, then?"

"Something like that." He nodded. "Whereas I was primarily responsible for carrying out orders."

"What can you tell me about this *HIVE-D*?"

Adrian felt his heart tighten painfully, but he tried not to let on.

"Depends." He cleared his throat. "What do you want to know?"

"We were not aware of the existence of this unit," Feystaal replied slowly. "A fact that causes me great headaches, since Rossur was colonized under the authority of *Aegis Dawn*. Actually, we should have known about it."

"That's why there's that word," Adrian replied. "'Actually' is the end of any certainty."

"Wise words." A smile tugged behind Feystaal's powerful full beard. "Our technicians are keeping this *HIVE-D* under isolation for the time being, and we won't do anything about it without your explicit consent. Still, it would help us greatly if we knew what exactly it is. Initial investigations have yielded disturbing results."

"Didn't Toussaint tell you?"

"She sent me to you."

Adrian snorted bitterly. "Of course she did. *HIVE-D* stands for Human In Vitro Embryo Database. It was intended as an emergency measure to repopulate Earth in case our reproductive capacity was insufficient. It contains about 1,000 genetically modified human embryos that have been bred to grow and reproduce as quickly as possible. They are genetically identical, fully compatible and healthy. With each generation, the genetic diversity grows until, after ten generations, the first real humans emerge."

Feystaal blanched.

"I know," Adrian continued. "I myself learned of their existence only a few hours before the *Genesis* mission began."

"And why did you bring it along?"

"Because one of our scenarios assumed that there were no humans living here and the signal was just to put us on the right track. Rossur as a surrogate Earth, so to speak."

"I see." Feystaal nodded. "Thank you very much for that information. If I may, I would like to request a more detailed report for our technicians."

"I'll see what I can do."

"Thank you."

He turned to leave.

"Feystaal!" Adrian was already reaching out to hold him back, but then didn't touch him. "Wait - what happens now?"

"Miss Toussaint will inform you of the next steps in due course. Until then, I suggest you gather your strength."

Chapter Fourteen

ROSSUR WAS A PRISON. Just like this facility and ultimately also the quarters in which Adrian was wasting his time. If he had understood the first days on this planet as a forced break due to the circumstances and had pushed aside his misgivings with a mixture of trust and sheer joy about human life on this strange world, he now found this more difficult with every hour.

He had long since been tempted not only to agree with Aacken's worst fears, but also felt them himself. They were being held here without being put in chains. A dungeon with open doors that made any attempt to break out pointless from the start. Why this was so, and what Feystaal and the people on Rossur hoped to gain from it - these were questions he could not answer. Perhaps even questions to which he could find no answer at all, since the foundations of his own thinking lay entrenched in a time that had passed for centuries.

Monotony, lethargy and absolute uniformity determined every single day in this prison. Meanwhile, Adrian found no comfort, much less distraction, even in the technological gadgets of his quarters. They were little more than opium for the senses; apparatuses created solely to numb the mind and suppress every thought and every doubt.

With his eyes closed, he sat cross-legged on his bed, his chin towards his chest. His attempt to go within and find refuge in the depths of his mind. Aacken was also right about another thing. Those black figures that incessantly patrolled the corridors, and the signals they continuously sent out - he was sure they served the sole purpose of wearing them down and making them compliant. For days he had been paying close attention to them, and for just as long he had felt a constant pain on the edge of perceptibility trying to keep him from thinking. A pain that always grew stronger when the figures were near him. Some form of sound waves, perhaps; a constant overloading of his hearing? Or even a signal drilling directly into his skull?

Adrian took a deep breath and held his breath. Just in those seconds, the pain once again became more intense. One of the figures had to be directly in front of his quarters. He even thought he could hear the high-pitched sound. He still did not know what these things were, but based on their incessant patrols and precise movements, he assumed they were some kind of drone. Very complex devices.

When the pain finally faded a few minutes later and once again retreated to the confines of his consciousness, Adrian stood up, removed the clothing he had been provided, and put on his spacesuit. How clunky and outdated the technology suddenly seemed to him, he had by now become accustomed to what was considered standard on Rossur. But for what he was about to do, the suit was not only sufficient, but essential.

He opened the door, took a quick look out into the hallway and made sure that neither one of the drones nor anyone else was in sight before marching with quick steps to Aacken's quarters. A quick knock and not a second later the German and Sato were standing in front of him - also in their spacesuits. They had deliberately decided not to put on the suits until after the drone patrol, since they couldn't rule out the possibility that these things had some kind of sonar and thus learned of their plan. That is, if the quarters weren't being monitored anyway. A one in a thousand chance, but still in their favor.

"That way."

Without hesitating for a single second, Aacken ran off. Adrian and Sato followed him on the spot, and together they picked their way through the unnecessarily sprawling maze of corridors in which they had been placed. The German had spent the last few days exploring the facility and the area of the dome behind it as precisely as possible, memorizing the various paths and junctions, just as he had memorized the routes of the drones. Time Adrian had spent - or rather wasted - writing as meaningless and useless descriptions of the *HIVE-D* as possible to satisfy Feystaal. As long as he didn't know what was going on, he certainly would not provide him with a manual on how to use it.

Each of them was officially allowed to leave the facility and look around the dome, but Adrian still thought it would be better if no one found out about their plans if possible. That Feystaal was keeping something from them was an open secret. A secret that was not least due to the fact that he was the only person they had met here so far.

He would have liked to take Toussaint along as well, or at least let her in on their plan, but neither would have been wise. For Feystaal, she was considered the official representative of the *Genesis* mission and was accordingly in close coordination with him. What they talked about for hours almost every day, he didn't know, and he couldn't imagine for the life of him that these conversations had any purpose except to elicit information from her that she would not otherwise reveal.

Adrian bit his lip and silently cursed. He should have become suspicious much earlier, should have done something much earlier. Something to regain the initiative. The devil alone knew what Feystaal wanted from them and planned for them, but every scenario that came to his mind ended badly for the survivors of the *Genesis* Project. His only glimmer of hope was in what they were doing right now; in trying to get out of the facility, and ideally the dome itself, and find all the answers Feystaal was keeping from them.

"Through here!" Aacken's hissed command made Adrian wince. "Quick!"

With those words, he opened a nondescript door at the end of an equally nondescript but oddly elongated corridor, and stepped into the darkness beyond. Adrian did the same and was about to activate his helmet light, but Aacken told him with a quick hand signal not to do so, and to follow him instead.

It took a few seconds for Adrian's eyes to adjust to the darkness, but when they did, he could make out rough outlines all around him. Within the gigantic dome existed only a few light sources, none of which had the purpose of illuminating it. Rather, the little light came mainly from the position lights of hundreds of automated flying machines that flew around among the massive buildings, and from red and green lights on conveyor belts and other transport equipment, presumably indicating their functionality.

Now, as Adrian followed Aacken running through the almost complete darkness, he noticed for the first time how much the air stank. No. Even that word didn't even begin to describe how horribly bad, stale, and chemical-laden the gas smelled that he sucked into his lungs with every breath. He would have loved to put on his helmet and fire up the oxygen tanks, or at least the filters, but he couldn't do that. They would still need the equipment and their more than limited oxygen supplies once they left the dome.

If they managed to do that at all.

"Is it still far?" gasped Sato, audibly disgusted.

"How should I know?" snorted Aacken. "It's my first time out here, too."

"But I thought you..."

"I said I was sure we'd find a way out of here," he interrupted her in a cutting voice. "Nothing more, nothing less. There's a way on from here and a way out - and that's our ticket there, I think."

He raised his hand and pointed at the flying machines whirring through the air a few feet above their heads, following their set trajectories. Most of them were far too small to be controlled manually, but at the same time seemed powerful enough to move containers, some of them very large. Parts of a single, large fabrication system. Inside the dome, space was scarce and correspondingly valuable, so it was probably necessary to make the best use of the free air space.

Adrian frowned and watched one of the flying machines disappear into a building, its position lights illuminating for a moment a kind of entry airlock and a whole row of grappling arms concealed within. He was fully aware that Aacken was correct in his assumption. This dome represented Rossur's manufacturing center and, accordingly, resources had to come in and waste had to go out at some point. They just had to find it.

The question was why this dome was necessary at all. Was it to protect them from the magnetic storms they had encountered on the *Hercules*, or were the planet's climate and atmosphere much too harsh to be exposed to them without protection? As far as he knew, Ross 128 b received considerably more solar radiation than Earth, which made it correspondingly more difficult to stay outdoors. But was that reason enough to retreat into such a dome?

Involuntarily, he shook his head. Questions upon questions. Feystaal was not exactly generous when it came to information, and Toussaint had not yet given the impression that she had learned more from him. It was obvious that he didn't want to tell anything about the dome, the planet and the people here. But why not? What was so secret that they were not allowed to know? After all, they were supposed to find a future for themselves here. Or was it not?

Adrian cursed silently. After all that had happened - how could anyone be responsible for behaving like this? Earth was lost, *Genesis* had failed, and Rossur seemed to be struggling with more than enough problems. So why this secrecy? Right when mankind should stand together and...

"There!" Aacken's voice made him flinch again. Immediately he raised his head and looked in the direction he pointed. "That's where we're getting out!"

Adrian narrowed his eyes. A short distance away from them, at a height of about twenty yards, was a larger square structure, which, just like everything else, could only be recognized by its outline, but which nevertheless inevitably led outside. At least, the transport machines that flew out of it at regular intervals into the interior of the dome allowed no other conclusion.

"So how do we get up there?" asked Sato tonelessly.

"Can you climb?" asked Aacken.

"Up there?! Certainly not!"

"Can you or can't you?" he growled. "The dome runs almost vertically up here. So we're climbing without an overhang. If you basically know how to do it, I can overload the servos on our suits. It's not good for the system, but with any luck it'll work long enough."

"And if it doesn't?"

"Then it would be good if you can fly."

"Goddamn it, Aacken, you..."

"That's enough!" hissed Adrian. "Aacken is right. This airlock is the best way out of here, and we can get to it with relative ease. See those crossbars that..."

"I don't see anything!" hissed Sato. "And you can't tell me you see more!"

"I see quite well." Aacken took a clearly audible breath and made an equally audible effort to keep his voice steady. "Sato, you must trust us. This dome seems to be made of individual elements connected by cross and longitudinal struts. I think we can climb up it."

"I can't climb if I can't see anything."

"Then we'll activate our lights," Adrian suggested. "We're right out of here and so far no one has stopped us. I can't imagine anything happening now."

"All right." Aacken nodded, but didn't move.

"What is it?" asked Adrian immediately.

"I want us to be really sure of what we're doing," he replied slowly. "And that we look over the consequences. If we go out there, we may never come back. And if we do, I'm sure Feystaal won't let this go unpunished."

Adrian nodded. "I'm aware of that. I didn't come here to die in my quarters. We should be dead by now; we have outlived our time and our purpose in life. There is little left for us to lose."

"I see it that way, too," Sato agreed with him. "If you ask me, it's only a matter of time before Feystaal has us all killed anyway. Let's do it. I'd rather die out there than wait in here for my end."

Aacken nodded, stepped first to Sato and then to Adrian, opened the controls to the servo motors on their life support units, and made a few quick inputs. Almost instantly, the servos began to buzz audibly, and an increasingly loud hum emanated from the power module. The incomparable feeling of carrying a ticking time bomb strapped to your back. But if it got them out of here, they could handle it.

One by one, they now began to climb the hull of the dome, shimmying from strut to strut. An endeavor they easily accomplished thanks to the overloaded servos, and eventually they actually reached the structure through which flying machines kept entering the dome. A screeching and at the same time strangely muffled howl reached them from outside; it became louder and louder, only to fade away again immediately. This had to be the airlock that let the machines in. It seemed to open for barely ten seconds each time. Not much, but enough time for them to slip out - if they managed to enter the structure now and squeeze past the machines.

While Aacken set about opening the access to some sort of maintenance shaft, Adrian looked around as best he could, trying to catch a glimpse of the dome's buildings and facilities behind him, but even from here he could make out little more than outlines. A world upon a world, shrouded in eternal darkness, empty and completely silent except for the rumbling of machinery. What if there were almost no people left here? Or if they eked out an existence deep underground and only those who couldn't help themselves worked up here? Questions to which he hoped for answers outside the dome. He could not imagine that there should be something only here. Such a dome could have been built on other planets. Ross 128 b was considered habitable. So why did they lock them up here?

GLARING sunlight burned down on Adrian with merciless force, penetrating even the aperture of his visor with playful ease. He had to hold a hand in front of his eyes to keep from being blinded, and even so he barely managed to protect himself. Even the cooling units of his spacesuit were howling under maximum load within seconds. But that was okay. They had made it. They had left the dome and entered Ross 128 b. Their boots stood on dark brown desert soil; the wind sent grains of sand pattering against their helmets.

Breathing heavily, Adrian lowered himself to the ground and stroked his visor with one hand, almost as if to wipe the sweat from his brow. Sweat that had long since run down his face and burned in his eyes. He was exhausted and the heat was getting to him, but nevertheless he was relieved to have finally left the dome.

He laughed softly into his helmet. How they had managed to slip through the airlock and squeeze past the flying machines, he himself was not quite sure. Between the noise, darkness and light, he had just run, doing what his instincts told him to do, hoping it would work. And it had.

After a few seconds of just breathing and trying to calm his frantically beating heart, he struggled back to his feet, turned and looked up. Dozens, if not hundreds, of flying machines were buzzing through the sky, but they were not coming from remote corners of the planet, as he had suspected, but were leaving massive carrier ships that were pushing their way across the horizon like titans turned to steel. Flying factories, perhaps? Mobile mining units?

"Well, in any case, we won't be getting back in that way," Sato summarized, looking up as well. She probably mistakenly assumed his gaze was on the airlock, which lay unreachably high and protected by the mirror-smooth outer shell of the dome behind them. "Well, there are worse things."

"I agree," Aacken agreed with her. "Still, it feels like a crap idea."

"We have to," Adrian said, averting his eyes. "In the dome, we were prisoners. Out here, at least we're free."

"What if we don't find anything?"

"We'll find something."

"Morris." Aacken stepped up to him and grabbed his arm. "I trust you and you know it. Otherwise, I never would have undertaken this madness with you. But we need more than hopes. Did Toussaint say anything when you spoke? Feystaal must have said something! You wanted to leave the dome at any cost; I would have looked around inside first. So - what do you have?"

Adrian fell silent and looked around. It was a good question. When they were brought in after they landed, he had not had a chance to scan the surface of the planet for possible settlements, let alone memorize any features. Nevertheless, there simply had to be something; such a huge structure as the dome could not operate completely autonomously even with the greatest automation measures - not to mention that there was no point to it either. There simply had to be people somewhere. They just had to find them.

"Those ships are manned for sure," Sato said, pointing to one of the massive flying machines gliding over the foothills of a sheer titanic mountain range a few miles away from them.

"So you can fly after all?" caustic Aacken.

"Shut up! I ..."

Adrian was about to raise his hand to deactivate his radio

to avoid the looming argument, but then paused as his fingers touched the radio controls. As they had held position in orbit around the planet and tried to scan the surface, they had picked up more than enough scraps of signal. Scraps of signals that might indicate life - and of which he received absolutely none here, in the immediate vicinity of the dome.

Without a second's hesitation, he marched off, motioning to Aacken and Sato to follow him with a quick wave of his hand. Perhaps the dome's exterior or the mountains were deflecting signals so that they couldn't pick up anything in their immediate vicinity? He wouldn't have been surprised, because the foundations of the massive structure were embedded in deep trenches, next to which the rock-strewn rubble was deposited dozens of yards high. No chance of receiving anything down here.

Unfortunately, Aacken had already reversed the overload on their servo motors, so finding a way over the steep piles of rubble proved to be much more strenuous. Nevertheless, after a few attempts, Adrian managed to locate a halfway passable path, and Aacken and Sato also followed him at some distance.

He was fully aware that he had little to show for it except the vague hope of receiving signals. The escape from the dome was due less to a concrete expectation than to a simple deduction: Feystaal had allowed them to move freely within the facility and the dome itself. This meant, therefore, that there was hardly anything outside their quarters that could help them in any way - not to mention the fact that it was utterly impossible to move through the virtually absolute darkness.

The only logical consequence was to take a step further and leave the dome completely behind them. There was no guarantee that there would be anything outside its protective shell - especially people - but given the circumstances, it was still the only option if they did not want to spend any more time waiting uselessly. Not to mention that Feystaal certainly had not expected them to escape, and Adrian took immense satisfaction in that thought alone.

He could not begin to say what it was, but the more he had dealt with Feystaal, the less he could stand him. At the same time, the High Commissioner, as he had imagined, made every effort to remain polite and to make their stay pleasant. And that was exactly what made Adrian suspicious.

At some point, breathing heavily, he finally reached the top of the pile of rubble that stretched all around the dome. For a moment he paused, breathing heavily, trying not to vomit from heat and exhaustion, which he scarcely succeeded in doing. Only with great difficulty could he choke down the hot bile that had long since made its way down his throat. He...

Suddenly a touch on his helmet. Sato, tapping against his visor. But before he could say anything, she reached out and pointed to a row of dark gray objects at the base of the mountain where the dome was embedded in its back. Objects that Adrian recognized as buildings only at second glance, rising like stones from the ubiquitous dark brown of the desert. Gray clouds of smoke also rose from a few, and he even thought he saw something like vehicles here and there.

"A village," Sato whispered as incredulously as triumphantly. "That's a village!"

"Unbelievable," grumbled Aacken. "I swear, I would have bet anything that there was nothing out there."

"We need a plan. Adrian, you're our old module leader. You've been trained for situations like this. What do you say?"

"Difficult," Adrian muttered more to himself than to her, shaking his head involuntarily as he continued to gaze at the houses at the base of the mountain. They stretched to the horizon and their sheer mass made it impossible to even estimate how many there were, but either way there had to be hundreds of thousands of people living down there. People who braved the heat outside the dome.

"Is that all you have to say?"

"There are too many possible parameters," Adrian

replied. "This is not a disaster scenario like on Earth. None of us were trained for a situation like this. It may sound a little over the top, but at the end of the day, this is nothing more than first contact. These people were born thousands of years after us. We don't even know if they were aware of our arrival."

"That would be good, wouldn't it?" asked Sato. "Then we could mingle with the people."

"In spacesuits?"

"We'd have to get rid of those, of course."

"Sato's right, Morris," Aacken agreed with her. "While I have no idea how long it will take for night to fall here, I suggest we wait until nightfall and enter the settlement. It will be at least a couple of hours before we descend. Somehow we'll get some clothes then."

"Agreed," Adrian said. "But we must act with extreme caution. We can't risk a riot. If something goes wrong, Feystaal will know where we are."

"Don't you think he already knows?"

"No. If he knew, we would never have gotten this far. I don't think he could have imagined that anyone would succeed in leaving the dome - or that anyone would even try. Just because he has superior technology doesn't mean he can foresee every possible scenario. Right now, we have the advantage. Let's use it."

"Of course we're going to use it," Sato snorted. "There's no way back. Proverbially or literally. If we don't take this chance, it's all been for nothing. So lead the way, Morris."

Adrian hesitated for a brief moment, but then nodded to her and picked his way down - which turned out to be considerably more complicated than the way up. The pile of rubble around the dome wasn't completely loose, but it wasn't so solid that it was easy to find a foothold. Eventually, he shifted to sliding mainly downward, avoiding the larger rocks as best he could.

As before, countless flying machines passed over their heads; some toward the dome, others back toward the massive carrier ships. They floated through the air like whales of metal and technology, slow and almost majestic. It was hard to gauge their actual size, since even the closest ones were several miles away. But despite the distance, there was no mistaking what huge behemoths these machines were.

Although Adrian needed most of his concentration to keep his balance and find a way down, he could not help but to keep glancing at the ships and staring at them like a child. They fascinated him. Not only because of their size and majesty, but mostly because he would never have thought something like that was possible. How they kept themselves in the air despite their surely immense weight while moving only minimally was a mystery to him. Just like the question of what in the world they were propelled by. Antimatter perhaps? Did they possibly use atmospheric peculiarities of the planet? He had no idea.

Only their purpose seemed obvious to him: they served as a focal point for the automated drones that supplied the dome; possibly even as a kind of semi-mobile intermediate base; a place where the drones refueled their engines and sorted raw materials.

"I don't get it," he spoke tonelessly into the radio at one point as he finally left the rubble pile and entered the regular mountain face covered by rounded, flat rocks. The way down here was just as steep, if not a little steeper, but at least the ground was much better, so he didn't have to expect to slip with every step. "These are immense amounts of raw materials. What do you need that for? Even in the dome, there aren't enough facilities to process such quantities."

"You don't know how deep it goes into the ground under the dome," Aacken replied dryly. "I don't think it's out of the question that the actual production and processing capacity is underground and only delivery is done inside the dome."

"If that's true and most people are living outside the dome at the same time, I don't want to know what exactly they're doing down there," Sato grumbled. "God, do you feel so incredibly alien right now, too?"

Adrian nodded, even though he knew she could not see him. Alien. Yes, that was the appropriate word. When they had gone into cryostasis and left Earth, he had been excited, nervous, and certainly afraid. Many of the scenarios he had imagined had not turned out well for him and the others, but he had not felt alien in any of them. That was probably why this realization hit him all the harder now.

Apparently, you could become alien to other humans. Not in the way they had been on Earth in the past; not in the sense that you did not know someone or feel connected to them. The knowledge of inhabiting the same planet, breathing the same air, and resembling each other in so many ways had always bound people together, despite their differences. It had been a kind of inseparable bond. But here? Here it was completely different.

Adrian took a deep breath and held it in his lungs for as long as his frantically beating heart would allow. At this moment, it would not have made any difference if he had truly been an alien in the classic sense; if he had antennae on his head, green skin or tentacles. Time and space separated him enough from the people here that he was an alien to them. A being from an unknown world and a time long past. A relic that emerged from the fog of oblivion and tried to find its way in a present that was no longer his own.

Chapter Fifteen

It was deep in the night when they finally reached the settlement. Adrian was not sure if this was not just a fallacy; an attempt of his mind to understand this planet by earthly standards. There was no moon here to reflect at least some of the sunlight onto the surface, and no other object in the sky to serve that purpose. Accordingly, within a very short time after sunset, a merciless, almost impenetrable darkness had settled over the planet, burying absolutely everything beneath it.

Nevertheless, Adrian still hesitated to activate his helmet light. Under no circumstances did he want to draw unnecessary attention to himself and the others. As long as they did not know whether they could trust the people here or at least stay halfway untroubled in this settlement, every interaction held a risk. Feystaal and his drones must have noticed by now that they were gone, and probably that they were no longer inside the dome.

If he was honest, Adrian was still surprised that they had come this far at all, and that no search operation had started yet. At least none that they would have noticed. Either they had taken Feystaal by surprise with their escape, or he had no way of tracking them down out here. He might even have thought that they had died. He would not have been surprised. Without their spacesuits, they would not have made the descent, nor endured the heat for so long.

Nevertheless, now was the time to at least take off their helmets. Not only were their oxygen supplies running low and their filters on strike in the face of the immense amounts of dust and sand, but he also wanted to avoid scaring anyone at all costs. Screaming was something they could not afford under any circumstances.

Adrian took one last deep breath and memorized the smell as best he could before opening the latches one by one and finally pulling the helmet off his head. He already knew that he could breathe the 'air' out here, though the concentration of pollutants was off the charts. Not exactly something he wanted to do to his lungs. Then again, he didn't have much to lose anyway.

"God, it stinks," Sato choked, barely pulling off her helmet and coughing a few times. "Imagine having to live like this."

"We have to live like this," Aacken replied laconically.

"True, I guess."

"It won't kill us," Adrian said. "According to suit sensors, mostly ammonia, sulfur dioxide and various nitrogen oxides. It's not pretty, but we'll get through it. At least for now."

"Says the optimist."

Adrian snorted, but didn't reply. It was clear to him, as it was to her and Aacken, where these pollutants came from: they were a byproduct of terraforming, especially when it did not go according to plan. And that was reason enough for suspicion. The concentration of pollutants was within acceptable limits, at least for terraforming, but it was still an undoubted indication that something was going very wrong. Especially since this colony had existed for several centuries and should have had a stable ecosystem for a long time.

At least in theory.

Was that possibly the reason why Feystaal had put so much emphasis on keeping them inside the dome? Did he want to cover up the failure of the colony and possibly the entire terraforming process? Or - thinking further - was that possibly the reason why they had been brought here? After all, Feystaal had assumed that the entire crew of the *Genesis* would come here. Along with their engines and equipment.

"It was never about us," he finally whispered. "They want our equipment."

"I was just thinking the same thing," Aacken growled. "Goddamn. Then we're lucky they didn't shoot us on the spot."

"They need someone who knows about the *Hercules* terraforming unit."

"Right."

"And how the hell do you screw it up so massively?" murmured Sato, looking around almost as if she hoped to spot the cause of the problems somewhere. "Terraforming is a complex process, I understand that, but most of all it takes time. You can't go too far wrong, especially when a planet like this is basically habitable and, more importantly, not pre-stressed!"

"Maybe their technology was simply defective," Aacken opined. "Or local conditions threw a wrench in their plans. Possibly even those magnetic storms? We..." He paused.

Adrian had heard it, too. A soft sound, not far from them. Footsteps. Someone who must have stopped when he noticed them. Immediately his heart contracted painfully, pumping a charge of adrenaline into his bloodstream as he strained to make out something amid the merciless darkness, but there was nothing.

For a tiny moment he hesitated, but then grabbed his helmet, activated his light and held it in front of him like a flashlight. On the spot, the cone of light fell on a woman peeking out from behind the wall of a house just a few yards away from them, staring at them with wide eyes. Contrary to expectations, however, she did not retreat, but stepped out of her hiding place and raised her hands.

"You're the ones who came," she whispered, "aren't you? The ones from Earth?"

Adrian looked at her and eyed her from head to toe. Unlike Feystaal, she was not particularly tall, but a good deal shorter than he, and also wore anything but elegant clothing. A gray-brown work outfit with heavy boots and some exposed tubing leading into a small device on her shoulder. Her skin was tanned, but at the same time looked unhealthy and sallow, and her eyes also made anything but a good impression. They possessed a yellowish hue and the pupils shimmered whitish in the light.

"That's right," he finally replied, dimming the light and handing Sato his helmet before taking a step toward the stranger. "My name is Adrian Scott Morris. This is Iris Sato and Lars Aacken. We're from Earth. What's your name?"

"Lyra." A smile twitched across her lips. "My name is Lyra. I'm from Sector 12, and I don't even know what to say. I was so hoping to meet you, and when I saw you at the dome..."

"You saw us? How so?"

"I'm watching the dome. I..." She paused, grabbed her forehead with one hand, and looked down at the ground.

"Sorry," she whispered now. "You must have many questions. I have many questions, too. Do you want to come with me?"

Adrian gave Aacken and Sato a quick look. Both nodded.

"All right. Lead the way."

"Thank you for your trust." Lyra nodded as well and gestured to the alley behind her. "It's not far, and the air is better inside. Come."

With those words, she turned and walked. Adrian followed her on the spot. While he couldn't claim to have a complete grasp of the situation, he was still aware that Lyra was his best chance for now to find the answers he was looking for out here. And she, as a local, surely knew how to further elude Feystaal.

Nonetheless, he kept looking around, trying to memorize the way through the alleys as best he could in case, for whatever reason, they needed to get out of here quickly. His gut told him that they could trust Lyra, but he did not want to rely on that alone. It was entirely possible that she was working for Feystaal.

It didn't take long for the local to stop in front of a nondescript, windowless building. Just like all the other houses here, it had only a single story, a square floor plan, and a flat, but apparently relatively massive roof. Lyra heaved open a heavy metal door that made such a deafening squeal that it must have woken everyone within a radius of hundreds of yards.

Behind it, a spartan but lovingly furnished home awaited them. The core of the small room was a water-filled depression in the floor, surrounded by a stone bench, and from which some kind of plant grew up to the ceiling. Next to it was a downright tiny kitchenette, a small bed that folded into the wall, and several shelves of all sorts of junk technology and crudely made gadgets. Lyra was obviously a tinkerer.

"It's not much," she said, gesturing for them to enter with a nod of her head. "Sorry about the mess."

"I'd prefer this a thousand times over my quarters in the dome," Aacken murmured, stepping through the door first.

"Lyra," Adrian interposed when he had also entered, glancing at her as she closed the door behind them, but then paused. He didn't have the slightest clue what to say, what questions to ask, or how to explain everything. Hell, he had no idea where to even begin! "I, we..."

"You came from space," she took over, sitting down at the water-filled depression. "From the old home. From Earth. I know the stories of the old days. You are the ones who were left behind. The ones who were supposed to rebuild."

"That's right."

"And you have come. The signal reached you. I didn't think it was possible - no one did. You've done the impossible."

"We had no other choice," Adrian said softly, sitting down across from her. "The earth died. We left our companions behind and went on our way. It feels like yesterday."

"Cold sleep?"

He nodded. "Cryostasis."

"That's how our ancestors got here, too."

"We know that. One of the few things Feystaal told us. Do you know him?"

"The High Commissioner. Yes, I know him."

"Lyra, I..." He sighed softly and shook his head. "I don't know what to say. Since we arrived, we've been stuck in the dome, learning nothing. We left it to find out what's going on, and now we're here. We don't understand Ross 128 b - Rossur. All we know is that the air is not good. What happened? Are there problems here?"

She looked down at the ground. "The planet itself is the problem. We are barely managing to keep the atmosphere stable. We abandoned the idea of living a healthy life centuries ago."

"What happened?"

"We don't know exactly. It just doesn't work, even though everything fits."

"How can that be?"

She laughed bitterly and looked him straight in the eye. "Rossur is not Earth. We don't live here like our ancestors. Life has always been hard and most of us don't live very long. Climate, radiation and poisons take an immense blood toll every day. A single human life doesn't count for much here. It used to be different. Not better, but more bearable. But since the new council has been in power, things are getting worse."

"The council that Feystaal belongs to? That's your government?"

"Exactly. Fifteen Commissioners and the dual Chancellors. It's not a dictatorship in the true sense, but it's not an elected government either. When our ancestors reached Rossur, they decided to tie politics to extremely pooled executive powers in order to speed up decisions and increase our prospects for survival. Since then, every twenty years they re-evaluate whether this is still necessary."

"And I assume it's necessary?"

"Of course it is. And I also doubt that it will ever change.

The old councils were harsh in their decisions, but they at least tried to protect life. The current council... They don't care about us. Workers. Nothing more, nothing less."

"So you are being kept ignorant?" asked Sato quietly.

"Yes." Lyra nodded. "That's one way to put it. Life expectancy is just 35 years in the last few decades. There is no time for education. Education begins at eight, work at twelve. From sixteen on, a woman must give birth to a child every three years, but very few make it. I was lucky enough to escape this. My father was a technician at a terraforming station at the planet's north pole. His influence made it possible for me to escape the system."

"Feystaal didn't look like he was in bad shape," Aacken grumbled. "And he didn't look sick, either."

"He's one of the Fives."

"Fives?"

"I see." She twisted the corners of her mouth into a forced smile. "You wouldn't know that. The Fives are the most genetically fit people of each birth cohort. They are taken to the dome. It's easier to keep radiation and toxins away from them there."

"And why?"

"Well - for reproduction. About four generations after arrival on Rossur, the first genetic effects from toxins and radiation were detected. The rate of non-viable children is correspondingly high. Both endanger the continued existence of the colony. That was the reason why the dome was built. Genetically fit children grow up there and receive higher quality education. A few of them later remain in leadership positions or become scientists, but most return at sixteen to produce as many healthy children as possible. Probably that's the only reason we're still around."

"That's terrible!" breathed Sato in a quivering voice. "We were in the dome! There are more than enough resources there! Why leave you out here to die when you could just..."

"It is what it is," Lyra interrupted her. "We're not worth it."

"And..."

"And what?"

"Is that why you were waiting for us?"

Lyra was silent for a brief moment, staring into the water, before finally nodding, barely perceptibly. "Yes. Ever since I learned that a signal was sent to you centuries ago, and that you were to arrive now, I've been waiting for it."

"And what should we do?"

"Help us. Save us. Rossur is dying. Even with all the Council's measures, we have only a few decades left before either our own genes kill us or the atmosphere does. Our attempts to terraform the planet have failed. Even if the Council won't admit it."

Once again, Adrian looked to Aacken and Sato. So then that was really the reason for Feystaal's interest in their equipment. Rossur needed a functioning terraforming unit to start from scratch. And the *HIVE-D* was a bonus that was more than convenient for him. The genetically flawless embryos would be able to populate the planet with healthy humans where the current population had been ravaged by disease and poison. A fresh start as on Earth. And once again humans were responsible for all misery and suffering.

SILENTLY, Adrian sipped the strong, malt-tasting and slightly sweet-smelling drink Lyra had handed him, but he couldn't bring himself to drink properly, despite his thirst. His throat felt as if he had swallowed dust, and no matter how hard he tried, he could not get his lips to drink.

Actually, the decision was obvious: they had to return to the dome, face Feystaal and offer their help in saving the planet. The sooner they began evaluating the terraforming efforts already in place and incorporating them into their own efforts, the better their chances were of not only saving the atmosphere and climate, but actually making Rossur livable.

Logic would even have dictated promptly deploying the

HIVE-D and breeding such a large reproductive potential via the outgrowing proto-humans as quickly as possible so that the genetic disadvantages of the existing population could be eradicated within a few generations.

Only that was precisely the problem. Every fiber in Adrian's body resisted doing any of these things. Not because he did not want to help the people here, but because that would also have meant helping Feystaal and his council. The Fives, as Lyra called them, would benefit the most by far. Not only would most of them live long enough to see the results of a restored planet, but they would be among the privileged ones who shaped the future of Rossur - while everyone else perished. Adrian would not even have been surprised if they were simply destroyed.

He would have loved to scream in frustration and anger right now. He knew there was only one logical choice. That the continued existence of humanity justified many, if not all, ways and means. That the ultimate goal of the *Genesis* mission had been, and remained throughout his own life, to give humanity a second chance. And if Earth was too contaminated and destroyed to do it there, it could inevitably only be done here.

Logical. All at once this word seemed to him like sheer mockery. Was it really logical? It was obvious that Lyra was ill, as was the fact that she did not have long to live. A few years at most, and maybe a few more if she received medical help. But did that justify her living in this hole? That she had nothing but these barren, windowless quarters? That her health was only worth as much as the work she could do? Was it okay to wear out and consume hundreds of thousands like tools just so a few could live in luxury and health?

No. No, it wasn't. No matter how he twisted it, he could not imagine that anything would change. It was completely irrelevant whether the planet would turn into a paradise or hell itself. Those who possessed power and wealth did not give both up voluntarily, especially not when they were sitting in a made bed and only had to watch others do the dirty work.

This meant that every step taken to save the planet would pave the path to continued injustice. It meant that humanity faced a future of servitude and imprisonment; that the individual was catapulted back into an early capitalist state where only those who worked could live.

On the other hand... Perhaps future generations would find the strength to throw off their shackles and stand up to their masters, no matter how unlikely that seemed now. Was one allowed to squander such a chance without having waited for it at all? Didn't the very existence of humanity weigh more than servitude and slavery anyway?

"I have made you unhappy," Lyra's soft, careful voice reached Adrian's ears at one point. "I'm sorry for that. Please accept my apologies."

"You didn't," Aacken replied before Adrian could say anything. "It's just in the nature of things that we are thinking."

"What are you thinking about?" asked Lyra much more cautiously; almost as if she feared making them angry. "It's obvious what you have to do, right?"

"If we use our technology to save Rossur, we make it possible for this to continue," Adrian took over, making a sweeping gesture with his hand. "I doubt your council will relinquish power and allow you to live properly."

"And?"

"So?" he repeated incredulously, staring at her. "That's not living! You are labor slaves, subjected to disease and death, and..."

"It is what it is," she interrupted him. "Better this than no life at all! It is your duty to save Rossur!"

"Our duty?"

"Yes, your duty!" she repeated, much more emphatically this time. Almost angrily. "Anyone who can help and doesn't help is a thousand times worse than someone who can't help! You have ways and means to do what we have failed to do! I know about the possibilities of the *Genesis*! What does it matter how it continues, as long as it continues at all!"

"It matters a great deal," Sato murmured. "We're not saying we won't help you, but if we do, we'll give Feystaal and the other commissioners the whip to drive you with. We have to at least try to change something! Even if we can't help you and the others here anymore, your children and your children's children deserve a better life!"

"That's not your decision!"

"Yes it is! We might not be able to afford not to help, but that doesn't mean we have to accept the way things are without contradiction! Feystaal and the Council haven't a clue how to save the planet! Damn, it was already clear centuries ago what was going to happen! Otherwise they wouldn't have sent a signal to us! And what has happened in these centuries? Nothing! Even if they couldn't terraform Rossur, they could have easily built more domes in that time! Why didn't they do that? You want to know something, Lyra? You guys are getting screwed! The Council and the Fives are living in luxury! In a luxury they would have to give up to give everyone a good life! Nothing more, nothing less!"

"So what!" roared Lyra, jumping up. "Who are you to decide that? That's easy for you to say! Look at you! Core-healthy you stand before me and presume to rule over my life! You've only been here a few days and you think you know more than I do!"

"You're right," Adrian said, gesturing for Sato to remain silent. "You're right, Lyra. We're not in your shoes. We come from a faraway place and time, and we meet you and your homeland with our standards. But please try to understand us as well. We have been trained to create a new, better earth. A home for all people. Not just for a privileged few. It's hard for us to accept that this is the way it's supposed to be here."

"It used to be different," Lyra whispered in a suddenly soft and melancholy voice. She stared at the plant growing toward the ceiling for a moment before leaning forward, scooping up some water with both hands and dripping it onto the leaves. "Not too long ago. My father saw it with his own eyes."

"What are you talking about?"

"Of our successes. Of the bright spots of terraforming. About 120 miles from here is a canyon. It stretches over almost a quarter of the planetary surface and is the only place where we have managed to establish a permanent surface water supply. There, in just five years, we managed to grow enough greenery to sustain us without underground green-houses. At the same time, there were local breakthroughs in other places. My father told me that it had happened before. Time and time again, there were small successes. And time and time again they have passed."

"And why is that?" asked Adrian. "What you say are not insignificant achievements. Especially with a water supply like that, plants should be almost self-sustaining."

"We don't know," she replied. "It's as if the planet itself has conspired against us. No sooner do we manage to stabilize it locally than the atmospheric levels change and it collapses again."

"Has data been collected? Have samples been taken, measurements performed? Your analysts must have noticed something! An ecosystem doesn't collapse that easily!"

Lyra was silent.

Adrian already opened his mouth to follow up, but then let it go. There was no point. If she or anyone else had known why such problems were occurring, there would never have been any need to wait nearly 600 years for the possible arrival of people who they didn't even know were alive for certain, let alone if they would draw the right conclusions from a signal.

"Sato," he finally said, looking around for her. She was sitting on the bed with her legs drawn up, staring ahead of her. "You're a chemist, biologist, and physicist. Any idea what that might be about? Is it related to the magnetic storms, maybe?"

"Hard to say," she murmured, returning his gaze. "There definitely have to be effects on the technology, but how they ultimately turn out is hard to gauge. So far, we've noticed little to nothing on the surface. The increased radiation levels shouldn't really have such a serious impact. Frankly, I'm more concerned about whether it's not really the planet itself, as Lyra said. Our terraforming units were designed for Earth, and the same is certainly true of the equipment the colonists brought with them. It is within the realm of possibility that it is simply impossible to succeed with it here. At least not without extensive modifications. However, both climate and atmosphere still exist. So it cannot have failed completely. I ..." She paused for a moment. "Morris, even with the resources of the *Genesis*, it would take years to determine the causal chains, and considerably longer to find a solution. We can't possibly do anything with our one terraforming unit. I hate to say it, but if we're going to have even a chance of making a difference, we're going to need Feystaal's help."

"I was afraid of that."

"So you'll help us?" asked Lyra cautiously.

"It looks that way," Adrian replied. "We didn't come here to watch you die. This is the last bastion of humanity, even if we don't like it. How do we get back to the dome?"

"I can ask one of the foremen to inform the dome staff in the morning. They will come and get you then."

"All right." Adrian took a deep breath. "Then it's settled."

"Thank you for doing this. You are our last hope."

"Again, I doubt that with all my heart." He bit his lip and stifled another comment. He may not have a full grasp of the situation and, of course, did not have access to any scientifically robust data, but nonetheless, he doubted that was the whole story. This planet had been inhabited by humans for centuries, and despite misery and disease, the population was thriving. If terraforming had failed completely, none of this would be possible. Some basic backup of atmosphere-forming measures still had to be intact and active. Only with difficulty did he manage to keep himself from throwing his hands up in disbelief, but he didn't want to upset Lyra any more. She already looked absolutely miserable. The very idea that they could refuse to help her seemed to have affected her deeply. Understandable, after all, Rossur was her home. This was where her friends and family lived. He himself would have given anything to save Earth, too.

And that was exactly why they had to be careful. Not only when they offered Feystaal their support, but especially afterwards. The ridge they were walking on was narrow, and on either side they were in danger of falling deep. If they did not have a complete overview of the situation, or if Feystaal even tried to mislead them further, their efforts could quickly fail - or result in even greater suffering.

All the images that had flashed across the wall-sized screen in his quarters, all the footage of such fantastic and alien places, now popped back into his mind and drove hungry animals like their fangs into his consciousness. What he had seen had not seemed artificial to him, but real. Real landscapes, successes of terraforming, evidence of the colonists' successes on Ross 128 b.

Why had they been shown these images incessantly? Was it an attempt to create the illusion of a world that did not exist? Successes that had long since passed; a desperate clinging? Or rather, hope for a better future; brief glimpses of what might one day be, if only the remaining participants in the *Genesis* Project decided to help Feystaal and the Council?

"The Fives aren't bad people," Lyra said suddenly. "They are not evil just because they are Fives. Our world and our society may be unjust, but earthly societies weren't just either. It's just more obvious here. Still, that doesn't mean that every person who escapes this life is bad. There are good and bad here as well as there."

"What are you trying to tell us?" asked Aacken.

"That you should not make a mistake that you can avoid. Exclusion and hatred help no one. But you should know as well as any of us where this can lead. I think about that a lot. About justice and fairness. I don't think I know the answers to these questions, but I believe that many things have their meaning. And maybe we should learn here to treat each other with respect and goodwill despite such differences and the injustices of life. A lesson from what has happened on earth."

Chapter Sixteen

IT WAS a bizarre picture that presented itself to Adrian. The High Commissioner Gunthar Feystaal was sitting in an elevated position at the head of a steel table that had two levels. The highest, where he was seated on a kind of gallery, flanked by two of the faceless drones, and another, considerably lower, where Cassandra Toussaint was seated on one side and Aacken, Sato and Adrian himself opposite her. The two levels were connected by a steeply sloping metal plate, which had been polished so intensively that it could have functioned as a mirror.

Had the situation not been so serious, it would inevitably have seemed ridiculous in its absurdity, and even so Adrian had to stifle a half-mocking, half-bitter snort more than once. On Earth, most rulers had at least taken pains to legitimize their authority and, at best, subtly flaunt it. This was just idiotic. Feystaal didn't use the proverbial picket fence to wave, but thrashed it at them.

By now they had been sitting here for a good ten minutes, in silence of course, while men and women in sober and unadorned black uniforms kept entering the room and handing Feystaal data carriers. Obviously adjutants and thus probably the first Fives other than the Commissioner himself that Adrian had yet laid eyes on.

"You're putting me in more than an awkward position," Feystaal said suddenly, glancing at some sort of tablet in his hand before setting it aside and clearing his throat. "We have done everything in our power to make sure you all have as comfortable a stay as possible during difficult times. As High Commissioner of the Rossur Council for the Repatriation of the *Genesis*, I am fully aware that our world seems alien to you - in more ways than one. Personally, I would have liked to leave it at a simple debate, but the Council asked me to issue an official warning. A justified reaction."

"We...," Aacken continued, but Feystaal immediately jerked up a hand, causing him to pause.

"Please be silent," he said quietly, looking to Toussaint. "Miss Toussaint, I have already explained to you the jurisdiction on Rossur. You are the representative of your people and therefore responsible for them. I hereby issue an official warning. The behavior of your people is unacceptable, violates our hospitality, and could have had serious repercussions on the dome."

Toussaint turned her head and looked Adrian firmly in the eye. "I understand."

"Good. As an immediate punitive measure, your entire crew will be revoked permission to leave their quarters until further notice and..."

"For what purpose?" Adrian stood up. A movement that the two drones instantly responded to by turning in his direction. "What's the point of..."

"Mr. Morris, you will remain silent or ..."

"No!" he shouted. "No, I won't! Ross 128 b is dying! Your terraforming has failed and your people are dying outside the dome! Don't take us for fools! Your ancestors sent the signal to Earth because it became apparent almost 600 years ago that you would not be able to stabilize the atmosphere! We're only here because you want our technology!"

Toussaint's eyes widened and her mouth opened ever so slightly. So Feystaal had not told even her of his intentions.

"Feystaal." Adrian took a deep breath and made every

effort to keep his voice as calm as possible. "We are not your enemies. Each of us has been trained since early childhood for situations like this. We can help. But we will not, under any circumstances, allow ourselves to be held hostage any longer."

"What do you know?"

"What does it matter?" he snorted. "Do you want to weigh what lies are necessary to explain this insanity?"

"No." Feystaal sighed softly, frowning, looking all at once fifty years older. He raised a finger barely noticeably, whereupon the two drones left the room. "Let's just say I have a personal interest in knowing who you've been talking to."

"Does it matter?" hissed Sato. "Are you going to punish her?"

"Punish?" Feystaal shook his head. "No, not at all. But I'm sure 'she' is Lyra."

Silence.

"Don't worry about it." All at once he sounded amused. "For one thing, we're neither brutes nor an unjust society - though you probably think otherwise - and for another, I'm certainly not going to harm my own niece."

"Your niece?"

"My sister and I were fortunate enough to be chosen as Fives. While she had to leave the dome to stabilize the gene pool, I stayed and became part of the Council. Lyra is their sixth child. A smart, shrewd woman. I would have given a lot to be able to nurture her talent."

"And why don't you?"

"Promote her just because she's my niece? I can't. There are many talented people living outside the dome. We don't have the resources to..."

"Don't talk shit, damn it!" hissed Sato.

"I'm not, Miss Sato," he said tonelessly. "Believe me, I am not. It may seem like injustice to you, but just about everything we do is for the purpose of securing life. Yes, the dome has significantly more resources at its disposal. That's necessary to keep harmful environmental influences away from the

Fives and allow them to continue to keep our society - and species - alive in the future. At the same time, you can imagine that people forced to live here need different employment opportunities and distractions than on the surface. Then there are the medical treatments and genetic stabilization interventions. Unfair? Certainly. But necessary."

Adrian opened his mouth; every fiber of his body demanded that he say something back and contradict this skyscraping justification, but no matter how hard he tried to say something, he could not.

"We will do what it takes," Feystaal continued. "Even if it's not pretty. Some of the Council may see it differently, but I personally would give a lot if we could offer a better life to more people. And, yes, maybe someday, we can."

"So why did you try to keep us locked up here?" asked Adrian. "Why did we have to break out to find out what was going on? Hell, why did you lie to us? What's the point of all this?"

This time it was Feystaal who remained silent. He stared ahead with an almost glazed look, but it didn't look like he was trying to make up a lie as an explanation, but rather as if he had to wrestle with himself to answer him at all.

"Some members of the Council feared you would refuse to help." The High Commissioner swallowed hard, stood up and left his podium before stepping around the table and sitting down in the last remaining chair between them and Toussaint. "It's a concern I can at least relate to. We only know part of the protocols your mission follows, but what we do know was cause for concern. It was never intended to lie to you. Rather, we wanted to slowly introduce you to the reality on this planet and convince you that help is essential. An endeavor in which we have failed."

"And..." Toussaint paused for a moment and held his gaze. Probably an attempt to gauge which questions would get her the most answers. "So what happens now? How do we proceed?"

"I will provide you with a detailed report and all relevant

data on our terraforming efforts to date." Feystaal nodded to her. "Atmospheric analyses, soil samples, raw material and water deposits, spectral analyses. Anything you might need. In addition, I will request our best scientists and technicians and inform the Council that you have agreed to cooperate. However, I must ask you not to attempt any more escapes or anything similar." With these words, he stood up and left the room.

Toussaint remained in her seat for a moment, staring alternately at Adrian, Aacken and Sato, before she too stood up and followed suit.

Involuntarily, Adrian narrowed his eyes and watched her go. He had firmly expected her to stay and talk to them. After all, they hadn't had time to talk to her since their return to the dome, or even to tell her what they had learned. But she seemed to have no interest in that. More than that, when she had left, she had seemed upset. Angry. Maybe even disappointed?

He didn't know. Either way, he could not understand why she was acting this way and not even allowing them to explain themselves. Had she perhaps been trying to break the deadlock in the background and they had exposed her by running away? Possibly. However, she was not their superior and even if she was, she could never have expected them to expose themselves to such confinement, for better or worse.

Finally, Adrian, Sato and Aacken also left the room and - escorted by two drones - went back to their quarters. It was better that way. After Toussaint stormed off, he had no interest in getting snapped at by her in private. It was better if tempers settled a bit first.

When he finally reached his quarters and closed the door behind him, he instantly noticed a tablet glowing at him from the chair. With a quiet, surprised laugh, he picked it up and sat down on the bed. A small, yellow-bordered notice in the upper right corner of the display told him that the bulk of the data had yet to be transferred, but there was already a considerable amount of information on the little device. Admittedly, he hadn't expected it to happen so quickly. Feystaal did not seem to have bluffed. Had he actually intended to inform them?

Concentrating, he worked his way through the data and records. Obviously, the colonization and terraforming of the planet had gone more or less well within the first few decades. The rate of progress of the terraforming effort, while at the low end of the scale, was still within basically acceptable parameters, especially considering that the colonists had faced some not inconsiderable and, more importantly, unforeseen problems.

Ross 128 b was within the habitable zone of the system due to its proximity to the sun, had acceptable gravity, and sufficient water resources in the soil and atmosphere. However, this seemed to be the biggest problem at the same time. Not only then, but still today. The planet's ionosphere contained immense amounts of ions and free electrons; a fact that seemed to have been known in principle. However, during the transformation of the atmosphere into one usable by humans, a kind of chain reaction had then occurred in the ionosphere and magnetosphere, resulting in a particular susceptibility to magnetic storms. Storms that had permanently disrupted terraforming efforts and continue to do so to this day.

Adrian took a deep breath and slowly exhaled. He was no physicist and understood at best the basics of atmospheric peculiarities and properties, but even he realized that this was a worst-case scenario. Terraforming, while fundamentally a very robust and low-disruption process, was built on the premise that it could occur over an extended period of time without serious catastrophe. Since the decision had apparently been made on Ross 128 b to invasively affect the atmosphere through targeted interventions due to time constraints, this part of the process had been made vulnerable.

All other terraforming processes seemed to be affected or

at least delayed. Or to put it another way: There was sheer chaos. Nothing was right anymore, nothing worked in harmony. At this point, efforts were concentrated almost exclusively on keeping the atmosphere reasonably stable. This was achieved through the large-scale use of specially cultivated plants and the targeted injection of various chemicals into the atmosphere, made possible by immense amounts of resources. In other words, precisely what was not exactly conducive to sustainable habitability, to put it mildly.

As Adrian continued to work his way through the data, each line cemented his worst fears. The planet was not uninhabitable in the strict sense, but had degenerated into such a mess over time that fixing and resetting it alone would require more effort than rebooting afterwards. If that would even be possible. Damn it, how had those responsible allowed it to get to this point in the first place?

"You mustn't blame them," a soft voice suddenly said at the door.

Toussaint, who was leaning against the wall with her arms crossed, looked at him with an indefinable expression on her face.

"How the hell did you get in here?" was all he asked.

"I knocked, you didn't say anything, and I walked in," she replied. "You must be pretty deep in thought."

"You can obviously read."

"You can hardly avoid blaming them."

"And why shouldn't I, then?"

"Because almost none of them were trained for the mission." She tried to smile, but could not. "Feystaal told me about it. The colonization of Rossur was planned similarly to our mission. They wanted to select the crew specifically and train them from an early age - however, the great war came sooner and more violently than they had feared. They had no more time for extensive preparations. And so they filled some of the slots with the parents of the intended children to bring in healthy genes. The rest of the colony ship was filled provisionally with specialists, scientists and technicians. You can imagine that these were not good conditions. None of them were trained for this, and hardly anyone was prepared or even capable. And for that, they did at least a respectable job."

"So you did know what was happening here?" was all Adrian replied.

"Partially. Feystaal didn't tell me how extensive the problems were."

"Then I'll just blame him."

"Is it really that bad, Adrian?"

He lifted the tablet. "You read it, too, didn't you?"

"Yes. But I was hoping you, as an engineer, would see a solution."

"I do."

"But?"

"But it's going to be hard." He took a deep breath. "Damn hard. And there's no guarantee of success."

"What do we have to do?"

Adrian sighed. "Well, first of all, we need to clean up this mess. I need to get an overview of active terraforming stations and their capacities. Then it will take more detailed atmospheric analysis. These magnetic storms pose an immense risk."

"Is there anything we can do about it?"

"Maybe."

"Maybe?"

He nodded. "Yes. Cassandra, this is pure speculation. I'm not a physicist and I can't calculate this. But practically speaking, our goal must be to reduce the amount of ions and free electrons in the ionosphere. This would give the magnetic storms less surface to attack and perhaps not necessarily make them less frequent, but at least weaker. One possibility would be to artificially induce an ionospheric storm - for example, by depriving it of elemental oxygen. This is really highly speculative and just my opinion. Sato and Nikolaou should be able to say more about this. As for the rest, give me a few days."

THE FEW DAYS Adrian had originally estimated for working through all the data and coming up with a plan soon turned into a week - and then finally two. Two weeks that he spent mostly alone in his quarters, taking notes, making calculations, and working through various solutions. He had contact with the others only when it was a matter of getting opinions and coordinating.

To say that he was making good progress would have been an outright lie. The more data he received - both from the past and from current measurements - the more complex and convoluted this already more than complicated problem became. Countless individual factors had to be put into relation with each other and their respective interactions within planetary effects had to be kept in view. A Herculean task, if you will. Fitting, after all, they had come here with the *Hercules*.

One of the biggest problems, however, was not even the sheer complexity of the issue, but trying to even figure out which measures had already been taken over time and which of them were still active. Even the Council had only a limited overview at best. Actually, it bordered on a miracle that it had been possible to keep Ross 128 b habitable at all for such a long time. Most of that was due to the lingering initial successes, combined with the desperate, but in some ways still working, current efforts.

Shaking his head, Adrian put the tablet aside, reached for his water bottle and took a few sips. Contrary to expectations, he had actually gotten used to the taste and no longer felt total aversion when drinking. Which, of course, didn't mean that the water tasted good.

Right now, he felt like he would never finish. Not as if he wouldn't be able to come up with a plan, but as if it was just way too much. As if one human life would simply not be enough to think about so many things and make all the necessary calculations.

He had long since felt how much strength it cost him. Hours and hours of endless work, countless, often enough unsuccessful calculations and brainstorming. Hypotheses and theories determined every waking minute and kept him busy even in his sleep. Much of the work would have been at least somewhat easier had they been able to fall back on the very high technology that Feystaal had so meticulously presented to them so far, but unfortunately even that was a castle in the sky.

The absolute majority of the work on Ross 128 b was not done by machines, but by legions of simple, untrained workers, often enough with the simplest of means and not infrequently without a basic division of labor. Inefficiency and incompetency determined almost every step of the work. The mirror of a society that lived from one day to the next, never knowing when the fragile balance to which it owed its very existence would finally collapse. Even the flying drones and the titanic carrier ships were mere relics of the past, kept functional only with the greatest effort.

Any major action to save and stabilize the atmosphere could only be done with the direct or indirect use of countless workers - with all the consequences. Already, dozens were dying every day during the most basic activities. There was a lack of protective equipment, tools, machines. Everything. Just imagining the toll of blood that planetary measures would take made Adrian shudder. But no matter how hard he looked for an alternative, he found none.

"Morris?" Suddenly, a knock at the door. It was Aacken. "Got a minute?"

"What's up?"

"I got that directory of terraforming stations you wanted." He pulled a disk from his pocket. "It's worse than I feared."

"That's what I thought."

"It's bad."

"How bad?"

Aacken leaned against the wall beside him and crossed his

arms in front of his chest. "We don't have the basics for comprehensive terraforming."

"In what way?"

"Efforts on Rossur are currently based on two factors," he grumbled. "One is oxygen production. The plants are highly efficient, I'll give them that, but they're already barely enough to saturate the atmosphere. They seem to have failed to permanently prepare larger areas of soil for growth. Earthly bacteria do not survive here for long. At least not the ones that matter. The production facilities are shielded from the outside world. Gas exchange occurs only in the course of photo-synthesis."

"That means we can't rectify oxygen to trigger ionospheric storms?"

"Not to a sufficient degree, no. And that brings us to the second factor: the atmospheric injectors, as they call it. Currently there are only two in operation. One at the North Pole and one at the South Pole. They're good for keeping the present atmosphere reasonably stable, but they're useless for our purposes."

"Feystaal said there was sufficient capacity," Adrian replied tonelessly.

"Well." Aacken snorted bitterly. "Feystaal was wrong."

Adrian bit his lip. "Still, it must be possible. They've survived for centuries. This wouldn't have happened if they couldn't make anything happen! Somehow they managed to keep the planet habitable!"

"Yup." Aacken gave him a meaningful look. "That's exactly the point I'm trying to make."

"What are you talking about?"

"Morris, what we're seeing and what we're experiencing don't match up."

"You think Feystaal is lying?"

"If he's lying now, we're all doomed," he snorted. "No, I honestly don't think so. The terraforming data is correct. For the most part, they match what we calculated ourselves. But they just don't match the optical findings, if you will. What the colony does in terraforming is not enough for a whole planet. Especially not over such a long time. This is also true for the atmospheric chaos. Only by these measures you can't explain it. At least not on this scale. I've talked to Sato. She sees it the same way."

Adrian took a deep breath, stood up and stepped to the opposite side of the room, where he also leaned against the wall. "I would have explained it by the successes in the early days," he said.

"For a hundred or a hundred and fifty years, yes." Aacken nodded. "But not for more."

"And what does that mean?"

"It's one thing to lie, and another thing not to tell the truth."

"Aacken ..."

"No, Morris, I'm serious! You already didn't believe me last time! Don't make the same mistake this time! Damn it, you're not stupid! You've got to realize that this is wrong front and center! Something on this planet keeps the climate upright - and that's guaranteed not these miserable stations the Council has built! The colony ship was financed and sent by *Aegis Dawn*. *Aegis Dawn*, who also smuggled Toussaint aboard the *Genesis* and financed the mission significantly! We were the backup for humanity and Ross 128 b in turn was the backup for us if we failed. Don't you think such an influential industry association wouldn't dream up more kinds of rearguards?"

Adrian was already opening his mouth to retort, but then paused. He wasn't ready to claim that Aacken was right, but what he said still made sense. Especially when considered against the backdrop of the data he himself had been working through over the past two weeks. After the landing of the colony ship, the colonists had managed to make more than considerable progress surprisingly quickly. Even on the premise that they had significantly advanced technology, that was an absolutely remarkable success. But also an unlikely success? After all, the achievements had quickly collapsed.

"Assuming you're right," Adrian finally muttered, giving the German a penetrating look. "Then that would have to mean that the planet was already at least partially terraformed when the colonists arrived."

"Exactly." Aacken nodded. "The *Hercules'* terraforming unit is a relatively small, compact all-in-one device. Not nearly as powerful as what we had on the *Genesis*, but it gets the job done sooner or later. So what if *Aegis Dawn* sent over an advance party or a fully automated system to prepare for arrival and make the colonists' first years easier? Not terraforming in the strict sense, but preparing the way?"

"And you think the colonists didn't know about it?"

"No more than we knew anything about Toussaint. Or the *Hercules*. Or the *HIVE-D*. Or this planet. Even Feystaal was surprised that only we came and not the entire *Genesis*. In my eyes everything speaks for it. The ship was sent out in a hurry at that time. I think it is possible that there was simply no one on board who knew about it. That's the only way they could have survived to this day, despite their bungling."

"God dammit." Adrian put his hands over his mouth and breathed into his palms a few times, but not even that was enough to calm his suddenly frantically beating heart. "God damnit."

"Yup."

For a few minutes Adrian just stood there, breathing further into his palms, trying to calm himself and push back the cascade of thoughts that had long since threatened to overwhelm him, but he barely succeeded. And the more he thought about it, the more logical Aacken's conclusion seemed to him - and the more idiotic he felt himself to have believed Feystaal's explanations so blindly. He doubted that the Commissioner had deliberately lied to him, but that did not make the factual situation any better - and under certain circumstances it also explained the complete chaos that prevailed on the planet.

So, assuming that somewhere on Ross 128 b there was indeed a machine of some kind that had been sent here to prepare the planet for the arrival of the colonists, and assuming that it was still active, it was most likely the piece of the puzzle to solve this dilemma. Or at least to make a good bit of progress.

"We have to find it," Adrian finally said. "This terraforming unit. Or whatever it is."

"I agree. But how?"

Adrian gritted his teeth. That was a good question. The obvious solution would have been a sensor sweep from orbit, but aside from the fact that getting the *Hercules* module back in orbit would require the greatest effort, the magnetic storms would have made such an endeavor impossible anyway. This left only a search on the planet's surface. However, since Ross 128 b had just under one and a half times the radius of Earth, that would not be a quick mission.

"Have Sato try to locate an origin point via the current atmospheric readings," Adrian murmured. "Have Nikolaou help her. Maybe they can at least narrow it down. Someone on the crew is bound to be a geologist, too. Perhaps a particularly suitable point for such a machine can be located. And we need to talk to Feystaal. Perhaps there are old reports or maps we can..."

"We need Lyra," Aacken interrupted him. "I think if anyone might know something about it, it would be her. When we were with her, I had a feeling she knew more about this planet than Feystaal or anyone else."

"All right. Then you take care of our people and I'll try to get us a plane or some other transportation."

"Understood."

Without a single second's hesitation, Aacken marched out of the room. Adrian followed him on the spot and made his way to Toussaint. No one but her had a direct line to Feystaal, and if they were going to even have a chance to get started on their search in a timely manner, it would have to be with her help.

"Morris!" a voice suddenly sounded behind him, vaguely familiar. He looked around. It was Kowaliw, rushing through the corridor with quick steps, looking more than just stressed. "Morris, wait!"

"Kowaliw? What's wrong?"

"I need your help." She gave him an oddly serious look and stopped at a more than respectful distance. "I..."

"Is it urgent?" he interrupted her. "I'm looking for Toussaint right now."

"Yes, it's urgent," she growled. "Listen, I know you're busy, but it's really important. Feystaal has asked me to work with some local scientists. They're looking for ways to reduce or even cure the genetic damage from the radiation. Even through the Five system, the collapse of the local gene pool can only be delayed."

"Okay? And what can I do about it?"

"I need full access to the *HIVE-D*."

"Excuse me?" breathed Adrian. "Are you aware of what..."

"Yes, I am." she interrupted him. "Morris, I know what I'm asking of you. But this is really important. The *Genesis* was populated with 900 people who were as healthy as a horse and as genetically diverse as possible, and as far as we know, we can consider that the absolute minimum for a stable population. On the whole of Rossur there are not even half as many people whose genetic makeup has not yet been permanently damaged! We must act! What's the point of saving the planet if there aren't enough people left to produce viable offspring!"

"And what do you need the *HIVE-D* for?"

"Seriously? You ask why geneticists need genetically modified embryos? Morris, the *HIVE-D* is a god machine! With it, I might find a gene therapy to help the people of Rossur!"

"The *HIVE-D* is sealed and completely shielded from environmental influences," Adrian whispered. "If I grant you access, the seal will be irretrievably destroyed."

"So do you plan to move it to another planet? Morris, if not now, when?"

Adrian was silent for a moment, but then nodded. "You're

right. I'll grant you access, but solely for medical purposes. It's possible we may need the embryos later. Let Toussaint know. And, Kowaliw?"

"Yes?"

"It's your responsibility. Make sure neither Feystaal nor any other Fives do any bullshit with it. The *HIVE-D* stays under our control."

Chapter Seventeen

Once again, they set out on a quest. Once again, they crossed a desolate world. And once again they did not know what awaited them at the end of this search. It was like back on Earth, in that distant past that was not so long ago. The parallels were unmistakable. There a planet devastated by human hands on the brink of death and a desperate search for even the faintest glimmer of hope - and here a planet also shaped by human hands, which faced a not dissimilar end if they did not succeed in finding a solution to all the serious problems.

Here, as there, the continued existence of humanity was at stake. If they failed, they faced consequences far worse than anything that could befall them along the way. In some ways, the initial conditions on Ross 128 b were much worse than on Earth. Here, they did not have hundreds of specially trained specialists and the resources of an entire space station at their disposal, nor did they have the home field advantage. At least, if one disregarded the developments at *Sarasvati*. No. Ross 128 b met them with all the power of an alien planet.

And yet it felt unimaginably liberating. At last they became active; at last they left the confinement of the dome; at last they did something besides surrendering to lethargy and monotony.

Slowly, almost reverently, Adrian stroked his fingers over

the hull of the transport plane they had been given. A completely alien machine - one like he had never seen before. Had he not known that it had been humans who had built it, he would have thought it was the ship of aliens.

While he had always understood any form of vehicle as a tool, a means to achieve a set end, he could not help but admire the shapely elegance of this machine. Possibly an emotion due primarily to the fact that it stood in such stark contrast to the rugged nature of the planet itself.

In its shape, the transport plane - though Adrian was tempted to describe it as a spaceship, even if it was not one - was reminiscent of a curved hand axe, with the blade pointing toward the ground. That was where the craft's primary propulsion system was located: four antimatter engines that used thrust vectoring to enable vertical takeoff, precise maneuvers, and holding a position in the air. They were supported by two additional stabilizing thrusters at the tail. Between them were modular tethers and multifunction tool arms. The cockpit itself was about five yards above the primary engine and had the shape of a horizontal semicircle, providing an impressive panoramic view.

"It's a dream, don't you think?" asked Aacken at one point, also approaching the aircraft. "Better than anything we had on Earth. The maximum speed is only 990 miles per hour, but the antimatter tank - a very sophisticated magnetic trap - will last for nearly 37,000 miles."

"It makes you actually realize we're from the past," Adrian said. "This is the future. So far, I've kind of had a hard time grasping it like this, but... God ... you and I, we were born almost 3,000 years ago. This colony is perishing and can barely sustain itself. And yet it is able to build such machines. That means this technology is so basic that it can be produced even under such circumstances. Just imagine what would have been possible on Earth during that time!"

"It's bitter to think about," Aacken muttered. "Probably by now they could have cured every disease and at least colonized the solar system. But instead, they decided to wage war once again. Without sense or limits. And that's why we're here now. You know, if it wasn't so incredibly sad, you could almost laugh. Sometimes I wonder what it's all for."

"You doubt that we'll make it?"

"It's not that. If anyone can do it, we can. No, it's more a question of what's to come. Of course, I hope for humanity to recover, establish a just society, and live in peace, but sometimes I just don't believe it. Don't get me wrong: maybe it took a boom like this. Maybe it's good that there are no more states and no more ancient history; no more hatreds that go back centuries. Without covetousness and sensitivities, circumstances force us to get along. But still, when I think about what weapons might eventually be developed, I shudder."

"I know what you mean."

"You've thought about it, too?"

Adrian nodded. "More than enough."

"So?"

"I don't think it's our decision," he replied hesitantly. "Lyra is right: if we can help, it's our duty to help. Nothing more, nothing less."

"That doesn't sound like the Adrian Scott Morris I know, though."

"That's because part of him died on Earth," he returned. "And maybe that was just as well. When do we leave?"

"Everything's ready here." Aacken tapped his hand on the hull of the machine as if he were patting a horse. "Fliers, spacesuits, equipment - and even official permission from the Council as icing on the cake. As soon as the others arrive, we're ready to go."

Just at that moment, a low rumble sounded at the other end of the brightly lit hall. Immediately Adrian turned, only to see Lyra and Toussaint step through the gate and march toward them. The former was clad in a yellowish protective suit, while the latter wore her old space suit. Involuntarily, Adrian narrowed his eyes. Toussaint? Actually, it had been agreed that Sato would accompany the mission. What in the world was she doing here?

"Cassandra?"

"I'm overseeing your mission, Morris," she replied coolly.

"Oh, now I'm suddenly Morris again?" repeated Adrian incredulously. "You're not serious, are you? What did I ever do to you?"

"Nothing."

She was about to step past him, but he grabbed her arm and held her back.

"Let go of me right now!" she hissed.

"I won't do that." He shook his head. "Not until you tell me what the hell is going on all of a sudden."

"What's going on?!" She snorted bitterly, jerked away, and took a step back. "Do you have any idea what repercussions your little walk has had?"

"Repercussions? Are you mad about the warning? We talked about this, didn't we? I thought we..."

"I don't give a damn about the warning!" she suddenly roared, jerking her hands up and clenching them into fists. Though she looked like she'd like nothing better, she didn't strike. "God in heaven, Morris, you don't get it! We're outsiders! This planet is not our home and neither is the society here! We have to act very carefully so as not to cause any problems! We have to gather information and weigh our decisions carefully! And you just waltz into this village and put everything in danger!"

"In danger?" Adrian slapped his hands over his head. "Tell me, are you actually haring yourself? What in the world is wrong with you all of a sudden? It's not our damn job to take any sensitivities into account! We are supposed to save humanity! If Feystaal had spoken openly with us, this would never have been necessary! It is not our problem that the society here is unfair! If anyone is putting anything in danger here, it's the Fives and their slaveholding regime!"

"It is what it is!" hissed Toussaint. "We're not saving humanity by provoking a planetary uprising! Most people here didn't know about us, but now suddenly it's all over the place that we were sent to save them! Can you imagine the developments that have been set in motion by this?"

"That's exactly our job, too!" shouted Adrian. "That's exactly what the job description says! I... God, what am I even arguing with you for? I thought we had all this figured out!"

"But that doesn't mean your trip was without consequences! All hell is breaking loose out there!"

"The only consequence I care about is the survival of humanity! But you're an *Aegis Dawn* agent! You can't even understand that!"

Toussaint glared at him. All at once her face turned chalky white and she moved her lips as if to retort something, but no sound left her throat. For a few seconds she just stood there, horrified and stunned, before she finally rushed past him, bumping his shoulder with such force that he almost crashed into the plane.

Adrian had opened his mouth to say something to stop her and apologize, but then let it go. He didn't actually want to. He stood by what he had said. It was not Cassandra Toussaint, a member of the *Genesis*, who had just spoken to him, but Cassandra Toussaint, an agent of *Aegis Dawn*. Two obviously fundamentally different people, after he had believed until now that she could reconcile these two affiliations.

Finally, Aacken stepped past him, patted him on the shoulder, and pulled the corners of his mouth into a forced, somehow encouraging smile before following Toussaint aboard. Lyra did the same, but kept her eyes stubbornly fixed on the ground.

With a silent curse on his lips, Adrian now turned around and climbed aboard. Was he the bad guy in this story? So far, he hadn't had the impression that his visit to the settlement at the foot of the dome had had such consequences; after all, Lyra was the only one who had even noticed. But even if someone else had noticed - what should he have done? Hide in the dome and wait for Feystaal to come clean in his infinite mercy? Toussaint wasn't stupid; she had to know that would never have happened. If he hadn't escaped with Aacken and

Sato, they would still be sitting in their quarters twiddling their thumbs!

Had he possibly misjudged her completely? After he had suspected her of sabotaging the *Genesis* in the beginning, he had learned to trust her - and he had also had the feeling that she trusted him. That she had left her past with *Aegis Dawn* behind and become a member of the *Genesis*. Had he really been so wrong about her and she was really just a... What was she anyway?

There was no point to it. For reasons he obviously could not comprehend, Toussaint had decided to be angry with him and put their friendship at risk. He might not like that, but there was no way he was going to apologize for his views. And certainly not for what he had done.

With a quick glance over his shoulder, Aacken made sure that each of them was in their seat, and then powered up the engines. Almost instantly, the aircraft lifted off the ground and held position at an altitude of about six feet, while a second, but this time much larger, gate opened diagonally above them. Adrian was already expecting glistening sunlight, but instead they were greeted by total darkness. How quickly one lost track of time underground.

"The area within a radius of about 400 miles around the dome has been completely mapped," Lyra now said carefully into the silence broken only by the whir of the engines. "And there are regular survey expeditions within a radius of about 2,500 miles to locate and develop new raw material deposits. As a rule, they're pretty reliable and accurate. The area around the canyon has also been explored."

"So we have to fly a good bit before we get to the relevant search areas," Adrian grumbled. "If we at least knew when this forward team left Earth, we could calculate a landing zone. Did you witness or hear anything? Were there any anomalies in the earlier terraforming attempts, perhaps?"

"Not that I know of." Lyra shook her head, looking wide-eyed at the two screens installed in front of her seat, incessantly displaying a wide variety of readings and data. "Did Feystaal give you data?"

Toussaint nodded.

"Can I see it?"

"Hold on." She pulled a small data carrier from a pocket of her spacesuit and inserted it into a port beside her. "Here. You have full access."

"Thanks."

"Didn't Feystaal say anything?" asked Aacken suspiciously. "There are scientists here, after all. They must have noticed something! Or what about those huge flying ships? Do they have sensors?"

"The assemblers." Lyra shook her head. "They have only basic navigational equipment, so they don't crash into mountains. They don't have sensors. Their job is to pick up the drones from the mining stations and bring them to the dome."

"Council scientists have no significant information," Toussaint added tonelessly. "Which they also never explicitly looked for a hypothetical predecessor terraforming unit. Given the time that has elapsed since then, we have to assume that it may have been buried. Major seismic events occur periodically on Ross 128 b. At the same time, magnetic storms make long range scans nearly impossible. Just about all the information about the planet and its nature has been gathered locally or calculated and inferred indirectly."

"So we have nothing," Aacken summarized their statements. "Super. Let's keep our eyes open, then. Do you think they at least put up a sign so we would know when we've found the site? Or a flashing light at least? I mean, *Aegis Dawn* certainly wouldn't have sent anything here and then rendered it useless."

"You're right." Adrian leaned forward toward him and glanced at the plane's controls. "I'm sure that's not the case. So let's think about this from the other side: the unit should be able to be tracked down if you know of its existence. That's the only way to include it in the ongoing effort. So how does one find it?"

"In any case, there is no signal sent throughout," Aacken said slowly. "That would have been tracked somehow even with the magnetic storms. So maybe we need a ping to get a response?"

"I agree. Can you do it?"

"I think so." Aacken nodded. "I'm transmitting on all frequency bands. Let's see what we can get in."

"You don't have to," Toussaint said suddenly. "I would bet money that the signal is over 100 terahertz."

"Over 100 terahertz?" repeated Aacken incredulously. "That would be..."

"A call signal." Toussaint nodded. "The *Exodus* signal."

TOUSSAINT WAS RIGHT. After Aacken began sending out a ping in the 100 terahertz range every few seconds, it had taken only a few hours for them to receive a response. Because of the flier's inadequate equipment, it was not possible to derive more precise information from the signal, but the systems were at least capable of converting variations in signal strength into a kind of echo sounder. And if those calculations were correct, the signal was coming from a point a good 4,300 miles away from them, in what Lyra said was an unmapped section of the planet. A flight of more than four hours. More than enough time to prepare.

Adrian would have liked to claim that it was surprising that the facility had not been found for so long and at the same time that they had managed to track it down so easily. Only, unfortunately, he could not. Signals in such a high frequency range were simply not used. One of the reasons why they had been used as a basis for the *Exodus* signal. If this connection was not known, it probably would not have come up at all. Another reason was that most com systems were not even capable of it. The technical effort was too great. Even now, the onboard systems had suffered massive damage. But it had served its purpose and that alone was what mattered.

While Aacken piloted the plane over mostly desolate rocky and desert landscapes, occasionally dodging massive mountain ranges, Lyra worked to gather as much data as possible about their surroundings through the machine's sensors. An attempt to find conclusions about the past effects of terraforming, perhaps aiding her own efforts.

Adrian would have liked to do something similarly useful, or at least meaningful, but that was not the case. Instead, he just sat and stared out the window. No matter how many times he tried to force himself to work, he just couldn't. All the discipline that had always encouraged him to keep going seemed to have suddenly disappeared. Why? He could not say. Maybe it was just exhaustion, or maybe it was resignation.

Resignation. Yes, this feeling had been with him ever since he got on that plane. Probably even longer. The initial enthusiasm about having deduced the existence of an unknown terraforming module and having finally found out where the problems of the colonists came from had only hidden it for a short time. What else should he feel in the face of this blatant mockery, which he encountered again and again.

In the second half of the 21st century, 900 people had gone to the *Genesis* to be put into cryostasis for an indefinite period of time. None of them had had a childhood or a life outside of education. Nor had they had a choice about whether they wanted it at all. Their lives as insurance to the collective conscience of humanity, who knew full well that they possessed the means to destroy themselves in a very short period of time.

He may not have liked it, but he had always accepted his fate and submitted to a higher purpose. Always knowing that his first breath after cryostasis meant that humanity had perished. Meant that reason and charity had finally been defeated by madness and hatred. That he would always face his life under the most adverse conditions until his own death.

But if those in power in the old world had been so sure that everything would end - why had they not done more against it? Why had they not tried to fight for a better tomorrow, a better world?

Instead, they had apparently not given even the *Genesis* mission enough of a chance to fix the global cataclysm, and had decided to spend even greater resources on yet another back-up. If they had been the back-up for Earth, the colonists on Ross 128 b were the back-up of the back-up. A double back-up. One of many, perhaps?

A laugh, as involuntary as it was bitter, made its way through Adrian's throat. He would not have been surprised. Colonization of the planet could not have been particularly obvious. After all, it had been considered necessary to send an automated terraforming unit here in advance to process the planet so that it could be colonized at all. So, what if there were other colonies out there that no one would ever know about, simply because that had never been planned?

After all, there were more than enough candidates for that. Proxima Centauri b, several Trappist and Kepler planets, and all the habitable planets that had certainly been found in the meantime. Maybe there was an advanced human civilization out there somewhere that no one knew about?

"A penny for your thoughts, Morris?"

"I thought you weren't talking to me anymore, Toussaint?"

"Really?" She raised her eyebrows. "You want to get childish? Now?"

"You tell me."

"Goddamn it, Morris..."

"Toussaint, I'm not interested in a fight," he interrupted her. "But you're not my superior. In fact, I thought you were my friend. It's your choice what it should be, but if you think I have to justify myself to you, you're wrong."

"Is that what you think I'm upset about?"

"I'm pretty sure of that, yes."

"Morris - Adrian - I personally think what you've done is good, especially in terms of Feystaal finally being honest with us now. But still, I stand by what I said: None of us will get out of this alive if a riot breaks out on the planet. The social situation is tense enough as it is. The people here are not stupid. They know what's happening. And if we suddenly show up now and they think we're their saviors, it will only lead to unrest and maybe even riots - and we don't need that. For what's ahead, we need everyone to work together."

"May I speak for a moment?" asked Lyra, before Adrian could reply. "I can understand those concerns, but I think they are unfounded. As you said, the people of Rossur are not stupid. And that is precisely why we know that even your arrival will not solve our problems overnight. No one is going to start a civil war over this."

"We can't say for sure, though," grumbled Toussaint. "Even Feystaal is concerned about social injustice. How much do people have to lose who are about to die of disease and radiation anyway?"

"Their lives. Just because we don't have much of a life doesn't mean we don't like to live."

"I... That..." Toussaint took a deep breath. "I didn't mean it that way."

"I'm aware of that. I wanted to say it anyway. I think you did the right thing. Feystaal isn't stupid, and the rest of the Council isn't interested in letting the planet perish either. I think their hesitation was due to a mixture of shame and doubt. Partly because far fewer of you have come here than anyone hoped all those centuries ago, and partly because no one likes to admit that there's nothing you can do about the collapse of the atmosphere."

"It was stupid," Adrian said laconically. "Either way. We can't afford delays."

"So?" asked Toussaint.

"So what?"

"Can we make up?"

"Your call."

"Adrian, please."

"I'm serious. You were the offended one. You started calling me by my last name again. So, it's your decision how to proceed, too."

She sighed. "I'm sorry, Adrian. Okay?"

"So am I. I didn't mean to put you on the spot."

"Thanks. So? A metaphorical penny for your thoughts?"

"I was just wondering how many back-ups there might be," he replied.

"We didn't know about Ross 128 b. Who's to say there aren't more?"

"Do you think that's possible?" She asked

"At the least, I don't think it's out of the question."

"Hmm," she went on, "difficult question."

"That's it?" interjected Aacken, snorting derisively. "Oh come on, Toussaint, you belong to *Aegis Dawn*! You must know more than that!"

"You're right." She took a deep breath, was silent for a moment, and then gave a long-drawn-out sigh. "There was a third plan. Proxima Centauri b. About two years before our cryostasis, they sent out a wooden rocket full of human-Earthman hybrids."

"Oh, I'm laughing my ass off."

"The German recognizes humor? Unbelievable, this really is the future!"

"You sure they didn't go off in a space baguette?"

"Oh, are we really bringing it to that level?"

"Enough!" hissed Lyra suddenly. "Stop!"

"What's the matter? I was just kidding!"

Lyra didn't answer, but returned her attention to the sensor data, and although Aacken and Toussaint still exchanged meaningful glances, they left it at that, so that silence once again settled over the cockpit.

The next few hours passed mostly uneventfully. Apart from a few air pockets, more turbulence and the occasional evasive maneuvers when mountain massifs once again blocked their path, nothing out of the ordinary happened. In the meantime, the sun had risen and illuminated the surface of Rossur, but since there was nothing worth mentioning anyway except for dark brown rocks and sand, this did not change the omnipresent monotony.

Adrian had actually hoped to find traces of old terraforming attempts somewhere, or at least hints that the planet was not completely dead, but this hope was disappointed again and again. There was nothing out there. No water, no plants, and certainly no animals. Only wasteland and more wasteland. Truthfully, it bordered on a miracle that people lived here at all.

The only thing that occasionally broke the monotony were colorful flashes of light in the sky, which lit up at irregular intervals. Some of them flickered only for fractions of a second, while others shone in the sky for several seconds. Had the planet not been so terribly desolate, it could have been a beautiful and downright magical sight.

"You only see them in the morning and evening," Lyra said softly.

"They're beautiful," Adrian whispered. "Do you have a name for them?"

"Geomagnetic lights. On Rossur, there are an incredible number of electrometeors. You would say northern lights for them. Lightning, of course, St. Elmo's fire, airglow, and sprites. But there are also things that didn't exist on Earth. We call them Valkyries."

"Valkyries? Tell me, what are they like?"

"They look like broad flashes of lightning. They're usually blue and stay in the air for a few seconds, where they keep spreading out and then suddenly disappear. When I was a kid, I used to sit outside for hours at night and watch them. They are rare around the dome, but you still see them from time to time. It was beautiful. I dreamed of being able to fly to them one day. Since I've grown up and learned more about the planet's problems, I can't enjoy them anymore."

"Because..."

"Because they make everything go wrong," she interrupted him, nodding. "They're not solely responsible for it, and I also know they're just a natural phenomenon, but I'm still angry with them. We could be good by now, but the magnetic storms are keeping us down. Did you know there used to be a space station in orbit?"

"We saw it on the sensors when we arrived," Toussaint replied tonelessly. "What happened to it?"

"We don't know for sure to this day. It was clear from the beginning that it would be difficult. The Council's scientists invested decades in preparation. A wide variety of protective measures against the storms were tried, and in the end they were confident that it would work. Unfortunately, I don't know which way they chose. When the shuttle took off with the astronauts, I was 11."

"And then? Did they arrive? What was the purpose of the station?"

"They arrived." Lyra nodded. "The station was in operation for almost three years. There were problems here and there, but nothing serious. We, that is, the whole planet hoped that everything would get better. The magnetic storms made it almost impossible to send signals from the surface, and even more difficult to receive any. We were almost completely shielded."

"So the station was a sort of transmitting station?"

"Exactly. Some people hoped that perhaps humanity on Earth had survived after all - or that you might succeed in saving Earth. We didn't know you were still in cryostasis. At the same time, we wanted to try to better understand the magnetic storms and find a way to reduce them. But then contact broke off."

"Contact broke off?" repeated Toussaint. "Just like that?"

Lyra nodded again. "Yes. We don't know what happened. Suddenly there was no contact and no other activity that could be detected. However, there was also no cosmic event strong enough to do anything to the station. We suspect that they were just unlucky. That there was a critical error."

Toussaint said no more, and Adrian was silent as well, although he would have liked to say a few words of comfort to Lyra. That their ancestors had at least succeeded in reaching Earth and with it the *Genesis* mission. And that the *Hercules* module had at least managed to survive the journey here. That there was hope now. Hope for solving the problems and making this planet livable.

But he could not.

Yes, there was hope. Yes, they would do everything they could to track down this terraforming advance unit and with its help try to fix the chaos on the planet. They would fight to the last second to push back the magnetic storms, or at least balance them out, and create a future for the people here. Unfortunately, that was all there was to it. Nobody could say whether these hopes were justified; whether they turned out to be daydreams in the end and there was no salvation for Rossur in the first place. Or whether another catastrophe would occur that would destroy all their efforts.

Nevertheless, hope was all they had.

Chapter Eighteen

AACKEN LANDED the mighty flying machine at the base of the last foothills of a vast mountain range. With a dull jolt, its steel landing skids extended, and with one more jerk the plane touched down. It kicked up so much sand and dust that even the light of the sun was unable to reach them for a few seconds.

The origin of the signal was somewhere within a few hundred yards. Perhaps even within a mile or so, if inaccuracies and interference were considered. The fact of the matter was that there was no way they could get any closer from the air. They would have to set off on foot and search - and Adrian hoped with all his heart that a major salvage operation would not be necessary. If the terraforming unit had been buried or even dragged down by the masses of rock... He did not even want to think about that.

While Toussaint and Aacken were still busy undoing their harnesses and sealing the fasteners of their spacesuits, Adrian stood up and walked to the hatch in the side of the hull. He had no idea what was waiting for him out there - and that made him nervous. He was not even thinking of the uncertainties and dangers of an alien planet, but rather the dangers he might face because of the terraforming unit. No one could say what technical basis it used. It was possible that he was about to be hit by toxins or a form of radiation that he could not even imagine.

What worried him most, however, was whether the machine would still be usable at all, and if so, what condition it was in. There was a world of difference between its existence and its actual practical use. In the worst case, its effects could even turn out to be negative, which in turn meant that they would have to find a way to...

Adrian shook his head and forced himself to concentrate. All the worries and thoughts in the world were not helping him right now. He had to get out there, search and see for himself what was there. No more, no less. And when the airlock finally opened and he climbed down the steps embedded in the hull, he kept reminding himself of this. He was an engineer, not a philosopher.

"Aacken?" he finally asked, looking back at the German, who was also climbing out of the aircraft at that very moment. "What's the situation?"

"The signal is coming from here, but I can't tell you exactly where 'here' is. Considering the measurement inaccuracies of the sensors and the rough resolution of our makeshift sonar, I would narrow the radius down to around 400 yards. However, since we haven't seen anything on the surface, at least from the plane..." He paused and sighed softly before pointing in the direction of the jagged mountains.

Even the foothills at the bottom of which they had landed were dozens of yards high. It almost looked as if an angry god had cut notches into the rock with a sword.

Adrian struggled to stifle a curse. That was what he had feared. Even without knowing the exact composition of the rock, it was obvious that the signal had been at least partially reflected by the rock faces, which in turn meant that it must have originated somewhere in this direction. A signal in the terahertz range penetrated many materials, but not all of them. Even a small amount of metal in the rock or a large amount of water in the ground could distort the readings.

For a moment, he wondered whether this could be used to

their advantage. While metal reflected terahertz rays, water only attenuated them and was even heated by them. It should be possible to measure this effect with a signal around 100 terahertz. Although their suits shielded them from the radiation and prevented their bodies from heating up, each of them had a small water tank in their life support module. So...

Adrian shook his head. No, that was pointless. The radiation was too wide-ranging and the heating could not be measured in any meaningful way. He also thought it would be pointless to locate it using other sensors on their suits. A terahertz signal would probably simply fry the radios - which would also prevent communication. This meant they could not use technical aids.

"We'll form teams of two," he finally said. "Aacken, you with Lyra, Toussaint with me. We have to search the area the classic way. We can forget the radio."

"Do you think the signal is interfering with communication?" asked Toussaint, glancing at her helmet. "I thought these things were pretty robust?"

"Morris is right," Aacken agreed before he could reply. "Our equipment isn't designed for signals in this range. One or two terahertz, maybe a dozen - no problem. But a hundred? We..."

"Mine is," Lyra said suddenly.

"What?"

"Mine is," she repeated, lifting her helmet a little. "Since the magnetic storms sometimes rage very intensely for days on end, we had to adapt our equipment and strengthen our technology. On Rossur, it's survival of the fittest. This terahertz range is no problem, at least for a short time and at close range."

"Can you make a tracking device with it?" Toussaint asked immediately, looking at Adrian.

"We don't need to." He shook his head. "If she picks up the signal, she just has to pay attention to where it gets stronger and where it gets weaker. Good, then we'll stay together for now and hope it works. Lyra - you lead the way."

While Lyra put on her helmet and began to walk a wide circle around the flier, Adrian attached his own helmet to the side mount of his life support module. He had no idea what he had expected, but the fact that they now had to resort to such improvised methods to track down the terraforming unit frustrated him. If Lyra had not been with them, they would not have been able to even pick up the trail. He had secretly hoped that they would find some kind of facility or at least obvious traces. The fact that this was not the case and that they were now once again forced into a possibly long search ...

More involuntarily than deliberately, he sank to the ground, put his head back and looked up at the sky. Once again it was a perfectly clear, cloudless day and the sun's rays felt so warm that he could hardly bear them. There probably was not nearly enough water in the atmosphere on Ross 128b to make clouds possible. Or the air pressure conditions weren't right. Whatever it was, it looked weird and felt even weirder.

Lyra continued to walk around the aircraft, sometimes a little closer to it and sometimes a little further away. If Adrian interpreted her movements correctly, then it was already apparent that their path would take them somewhere to the right, past the foothills of the mountains, but Lyra did not yet seem sure enough to send them in that direction.

What if they found nothing? What if the unit had been destroyed or had to be destroyed to save the atmosphere? An icy shiver ran down Adrian's spine. What if they failed to save the planet? Failure had always been a possibility on Earth, and death was an ever-present, if not immediate, threat, but right now it felt so imminent. The idea that it ended just like that. Human life. Perhaps even all intelligent life in the universe. Every cell in his brain seemed to be resisting the thought; he found it difficult even to think about it. Not surprising, considering he was questioning existence itself, denying everything they did.

He clenched his hands into fists, turned his eyes to the ground and forced himself to use self-control. God, what was wrong with him? At times like this, he felt as if he was losing control of his own thoughts. Fears, worries and doubts dug into his body like pinpricks and there was nothing he could do to ward them off. He had to endure them, even if he hardly knew how. The fears robbed him of his strength; they paralyzed him.

What was different here than on Earth? There, he had somehow managed to keep his nerve. Even when they had received the first indications from *Sarasvati* that Earth could no longer be saved. Had it been the feedback loop and the knowledge of Ross 128 b that had made it easier for him to shoulder this burden? The hope that things would go on without the *Genesis*? A hope that he no longer had, now that there was no evidence that a third back-up existed?

"That way." Lyra raised her hand and pointed - as expected - past the rutted foothills to the right, while with the other she raised her helmet just enough to speak. "I'm sure that's where we need to go."

Adrian nodded to her, struggled to his feet and caught up with her, even though his entire body suddenly felt as heavy as lead. Together with the others, he made his way through the brown, dusty desert of the planet. There was no wind or anything else to be felt. Just the omnipresent, monotonous, oppressive heat. Even the air out here tasted different to that in the dome and its surroundings. Thinner. Like a high mountain range.

As they picked their way past the rocks, Adrian kept glancing over his shoulder in the direction of their plane. He was unable to say why, but every fiber of his body resisted moving so far away from it. He was afraid of getting lost in this wasteland if he lost sight of it. Ridiculous, he knew, but there was nothing he could do about it.

"Lyra?" asked Toussaint at some point when they had been walking for a few minutes. "How is it that you're so good with technology?"

"I'm observant," she replied, giving her a quick glance. She was currently holding her helmet in her hand and marching quickly through the oppressive heat. "And my father taught me everything he knew before he died. He wasn't one of the Fives, but over the years he trained as a technician. It was hard for me at first."

"Hard?"

"I didn't fit into the system anymore." She shrugged her shoulders. "At least I think that was the reason. Everyone around me had to work and most of them died in the process. I'm almost forty now and still relatively healthy. Few people live to be that old. I think many people envy me for that."

"Can you blame them?"

"There are two sides to everything. Yes, I'm older than most, but I've seen almost every one of my friends die. Even my friends' first children are already dead. I spend most of my days maintaining the equipment and machinery around the dome, trying to find out more about us and this planet. Most of the time, it's just a few steps, but over the years I've accumulated a lot of knowledge. In fact, I think few people know more about current technology than I do."

"And..." Aacken began, but then paused.

"Speak freely."

"No. I think I would offend you."

"I'll manage."

"Well - has it never occurred to you that the failure of your terraforming might be related to the fact that another facility is active on the planet? That the efforts are intersecting?"

"To be honest, yes. I've made that assumption and the Council has even sent out a search party."

Adrian narrowed his eyes. "And they didn't find anything? They must have come up with a signal scan, right?"

"That's what's troubling me at the moment."

"And what do you think?"

"Well." She stopped and turned to them before letting her gaze wander over the surrounding desert and making a sweeping gesture with her hand. "This planet is huge. I don't know if they were here. And even if they were. Our communications don't usually operate in the terahertz range. I don't even know if they would have been able to generate such a signal."

"Why didn't you say so earlier?" asked Aacken.

"Would it have made a difference?"

"No, probably not."

Adrian followed Lyra's gaze and also looked out into the vastness of this planet. A signal scan was actually part of the standard procedure for any search operation, especially if you knew you were looking for something technical. Even all those centuries ago, when he had gone into cryostasis with the others, just about every device and machine had been able to respond to such a ping. If it could. Even a terahertz frequency could not explain the fact that nothing had been found. There should at least have been some clues.

So why was that not the case here? He refused to believe in coincidence. Nor in bad luck. The survival of the planet was at stake and that had already been the case back then. They could not afford to be negligent or to search selectively. Just as little as they could afford incompetence or human error. That meant there had to be another reason.

But what was it?

Adrian bit his lip. There were many possible explanations, with varying degrees of probability, of course. He could discard most of them as practically unthinkable to impossible - while one explanation seemed to make more sense to him than all the others: What if the system had simply not reacted to signal pings before? What if it had only now been enabled to communicate with the outside world and be detected accordingly? Now that they had arrived here?

But why? Why would *Aegis Dawn* have installed such a function? It was an open secret that the reason for this was the arrival of the *Hercules*. But had anyone really expected this development? That Earth was irretrievably lost, that part of the *Genesis* would flee and arrive here at some point? But why? Why condemn the colonists and their descendants to a life of illness and repeatedly failing efforts when they could have been helped right away?

No, he couldn't imagine that. Or at least he did not want to. No one could risk the continued existence of the entire human race so lightly, no matter what the reasons. Especially since this development had been anything but probable or even foreseeable. The fact that they had not only investigated the feedback loop in Greenland, but had also flown to India, traced the signal back to Ross 128b via a completely devastated radio telescope and then survived an almost 600-year cryostasis journey across space had been impossible to predict. There simply had to be another reason for the sudden activation of the signal.

But what if there was none?

ADRIAN HAD EXPECTED MANY THINGS, but not what he now saw before him. In the middle of the rutted rocky landscape, a huge steel tube emerged from the ground. A tube that stretched hundreds of yards through the foothills of the mountains. It lay there like a snake in the middle of the rock; partly exposed and covered only by a thin layer of dust, partly buried yards deep under rock. It was completely impossible to find out where this huge structure led, because although they had found it a few minutes ago, they had not yet managed to make out a beginning or an end.

However, it wasn't even the construct itself that puzzled Adrian, but rather the fact that he could actually see it in front of him. It was a *MIDGARD*; a *Modular Incursion Device for Ground Access and Resilient Durability*. A shitty acronym. Back on Earth, when he was still training, he had spent some time working on prototypes. Especially with regard to cryonics and potentially extensive changes to the topography and other ground conditions, it was necessary to keep old facilities as accessible as possible - or to create new access even under the most adverse conditions. Nothing more than dreams of the future at the time. The best prototypes had used compressed air and plastic membranes and had been correspondingly easy to damage.

But this one... He could not help but grin from ear to ear. Obviously, it had not only been possible to construct a significantly larger *MIDGARD*, but also to enable it to withstand the most adverse conditions on alien planets. The technical finesse alone that must have been necessary for this was impressive, not to mention the implementation itself.

The principle was very simple: the aim was to keep an object - be it a plant, a spaceship, a bunker or a vehicle - accessible under as many conditions as possible. It was completely irrelevant whether it was buried, under water, in the middle of a desert or overgrown with plants. No matter what happened over the centuries, access was the most important thing. And the simplest practicable option was a modular entrance, constructed using a series of technical gimmicks so that it would remain on the surface under as many conditions as possible.

"Adrian?" Toussaint's voice reached his ear. "Is that what I think it is?"

"Yup."

"And what is it?" Aacken asked.

"A *MIDGARD*."

"Really? That's a *MIDGARD*? I always imagined it differently."

"How could it be?"

"I have no idea. Like some kind of buoy, maybe. Definitely not like that. So, we just have to look for the end of the thing?"

"Exactly."

"Wouldn't it be easier if I go back to the plane and get a plasma cutter before we run around the entire mountain range looking for the entrance?"

Adrian was just about to reply when he suddenly spotted a relatively fresh-looking deposit of rubble and boulders. It was a good distance away from them, but was remarkable if only because they hadn't seen anything like it anywhere else in the area - and that in turn suggested that the entrance to the *MIDGARD* might be nearby.

Without hesitation, he set off - and indeed, just a few minutes later he spotted a hexagonal metal capsule about twenty yards in diameter protruding from the rubble. It too was almost completely covered in dirt and dust, but unlike the rest of the *MIDGARD*, it was not buried. A constant, deep hum emanated from it, accompanied by a slowly pulsating, high-frequency whistle. The mechanisms that kept it on the surface and at the same time solidified the ground beneath it.

While the others caught up with him, Adrian climbed over the rubble and took a closer look at the capsule. It had a narrow hatch on each of its six side walls, just big enough to climb through, and on its surface were several balloon-like structures made of a material he did not recognize, which were collapsing at that very moment.

"Brilliant!" he exclaimed as he continued to stare at the capsule, spellbound.

While he could only speculate about its exact workings and the technologies responsible for them, so far at least it looked like it used some kind of pressure equalization and spontaneous gas expansion within these balloon-like containers to clear its surface of debris. And even though he could not see the underside from here, he was sure that it must have a similar system there, probably combined with a buoyancy device or even some form of thrusters.

"What a load of crap," Aacken murmured, stepping up to him with his arms crossed. "Unnecessarily complicated."

"What?" Adrian breathed. "What makes you say that?"

"Too complex. Too error-prone. These balloons are all well and good; I understand what they're good for. But I don't think they can move more than a few tons of rubble."

"They don't have to," Adrian replied. "The *MIDGARD* wasn't designed as a crowbar. It works continuously and exploits natural ground movements. There is extensive activity in the ground in any relevant operational scenario.

Maybe not right away, but even if it gets buried, sooner or later it can move back to the surface."

"And if a sufficiently heavy boulder hits it, it's scrap."

"Then everything else would be scrap too, Aacken. The fact is, we can get in here. If we manage to stop the planet from dying, you're welcome to work out a better system."

"Believe me, I will," he growled. "So - should I go back and get the flier, or what do we do?"

"It wouldn't be a bad idea to have the plane here," Toussaint said. "We could mark the spot and save the route in the onboard systems. Or do we need his help, Adrian?"

"That remains to be seen," he muttered and stepped up to one of the hatches, but no matter what he did, it wouldn't open. "It's probably better if he gets the plane."

Aacken turned on the spot, climbed down from the pile of rubble and marched back in the direction they had come from. Adrian watched him for a tiny moment and sighed silently. He could understand his objections. Such a complex system was always prone to error. But if they had decided to use it here, there must have been a reason for it. You didn't just throw an immature technology into the field and hope for the best. Even if it seemed that was exactly what had been done.

He stepped up to one of the other hatches, took a deep breath and tried to raise it, but nothing happened here either. Absolutely nothing. Although the lever came out of its holder without any problems and could even be turned, the hatch itself didn't move an inch. Adrian involuntarily narrowed his eyes and looked around, but for the life of him he couldn't see a lock or anything else that would explain this.

The third and fourth hatches did not open either, and he was tempted to yell in frustration. But with the fifth, he actually felt a slight resistance when he turned the lever. A resistance that increased with every turn until, after a few seconds, a metallic creaking sound was heard, closely followed by such a sudden and loud bang that Adrian immediately took a step back and threw his hands up to protect himself. What the hell was that?

He reached for his helmet to put it on as a precaution, but then he suddenly noticed a strange, acrid smell in the air. It was coming from inside the capsule. Clearly a chemical; some kind of gas, but he couldn't place it.

Toussaint laughed softly. "Scared? I didn't think you'd scare so easily."

"Shut up," he growled. "You'd flinch too if something exploded in your face."

"Nothing exploded, but..." She paused and grinned. "Oh God, you don't know what that is, do you?"

"Hell, no!"

"Adrian, what you smell is lithium perchlorate."

"Lithium perchlorate?" he repeated incredulously. "Wait - do you think that's..."

"Yup," she interrupted him. "Very simple oxygen candles. Makes sense when you think about it, doesn't it?"

"I didn't think they'd still be in use," he grumbled and carefully turned the lever, causing the hatch to open bit by bit. "We didn't even have oxygen candles on the *Genesis*."

"The *Genesis* was a controlled environment, with a stable power supply and monitored by a state-of-the-art AI, far away from any environmental influences," Toussaint replied, leaning against the capsule next to the hatch. "If they'd needed oxygen candles, the shit would have hit the fan, as they say. The things wouldn't have helped much there either. Whereas here..."

"They're perfect here," he completed her sentence and gave her a quick glance, which she returned with a nod. "Low interference, easy to use, reliable."

"And above all, durable and effective," she added. "Do you remember the incident on the second ISS in 2038? The crew survived for almost two weeks with just two lithium perchlorate-based oxygen cartridges."

"How do you know that?"

She remained silent.

"Toussaint?"

"Before the mission, I was terrified of suffocating in space," she murmured. "I spent days reading up on emergency procedures."

"That's cute."

"Cute? That's scary!"

"You know that of the hundreds of astronauts who launched before our mission, just three actually suffocated?"

"Yes. Soyuz 11 in 1971, but still. Fear is not a rational thing."

Adrian gave no reply, because at that precise moment the bulkhead finally swung open, revealing the interior of the capsule. He immediately put on his helmet, activated the closed breathing circuit as a precaution and switched on his lights before stepping inside and looking around.

The ravages of time had left far greater traces on the MIDGARD than had appeared from the outside. Apart from the bulkhead he had just come through and the one to the left, the mechanics of all the others had been destroyed from the inside. It was hard to tell at a glance, but it almost looked as if the metal had rusted away. The mechanical components of the remaining two hatches also looked anything but good. A result of the lithium perchlorate? He wasn't a chemist and didn't know the properties of the substance, but it would at least have been an obvious explanation.

But even apart from this damage, the capsule did not look good. The interior was dented in many places; in some places entire steel beams were broken and jutted out at him like spears. At least the entrance to the modular metal body - a simple hatch in the floor that was already open - didn't appear to have been damaged any further.

"I don't like this," he heard Lyra's muffled voice through his helmet. "I don't like this at all."

"Why not?" he asked, pulling off his helmet after she'd followed him without hers, showing that you could probably actually breathe the air in here.

"I can't tell you." She shook her head. "It's just a feeling."

"If you ask me, there's no point in us all squeezing in there anyway," Toussaint grumbled, giving him a meaningful look. "Right?"

"No, you're probably right. Lyra, you stay here and wait for Aacken. We'll go inside and see what's waiting for us. Maybe there's a better entrance somewhere else."

"Agreed." Lyra whirled on the spot and practically stormed out of the pod. "Good luck!"

Adrian snorted softly, knelt down and took a look through the hatch. Toussaint might be right in her assessment, but he didn't think that a bad feeling was sufficient justification for not helping to save their own home planet. But then again, Lyra wasn't much use to them if she lost her nerve halfway through the journey. It was probably better this way.

Under the hatch, a ladder led about twenty yards down to a point where the path seemed to flatten out again. It looked as if he would be able to move relatively unhindered even in his comparatively bulky spacesuit, but his desire to crawl for hours through a narrow tube was still limited. Unfortunately, he had no choice but to do so.

Eventually he climbed down. He was forced to put his helmet back on first; not because he needed it, but because he couldn't attach it to his suit under any circumstances due to the tightness. Toussaint followed him closely and together they climbed into the darkness. A darkness that felt like the maw of a monster. The distant screeching, creaking and howling of the metal increased to sometimes immeasurable echoes.

When Adrian reached the end of the ladder after what felt like an eternity, a winding, serpentine path opened up in front of him. Rungs were embedded in the floor, the walls and the ceiling; ways of shimmying along in any position. However, entire sections of the modular tunnel had been pushed in over and over; sometimes even boulders protruded like thorns through the weak points of the *MIDGARD*.

Adrian shook his head. All at once, it felt as if Lyra's premonition had been confirmed. Something was wrong here.

The purpose of a *MIDGARD* was to create the shortest and most effective route possible. That was definitely not the case here. They had already seen from the outside that the modules were drilling through the rock sideways for several hundred yards. Why? A mistake? Or perhaps even an attempt to counteract extreme tectonics?

Damn. Adrian felt his heart pumping a not-so-small charge of adrenaline through his bloodstream. The devil only knew what state this thing was in after all this time. If the entry capsule was already rusty, he didn't even want to imagine what it looked like in the deeper modules. In the modules that were exposed to much stronger forces - and over a much longer period of time. What if it was all in vain and at some point, they simply stood in front of an insurmountable rock face?

"Cassandra?"

"Yes?" her distorted voice crackled through the short-range radio.

"Do you think we'll find anything?"

"Yes."

"Why?"

"You're here." She laughed softly. "Ever since we woke up, you've always had the right gut feeling; you've intuitively made the right decisions. Without you, none of us would be here today. I trust you. If you don't see a reason to break off, then I don't see one either."

Chapter Nineteen

THE PATH through the *MIDGARD* was like a mixture of an obstacle course and a climb, held in a narrow, dark tube. In a narrow, dark tube from which there was no escape. Adrian hated to admit it, but even if he had wanted to, there was no way he and Toussaint would have been able to turn back. Countless rocks that had broken into the modules made the way forward difficult, but the way back virtually impossible. If they wanted to get back out at some point - if they stayed alive long enough - they would have to think of something.

Adrian had no idea how far they had already come. The darkness and the omnipresent rumbling that echoed through the modules at the slightest movement of the rock turned any sense of time into an indefinable vortex of exertion and exhaustion. Each yard felt exactly the same. An eternity that simply would not pass. An eternity that they had to conquer.

It was now obvious that something must have gone massively wrong here. Adrian had already been aware of this outside, but inside the *MIDGARD* itself it looked much worse than he had feared. The damage and obviously defective modules were one thing, but the fact that the machine had been moving practically horizontally for long stretches told him that the root cause lay much deeper. All that remained was to hope that the actual system could still be reached.

It couldn't be far now. Even though he had long since lost his sense of time, he had at least counted the individual modules they had passed on their way. So far, there had been 47 - a considerable number, given the logistical and technological requirements involved. The longer a *MIDGARD* became, the greater the chance of serious problems or damage that could affect the integrity of the entire structure. His gut feeling as an engineer told him that they must be nearing the end...

Suddenly, a yawning, abyssal darkness opened up at the edge of his light cone, and although the tunnel was practically horizontal at this point, Adrian instinctively clung to one of the rungs. In front of him, the *MIDGARD* modules continued for only about fifteen yards, only to suddenly disappear into absolute darkness. That had to be a cavern.

"Shit."

It took him more than a few seconds before he finally managed to get over himself and crawl carefully onwards. That probably explained the infernal rumbling that had accompanied them the whole time. Not rock movements from outside, as he had wrongly assumed, but rather echoes from here. Echoes that had only been amplified in the narrowness of the tunnel.

While Toussaint also began to curse almost inaudibly behind him, he continued to feel his way forward. With some effort, he managed to turn around and continue climbing with his legs in front of him. Under no circumstances did he want to risk losing his footing with his upper body first. The metal around him was already creaking so alarmingly that he wasn't sure how much longer it would support him.

The further he got, the more outlines emerged in his cone of light. What he had initially thought was a yawning abyss soon turned out to be the extension of a large cavity. A cavern that contained a large amount of debris from the *MIDGARD*. Many of it seemed to have been literally crushed by the force of the rock and torn from its moorings. Obviously there were considerable tectonic movements in this area. Or was this possibly even a consequence of terraforming? In any case, it explained the unusual path the machine had taken.

When Adrian finally reached the edge of the tunnel, which was creaking more than a little alarmingly, and took a careful look down, he recognized a huge pile of rubble, but also the shell of a larger structure next to it. Although he could only see a few square feet of it, he was sure that it must be the terraforming unit. At least at first glance, it looked relatively undamaged. Perhaps they had been unlucky?

"And how do we get down there?" Toussaint's voice brought him out of his short-lived elation and snapped him back to reality with merciless force. "Have you got a rope with you?"

Adrian bit his lip and shook his head, which of course she could not see. "No."

He refrained from saying that a rope would probably hardly help them anyway. Instead, he continued to look around and searched for a way they could still get down somehow. He was aware that this would inevitably lead to the question of how to get back, but he tried not to think about it. For now, it was important to somehow reach the unit and find out what was going on. Then they could take care of everything else. His hopes in this regard rested primarily on Aacken. On Aacken and a plasma cutter.

"There on the left," Adrian finally said, raising his hand and pointing to a narrow ledge that ran diagonally across the rock about a yard and a half below him. A relatively fresh break. "It won't be pretty, but it should work."

Toussaint squeezed past him as best she could and glanced down. "Are you crazy?"

"Can you think of anything better?"

"No, but that doesn't mean we have to do this! Let's break off and go back! Aacken is the specialist for situations like this! Let him..."

"I don't think we'll get back that easily," he said dryly. "You saw how badly the *MIDGARD* was deformed. It's one thing to go down, but even with the servos, we can't get back."

"You mean we're trapped here?"

"For the time being, yes. We can only go forward."

Toussaint mumbled something unintelligible, but said nothing more.

Adrian was fully aware that this was not the best solution, but there was nothing he could do about it. On Earth, the protocol for the *Genesis* mission would also have dictated that they continue in such a situation. When in doubt, achieving a mission objective always outweighed individual lives.

Finally, he stood up as straight as he could and stepped to the edge of the tunnel. Reaching the ledge was no problem, just like moving on from there - only getting back was an impossibility. But he could see no other way. And so he stepped onto the ledge and carefully felt his way along the wall. He found it difficult to keep his balance in his bulky spacesuit and especially with the life support module on his back, but after a few steps he found his balance and stepped to the side so that Toussaint could follow him.

But she didn't move from the spot.

"Toussaint?"

"I'm coming." She took a deep breath, which caused a low hiss in the radio. "God, I hate it."

With those words, she leapt to him and instantly clung to him, though she was standing so securely that she didn't need to. She remained transfixed for a few seconds before letting go of him and following him further down.

The rest of the way proved to be not nearly as difficult as Adrian had feared. Most of the anchors that the *MIDGARD* had driven into the stone were still in place, and where they were no longer there, they had made cracks big enough to climb along. After just a few minutes, they reached the shell of the facility, covered in scrap, debris and boulders, and more importantly, the entrance to the *MIDGARD*. Their ticket in.

"This facility is a lot bigger than I thought," Toussaint muttered as they picked their way across the hull. "If this is just part of it... This thing must be huge!"

"That was my thought, too." Adrian agreed with her.

"Although it's not surprising. Our equipment on the *Genesis* was relatively small and mobile, but there were people there to operate it and provide supplies. The manual work steps, logistics and so on - all of this has to be automated. Along with security measures, back-ups, resource depots and everything else."

"That's probably true. I..." She paused.

"What?"

"I think it's madness."

"What exactly do you mean?"

"All of it! This plant must have cost billions, if that's even enough! More like trillions! The technology, the research, the man-hours, everything! I just can't get my head around why you would take this on and at the same time not be able to prevent a war that would wipe out the life of an entire planet!"

"Not at the same time," Adrian replied. "But because."

"You think this was an act of... desperation?"

"Yes. In fact, I'm afraid this behavior is natural to our species. Basically, most people are good, kind and sincere. Only a few deliberately want to harm others. But as soon as it goes to a larger level - countries, nations, alliances - the individual no longer counts. No one could have wanted this war, but humans are good at creating mechanisms that inevitably lead to such events. Sometimes it's easier to do something like this than to try to prevent the cause."

"I don't see it that way."

"That may be, but it is what it is. You could have sat the Chinese and Mongols at the negotiating table thousands of years ago with the same reasoning. But the fact is that a gigantic wall was built. Reasonable people in the USA could have discussed the horrors of slavery and the economic advantages of a free system instead of letting hundreds of thousands of souls be torn apart in the blood mill of the Civil War. But they did not. Fear, hatred and ideologies usually outweigh reason. And this..." He stomped hard on the hull with his boot, causing a piercing, deep thump to resound.

"This is just the last resort of exactly the same inevitability. Sometimes it's easier to move mountains than to build a bridge. But what concerns me much more right now is why the *CONE* system knew absolutely nothing about this unit."

"Honestly?" Toussaint snorted. "That's more on your mind? Technical gimmicks in the face of the total annihilation of a planet?"

"Yes, actually," Adrian replied. "It's not our job to mourn the past, but to build the future. And to do that, we need to be able to rely on the tools that have been created to support us. The *CONE* system is the ultimate listening machine. It should have heard everything that happened on Earth; we should have known about Ross 128b, about the colonists and also about this terraforming unit. But we didn't. Why not? Can we even rely on that? What if there are other colonies? Maybe even on Mars? Or if information is also being withheld from us to save the planet?"

"You just said yourself that it's not our job to mourn the past."

"That's not the same thing," he growled. "It's not about mourning, it's about us getting fucked from top to bottom! How are we supposed to do our shitty job if we can't rely on anything? You can't tell me you don't see it that way! As an information technician, you of all people should know how important it is that every little part of a system works! Even a single bug can ruin an entire program! It's no different here!"

"I'm long past wanting to understand anything," she whispered after a moment's hesitation. "Adrian, I... It's probably because, unlike you, I wasn't trained for this as a child, but I find it hard to look at it all logically and rationally. That's something I envy you for. You keep going, you look for solutions and at least outwardly you keep your nerve. I notice every day that you live for this and that's remarkable. I, on the other hand, find it harder every day to understand or even accept anything. I..." She paused for a moment before suddenly spreading her arms out and turning in a circle. "I mean, look around you!" she shouted. "We're in the middle of a cave looking for a centuries-old machine! And on a planet eleven light years away from Earth! Eleven light years! That was over sixty-two trillion miles! Just thinking about it makes me dizzy, literally! I... I... Forget it, Adrian. Let's move on. I don't want to talk about it anymore."

With those words, she stepped past him and marched towards the *MIDGARD* module protruding from the hull of the terraforming unit a few yards away from them. Adrian followed her, but also said nothing more.

She was right. He was trying as best he could to approach all the problems and questions they faced with logic and reason; trying to focus on goals and outcomes rather than all the hurdles and obstacles along the way. But that's where she was also wrong, because he did it not because he was keeping his nerve, but in order to maintain it.

He, too, was only human. He too was afraid and found himself in weak moments. He, too, had doubts. Of course, he had ultimately been trained for just such a situation, albeit under different parameters. Nevertheless, that did not mean that all the horrors passed him by without a trace. The possible imminent end of humanity affected him too; he too mourned the loss of Earth and all those they had to leave behind. And he, too, sometimes wondered what the hell he was doing out here. And why he really presumed to want to save Ross 128 b with this terraforming unit.

Maybe it was better not to think too much about it.

THE TERRAFORMING UNIT was unlike anything Adrian had ever seen before - and unlike anything he could ever have imagined. It wasn't just any device, and it wasn't just a sophisticated machine, but a station. A station that was in no way inferior to the *Genesis* in terms of size or equipment. Fully automated, of course, but also designed to be entered and operated by humans. And even if he didn't like to admit it, he only had a rough idea at best of what most of the modules and systems were good for. They were too advanced and sometimes downright strange in terms of form, structure, function and operation.

Slowly and almost reverently, he made his way through the system together with Toussaint. It was impossible to estimate its size from the outside, but the sheer mass of corridors, ladders and machines inside suggested that it must indeed be as big as the *Genesis*. Maybe even bigger. It would take days to fully map it, and weeks to get through its structure. If that was even enough.

An omnipresent symphony of different noises echoed through the winding corridors, incessantly accompanied by the deep, monotonous whirring of powerful generators, which even after centuries still supplied everything with energy. Not only did the entire facility still appear to be active, it also looked fully functional. Adrian couldn't see any damage or even a hint of a malfunction in its systems anywhere.

Moreover, while he had initially assumed that it was more of an 'advance party' than a fully-fledged terraforming machine, he now realized more and more how wrong he had been. This wasn't just some atmosphere conditioner; not just a device to filter toxins from the air or initiate the first terraforming processes, but a real terraforming module like the one they had on the *Genesis*. This facility would have been capable of terraforming the entire planet without any problems, if only because of its size.

But why had it not done so?

Adrian bit his lip. It was difficult to find out more without further investigation. The only way to access all the different subunits and subsystems was through maintenance tunnels. He didn't see any consoles or computers. That probably meant that there had to be a central control unit somewhere that could be used to control the entire system. They just had to find it. A piece of cake.

"Do you think it's been buried?" Toussaint asked quietly at one point, just as they passed a row of transformers. Presumably part of the station's power supply. "That's why it's not working properly?"

"I don't think so," Adrian grumbled, shaking his head. "For one thing, I think it works exactly as it's supposed to, and for another, I'm sure that the parts leading to the outside also have *MIDGARD* technologies. Anything else would just be stupid."

"We didn't see anything on the outside."

"We weren't looking for it." He raised his hand and pointed upwards. "I'm sure the lines run through the entire mountain range."

"So we came here to explain the imminent collapse of the planetary atmosphere with a perfectly functioning terraforming module?"

"More likely that the colonists didn't know about it and made correspondingly bad decisions in their own terraforming. They..." He paused.

Just at that moment, they had entered a wider intersection and suddenly he recognized a piercing, bluish glow at the end of the corridor to his right. It was clearly a screen and exactly what they had been looking for. Bull's eye.

Without another moment's hesitation, he ran until he finally reached a sort of octagonal control room, with dozens of monitors and countless control consoles embedded there. An infinitesimally thin layer of dust had settled over everything, but apart from that, the equipment seemed to be fully functional - and as soon as he had stepped through the open door, a soft humming suddenly filled the air and the other screens lit up.

Countless lines of data gleamed at Adrian; status displays, measured values, information on power and resource consumption. Everything you could wish for. And although he had not been trained as a terraforming operator, he found his way through this jungle of data relatively quickly. The left-hand third of the monitors and consoles seemed to mainly display external readings and status displays of the internal systems, while the middle third mainly housed the control elements. On the right were almost exclusively directories for storage rooms, depots and silos - and for gene databases that were obviously available.

The most interesting feature, however, was a relatively small, inconspicuous machine that was centrally embedded in the control system. Unlike all the surrounding systems, it only had a single button, which was installed next to a hand-shaped recess. Adrian stepped closer. He could see dozens of small holes in the recess, which in turn appeared to contain tiny needle points. What on earth was that supposed to be?

"Cassandra, talk to me."

"You can conjure up a unicorn over there on the left," she hissed, stepping past him and sitting down at one of the consoles. "I have to familiarize myself first and ..."

Suddenly, the entire control room lit up in yellow light - and all the screens that had just gone up went black again. But before Adrian could say anything or even react, a whistling noise suddenly sounded.

"Welcome to this terraforming facility," came a computer voice that sounded exactly like that of the *Genesis'* onboard AI. "My name is *TAIIOS. Terraforming Artificial Intelligence Interface Operating System*. Or *TAI* for short. How can I be of service to you?"

"My name is Adrian Scott Morris," Adrian said hesitantly, looking around for something to look at, but again the voice was disembodied. "I'm..."

"Adrian Scott Morris," *TAI* interrupted him. "Engineer. Head of Module 22 of the *Genesis* space station. It's a pleasure to welcome you to this facility."

"You know who I am?"

"I have extensive databases on previous terraforming efforts. The arrival of members of the *Genesis* mission on Ross 128b was given a 25.6 percent probability according to the calculated scenarios. My protocols call for the following message to be played to you."

A soft, static noise sounded and the yellow light in the control room went out for a tiny moment, but before Adrian's eyes could even adjust to the sudden darkness, the slightly distorted image of an older, gaunt woman with stern features suddenly lit up on one of the monitors. An image that immediately made Adrian's heart skip a beat. It was Dr. Sara Abraham - the founder of the *Genesis* Project.

"Good afternoon," she said in the same monotone yet commanding voice that had characterized so much of his childhood. "If you see this message, it means that you have found a way to Ross 128b. And it also means that Earth is lost. A fact that saddens me deeply, as it means that both you and your mission have failed. I pray that this message will never be intercepted. If it is, we must find a way to open up a future for humanity beyond Earth. You are our best and possibly only tool." Dr. Abraham paused. Just as she had always done centuries ago to let her words sink in. "You will have many questions," she continued. "And despite my best efforts, I am not in a position to answer them all. The development of the future remains one of the last mysteries of mankind that we have never been able to solve, despite all our resources. Much time has passed since you went into cryostasis. Great discoveries have been made, catastrophic setbacks endured. Humanity is at the zenith of its existence. Many doubt the usefulness of the *Genesis* mission. They want to take the station out of orbit, wake you up and end our project." She pursed her lips. "A mistake I will not allow. I'm sure you've noticed by now that the *Genesis* is under the control of *Aegis Dawn*. We would never have been able to come this far and accomplish such an effort on our own. But even that is not enough. Ross 128b is the next step. Our reinsurance in case you fail. In case our descendants decide to destroy the planet, although I pray to God that won't happen. Let me start by saying that Ross 128 b is our only project of its kind. At least for the foreseeable future, we will not launch a second venture of this kind. So we must not fail here." She paused again. "In a few years, an autonomous, fully automated terraforming unit will be sent out. It will prepare the way. It is the unit you're in right now. It far exceeds the capabilities and capacity of the *Genesis* and should be able to turn Ross 128b into a habitable planet within forty years of its arrival. The colony ship will follow after extensive crew training, but no specific date has yet been set. As with each of you, it will take decades of precise selection of candidates."

"Does she always talk so much without saying anything?" hissed Toussaint.

"I must confess something to you that I don't like to admit." Abraham lowered his eyes for a moment. "The fact that you are here and see this message means, in almost every one of our scenarios, that something has gone wrong. That the colonists contacted Earth and you set off on your journey through space. That honors them, but it was a decision that will require bitter action on your part. *TAI*, the AI of this facility, is equipped with extensive sensors and will inform you of the necessities in a moment. But first, it's my turn to apologize." She took a deep breath. "During your cryostasis, extensive genetic modifications were carried out on each of you. Changes that you won't feel, but which will have a lasting effect on your genetic make-up. Genetically speaking, you are the best the human species has to offer. The latest technologies enable us to improve your genetic make-up even further."

Adrian felt his heart contract painfully. Once again, Abraham was silent for a moment, only to look directly into the camera again - and in a way that sent an icy shiver down his spine.

"Countless scenarios have been calculated, innumerable probabilities have been run through. Too many to explain here. *TAI* will tell you what to do. Always remember that your obligation is not to the people on Ross 128b, but to our entire species. Dr. Sara Abraham - over."

"What the hell..." Toussaint began, but she didn't get any further before the room was once again bathed in yellow light and the onboard AI reported back.

"My programming intends to provide you with extensive support from now on," said *TAI*. "We are currently in an Epsilon 17 scenario, sub-specification 14/27-F."

"And..." Adrian's voice broke. He cleared his throat, but barely managed to make it steady. "And what does that mean?"

"Hasty departure of the colonists from Earth. Inadequate preparation for the mission and the necessary terraforming steps, unacceptable ignorance of the necessary protocols, plus a serious genetic homogeneity. Chances of survival: Zero. Established contact with the *Genesis* mission with subsequent departure from Earth in the *Hercules* module, assumed uninhabitability of Earth. Survival of humanity on Ross 128 b must be guaranteed."

The button on the machine with the hand-shaped indentation lit up green.

"Please confirm."

"What?" Adrian breathed. "What do you want us to confirm?"

"The kill protocol."

"The what?"

"The kill protocol," *TAI* repeated. "The destruction of genetically inferior life on Ross 128b. According to my sensors, amateurish terraforming measures combined with the cosmic characteristics of the planet have resulted in almost the entire native population becoming ill in the process of genetic degeneration. It is therefore practically impossible for humanity to survive. The protocol is to release a pathogen into the air that attacks the natives on a cellular level and wipes them out within three months. Your genetic adaptation on board the *Genesis* makes you significantly different from them. A final adaptation of the pathogen to your DNA to ensure immunity is necessary as the pathogen will remain in the planet's water supply. After release, begin recolonization of the planet using the *HIVE-D* protocol."

"I'm not going to do that," Adrian said, shaking his head vehemently.

"Me neither!" Toussaint almost shouted. She stood next to him, fists clenched and breathing heavily. Her face was white as a sheet, her body trembling. "This is sick!"

"The protocol stipulates that a pathogen release can only be carried out after matching to your DNA and explicit clearance by a member of the *Genesis* mission. Please comply and then proceed with the repopulation of the planet as instructed."

"We're not going to do that!"

"In that case, I will be forced to take the entire facility offline. This will accelerate the collapse of the planetary atmosphere and also lead to the death of the people - including you. You will have four weeks. Bear in mind, however, that dying from radiation, toxins and lack of oxygen is a much more inhumane way to die."

"So you want to wipe out humanity?"

"No. You brought the *HIVE-D* to the planet intact and functional. Remote access to the database is possible and I have the capacity to birth the embryos and care for the humans long enough for them to fulfill their purpose. Before that, I can terraform the planet sufficiently. Your help is wanted, but not necessarily needed."

"Why didn't you just adjust your activities when you realized the colonists were failing?" cried Toussaint. "Why did it even have to come to this?"

"On Earth, they were able to eradicate virtually every disease and correct every genetic flaw. Humanity deserves a healthy future; a clean new start without the burden of hereditary diseases and mutations. You can become the progenitors of this new beginning."

"We won't."

"Your objection has been noted. I am programmed to give you a week to think it over. Then the system will be taken offline."

Chapter Twenty

Scenarios and protocols, calculations and probabilities. They determined the world. They decided what was and what was not. What would happen and what would not. They dictated how things had to be and what decisions people had to make for their own good. It was probably in the nature of things that humanity itself fell by the wayside.

Adrian sat motionless in one of the corridors of the extensive complex, surrounded almost exclusively by darkness and the pale light of a lamp flickering in the distance that reached him. He was alone. All alone. Toussaint was long gone. He didn't know where she had gone, nor did he care. He wanted to be alone. Alone with himself and alone with his thoughts.

Now everything finally made sense. Now he finally saw the big picture, which he had always thought he understood without seeing it. The earth, *Genesis*, *Sarasvati*, Ross 128 b. The missing data in Greenland, the mystery. Just everything. Hell, he wouldn't have even been surprised if that had ultimately been the reason for the system cascade. Who could guarantee that Abraham wasn't responsible for blowing up the modules? Perhaps the genetic transformation that had been carried out on all of them without their knowledge had failed in the modules? Worthless people, useless for big plans?

Adrian slowly turned his helmet, which he held in his

hands, until he saw his own reflection in the visor. He was a thing. A product. An artifact. Not a human being. He had been created. Not as a human being, but as an individual. From birth, he had been shaped, molded, trained and his every move predetermined. Everything he was, and everything he had, had been made by others. He was a tool with no free will, was bound and shackled by protocols and scenarios. And by thoughts that he could not even be sure were his own.

A soft, but all the more bitter sigh made its way out of his throat. Protocols. They were worse than machines, worse than any clockwork. A mechanical process did what it did because it could not do otherwise. A cogwheel could only turn and any machine, no matter how complex, was ultimately just an apparatus. A protocol, however, was worse. Its actions did not follow a blunt automatism, but were the result of meticulous considerations and calculations. It claimed to determine everything and to be beyond any doubt. Who needed morals or even free will when protocols dictated your actions?

It was actually ironic. Back when he had gone into cryostasis, protocols had been one of the few things that had given him security. Anchors to hold on to, lights in the darkness. The knowledge that, in his eyes at least, intelligent people had spent a lot of time trying to find viable solutions for every conceivable scenario under the most diverse premises.

And now? This.

He shook his head. Part of him still refused to accept what had happened. To believe what he had seen and heard. What the computer, *TAI*, had said was far beyond anything he could have imagined. And now he stood here, once again shackled by protocols and confronted with a decision that no human being should ever have to make - or even be allowed to make.

His task was to ensure the survival of humanity. To make a future possible and bring a long-dead species back from the grave. At all costs and against all odds. He existed solely for this purpose. Every breath, every heartbeat, every hand movement - simply everything he was, served this goal. He was the hammer that forged a new future; the plow that re-cultivated the fields.

And now he was also to be the scythe that, like a reaper, destroyed all those who were not good enough to experience this future?

He simply could not. It was wrong. No sane person could even contemplate such madness. Was it not exactly this kind of behavior that should be a thing of the past? In the past, delusions about genes, health and race had claimed countless millions of lives, just like every other form of hatred and exclusion. People had been enslaved, massacred and systematically destroyed because of their supposed inferiority.

And the future that ended all this was supposed to be based on just that? A pathogen that exterminated the people on Ross 128 b like vermin, simply because they had been unlucky enough to have been lied to? Because they weren't the right ones? Because their ancestors had had to flee too hastily?

No. That could not happen.

But what was the alternative? That he would sit here and refuse to do anything, no matter what happened? That he simply waited for *TAI* to take the facility offline, stop terraforming and kill all the people here just the same? The Council's facilities weren't doing nearly enough. Without the continued influence of this unit on the atmosphere, it was only a matter of a few weeks before everything perished. That could not happen either.

But was there anything he could do? His first thought was to simply destroy the *HIVE-D* or at least try to shield it from the AI's grasp. Even if *TAI* had ways of getting the module into the facility, he would at least have a basis for negotiation. However, there was also an undeniable danger in this plan. Only the devil knew what security measures were hidden somewhere deep in the systems. It was possible that *TAI* had long since taken control of the *HIVE-D* and even had remote access to the *Hercules*. Nothing would have surprised him.

"Hey." Suddenly a quiet voice in the darkness, closely

followed by slow footsteps. Toussaint, coming towards him through the corridor. Just like him, she had taken off her helmet and was holding it in her hand. "May I sit with you?"

"Go ahead." Adrian put his head back, took a deep breath and moved a little to the side so that she could sit against a flat section of wall.

"Thank you."

"So?"

"So what?"

"Where have you been?"

"I was just wandering," she whispered tonelessly, resting her head on his shoulder. "Without a destination."

"I was hoping you'd find a solution."

"Me too. The control room seems to be the only way to access it. At least as far as the system is concerned. *TAI*. All other access points are either purely mechanical or only allow limited local access to individual systems."

"You wanted to shut down *TAI*?"

She nodded barely perceptibly. "Yes. It's impossible. *TAI* has a kill switch. If I access it, the entire system shuts down. It will probably even be destroyed. It controls all the systems and every useless subroutine. There's nothing we can do."

"That's what I was afraid of."

"Then our decision should be clear, shouldn't it?"

Adrian snorted bitterly. "Should."

"But we're not going to do it."

"No."

"So we're going to die?"

"Looks like we are. Actually, it's funny."

"You think so?"

"Well." He turned his head towards her. "Funny is the wrong word. Ironic is a better word. We travel halfway across the universe to be killed by an AI that wants to force us to kill people to save humanity."

"You know Abraham better than I do," Toussaint whispered.

"As well as you can know someone like her," Adrian

replied. "To us, she was a mixture of mother, teacher and judge. Most people feared her as much as they loved her. On good days, she was the only one who showed us any kind of affection. We had practically no contact with our biological parents. But on bad days..." He sighed softly. "On bad days, I would have loved to hide from her. Nothing was good enough and no matter how hard you tried, it was never satisfactory. There was always something to criticize. Something we did wrong. She knew each and every one of us inside out. Our weaknesses, our strengths, everything. She controlled every aspect of our lives. And therefore every aspect of this mission."

"And..."

"And what?"

" Do you believe that she..." Toussaint raised his hand. "Well - that."

Adrian nodded. "Yes."

"That sounds convincing."

"I am convinced, Cassandra. If there's one thing I can guarantee you, it's that she knows you as well as any of us. Otherwise, you would never have come on board the *Genesis*. The station, the mission - they were her life. Through us, she sees herself as the progenitor of all future humanity. You are just as genetically flawless as any of us. It is perhaps to her credit that she was never concerned with ethnicity or ancestry. We had people from all over the world on board. But it was always about genetic perfection. What's happening here doesn't surprise me in the slightest."

"It's mass murder. Euthanasia."

"Yes, I agree."

"But why? Why does it have to be?"

Adrian took a deep breath. "I can't tell you. At least I don't know for sure. Abraham never had any children of her own, though there were always rumors that she once had some who died of hereditary diseases. I think she saw nature and evolution itself as her enemies. As something to be fought and conquered. She was almost obsessed with the end of the world and the new start through us. That's why we had to keep getting better. You can probably only come up with a project like this if you are inclined to be so radical."

"You're defending her right now, Adrian."

"No." He shook his head. "No, I'm not. I'm just trying to explain her."

"So she hates people because they're not perfect?"

"You could put it that way, yes."

"That's sick."

"Yes, it is."

"And this *HIVE-D*? Is what *TAI* says true? Could he use it to recolonize the planet?"

"I'm not sure, honestly." Adrian swallowed hard. "Possibly? The *HIVE-D* was always designed to be looked after by members of *Genesis*. Or at least by someone trained to do so. The embryos on board will grow to maturity within a few years of activation and will begin to reproduce, provided they have sufficient quantities of food. I don't think *TAI* is bluffing. This facility must have adequate supplies - or the capacity to produce sufficient food and water."

"Won't these embryos die if they're raised by a machine?"

"Cassandra, that..." Adrian paused for a moment and bit his lip. "They're not human. Not like you and me, at least. Abraham developed them personally. For the first ten generations, they're just organic reproductive machines. I was told they have neither free will nor consciousness."

"And you believe that? Do you really think you can just reverse engineer humans like that?"

"I don't know. Maybe? I only found out about it myself shortly before the start of the *Genesis* mission, but basically I believe Abraham is capable of anything. To be honest, I had always hoped that the *HIVE-D* would never be activated. That we wouldn't need it and that it would eventually be scrapped. And that these artificial people would never need to be activated."

"Then we'll destroy them." Toussaint stood up. "Come on,

let's go! We'll destroy the *HIVE-D*! If *TAI* doesn't have it as leverage, he'll have to find another solution!"

"Do you really think it's that simple?"

"If you'll allow me to interject?" Suddenly, the voice of the computer system echoed through the corridor. "The *HIVE-D* has long been under my control and is already on its way here. I will respond to any attempt to destroy it with an immediate deactivation of the facility in accordance with my protocol."

"Then you're destroying humanity!" shouted Toussaint. "That goes against your programming!"

"Negative. This reaction is in line with the applicable protocol. You are misinterpreting me and my behavior. As an active onboard AI of this facility, I do have behavioral routines and am capable of complex verbal interactions, but I am not an artificial intelligence as you may understand it. My behavior is bound to the respective protocols and my statements are limited to explaining them to you and requesting your cooperation, taking into account various factors. At this point I must emphasize that this is for you. Members of the *Genesis* mission. No one else."

"And if we hadn't come?" Adrian asked, as Toussaint was about to retort, and motioned for her to remain silent. "What if we hadn't received the signal? Or if Earth hadn't been destroyed? What if we had died on the way here? What would your protocol be in that case? Why did you allow humans to exist here for so long in the first place?"

"The probability of your arrival was ..."

"I'm not interested in that!" Adrian shouted and took a few steps into the corridor. "I don't want to hear probabilities, I want an answer to my question! What if we hadn't come?"

"In that case, the downfall of humanity on this planet would have been imminent. The local population is not capable of surviving on its own. Even with a stable atmosphere, their genetic disposition would lead to the collapse of the population within a maximum of 200 years."

"And if you had taken action earlier and worked with them?"

"It wouldn't have changed anything. The available gene pool was already insufficient when they arrived and still is. They were allowed to live because a technological breakthrough in genetics could not be ruled out during their existence, but it did not occur. Thus, only the current scenario offers a chance for the survival of the human species. If you had not come, humanity would have died out. Only the fact that you are here allows for a different outcome."

No MATTER how desperately Adrian thought about it; no matter how many scenarios and possible solutions he played through in his mind, in the end it all came down to one and the same decision: either he gave in to *TAI*, followed protocol and killed every human on Ross 128b, or he didn't and would still kill every human on the planet, including himself. Either way, the future was not built on humans at the end of millions of years of development and selection, but on artificially bred test-tubes, of which no one knew whether they would actually be able to procreate or even be viable, despite the highest expectations. Or whether they would actually produce fully-fledged, genetically diverse and, above all, conscious human beings in ten generations.

The decision was obvious, and even if Adrian still told himself he hadn't made it yet, he secretly knew what he would do: he would not give in to *TAI*. He would not give up his humanity and become a mass murderer, he would not be responsible for a planetary genocide. Perhaps, given the circumstances, it was better for humanity to perish anyway. Such hatred could not be allowed to persist, regardless of whether or not it was carried over from the past into the present. A person with an intact conscience could only make one decision. All logic, all protocols and all rational judgment could not change that.

Somehow it felt liberating. Even if he hadn't done anything yet. For the first time in his life, he was making a decision on his own responsibility. No. Not just that. He wasn't just making a decision, he was going against everything that had defined his life so far. He rebelled against protocols and the madness that underpinned them. He would have given a lot if it hadn't meant the probable end of humanity, but that was no longer in his hands anyway.

He and Toussaint had long since made their way out of the terraforming facility. Not through the *MIDGARD*, but via a narrow maintenance tunnel that ran alongside an atmospheric injector and would probably take them somewhere in the higher regions of the mountain range. But that didn't matter to them. The main thing was that they could finally leave this cursed place.

TAI hadn't tried to stop them and hadn't said another word to them. Why would he? It wouldn't have changed anything if he had kept them here and forced them to make a decision. He followed his protocol. An automaton, nothing more. If they left the facility and talked to the others about what they had found out, there was at least a chance that one of them would try to save their own skin and activate the kill protocol in their place. Even if Adrian doubted that with all his heart. Or at least wanted to doubt it.

Eventually, they reached the end of the maintenance tunnel. In front of them was a small hatch set into the side of the wall, which opened automatically as soon as Adrian stretched out a hand towards it. As expected, it led to a relatively high mountain spur, and as he climbed out and looked around, he saw dozens of small and large shafts, pipes, valves and other outlets all around him, blending almost seamlessly into the surrounding terrain. They too seemed to use some kind of *MIDGARD* technology, albeit on a much smaller scale.

"There," Toussaint said tonelessly, pointing down the mountainside to their right towards a metallic shimmer in the distance. "That must be Aacken."

Adrian squinted and tried to make out something in the

shimmering heat, but apart from the gleam, he couldn't see anything. Nevertheless, he was also sure that it had to be Aacken. It was a long way, but they had little choice. The plane couldn't possibly land up here.

"Aacken?" Adrian pulled on his helmet and activated the radio. At the moment, he didn't care whether the system's signal was still active and was destroying the technology or not. After all, there would soon be no one left to use it anyway. "Aacken, can you hear me?"

"Morris, is that you?" his voice rushed out almost instantly. "Where are you? Is Toussaint with you? We..."

"She's here," he interrupted him. "We're on the mountain and we're coming to you. Aacken, it looks bad. We..."

"I know."

"What?"

"I know, Morris. The system - *TAI* - has contacted us. We've been listening to your conversation."

"That..."

"You made the right decision."

Adrian fell silent.

"Morris, listen." Aacken took an audible breath. "The *Genesis* mission was already dangerous. The fact that we survived this suicide mission for so long is nothing short of a miracle. It was foreseeable that it would end sooner rather than later."

"And what about Lyra?"

"I heard it too, Morris," Lyra replied quietly. "You should do what it takes to save humanity."

"We should what?"

"You should release the pathogen," she whispered. "The computer is right. Our society is dying. Better this than a slow vegetation. At least this way we know that humanity will survive and someone will build on our previous work and create a home worth living on..."

"Lyra, we're not going to do this!" growled Adrian. "We didn't come here to kill you!"

"We're going to die either way. At least save what can be saved!"

Adrian was about to open his mouth to say something in reply, but then let it go and deactivated the radio link instead. He didn't have the energy to discuss it with her. With her or with anyone else. He could hardly bear the situation as it was.

Suddenly there was a brief touch on his shoulder. Toussaint, who reached out for him and held him back. She had pulled her helmet off her head, looked at him expectantly and finally gave him a barely perceptible nod. Sighing softly, he did the same.

"What is it?"

"What if we activate the kill protocol without activating it?"

Adrian narrowed his eyes. "What's that supposed to mean?"

"I've been thinking." She glanced over her shoulder, almost as if to make sure *TAI* wasn't listening to her. "In computer science, there's a way to crack a system that can't be cracked any other way: you follow its instructions while trying to trick it into doing what you want. So what if we try the same thing here? After all, we don't have much to lose. It doesn't matter if we die a few days earlier or later."

"What do you have in mind?"

"Well. *TAI* says the kill protocol must be activated by a member of the *Genesis* mission so that the pathogen is adapted to us and doesn't infect us. After all, it would be negligent to develop a substance centuries ago that is supposed to work so precisely today. So we can take advantage of this adaptation."

"And you think this machine in the control room is creating a genetic profile?"

"Exactly. You saw all the needles yourself."

Adrian was silent for a moment and looked down. "So we're not fundamentally immune to the pathogen, but some kind of exception is programmed into us. Something that is tailored to our DNA to spare us. Presumably the mechanism by which it enters cells. At the same time, all other people who do not share these characteristics are killed. So the exception is based on the genetic changes that were inflicted on us aboard the *Genesis*."

"Which means that the pathogen is basically adaptive," Toussaint took over. "A neutral medium, so to speak, that is adapted. All we have to do is establish the natives as the basis - or rather their DNA."

"Which would mean that we die."

"But they live."

"Don't you think *TAI* would recognize such an attempt at deception?"

"That's the point." A smile flitted across her lips. "We're not deceiving him. He's getting our clearance, just under different premises. He certainly has some kind of pattern of our DNA as a reference point, but we were in cryostasis in orbit around Earth for almost 2,000 years and then another 500 on the way here. Despite all the shielding measures, we have been exposed to quite a bit of cosmic radiation during this time. Don't even get me started on *Sarasvati*. What will *TAI* do if it doesn't like our genes? Kill us anyway?"

"Probably."

"Well. Then at least we've tried. Adrian, I know I'm not a geneticist. I don't know much about it; hell, I don't even know if it can be done. But if we have any chance of outsmarting *TAI*, this is it."

"Then we need Kowaliw," Adrian said simply. "She's our geneticist. If there's anyone who can help us, it's her. However..." He paused.

"What?" Toussaint asked immediately.

"We can't let any of the others find out about this." He gritted his teeth and clenched his hands into fists. The fact that he was even saying this disgusted him. "I trust them, but we can't risk ..." He fell silent again.

"I understand," said Toussaint quietly. "Lyra could be a problem."

Adrian nodded. Lyra certainly meant well in her own way, and her selflessness in the face of humanity's impending doom honored her, but ultimately she didn't understand much about the complex processes and problems that made up this situation. Her almost naive willingness to make sacrifices was easily capable of forcing *TAI* or a member of the *Genesis* mission to act - or even worse: to cause unrest among the local population. They could not and must not allow this to happen under any circumstances.

But what were they to do? Just abandon them in the desert? That was not an option. She had to understand how complicated and confusing the current mixture of facts and assumptions was in view of the complex underlying processes. It certainly wasn't going to be easy for her, but she simply had to understand.

"I'll take care of her," Toussaint finally said. "For now, I'm not particularly useful. You and Kowaliw need to find a way to make our plan work. Everything else is secondary."

"Let Aacken explain it to her," Adrian replied. "He can handle it. You need to talk to Feystaal."

"Do you think he'll help us?"

"Any other scenario means his death."

"True again." She snorted bitterly. "All right. I ... God, are we really doing this? Is this really happening?"

"We have no other choice."

"That's not what I mean," she muttered, sinking to the floor. "I just feel like a world is collapsing around me right now. It's so unreal. Do you know what I mean? Somehow you believe that everything has to be okay. That things won't turn out so badly. Regardless of whether you believe in God or not, somehow everyone is convinced that it has a purpose and has to go on. That it can't just be over. There is always someone who knows better. Someone who has the situation under control and knows what to do. Someone who knows a solution, even if it might not be pretty. And now? There's no one here. It's just us."

Adrian sat down next to her and put a hand on her shoulder, but said nothing. He knew exactly how she felt and would have given a lot to be able to say something comforting. But he couldn't. It wasn't that there was no one left. Quite the opposite: Abraham was still there and from the grave tried to direct the future according to her will. She knew what to do and it would have been easy to follow her and save herself while an entire planet died.

That is what made the decision to defy her so difficult and the consequences of her actions so unpredictable. They went against the only person who could present a viable solution. For the simple reason that this solution was wrong - in so many ways that you couldn't even name them all. Adrian didn't know of an alternative, and neither did anyone else. Perhaps there was none at all. But that didn't change the fact that the proposed solution couldn't be implemented without betraying everything that made humanity special.

After a few minutes of just sitting there, they finally got up and made their way to the plane, still shimmering in the distance. It was time to leave this mountain and with it this cursed facility for good. An escape, no less, even if they tried to disguise it as resistance.

Adrian was aware of this. He knew the consequences of his decision and the infinitesimal chances of success of any alternative. Nevertheless, it felt good. He knew with every fiber of his body that he was doing the right thing. And that he would rather live a few more weeks and die with his head held high than spend a lifetime knowing that he had wielded the scythe that would end humanity.

Chapter Twenty-One

"I'VE GOT to hand it to you, Morris." Kowaliw laughed softly. "You have courage."

Adrian looked up, but before he could return her gaze, she had long since turned around and gone back to her work. Her fingers flew across the keyboard, typing at breakneck speed, which he couldn't even begin to understand.

It was completely impossible to interpret her facial expressions. It was somewhere between stoic concentration and eyes narrowed in annoyance. Nevertheless, that had just been the first time in hours that she had said anything at all - and it hadn't just been an unintelligible mumble, but a sentence explicitly directed at him.

"I don't think it has much to do with courage," he said laconically.

"Yes, it does," she murmured without taking her eyes off the screen. "Courage is when you do something to help others in the face of the most adverse circumstances, even if it means harming yourself. That's the textbook definition."

"Then you're brave too."

"I should hope so," she snorted. "I'm programming our death here right now."

"So it's working?" he asked hopefully.

Kowaliw pursed her lips and paused for a tiny moment before shaking her head almost imperceptibly.

"No?"

"Morris, what I'm doing here is extremely complex genetics. Whether it will work or not, I can't tell you."

She grabbed the screen and turned it a little to the side so that Adrian could see a series of different data and a schematic representation of a double helix in which some segments were highlighted in red.

"This is my own DNA. After you gave me permission to work on the *HIVE-D*, I took a sample to assess the effects of cosmic radiation. To be honest, my jaw dropped at first glance."

"That bad?"

"Bad is the wrong word. More like unexpected. These are massive mutations in the genetic material that I actually thought were impossible. It's impossible to predict the exact effects in such a short time, but what you said explains it. I was obviously subjected to intensive gene-scissor therapy. There is no other way to explain such radical changes. The same thing must have happened to you and the others. And therein lies the problem."

"You can't decode it?"

"At least not as precisely as I would have to in order to get a reliable result." She sighed, leaned her head back and massaged her temples. "It would take too much time to explain everything to you, but roughly speaking, I don't know which segments this pathogen will target. It's definitely a biological warfare agent. Something that acts quickly and is difficult to treat, plus it spreads easily via water and perhaps aerosols. *TAI* has access to both. In addition, the agent must not mutate so that it does not pose a threat at some point in the future. The genetic focus narrows it down further. Specially bred spike proteins would be possible. I'm going out on a limb here, but my personal guess is massively reengineered prions."

"So the pathogen attacks the brain."

Kowaliw nodded. "Exactly. Morris, what I'm seeing here is - to me - absolute madness. Genetics must have made immense progress during our cryostasis. Normally I would have had all the time in the world to read out the data from the *CONE*, but like this ... We can forget it. We simply don't have that much time."

"Kowaliw, I need a statement. Can you do something or not?"

"Maybe. With a big question mark. Before *TAI* took control of the *HIVE-D*, I was able to collect some data on the embryos and their genetic characteristics. They have the immense advantage of partially adapting to existing environmental conditions. A rather complicated process. I can definitely work with that. I will use my own DNA as a sample."

"Do you have any native reference points?"

"Feystaal has provided me with extensive databases."

"Good, then..."

"Morris, wait." She grabbed him by the arm and held him back as he was about to stand up. "This is important. On Rossur, there is not one genetic change that affects all humans, but many different ones. I'll do everything I can to find the most general and widespread factor possible, but even in the best-case scenario, tens of thousands will die."

"Better tens of thousands than hundreds of thousands." Adrian gritted his teeth. "Do what you can."

With these words, he stood up and left the room crammed with computers, laboratory equipment and other devices, where Kowaliw had been working for three days without sleep or rest to put Toussaint's plan into practice. Given the extremely short time and the sheer recklessness of what they were about to do, she had come a long way, but still not far enough.

The one week *TAI* had given them to think it over was already half over. And although Adrian was doing his best to remain hopeful and was doing his utmost to further their efforts, he could feel himself getting increasingly nervous.

They were running out of time. No, it wasn't just running out. It was slipping through their fingers like water.

Toussaint had persuaded Feystaal and, through him, the Council, to place all available resources at their disposal, but by God it still was not much. Not only were there hardly any geneticists on Rossur capable of even assisting with such complex analyses, but the planet's genetic research as a whole was at best on par with what had existed on Earth in the past. Quite apart from the fact that they could not allow the Council to collaborate on a large scale anyway, they did not want to risk *TAI* finding out about their plans through possible system access.

At the same time, the *HIVE-D* was probably the most effective tool they possessed. *TAI* had actually succeeded in bringing it under his control. According to Feystaal, the dome's drones had gone AWOL during their absence. While the majority of them had crashed and caused chaos, some of them seemed to have lifted the *HIVE-D*, which had been loaded into a hangar in the dome, and carried it away. A demonstration of power by the AI, as Adrian was fully aware. The embryo database itself was of secondary importance at best, but this action was intended to show him and the others what kind of opponent they were up against.

Groaning softly, Adrian sank into a small seat in the wall, leaned back and buried his face in his hands. Like Kowaliw, Toussaint and everyone else who knew about their plan, he had been on his feet for days. Right now, he would have given anything to have more to show for it. But while he hated to admit it, it looked bad.

The uncertainty as to whether Kowaliw would be able to produce reliable results was one thing, but even that was only one of far too many problems. *TAI* had effectively check-mated them - and with such playful ease that Adrian would have liked to scream. The fact that the AI was only following protocols that had been tailored precisely for situations like this didn't make things any better, but actually underlined his helplessness.

Even if everything worked as they had imagined, no one could guarantee that *TAI* would not see through the deception. Although he would also strictly follow his protocols for the release of the pathogen and the preceding genetic analysis, this was precisely what posed such a great danger. Depending on how extensive and precise his analysis skills were, he would see through them and then react as instructed, which in turn would result in the death of every human on the planet.

It was actually a battle they could not win. And the fact that they had to fight it at all was blatant madness. How could it be that supposedly intelligent and foresighted people had not only planned such madness, but also pursued its implementation with such merciless determination? Humanity even managed to hate and destroy itself from the grave.

"Morris, is that you?" a voice suddenly echoed through the corridor. He leaned forward, only to catch sight of Sato marching towards him with quick steps. She was wearing her spacesuit with her helmet in one hand.

"What are you up to?" he greeted her.

"Can't I go for a little walk in my work clothes?" she replied with a grin, but he immediately saw how difficult it was for her to feign a good mood. "I've just come from one of the Council's shipyards. I had a look at the ships. And I have an idea."

"An idea?"

"Mmm." She leaned against the wall opposite him and folded her arms in front of her chest. "The *Hercules* is more or less mothballed. The module can barely take off under its own power, but is otherwise fully functional - and still has the cryo-capsules and our portable terraforming unit. So what if we could avoid our imminent and seemingly inevitable death after all?"

"And how do you envisage that?"

"We go back into cryostasis. The *Hercules* is explicitly designed for this and still has enough antimatter to keep the module active for almost another thousand years. The necessary repair work is limited. And although the Council's ships are not designed for interplanetary travel, they are capable of taking us into orbit and past the magnetic storms."

She paused for a moment.

"Morris," she whispered now, looking him straight in the eye. "I've done the math. We could make it to Proxima Centauri. A new planet, no legacy of Earth. It won't be easy, but with the *Hercules* as a base and the mobile terraforming module, we could make a new home."

"You really think we're lucky enough to survive a century-long cryostasis for a third time?"

"It's a better alternative than waiting here to die. If *TAI* releases the pathogen, we have our suits to protect us from it for the first few hours. But if I've understood correctly, this stuff stays in the water permanently. We can't stay here either way. So why don't we risk it?"

"We'd have to tell the others what's going on."

"So you really don't trust them?" All at once, her face turned deadly serious. "Morris, we grew up with these people! If we ever had anything like a family, it was them! Every one of us was trained to give our all and save humanity! If you don't trust them, you can't trust Toussaint or me!"

Adrian remained silent.

"What's going on?" Sato asked immediately, giving him a suspicious look. She stepped away from the wall and straight towards him. "Damn it, Morris, what's wrong? What did I miss?"

"Nothing," he replied after a moment's hesitation. "You didn't miss anything."

"Then what's going on?"

"I don't know. I'm tired and exhausted. Somehow I can't even imagine that anything is still going well."

She squatted down and took his hand. "Then trust me."

"I'll try," he said, trying to force himself to smile, but he had no idea if he succeeded. The corners of his mouth felt leaden.

"Not to mention that we're going to die either way," she

grinned and stood up. "I'll prepare everything and let the others know. And if anyone tries to give *TAI* the go-ahead for mass murder, I'll break their nose myself, I promise."

"Well then," Adrian grumbled. "Do you need help?"

"The *Hercules* is practically ready to take off and I can manage the little things that still need to be done on my own. The Council's engineers have already been working on getting it back into orbit anyway. Now it's just a matter of making the rest work."

With these words, she turned around and marched back in the direction she had just come from. And when she finally disappeared around a corner, Adrian suddenly felt a wave of relief wash over him. Until now, he had been so firmly convinced that the *Hercules* could no longer take off anyway that he hadn't even considered the possibility. Although he dreaded going into cryostasis again and once more exposing himself to the waves of fate, it was still a thousand times better than dying here.

Proxima Centauri it was. There was probably no other planet that had been so glorified for potential colonization, even though hardly anything was known about it. Even the mere suspicion that life was possible on it had made it the focus of countless books and films thousands of years ago. However, even being classified as a habitable planet did not mean that the local conditions guaranteed that it was habitable. It was just a possibility.

Adrian laughed softly. He felt a little like he was playing Russian roulette: ever since they had woken up, they had been putting the proverbial gun to their temples and pulling the trigger. First with the risks they had taken on Earth and especially in *Sarasvati*, then with the flight to Ross 128 b and now this. Even if they were outrageously lucky and actually survived the journey to Proxima Centauri, it would take nothing less than a goddamn miracle for them to make the planet habitable with nineteen people and a single terraforming module.

But only the devil knew whether they would even get that far.

He shook his head and stood up. It was idiotic to worry about it. First they had to solve the many problems on Ross 128 b before they could worry about something like that. And they still had a lot of work to do before they could do that.

TEN HOURS until the deadline expired, *TAI* took the facility offline and condemned every living being on the planet to death. Hardly enough time to even reach the terraforming facility, let alone enter it and put their plan into action. But that wasn't even the biggest problem. No. The biggest problem was that they still had nothing to show for it, apart from the *Hercules*, which was ready for launch and mounted on a Council carrier ship.

Sato had been right. None of the crew had uttered a single word of doubt or even contradiction. Instead, the others had also worked day and night, doing everything humanly possible to support Kowaliw in her work. Unfortunately, they had not been able to contribute much and by now the geneticist had been locked in her study for more than a day.

Adrian knew that the others were becoming increasingly nervous. The expiry of the deadline and the impending atmospheric collapse were fraying their nerves, and the knowledge that they were ultimately sacrificing their own lives in vain and solely for the sake of moral integrity did the rest. Nevertheless, they kept calm, endured the gnawing uncertainty and faced the impending end without fear. That alone honored them more than anything else.

Adrian was no different. Together with Toussaint, Sato and Aacken, he stood by the plane, fully equipped and ready to take off as soon as Kowaliw called. If she did. So far there had been complete radio silence and she had not responded to any attempts at contact, but she still had some time. 27 minutes, to be precise. Then they would take off without her and make one last attempt on site to stop *TAI* by blowing up the control room. With any luck, they would then be able to get the facility back online, even if they didn't have the faintest idea how that would work.

Adrian knew that this plan was nothing more than a chill pill. Something they told each other to cling to. A last hope that kept them from drifting off into the sea of despair. But it was fragile and he felt it with every fiber of his body. He was trembling. He had been since yesterday. And his heart was racing constantly. It was a state of incessant, omnipresent, merciless tension.

"She won't come," Toussaint growled when Kowaliw only had ten minutes left. "Even if she reports now, we won't be able to load her equipment in time."

"She'll come," was all Aacken said.

"How can you know that?"

"I've been praying."

"What?" she snorted derisively. "You can't be serious!"

"It's better than not praying."

"It certainly couldn't have hurt," Sato grumbled in a voice that was far too thin. "Come on, Aacken, let's get everything ready."

The two climbed into the plane.

"What do you think?" Toussaint now asked, looking at Adrian. "You know her better than I do. Do you think she..."

She paused, because at that very moment the gate to the hangar suddenly opened and Kowaliw came running towards them. Her eyes were bloodshot and had circles so dark that they almost looked painted on, but a triumphant smile graced her lips. Adrian immediately turned around, climbed aboard and held out his hand to the geneticist so that she could pull herself up. And no sooner had Toussaint followed them than Aacken let the engines roar to life and took them out of the dome and into the air in a breakneck maneuver.

"And?" Sato demanded to know. "What have you got?"

"I have incorporated some of the mutations shared by

large parts of the native population into my DNA and coupled them with the modifications that were inflicted on us in cryostasis," replied Kowaliw, breathing heavily. "If my calculations are correct, we will save about 70 percent of the people on Rossur."

"Wait!" Adrian said immediately. "You've incorporated the mutations into your DNA? Doesn't that mean that you..."

"Mhm." She closed her eyes. "Believe me, I feel the same way. But that's okay. If I can stop this shit like this, I'm happy to."

"Can't you undo it?" asked Aacken from the front. "You got the mutations into your DNA - can't you get them out again?"

"No. It's a rapidly progressing genetic degeneration. The natives have adapted to it to some extent over the years, but that doesn't apply to my body - especially as I had to retain the existing changes. Think of it like when Europeans first came to South America: Diseases that they got away with relatively easily almost wiped out the indigenous people."

"Can't we treat that? We have doctors with us! They must be able to do something!"

"You can only delay the inevitable." Kovaliv took a deep breath. "But I don't want that. I'm not coming with you when you leave. I'm staying here."

"Kowaliw ..."

"I won't discuss it, Aacken," she replied calmly. "Thank you for your concern, but my mind is made up and I want you to respect it. I've worked far too hard to argue with anyone now. Let's get this over with."

Adrian looked at her. Only now did he notice how pale, exhausted and sick she looked. Her skin reminded him of Lyra's, and her cheekbones were much more prominent. Even through her suit, he could see how hard she was breathing and how much strength it was costing her. Beads of sweat glistened on her forehead. Was it possible that the genetic deterioration was progressing so quickly? That her body was collapsing so quickly? He didn't know, but he hoped with all his heart that there had been no other way. That it was not just the crunch for time that had forced her to make this sacrifice.

There was a heavy silence for the rest of the flight. No one said a word, even though it felt like there were a thousand things Adrian wanted to say to Kowaliw. Words that expressed his gratitude; that told her that he appreciated what she was doing, even if that was far too weak a word. Perhaps something he could comfort her with. But no matter how hard he tried, he could not manage to say anything. The silence had an indescribable power.

At some point, Aacken finally began the landing approach, but Adrian immediately saw that he was not heading towards their last landing site or the entrance to *MIDGARD*, but towards the mountain spur where he and Toussaint had left the facility a week ago. A daring maneuver, but given the ever-shrinking time window and Kovaliev's obvious exhaustion, it was the only option left to them.

"This is as close as I can get you!"

"That's enough!" Adrian leaned to the side and opened the hatch. There was a drop of almost two yards next to the plane, but at least the surface there wasn't too steep. "We'll stay on ambient air as long as we can! As soon as *TAI* releases the pathogen, we'll switch to our tanks. If all goes well, we'll make it to the *Hercules* in time. Let's go!"

With these words, he dropped out of the plane and hit the ground almost instantly. The servos of his suit howled, but with their help he managed to keep his balance. Toussaint was the next to jump, and together they caught Kowaliw, who followed a few seconds later. Sato was the last, and no sooner had she left the plane than Aacken turned and held position a few dozen yards away from them.

Adrian immediately heaved open the access they had come out of a week ago and climbed down. This time it was Kowaliw who followed him first - if she lost her strength, he was best placed to support her. The narrowness of the shaft and his servos should be enough for that. Nevertheless, he hoped that it would not come to that and that she would make it under her own power.

"*TAI*!" he shouted as soon as he reached the end of the shaft, and Kowaliw plummeted as soon as she had left the ladder. Although she was still standing on her own two feet, she was clearly swaying despite her suit and the servos. There was no way she was going to manage the remaining distance under her own steam. "*TAI*! This is Adrian Scott Morris of the *Genesis*! We've come to activate the kill protocol! Do you hear me?"

"Welcome back, Adrian Scott Morris," *TAI* replied. "It is my pleasure to welcome you back to this facility. Please identify your companions."

"Iris Sato, Cassandra Toussaint and Irina Kowaliw."

"Your presence alone would have been enough to activate the kill protocol, Mr. Morris."

"I am the last remaining geneticist on the *Genesis* mission!" Kowaliw suddenly said in a surprisingly firm voice. "We discussed the activation of the protocol at length and came to the conclusion that I alone am responsible for it. The *HIVE-D* is my responsibility and therefore also the recolonization of the planet - with everything that is necessary for it."

"Adrian Scott Morris has been identified as the primary interactor of this facility."

"Adrian Scott Morris is not responsible for this!" barked Kowaliw with unmistakable anger in her voice. "I may not be a module leader, but I alone am responsible for this decision! Besides, I have studied the genetic disposition of the surviving crew members in detail; my DNA is best suited for adapting the pathogen!"

"Please wait a moment. Your statement is being processed."

"You don't have to process anything!" shouted Kowaliw. "An Epsilon-17 scenario with the subspecification 14/27-F is still ongoing! It envisages the native population being wiped out and the *HIVE-D* being activated under our supervision! The probability of survival of mankind increases immensely

BRANDON Q. MORRIS & DOMINIK A. MEIER

if we as humans control the growth of the test tubes! You will accept my DNA!"

TAI did not respond. Adrian immediately felt his heart begin to beat even faster than it already was. He looked around for help, but neither Toussaint nor Sato seemed to know what to do with the situation. Damn it, what if the AI refused? What if there was a protocol for this exact situation and it saw through their deception? What if...

"Confirmed," *TAI* finally said. "Deviations from protocol and scenario are within acceptable parameters. Irina Kowaliw is designated as the primary interactor of the facility. Please proceed to the control room and activate the kill protocol. The time limit set for you is hereby paused until the protocol is activated."

"Is the *HIVE-D* okay?" asked Adrian as he and the others made their way towards the control room. He wanted *TAI* to believe at all costs that they were serious, and that meant they had to behave as a possible protocol had calculated their behavior. So if they really wanted to activate the kill protocol, the future of humanity rested solely on the *HIVE-D*.

"The database is intact and undamaged. It is located in a separately protected part of this facility and will be released once the kill protocol has been activated."

"We'll continue to use the planet's old infrastructure for now," Toussaint said. "Especially the dome. The protected environment increases the embryos' chances of survival and reduces harmful effects from the radiation. Once the protocol has been activated, you will take the *HIVE-D* there."

"Understood. However, please keep in mind that this facility is easily capable of providing care."

"We are aware of that. The dome is still more suitable. We had the opportunity to inspect it in detail. Above all, the auto-mated production capacities allow us to quickly terraform the planet. We need your help with this. The climate and atmosphere must be stabilized and further improved as quickly as possible."

" Affirmative. I will provide you with override modules.

306

Install them in the control systems of the existing terraforming facilities. I will add them to my measures if possible or take them offline if necessary."

"And how long will it be before the planet is habitable?"

"Earth-like conditions will be achievable within about forty years. According to my records, the colony ship was in possession of extensive gene databases of various plants and animals, just like the *Genesis*. I propose to use this facility to begin cloning and reintroduction in thirty years according to the *Genesis* terraforming protocol."

"Understood."

Adrian bit his lip, but said nothing. He wanted to believe that everything would be fine, but he doubted that he was lying to himself. Right now it looked as if they would succeed in deceiving *TAI*, but sooner or later the AI would find out what was going on. That the *Hercules* was gone and only the locals remained on Ross 128b. What would happen then? Was there a protocol for that too? One that included the fact that the AI had been tricked? He would not have been surprised. The only question was whether Abraham would accept it or destroy everything in her anger.

Unfortunately, that was something he could not discuss with the others. Right now, they could only do what they had come to do. And by now they had reached the control room.

Kowaliw now stepped hesitantly towards the machine in the middle of the consoles. She barely managed to stay on her feet, but when Adrian tried to help her, she immediately told him not to. Instead, she looked back at him one last time, made eye contact and smiled before taking off her glove and placing her hand in the recess. A soft, rapid clicking sound was heard on the spot. She sucked the air between her teeth with a hiss, but after just a few seconds there was a bright beeping sound and the button next to the well lit up green. She pressed it without hesitation.

Adrian immediately reached for his helmet and put it on, just like Toussaint and Sato. Only Kowaliw remained motionless in the center of the control room before she staggered to the side and slumped to the floor at one of the consoles. Her lips were blue and her face almost snow-white. And although pain and exhaustion were clearly written in her eyes, she smiled.

"So you sacrificed yourself for the people on Ross 128b," a voice suddenly rang out, almost making Adrian's blood run cold. Dr. Abraham's face flickered up at him from one of the screens. "I didn't think it was possible, but here we are and you're hearing this message."

"This can't be happening!" Adrian exclaimed. "Good God, this simply can't be true!"

"Part of me is angry that you are so recklessly jeopardizing the future of humanity and disregarding my clear instructions," Abraham continued undisturbed. "Your entire existence serves this one purpose alone. You are to save humanity. However, I must admit that I appreciate your finesse, as well as your will to protect your fellow human beings from harm. That is something very human."

She paused for a moment and finally raised a stack of papers to the camera.

"I've got a good eighty pages of calculations here about what I should do now. Each of them concludes that I should release the pathogen in an unstable wild form to cleanse the planet. You and your comrades will die anyway. Actually, I should bet on the *HIVE-D* and start all over again in ten generations with *TAI*'s help. But I won't. I've been watching over you and *Genesis* for decades now, and in that time I've realized that no matter how many protocols I work out, in the end I won't be able to steer the future in the right direction. I have to trust. In those who are yet to come - and in you. If you see a reason to do what you are doing, then I have to trust you and hope that you see opportunities that I can't." She paused again. "When this message is played, all logs and scenarios will be erased from *TAI*'s database and its functions will be limited to saving the planet and making it habitable - regardless of who inhabits it. I would be lying if I said I wanted this outcome, but it is what it is. I have done what I can to create a future without disease and suffering. A future with as many opportunities as possible for our species. You have decided that it should not be like this. You bear the responsibility."

The transmission ended. For a moment there was a droning silence in the control room, but then a muffled noise sounded. It was Kowaliw, who had slumped to the floor. She was dead.

Epilogue

ONCE AGAIN, Adrian looked at the prepared cryogenic capsule. Everything was different and yet so much the same. Once again, he would climb into this cold, dark coffin and fall into a deep sleep, not knowing what awaited him when he woke up - or whether this time the infinity of the universe would swallow him up for good on his way. Nevertheless, it was different. This time he knew it would be his last journey. Not only because he would not undergo the rigors of cryostasis a fourth time, but mainly because the technology and machinery were not up to the task.

But that was okay. No matter what happened and how it ended, it was okay. He had done what he had to do; he had done what he had been trained to do. Not on Earth, but here on Ross 128b, but that made no difference. The goal of the *Genesis* mission had always been to save humanity, and even if he couldn't say that for sure, he had at least given it a chance. That was all he could do; his raison d'être had been fulfilled.

And now? Now he had to find a future for himself and the others. After Kowaliw's death, only 18 of the 900 were left. The vast majority had died centuries ago on Earth; a few had not even survived the initial cryostasis, and they had buried Kowaliw at the foot of the dome. A few hundred lives for all that was to come. A fair trade. They could not claim never to have doubted or despaired, but they had faced all their worries and fears and overcome them. They had made decisions that had put their own lives in danger and often cost them. And even though they and their mission would probably be forgotten in a few generations, it was something they could be proud of. Everything that came next was their work.

They had decided to leave the *HIVE-D* on Ross 128b in the care of Lyra and those she deemed suitable and trustworthy. As soon as the atmosphere stabilized, they would activate it and introduce the offspring into the gene pool of the native population. That was all they could do for the planet and humanity. A justified hope that it would be enough, but ultimately, just like everything else, just a hope. One chance among many. Something that Kowaliw had given her life for. It had to work.

No one could say exactly what the future would bring for Ross 128b. The Five System and the severe social inequality were based on the planet's hostility to life. If this disappeared and the *HIVE-D* introduced healthy genetic material into the gene pool, the system was bound to collapse. Whether for better or worse, no one could foresee. But that was how life worked. It was change. A perpetual selection. Not only of individuals, but also of everything they created.

Adrian felt a smile flit across his lips. There was a certain anticipation in him. An anticipation of Proxima Centauri and what they would find there. The thought of terraforming a new planet for the first time without having to consider the legacy of old wars and tragedies was exciting, even if they only had basic and at best limited options at their disposal. Even there, no one could say whether they would succeed, but the very thought of such a carefree new beginning held an undeniable comfort.

"So, here we are." Toussaint stepped up to him. A smile graced her pale, exhausted face, but not even her smile could hide the tiredness in her eyes. Just like Adrian himself and everyone else on board the *Hercules*, she was wearing only her underwear, ready to go into cryostasis. This ship was the last place on the planet where they could breathe without masks. "It feels weird."

"Yes." Adrian returned her smile. "Yes, it does. But it's also good."

"Are you nervous?"

"I'm not sure if it's just nervousness or fear."

"I can understand that. I feel the same way. I've just spoken to Feystaal and the crew of the ship that's taking us into orbit. We' ready. As soon as we give the signal, they'll take off. Sato has programmed the course to Proxima Centauri."

"Do we have a tolerance for delays?"

"Forty years. Plus-minus."

"Not exactly a lot."

"No," she sighed, "I'd prefer a hundred, but it is what it is. We've come this far, it just has to work out. It's not like we have any other choice. Feystaal has even offered to refill our tank with antimatter that they extract locally, but Aacken says the systems aren't compatible."

"They are compatible," Adrian replied. "It's just that we don't have enough time to adapt them. It's okay. Forty years is a long time. I think it's like you said a few days ago."

She returned his gaze with wide eyes. "What did I say?"

"That it can't just be over. I think you're right. You can never control what happens. Sometimes you're lucky, some-times unlucky. So much and yet so little time has passed since we woke up in orbit around Earth. We have achieved unimag-inable things and overcome immense obstacles. I want to believe that we have earned it, that things are going to go well. And if not... well. We won't be awake to see it."

"That's what I think, too." She laughed softly. "But I'd like to live a little longer. Adrian, can I ask you something?"

"Always."

"When we get to Proxima Centauri - if we get there - and if all goes well ... Do you think you and I... We..." She paused.

"Are you asking me out right now?"

She looked down and blushed. "Yes. None of us can

foresee what age we will reach. We could die at any time. Kowaliw's death showed me that even with the best intentions and plans, we can never know what will happen. Or what we have to do so that the others survive. I don't want to be just a tool, Adrian, I want to be a person. And I don't want to spend what little life I have left alone."

"I'd love a date," Adrian replied quietly. "That's a nice idea. Now I have something to look forward to when I fall asleep."

Toussaint smiled. "Thank you. It's almost time now, isn't it?"

"We can leave anytime."

"Why don't we?"

"You know that feeling when you're a kid and you don't want to sleep despite all the tiredness? When you feel like you're missing out on something and just can't bring yourself to lie down? That's how I feel right now. I'm waiting for something that I know won't happen. I've been hoping all along that Feystaal or someone else will come through the door and tell us the pathogen is gone. But that's not going to happen."

"At least not quickly enough," Toussaint whispered. "I've also thought about whether we should just stay on the planet or in orbit and wait for it, but the devil only knows how long the pathogen will stay in the water. We have no future here."

Adrian took a deep breath. "Then we shouldn't waste any more time."

"I agree." All at once, her face became completely expressionless. "I'll let the others know. Will you give Feystaal's people the signal?"

"Yes. And Cassandra?"

"Yes?"

"Good luck. I'll see you soon."

"I hope so, Adrian. I hope so with all my heart."

Afterword

Dear readers,

Thank you so much for following the dramatic story of Adrian Morris, which Brandon Q. Morris and Dominik A. Meier have written for you - and for us. We, that is Joshua Tree and Brandon Q. Morris (the very same), the founders of the publishing house that published this book.

As we ourselves are internationally successful with our books, we want to open up this perspective to other authors from all over the world. We bring exciting science fiction books to the market.

We also have a request: Did you like the book? Then please leave a review, the easiest way to do this is via this link: a7books.com/links/4047916

Thank you!

Joshua Tree & Brandon Q. Morris

Extract: Sol in Flames

10-11-2210, Elysium City, Ares Corporate Republic, Mars

THE SOFT SOUNDS of music caressed Kareena Toran's auditory center, freeing her neurons from the hectic activity of the previous workday. All the dossiers, status reports and crisis meetings gradually disappeared from her typically hyperactive mind. A majority of her colleagues used Lullaby or other tranquilizers to quiet their synapses tormented by the constant flood of information. Kareena resorted to the blessings of modern pharmacy only in emergencies. She doubted the product reviews from the advertising strategists, according to which the development of any physical or psychological addiction had been completely ruled out, even with regular use. Observation of her milieu fueled her mistrust, as many of her acquaintances could not sleep at all without sedatives. Kareena preferred music in order to put the stress and strain of the past shift behind her. Preferably, neoclassical works like Janarov's symphony 'Lost World', which she was listening to now. It was one of her favorite pieces. She had stored it directly on the internal memory of her cortex implant. This was not technically permitted since the implant was property of the Cynarian Corporation, but she allowed herself this little insubordination with a reasonably clear conscience. Her job occasionally took her to areas where she could not access the ComNet from which she normally downloaded her music. In such remote places, she did not want to miss out on a few cultural comforts.

The tranquil harmonies of the Polish composer fed directly into the auditory cortex of her brain without a detour via the ears. True music connoisseurs branded this procedure a barbaric sacrilege, but Kareena did not especially care. She just wanted to relax after more than twelve hours on duty, and the neural interface certainly served that purpose.

She had closed her eyes and turned off all visual input from the interface, giving herself completely over to the melodies. Images of endless, untouched forests, meadows on gently rolling hills, villages scattered across the landscape with red gabled roofs and pointed church steeples appeared in her mind's eye. The whole scenery spanned by a blue sky over which the fluffy white swabs of fair-weather clouds drifted. She had once seen an interview with Ilian Janarov, in which the composer described how he had been inspired to write his music by old films and records. Although he passed away decades ago, he too had never seen with his own eyes the idyll whose indescribable beauty he wanted to reproduce with his compositions. Already in the early 22nd century, when Janarov had created his works, that world was irretrievably lost. Kareena herself knew it only from films and documentaries. She had already visited Earth, and what she saw there had made it seem impossible that the wonders the records showed had ever existed. The very title the Pole had given his symphony summed it up rather concisely. The song 'Lost World' had struck a chord and made his name immortal. Unlike Janarov himself, who, despite the wealth he acquired, refused up to the end of his life to submit to the cell refreshers and gene modifications that would have enabled him to continue his work even now. Instead, he had freely surrendered to the deterioration of old age and eventually death. His popularity had not diminished with his demise. Quite the contrary. He became the idol of the Naturalist movement, which labeled him the champion of their war against the alienation of humankind from its origins.

Kareena did not think much of these archaic ideologies. She had been born on Mars, and from early childhood involved in the world of the corporations, who pushed with all their might for the technological progress that the naturalists rejected. Of course, she too regretted that the paradise of Earth's past no longer existed. It would be nice to know that somewhere in the solar system there was a place where one could walk barefoot across dew-damp meadows, under the warming rays of the morning sun. But it was now in the past. And moreover, the past of a distant celestial body, far from her. Kareena did not approve of the militant enthusiasm of the naturalists. It was a pure waste of time and other precious resources.

The lovely sounds of the symphony faded away from one moment to the next. In its place, the implant fed a call signal into her audio center that abruptly ended the wandering of her thoughts. For a moment, Kareena felt disoriented. She had been on the verge of dozing off for good, and now she abruptly snapped back into reality out of the world of dreams. She had limited her accessibility status to emergencies only, so whoever contacted her had better have a good reason.

She opened her eyes, but only dimly perceived her surroundings. Sleep, which she had already halfway approached, would not let her go without a fight.

All right. The hard way, then.

With minimal concentration, Kareena sent a nerve impulse to the drug dispenser in her abdomen. Immediately, a cocktail of stimulants poured into her veins, spreading across muscles, organs, and brain with each beat of her heart. Within seconds, any semblance of fatigue and disorientation fell away from her. Her vision cleared, showing her the disarray in her quarters. She hoped no one would show up unannounced. It would take more than a few minutes to clean up enough to let guests in.

Pensively, she opened the call channel.

Her voice had not quite recovered from the wake-up call. The brusque "Yes?" left her throat with a harsh, ominous undertone that her throat microphone relayed unfiltered to the caller.

"Please excuse me, ma'am." She recognized the voice of Lieutenant Carrough, who had replaced her as shift supervisor about an hour ago. Following his voice, his image also appeared in the data stream. The implant projected it directly into her visual cortex. Carrough had the same radio implant as she did, but he used his workstation's ComLink, including the camera. The call's signature confirmed that he was in the Department of Internal Security's communications center. An official emergency call of the highest priority - it must be something extremely important.

"It's okay, Steve," she reassured her obviously flustered subordinate. He knew how she could react to unwelcome disturbances of her quiet time. She assumed he had thought it through before disturbing her. "What's going on?"

"We have a request from a task force from Sector Eight."

Sector Eight. Better known as Hades. The worst sector in the entire colony - a nest of squalor and rampant crime. A world of its own that gave the city's administration the finger. Not even the security forces went in there without a good reason.

"Which task force?", Kareena inquired. "The one that was supposed to be looking for the runaway mutant?"

"Affirmative."

She had supervised the launch of the operation herself. The sergeant in charge had years of experience and should have no problems with such a routine task. She had turned over responsibility for the proper execution of the job to Lieutenant Carrough without hesitation. It seemed that everything was not going according to plan after all.

"What happened? Is the squad in trouble?"

"No, ma'am, no casualties. And no difficulties. At least not in terms of its safety. But they did discover something ... unexpected. I think you should take a look for yourself."

"All right. Send it over to me!"

"It's better if you come here. The matter is potentially ... volatile. I recommend using only the highest security channel for this."

That meant the message could not be sent over public lines. This ruled out Kareena's radio implant as well as the ComLink in her private quarters. The highest security level was typically used only for messages that called into question the security of the colony itself. In her entire career, Kareena had experienced only a handful of such messages. And none of them had been addressed directly to her. For a moment she doubted Carrough's judgment, but the young lieutenant was one of the most conscientious members of her unit. He must have really come across something out of the ordinary.

"I'm on my way," she said as she rose from the bed. Then she disconnected.

Hastily, she once again donned the service uniform that she had carelessly thrown over the back of the chair when she arrived home. Fresh clothes would have been in order, but she was seriously perturbed by the distress call and did not want to waste time trying to gather new things in the general chaos of her quarters. She felt uncomfortable in the uniform she was wearing, as she always attached significant importance to an impeccable appearance. But an emergency was indeed an emergency.

Leaving her quarters, she dialed into the transport system via the ComLink in her head and ordered a top priority transport pod. Not cheap, but in such cases the corporation reimbursed the cost. With long strides, she hurried along the corridors. At this hour, the lights had dimmed. If there was no access to daylight, it was at least possible to maintain the illusion of day and night.

Upon her arrival at the terminal of the apartment block, the capsule was already waiting. The group of three standing in front of the boarding gate blatantly scowled at her. Because of Kareena's priority capsule, their transport was delayed. But none of the waiting people dared to say anything. The Internal Security uniform instilled enough respect in any civilian to keep their own opinions to themselves.

In a practiced motion, Kareena held her forearm with the implanted ID chip up to the scanner. Within half a second, it confirmed her identity and cleared access to the pod. She took a seat on one of the two opposite benches and gave the three civilians another apologetic smile as the hatch closed again. She had already set the destination when she ordered the transport, so the capsule began moving immediately.

"Maximum speed," she ordered. The controls of the transport tube responded immediately to her command. The capsule did its best to make the ride as bearable as possible for Kareena. With each acceleration and braking maneuver, it turned in such a way that the passenger was merely pressed into the seat and not thrown around wildly. Nevertheless, it required a stable stomach to endure such a ride unscathed. Kareena was fully occupied with keeping her dinner down while the capsule raced in a confusing zigzag course through the tube labyrinth of Elysium City.

Elysium City. The uncrowned metropolis of the Ares Corporate Republic. Home to nine million people, almost a tenth of the total population of Mars. Next to Selene City on Luna, it was one of the largest cities beyond Earth's surface. A sprawling collection of mostly subterranean habitats whose lack of urban planning revealed itself, among other things, in the wildly branching tunnels of the ever-expanding transportation system through which Kareena sped.

Four minutes later, the final braking maneuver indicated the end of the torture. Kareena rose from the seat and squeezed out as soon as the hatch opened. Two heavily armored guardsmen from the USI affiliate InterSec watched her closely. The one on the right raised his hand in salute.

"Captain Toran," sounded from the helmet speaker.

She knew the voice but could not assign a name to it offhand. To use her internal memory would have taken several seconds, which she did not want to invest currently. She limited her answer to a curt nod and strode toward the entrance to the communications center. The ID scanner once again scanned her forearm and released the door when it was sure that she had the necessary authorization level.

There was obvious commotion inside the control center. Typically, only the low hum of the air conditioning filled the room, as all communication took place via the implants that every employee possessed. But today, more than half of those present had left the ergonomic recliners, and were standing in a frantic cluster around the workstation of the shift supervisor on duty. The animated discussion died down when Kareena entered the room. All faces turned toward her. Deep relief showed on Steve Carrough's features. So far, she had come to know the young officer as exceptionally competent. Seeing him display such emotion troubled her.

Briskly, she approached the group. "Ladies and gentlemen. What seems to be the problem?"

Lieutenant Carrough saluted curtly. Some of the others also straightened themselves halfheartedly. As Kareena ignored the salute, the rest of the security team also put protocol aside.

"It's best if you look at it for yourself." Carrough pulled a data cable from the headrest of his chair and offered it to her. She took it and, without hesitation, plugged it into the jack behind her ear. It was a bit reckless to start a full sensory simulation while standing. But it seemed inappropriate for her to sit down in the chair while everyone was standing around her. She held onto the neck rest with one hand. That would have to do.

The interface recognized her after a quick neural scan and transferred the overview menu to her brain. The priority message from the patrol in Sector Eight dominated the display. She opened the channel and was immediately connected to the patrol leader. The image from his helmet camera fed into her visual center. The connection was not good at all. Amongst the constant image interference, she made out the heavy body armor of the security team. The cones of light from their helmet lamps fell on the walls of a narrow room crammed with all sorts of objects that she could not identify at first.

"Captain Toran," the patrol commander greeted her. The nervousness in his voice was unmistakable. "Sergeant Martinez here. Good to see you."

"What's going on, Martinez? Have you found the fugitive?"

"No. Not yet. But we've made a discovery here ... I've prioritized this and called off the search for the fugitive for now."

Slowly, Kareena grew impatient. "What did you discover?"

"It's best if I just show you."

He pushed one of his men aside. Several people became visible from behind the hulking body armor. They squatted on the bare floor of the room among stacks of empty fast-food wrappers and other nondescript clutter. Foremost, a woman sat there. The loose coveralls she wore could not hide her stocky physique. Her nearly hairless, angular skull covered with grayish skin left no doubt. She was a mutant. Beta-class. A worker, and possibly an escapee as well. Many escaped mutants hid in Sector Eight. However, she was not the person the patrol had been looking for, as Kareena remembered that it had been a man. So far, still nothing special.

Behind the woman, two other figures crouched, looking fearfully into the policeman's spotlight. They were smaller and wore little more than rags on their bodies. Their skulls were also covered only by a few hairs. Their skin possessed the typical gray coloring. A thin plaited braid fell over the high forehead of one of the two. Kareena had seen mutant children before. But so far, only in the breeding farms of the corporations that produced them. A terrible suspicion took hold of her.

Her eyes fell on the woman again. She was carrying something in her arms. A bundle of rags and plastic. She held it close to her chest, trying to hide it from the beam of the spotlight that shone in her face. Sergeant Martinez's armored hand came into view. Relentlessly, his steel gloves grasped the bundle. The woman struggled, twisting to the side to protect the thing in her arms. Martinez grabbed her by the shoulder and pulled her forward again. "Easy. I'm not going to hurt him," his tinny voice rang out from the helmet's speaker. Gingerly, he reached out two fingers to the bundle and carefully pushed aside the top layers of plastic wrapping. A small nose emerged, a pair of narrowed eyes. With a distorted grimace, the tiny creature complained about the harsh lighting. A tortured mewl sounded from the toothless mouth. Martinez had now fully exposed the baby's head. The angular skull shape was unmistakable. The gray skin stifled even the last doubt. "Shit," was all Kareena could say. "Fucking shit!"

10-13-2210, King Christian X Country, Greenland, Earth

The rain pounded relentlessly upon Skip as he marched across the bare rocks. Each of the freezing drops bounced against his skin like a projectile, driven by the hurricane-like storm that swept over the prospectors' camp. Like his two companions, he was clad in thick protective clothing, but unlike the others, he had not closed the visor of his helmet. At the beginning, his inclination to subject himself to the unleashed elements of the earth without necessity had been met with a general lack of understanding. Some had smiled at him; others had thought him downright mad. Meanwhile, most accepted that he simply wanted it that way. That he wanted to feel the world that surrounded him with all his senses. For that, he was also willing to endure pain - only to a certain extent, of course. He was not a masochist. The pinpricks of the raindrops on his face, however, still belonged to the category that he found distinctly pleasant. The water on his skin connected him to the rain, to the wind that swept the drops almost horizontally across the land, to the low-hanging clouds that the storm swept overhead. Even to the sea from which the clouds had been created. He was part of a world in which everything was interconnected. He felt this world so directly that it made him shudder.

He set the welder down next to one of the truck's eight man-sized tires. Mace silently lowered the new drill bit next to it. The giant swayed his head left and right. The cracking of his neck vertebrae drowned out even the whistling wind. Jorge, meanwhile, climbed silently into the cab of the crane, started the electric motor and swung the boom to the side. He lowered the boom until it dangled above the ground at head level. Skip gave him a thumbs up. The hum of the engine died, and Jorge came back down. He paused briefly as a particularly strong gust nearly blew his helmet off his head.

"Crap weather," he grumbled.

Skip grinned as he got the welding torch ready for use with well-practiced movements. Unlike Jorge, he could hardly get enough of the unfettered forces of nature. For most of his life, he had shut himself off from his surroundings. He had had no choice. The hostility of outer space to all life prevented any closeness. Even the thick skin, sturdy bones, and increased cell regeneration that the genetic designers had given him could not protect him from solar storms, near-absolute zero temperatures, and the vacuum. His life had been dependent on the thick armored bulkheads, electromagnetic radiation shields, and pressure locks that had always isolated him from his environment.

But now he found himself on Earth, there was breathable air everywhere instead of the unforgiving, hostile void that lurked beyond the outer hull of the interplanetary tanker that had been the closest thing to home for him until six months ago. To be sure, in some regions of the globe, contamination with toxins and the radioactive remnants of the nuclear adventures of the 20th and 21st centuries were quite hazardous to humans. But during that time, Greenland had still been a nearly deserted frozen wasteland, largely spared from the escapades of mankind. Moreover, Skip's cells were far more resistant to the effects of radioactivity than those of natural-born humans. For him, the fresh air was harmless. Even though this was something that he first had to learn with some difficulty.

He still remembered well the panic he had felt when he had stepped outside for the first time in his life. He remembered the effort it had taken him to brave the open sky, and the indescribable feeling of the cold wind on his hands, on his face. It had taken him almost an hour to build up the resolve to pass through the door that separated the safety of the interior of the building from the unruly world outside. But with each day he spent on Earth, his instincts had made it easier to accept that leaving the protective shell of steel and concrete did not mean immediate death. Even after more than half a year, the unfiltered sight of the sky and the sheer vastness of the open landscape still filled him with trepidation, but he had learned to channel the fear and banish it to a region of his mind where it did not interfere with his actions. Despite his success so far, it was not nearly enough for him. He wanted to rid himself of that fear completely. And what carried him further to that end was direct confrontation with the object of his fear. Meanwhile, he enjoyed the fight against instinct which had long been instilled over decades spent in pressurized capsules and hermetically sealed habitats. He had now pushed his limits in terms of overcoming fear to the point where his need for protection against the onslaught of Earth's atmosphere was in some areas even less than that of his comrades who had grown up here.

And incidentally, this was how he had earned his reputation for being one tough son of a bitch.

Skip pulled the darkened goggles down from his helmet and over his eyes, then turned on the plasma torch. The heat from the flame, barely the size of his fist, hit his face which was unprotected except by the welding goggles. The bright, flickering light was reflected on the helmets of his companions, who pressed the two pieces together. Jorge held the frame that hung from the crane in place. Mace closed his giant hands around the new chisel and heaved the heavy piece upward by a foot until the edges rested on top of each other. Skip positioned the radiant blue flame and joined the two pieces together. Wisps of steam rose where the rain met the glowing metal. The weld was certainly not a masterpiece, but it would hold. Mace twisted into another position to keep the rain off with his massive body. It only helped to a certain extent. After a minute, Skip could see the giant's arms begin to shake under the weight. The Alpha-class worker made no sound, as usual, but he wouldn't be able to withstand the strain forever. Skip hurried to weld the last few inches, removed the plasma flame from the metal, and watched its color change from white, to red, to a dark, gritty gray in a matter of seconds. With his left hand, he gestured for Mace to carefully lower his load. He surveyed the weld from all sides as the tension slowly increased. It looked good.

Skip waved his hand, and Mace finally let go. The chisel held - at least when it was hanging loosely on the crane. They had done their part, but the drill crew would do the final stress tests. That certainly would not happen today, as the storm was getting stronger. This had also been the last work of the shift for the three-man repair team. Jorge was already making his way back to camp. Mace fixed the frame so it wouldn't be blown around by the wind. Skip took another deep breath of the ice-cold, rain-soaked air. Then he grabbed the welder and trotted after his giant comrade, back to the containers of the prospecting camp. The half-cylinder-shaped mobile shacks clung tightly to the bare rock. It almost seemed as if they were ducking under the storm. The beginnings of wet snowflakes mingled with the raindrops. Tomorrow morning, snowdrifts would probably pile up on the downwind side. The short Arctic summer was over and the ice that had held Greenland in its cold stranglehold for ages would soon return. At least for a fleeting interlude. In the long run, however, the ice would lose the refuge it had thought secure. Every year, the mighty inland glaciers retreated further. Sometimes only a few hundred yards. In warmer summers, sometimes several miles. And every year they revealed another strip of virgin land that no prospector or miner had ever seen. For resource-producing corporations like Skip's employer, Ascon Industries, Greenland was an unopened treasure chest. Hundreds of prospecting camps, like the one Skip was heading toward, pushed further inland each year, drilling test holes, drawing up prospecting plans and making profitability analyses. In their wake, mines, drilling stations and all the rest of the resource extraction infrastructure swept the country to satisfy mankind's insatiable hunger for the earth's treasures. Compared to the staggering yields of extraterrestrial mining in the asteroid belt and the other colonies in the solar system, this was peanuts, but Ascon and its terrestrial competitors did their part to at least somewhat reduce the dependence of terrestrial nations and corporations on imports. Only in this way was it at all possible for nations such as the European Federation, the Arctica Bloc, the American League, or the Yamato Empire to assert their political sovereignty against the transnational corporate giants of the colonies. The fact that Skip was thus countering the market leadership of his former employer, the near-omnipotent United Space Industries Corporation, had only seemed like treason to him at the very beginning. Ultimately, he didn't care who paid him. He was simply doing his job.

But that job was now over for six months. The six-month prospecting shift was nearing its end. The camp would soon be deserted for the winter except for a skeleton crew. Outside the entrance to the hanger container, Skip turned around one last time, closed his eyes, and enjoyed the sensation of the large raindrops on his face. What would the rest of the planet be like? He was looking forward to finally seeing more of the planet than the barren rock and ice deserts of Greenland. He already had plenty of plans for winter vacation before heading out again in the spring for the next shift in the Arctic. But one step at a time - for now, it was time to call it a day.

The roar of the elements disappeared in an instant as Skip closed the steel door and entered the narrow airlock with protective clothing lockers. Jorge had already taken off his helmet and was shaking out his long black hair. "Damn this shitty weather," he grumbled to himself. "I don't get paid enough fucking money for this shit."

His English, like most people raised on Earth, was quite ancient, without the Chinese and other inflections common in the colonies. Skip had no trouble understanding it from the start. But it had taken him great effort to adjust his own language to the point where the other person no longer stared at him blankly with every other sentence.

"Listen to that sissy!" retorted Mace in his inhumanly deep bass voice. He slapped Jorge on the back. "I've always said it: the Norms just can't take shit."

The look on Jorge's face suggested he was not in a joking mood. "Stay away from me, you oversized deformity!"

"I've told you before," Mace, as usual, refused to be provoked and continued talking calmly, "It's just the way I was made..."

"Yeah, yeah, I know," Jorge interrupted him, "they just pulled you out of your brood canister that way. I got it. Damn mutant vermin!"

Mutants. That was the title given to them. Mace and Skip and all the other products of modern genetic engineering. These days you still had to put a 'damn' in front of it and 'ver-min' at the end to make it an insult. It was unknown who had been the first to use the term 'mutants' for the new human races that came from the breeding farms of the genetics companies. In any case, it had been meant as a swear word in those days - even if it was factually wrong. Mutation was a random process. The changes that genetic designers made to their raw human material were purposeful and specific. Nevertheless, the term 'mutants' had caught on and was now even used by the producers themselves. Skip's old teacher, Dr. Huang, did not like the term and had impressed upon his students not to forget where the word originally came from and what the intention had once been behind it. Huang, however, was powerless against the general spread of the term. Skip used it himself without giving it too much thought.

Even Mace didn't seem to have an excessive aversion to being called a mutant.

"Oh, you're just jealous," he continued to grumble, "because you can't do this, now can you, little guy." He had taken off his thick anorak, exposing his massive biceps. The head-sized muscle traveled up and down his upper arm as he tensed it.

"Don't call me 'little guy,' you giant baby!" Jorge's tone was irritated.

"Will you stop with the bickering!" Skip had had enough of the eternal banter between the two. It didn't matter how they called each other names and teased each other; later, in the station cafeteria, they would drink and laugh together. But he couldn't get past the bickering. "Take off that junk and get the hell out of here instead of getting in my way! I want to get off work already."

"You got it, boss." Mace grinned broadly.

Jorge's expression was less friendly. He was still smarting from the fact that Skip had been appointed leader of the repair team. As friends and co-workers, he could accept mutants, but as superiors... that still gave him trouble. Without a word, he complied with Skip's order.

After all three had stowed their helmets and anoraks, they entered the hangar. Skip briefly reported on the successful maintenance mission to Ole Skarsgard, the lead engineer. After Skarsgard informed him there were no further urgent tasks, Skip announced to his two comrades that it was time to retire for the day, and all three dispersed to their quarters. He ran into Mace one more time in the communal shower, but otherwise they went their separate ways.

As team leader, Skip shared a two-bed room with Rosco, a black Norm who barely spoke a word. Skip was fine with it. He liked the quiet and was glad to no longer be confined to one of the usual rooms with four, or even six beds, where someone was always chatting or otherwise making noise. From his time on the freighter, he was used to living in close quarters with other people. But in the spaceship crews it was common not to bother one' s fellow crewmembers unnecessarily. Everyone respected the privacy of the others. Those who did not obey this unwritten law were strongly urged to conform or were otherwise removed from the crew - one way or another. Most learned quickly to adhere to the customs.

Here on Earth, however, such a code of conduct did not seem to exist. The thirty-or-so crew of the prospecting station was wildly scattered, and everyone seemed to urgently need to tell the others what they were thinking, what they had already experienced, and what effect the food today had on their digestion. Not that Skip wasn't interested in the life stories of his fellow crew members - quite the opposite. After all, he had come to Earth to learn about the cradle of humanity, and its inhabitants. But being bombarded with unsolicited boastful stories had quickly begun to get on his nerves. For this reason, he had gratefully accepted the offer to move into Rosco's quarters when he had been promoted two months ago.

At the moment, it was particularly quiet as his roommate lay motionless on the bed, data goggles on his eyes and an electrode net on his head. Whether he was meeting with his family in the virtual world or watching porn, it was impossible to tell from the outside. Rosco refused to have a neural interface implanted, even though it greatly increased the quality of the transmission. He was not a Gaian who demonized all modern technology, but he did value the integrity of his body. Skip could only partially understand this attitude. He didn't want to argue with the undeniable benefits of implants. But he had long accepted that he would not understand all the foibles of natural-born humans.

Skip didn't stay long. He put on fresh clothes and headed for the mess hall. The dining room generally served as a meeting place for the off-shift and, apart from the virtual world, was the only place that offered a bit of a change from the station's dreary daily routine. Now in the evening, a good half of the crew had gathered there. Most of them sat at the tables, a can of beer in front of them, and stared at the holoprojector in the corner. A news feed was playing. A Pure in corporate uniform was venting about some mutant program.

When Skip entered the room, faces turned in his direction.

"Well, well," Jan Hanssen, the warehouse supervisor, called out to him, grinning broadly, "another secret breeding bull! Let's hear it, Skip! How many little mutants have you brought into the world already?"

Skip was confused. "What are you talking about? Did I miss something?"

"Miss? I don't know how many mutant chicks you've given a roast in the tube." Hanssen punctuated his statement with an obscene gesture.

"Shut up, mama's boy!" Mace held up an extended middle finger to Hanssen. Then he turned to Skip. "Don't listen to the idiots, man! Somewhere on Mars they've discovered mutant children. Along with their mother. And now they think we've got nothing better to do all day than screw around and bring babies into the world."

"But we can't have children, can we?" snapped Skip involuntarily.

"Well, sunshine," Hanssen interjected, "we all thought that until today. But it looks like you've got something besides piss in your sack, too."

Skip turned to the news hologram and the others fell silent again as well.

"... must now investigate whether the children are really pure Beta-class workers or whether unmodified human genetic material has played a role," the corporate lackey continued. "Based on what we know so far, we can safely rule out natural insemination with two mutants as parents. It is simply not possible. Mutants are infertile by design. This means that the manipulation of their genetic material is more than likely. This has not changed since their introduction to the market some fifty years ago. Even the current generations can only be conceived by artificial insemination in breeding farms ..."

"Oh, don't bullshit me, man!" the corporate man, Hanssen, chimed in. "We've seen the brats, haven't we? They're not human, they're fucking mutants. No doubt about it!"

"Hey, you nipple sucker!" Mace heaved his half-ton body up from the chair and took a step toward Hanssen. Skip noticed that Norms and mutants - mostly giant Alphas like Mace - were sitting at separate tables today. Jorge, too, had joined his peers and was trying, with only moderate success, not to look too hostilely at his superior.

Hanssen stood up. He was more than a head shorter and, despite his stocky stature for a Norm, downright scrawny compared to the giant Alpha.

"We're human too!", Mace snapped at him. "Don't you forget that, or I'll have to teach you!"

"Easy, big guy." Skip put a hand on the giant's arm. Mace snorted again, but then sat back down.

"Everybody needs to keep a level head!" interjected Skip. All eyes were on him. "I have no idea what they found on Mars. But I've screwed plenty of Beta women and a few others, too, and nothing ever came of it except a little fun. And all the other mutants I know do the same. No rubbers, no pill. We don't need them. It's just the way it is. Somebody on Mars got the wrong idea. It's just a misunderstanding or deliberate misinformation. Don't let anyone tell you different!"

"And what about this?" Hanssen had rewound the news feed a bit. The hologram showed a blurred 2D image. It took Skip a moment to realize what it depicted, then he saw the same angular skull that looked back at him in the mirror every morning, only the size of an infant, pressed against the chest of a woman who was as clearly a Beta-class worker as he was.

"It's the spitting image of you, don't you think?" said Hanssen, gesturing towards the holoimage. "And while we're on the subject. You've only been here on Earth for six months, right? Where were you - say - nine months ago? On Mars, by any chance? Maybe it's your brat."

Skip took a deep breath. His designers had graced him, like all Betas, with great equanimity and patience. That helped him now to accept the provocations of the Norm.

"Nine months ago, I was on my way to Earth. Far away from Mars. And that one," he pointed to the hologram, "is just a mutant baby. There are tons of them in the breeding farms. I was one of those once. How the child got from the farm to that woman, I don't know. But that doesn't prove anything. We should all just calm down a bit. You don't give a shit about what happens on the other side of Earth, and now you want to go at each other's throats just because they found a mutant child on Mars? That's beneath even your level! So, end of discussion. I'm buying a round!"

He went to the drink machine and ordered twenty beers. Half of those present raised their tins appreciatively and toasted him. The rest, including Hanssen, somewhat reluctantly turned back to other topics. Someone turned off the news feed and switched to a music station. Slowly, the general tension gave way to the usual after-work conversations. The separation of mutants and Norms remained largely intact, however, and looks were exchanged from time to time that were somewhere between skepticism and hostility.

Skip grabbed a beer from the vending machine and sat down with Mace. "I got a real bad feeling about this," the giant confided to him in a whisper. "A real bad feeling."

READ MORE:
a7lbooks.com/links/3418764

Made in the USA
Coppell, TX
12 October 2024